HARRY, ME AND BOTTLED TEA

A farmer's boy in the 1960s

ANDY COLLINGS

ISBN
9781723959738

Books by Andy Collings

Harry, Me and Boiled Bacon

Print or die

Harry, Me and Bottled Tea

For Florence

HARRY, ME AND BOTTLED TEA

A farmer's boy in the 1960s

A TRACTOR with a cab. This really was a treat of enormous proportions and I couldn't wait to climb in to it and, when I was on board, I wanted the rain to hammer down, the wind to blow at hurricane level and a thousand incontinent gulls to gather overhead, so I could sit on my beautifully dry foam seat, wear a T-shirt and laugh at everything that was going on outside.

Not entirely sure where or why Harry acquired the Grey Fergie. It just appeared one day, parked under the barn and I spotted it as I was on my way to fetch a sack of ground barley for the milking bail's feed hoppers.

While I had seen plenty of Grey Fergies running around the countryside – it seemed most farms had either a Fergie or a Fordson Major, or even both - this was the first one I had actually managed to get within touching range and the very first one I had seen with a cab.

Not, it has to be said, did the cab do a lot to enhance its overall appearance. Painted battleship grey, like the rest of the tractor, the cab was constructed from flat sheets of thin tin that had been bent over and riveted to an inner framework and lacked anything that could have been interpreted as 'style', or, as I was to find out, much in the way of comfort, either. It crossed my mind even as I looked at it that a couple of corrugated tin sheets and a large hammer could have achieved much the same effect.

I dropped the sack to the ground and began to give the tractor a closer inspection, but I hadn't travelled any further than the windscreen when Harry strolled around the corner of the barn.

'What do you reckon, boy?' he asked.

'Well, it looks pretty good to me,' I replied. 'And it has a cab too.'

'Yes, well, I can't say I really wanted one but I suppose we can put up with it. We can always take it off if we don't need it; most probably will in fact.'

My heart dropped. 'No, no, I'm sure it will be fine,' I said, thinking about all the times I had been soaked, frozen and crapped on when driving tractors. 'I could have a try in the cab, if you like, just to make sure?'

'Yeah, give it a go,' Harry said, indifferently.

The trouble was there were no doors to open to allow me to climb in. At one point I had thought there may have been one on the other side, but there wasn't.

'I guess you just climb in through the back,' I said, noticing for the first time the rear of the cab was entirely open. A closer look revealed a canvas sheet rolled up and secured with straps somewhere near the roof which, when required, could be let down.

'That's what I thought too,' Harry said. 'Not that

6

I've tried it.'

I stepped onto the drawbar, grabbed the back of the seat and pulled myself into the cab, squeezing between the seat and the mudguard before I could place my boots on the foot rest bars which were on either side of the gearbox. There were no floor panels.

'It's not very easy,' I said, when I had untangled my legs and lowered myself onto a seat which, disappointingly, I discovered had a wet foam rubber cushion on it. But I was now sitting in my first tractor cab and staring out onto the world through an oblong front screen and, if I turned my head, there were translucent, plastic side panels that just managed to let some light in and achieve little else. And it felt pretty good.

'Start her up and see how she sounds,' Harry said.

I looked round for a key to turn or a button to press but I could find neither and, after exploring everywhere and sensing Harry's growing impatience, I had to concede that when it came to engine start up, this tractor had me beaten.

'Harry,' I said. 'Can you give me a clue as to how I should be doing this? I don't seem to be able to find the starter button.' I gave the area beneath the steering wheel another inspection, followed by a careful examination along each side, as far as the cab support frame would allow me to go.

'Well, I haven't driven it; the tractor was delivered by the dealer but I'd have thought it was pretty straight forward. There must be a button somewhere.' He climbed onto the drawbar and peered over my shoulder.

After a few more minutes of searching, which revealed absolutely nothing, I suggested he should have a turn in the cab. I needed to get on with the milking and I still had the feed hoppers to fill.

'I suppose I'd better,' he said, climbing onto the drawbar and starting to push his way in.

'No, I think it would be better if you waited until I'm out of it,' I said.

Harry stopped and looked surprised. 'Can't you slide out on the other side of the seat?'

'I shouldn't think so. Anyway, my legs are all tangled up and I don't think they will work if I try that.'

'Bloody cab,' muttered Harry as he stepped back down onto the ground. 'We always manage to travel with two or even three of us on the Fordson – it has mudguards big enough to lie down on. And now you tell me there's only room for one person? That's ridiculous.'

'It's the cab,' I said.

'Well, if it is...' Harry shook his head.

I left him to it and headed for the old stone barn where the ground barley was stored and, as I walked away I could hear Harry cursing as he hunted round for the elusive starter button.

'It's like sitting inside a gnat's bollock in here,' he said, as I walked into the barn.

When I returned with a loaded sack across my shoulders Harry was outside the cab looking at a booklet he'd opened up across the tractor's bonnet.

'It says here something about pressing a button on the side of the gearbox,' he said.

I lowered the sack to the ground and propped it against a bale before stepping up on to the draw bar and looking in. 'Yes, you're right. There's a brass button on the right-hand side.'

'Can you press it? Harry asked.

'Not without getting into the cab.'

He scoffed. 'Well that's a surprise. You'd better crawl in again.'

I really wanted to get on with the milking and I could hear the cows bellowing, as they waited for me to open the gate on the other side of the paddock.

Back in the cab, I leant down and tried to press the brass button with my hand but I couldn't manage it. 'What a stupid place to put a button,' I shouted to Harry who was still leaning over the bonnet studying the booklet.

'And on this page, it says you should use the heel of your boot to press the button and then push the gear stick away from you in the direction of the "S" moulded on the gearbox cover,' he said.

'It says what?'

Harry sighed and moved round and pulled open one of the small canvas flaps which, like letter boxes, were cut into the side panels and spoke through it.

'Press the button in with the heel of your boot, and then push the gear stick away from you in the direction of the "S",' he repeated slowly.

'It all sounds a bit complicated and anyway, what does "S" stand for?' I enquired.

'How does "Start" sound?'

'Well it could be, but it could also be "Stop".'

'I don't think they would want you to move the gear lever to stop the engine,' Harry said. 'It's not running yet.'

'Looking at it from here, it could be also be a "5" as in fifth gear.'

'Just do what it says in the book,' he groaned.

'It might stand for "Supercharger",' I said as I raised

9

the heel of my boot and pushed it against the brass button.

'Or even "Stupid suggestion",' Harry offered. 'Look, just press the flaming button and move the gear stick over to where the book says you should and see what happens.'

So, I did just that and, magically, the engine turned over and fired up.

'It's a good job we had the book to tell us what to do,' Harry said as I shut the throttle down to tick-over and crawled out of the back of the cab.

'It usually is,' I said, hoisting the sack of ground barley up onto my back again. 'But it takes all the fun out of it, doesn't it?'

CHAPTER ONE

July 1967
Homeward bound

WHAT WITH TRAFFIC jams, diversions and roadworks, the drive down from the York Agricultural Institute in Askham Bryan seemed to be taking an eternity.

I had thought an early start on a Saturday morning would have seen me avoiding the worst of the traffic, but the end of year celebrations had rumbled on into the small hours and the morning was almost history before I had loaded all my kit into the back of the pick-up and driven off the campus for the last time; my year spent learning about modern farming methods had come to an end.

And now, with the dashboard clock showing half-past two, I reckoned I still had at least another hour to go before I arrived at Storeton Green and turned into Church Farm where I hoped Harry and Alice would be there to meet me. On the plus side, there was plenty of time to soak up the July sunshine which today put temperatures in the high seventies and called for windows to be wound down all the way.

It had been a good year with plenty to learn and

plenty of new ideas to take back to Harry and see what he thought of them. There had been a pleasant group of fellow students to work alongside and socialise with and it was also a year when I celebrated my eighteenth birthday and was able to purchase and consume a legal pint of beer for the first time.

Thinking about it now, squeezing everything into just one year was a big ask and predictably, the coursework was pretty basic and split into livestock, arable crops and machinery all of which I soaked up with enthusiasm, that is, with the exception of anything to do with pig production; the number of times I'd spent cleaning out Harry's pigs had just about hammered out any interest I may have had in such animals.

I drove on, allowing my mind to wander over some of the events of the last couple of years not least, the day it all started when I cycled the ten miles from my parent's home to be interviewed by Harry Wilcox for a job on his farm.

It had rained all the way and I was more than just soaked by the time I walked up the steep pathway which led to Church Farm; I was drenched and dripping.

Not that rain seemed to be troubling Harry, a well-built forty something who had spent a lifetime working on the land; he just stood out in it and let the rain flow over him while I shivered and felt icy water running down my spine. After telling me several times I would be of no use to him at all he relented and agreed to give me a try for a few weeks to see how it went. But he'd warned me I would find it hard work.

And it was tough going. Much to Harry's amusement, my hands, which were as soft as putty, blistered as they were continually chaffed by fork handles, bale strings and everything else I was asked to move, carry or stack.

They were painful times and I have Alice, his wife, to thank for helping me through them but there had also been happier, memorable times like the day Harry announced he wanted to reduce the number of branches shading his greenhouse: 'Tomatoes don't like too much shade,' he had said.

Joining us in the orchard where the greenhouse stood had been Ronny, a vagrant teenager who turned up intermittently to give Harry a hand whenever it suited him. With the ladder too short to reach the offending branches we resorted to donkey power and used Pedro to pull Ronny up into the tree after we had tied a rope around him and looped it over the highest branch. Trouble was, when Pedro stopped pulling he turned around and the rope slipped off his neck and Ronny hurtled back down again into a pile of donkey droppings.

Then there was an unfortunate incident when we were loading a two-wheel trailer with hay bales. It was my first attempt at stacking a trailer and I was still learning how the bales should be placed so when the front half of the load fell off, the weight of the bales still on the rear of the trailer caused it to tip up and the rest of the bales then slid off the back.

But perhaps the most taxing occasion was when I was cajoled into taking Pedro to the harvest festival in the church. Having spotted the vegetable display he headed straight for the carrots and this was followed by a recurrence of his flatulence problem which proved to be all too much for those sitting in the front few rows.

Heavy stuff, but much as I loved life on the farm it was the cows I milked twice a day I really felt most for. Thrifty, the adorable black Angus cross, Horns with all her temperamental hang ups, Lucy who had just joined the herd as a freshly calved heifer and Matty, a Friesian who was a long serving member of the herd and was not averse to having a few words with me on a Sunday afternoon. And there were so many other wonderful girls each with their own characters and temperaments. I wondered if they would all remember me; I hoped so.

I turned off the main road and for the first time that day I saw a signpost with Storeton Green written on it. Just another five miles and I would be there. Already I could recognise some of the farms or at least, their farm gates and drives, and it wasn't long before I was passing the ten-foot gate tied up with bale string which marked the entry to Rose Hill Farm, the farm where Elizabeth's parents, grandparents and sisters all lived.

I had hoped to give Elizabeth, who was attending York university, a lift home but her biomedical science degree course wasn't taking its summer break for another couple of weeks. When she did make it home we hoped to have a good two months together before she returned to university.

Copse Hill seemed steeper than ever and I was down in to second gear before I reached its summit where the road was met by the driveway that led to the largest farm in the village. I wondered if Sam Jones, the farm manager, was still rushing around organising his team of tractor drivers and herdsmen.

I was half tempted to turn in and see the farm's line-up of tractor sheds once more; there must have been more than twenty of them and each shed was home to a tractor. And across the yard there were even more sheds containing an array of implements, some I had never seen before. This was farming on a big scale.

And not long after, I turned down into the centre of the village where the church of St Matthew with its tall spire dominated the scene. Built on high ground it overlooked not only the houses in the village but also Church Farm, which had its buildings and farm house on the other side of the graveyard wall.

I took the top road to the farm for about a quarter of a mile before slowing down to rumble over the cattle grid and after that, coming almost to a halt when I encountered the hens which had all settled down for their afternoon nap on the farm track. Having negotiated my way through them, I turned left through the gateway and coasted down into the yard. I was home.

The dogs, two border collies, were barking before I had the handbrake on, and as I opened the door they rushed up to me. Ross, with his long straggly coat, took one leap and splashed his great wet tongue all over my face while Bob ran up and down, wagging his tail furiously and letting out the wildest of barks and howls.

'Well, at least they remember you, boy,' said a voice

I knew so well.

'Harry! How good to see you; how are you keeping?' I lowered Ross to the ground and extended my hand towards him.

'How's it been?' he asked, when he had finished squeezing the life out of my hand. 'Have they told you how we should be farming now?'

I laughed. 'Shouldn't think so for a minute, but it's been good and really interesting.'

At that moment, I caught sight of Pedro who had made his way from across the other side of the orchard to see what all the noise was about and, before I could say anything, began to bray, great heaving brays that left my ears ringing.

I met him at the gate and gave his muzzle a welcoming stroke and then told him how much I had missed him as he used his teeth to give me an affectionate nibble on my shoulder. And then I saw Alice stepping out of the kitchen door, drying her hands on her apron and I ran down the path to greet her.

'Oh John,' she said as she put her arms around me and held me. 'We've missed you so much.' After a while, she pushed me a way and held me at arm's length. 'Let's have a look at you. You've lost some weight, but we'll soon put that right and while you're at it, a good haircut wouldn't be amiss.'

'Don't get all weepy over him, Alice,' Harry said, when he joined us. 'The boy's had a long drive and I should think he could do with a cup of tea and a sandwich or something.'

'Yes, of course he does,' Alice said, leading me to

16

the door. 'The kettle's on and Harry can slice some boiled bacon while I butter the bread.'

I carried my bags up to my room and stowed everything away before pausing to look out of the window at the graveyard; at the sheep grazing between the head stones, at the heavy, cast iron gate that creaked every time someone pushed it open, and at the neatly trimmed yew bushes, some large some not so, growing alongside the pathway as it meandered its way up the slope from the street below.

But towering over everything was the church with its sandstone walls, a spire which nearly touched the sky, and large stained-glass windows. This structure had been the dominant village feature for centuries, witnessing and participating in the life and times of people who dwelled within the parish of Storeton Green, many of whom now remembered only by fading inscriptions on weathered stones, and an entry in an ancient register.

'Are you still up there, boy?' Harry interrupted my thoughts with a call from the bottom of the stairs. 'You can give me a hand with the milking.'

I joined him in the kitchen where he was running warm water into a bucket; the water used to wash the cows' teats before the milking machines were attached.

'Have you fetched the cows in?' I asked.

'No, not yet but they're only down in Farm Close so we can soon have them in the yard.'

Farm Close was just a hundred or so yards further on than the other side of the graveyard and, if they were as I remembered them, they would all be waiting at the gate for us. But I was wrong; far from waiting at the gate, the cows seemed to have almost made a conscious effort to find the furthest point from it. And there they ignored all my calls and stood where they were until I had walked up behind each of them and, with the help of a gentle prod, suggested they started making their way towards the gate.

'Are they always like this?' I asked Harry.

'They weren't to start with but they've seemed to have become increasingly unhelpful over the last few months. It wastes hours every week.' He gave one of them a push to get her moving.

When they were eventually gathered together at the gate, I looked over them as Harry walked round to open it. I spotted Thrifty, Horns and Lucy along with a few others but while these were undoubtedly the cows I had loved and cosseted less than twelve months before, they were now a different group of girls who, under different circumstances I would have struggled to recognise.

The cows sauntered into the collecting yard and Harry started the Lister engine. As the vacuum built up in the churns, I listened out for the rhythmic hiss of the pulsators as they came to life.

'Still using the milking bail then,' I said, putting a scoopful of ground barley into the four feeders that were on the head end of each stall.

'Yes, it'll do us for a bit longer yet,' he replied. 'The word is that the dairy is going to be phasing out churns within a year or two and all the milk will then need to be in bulk tanks. So that's something we need to think about.'

'Sounds as if we're heading for a suckler herd, bearing in mind most of these girls are now classed as beef breeds,' I said.

'Well, we will have to see.'

I opened the gate and let four cows in to be milked. Harry grabbed the cloth and, having rinsed it in the bucket of water, washed their udders and then stooped down to attach the clusters to two of the cows.

'Well John, how do you feel about things?' he asked when he had straightened up.

I leaned back on the gate and took stock of the situation; I wasn't sure how this conversation was going to go. 'Oh, pretty good and all-the-better for being back home,' I replied, cheerfully.

'You don't feel as if it's a backward step, then?'

'What, coming back here? No, not at all. Why should it be?'

'I just thought having had a taste of how the big farms work and all the shiny new machinery that goes with them, you might feel as if you could be doing better than hanging around a small dairy farm.'

'I hear what you say but the answer is that I'm more than happy to stay here. There's a lot of ways we can work to improve things.'

'Well, if you're sure. Farming systems are changing and there's an awful amount of work we need to do to keep up with them. And I'm relying on you to tell me all about it.'

I looked at him. 'Harry,' I said. 'I'm back now and everything is going to be fine.'

Harry smiled and nodded before making his way

over to remove the cluster from a cow which had finished milking.

CHAPTER TWO

A disappointing start

I WOULD NEVER have believed it. The cows I was milking this morning were definitely not the same sweet-natured girls I'd left behind when I went to York; they were no way even near being like they used to be.

Alright, they were the same cows but they had changed from being my calm and untroubled girls who would take handfuls of nuts out of my hand and enjoy a gentle tickle behind the ear, to highly strung ladies which looked worried and stressed and showed it by emptying their bowels all over the collecting yard.

When Horns came in to be milked she was beside herself with anger and kicked off the milking units as many times as I replaced them. Lucy, the new heifer I had milked so calmly for the first time after she had calved was off her head and bounced about in her cubicle hating every minute of it. And as for dear old Thrifty, the cow I could sit by on Sunday afternoons and share a few words with, she was as distant as I've ever seen a cow.

In short, it was a big disappointment. Perhaps I was expecting too much but I would never have believed cows could have changed so radically and become so difficult and distant.

I said as much to Harry who just shrugged his shoulders. 'They have short memories and react to different people in different ways. You'll get them round again, just you see.'

When the last cow had been milked I looked at the sea of slurry spread all over the collecting yard. It was inches thick and I reached for the shovel to clear a path, so I could roll the churns over to the trolley without getting their bases covered in it.

Down in the dairy, I unloaded the trolley and set about cooling the milk using a water-cooling system which was passed cold water through the milk in metal tubes before spewing the now lukewarm water down the side of the churn and onto the floor.

While the milk cooled I wrote out the labels and tied them to the handles on each of the churns. To allow more time for cooling, I retrieved the churns that had spent the night in the large walk-in fridge and loaded three of them onto the trolley.

And then the moment had arrived: the time to make a trip down to the stand in the street and frighten myself witless as the trolley careered down the fearfully steep slope with three full churns on board and me clutching the handles with everything I had, pressing down hard on the skid to try and keep speed at a controllable level.

Once underway, there was no chance of stopping until I arrived on the stand – a few railway sleepers bolted together which brought its height up to near that of the milk-lorry's bed – and, as it happened, the milk lorry drew alongside it just as I arrived.

'Oh, you're back then?' the driver said, when he had

climbed out of his cab. 'Perhaps we can look forward to having the churns waiting for me rather than me having to wait for them.'

'Harry hasn't been keeping you waiting, has he?' I asked.

'I've been tempted on more than one occasion to drive on,' he said, his half-smoked cigarette bobbing up and down between his lips as he spoke. 'Harry doesn't know how lucky he is having me on this round.'

'Why didn't you drive off, then?'

'Just to prove I'm not the miserable sod you all say I am.'

'Oh, surely not. Why would anyone say that about you?'

'Well, just you make sure you have the churns down here on time. That's all I'm saying.' He looked around, counting the churns. 'Looks like you've some more to bring down.'

'Only another three,' I said.

'See what I mean? It's not good enough.'

I did my best to make it good enough and when I had slithered to a halt with the remaining three churns and they had been loaded on to his lorry, he jumped down, re-fastened the side panels and headed back to his cab without another word.

'Have a good day,' I said, as he slammed his door shut. 'You miserable old sod.'

'I heard that!' he shouted out of the cab window.

Harry was waiting for me when I arrived back at the dairy, having hauled three empty churns up from the street.

'How's Miserable Old Sod this morning?' he asked. 'Still enjoying his job to the full?'

'Oh, same as ever,' I replied.

'Well, never mind, let's have some breakfast.'

When I walked into the kitchen I was pleased to note there was still the joyful, refreshing smell of the blue soap I used to wash my hands and arms with and, as ever, there was the slightly damp hand towel hanging on a rail beside the sink to dry them on.

As I hung the towel on its rail, I turned and faced the kitchen, the space dominated as ever, by a large oak table with seven chairs set around it; three down each side and one at the far end where Harry always sat.

Flopped out in front of the Rayburn, enjoying the warmth, were two or three cats and a couple of dogs, none of which seemed remotely interested in moving when Alice told them to move out of the way while she carried a boiling kettle across to the teapot.

'It's their instant obedience which always impresses me,' she said, as she lifted the lid of the teapot and started pouring hot water into it.

I sat down and looked up at a sheep wandering past the window at the far end of the kitchen. The graveyard was about ten feet higher at the rear of the house than at the front and the view from the window behind Harry was limited to looking up at grave stones and the occasional sheep grazing on the grass growing between them.

Over to the right of the kitchen a large, walk-in alcove ran the length of the room and was home to a Rayburn which vied for space with a gas oven and an automatic washing machine. Polished, large diameter copper pipes attached to the Rayburn, led out of the alcove into the ceiling and headed for the hot water tank in the bathroom.

A hard-working farmer's wife, Alice was intensely house-proud and spent many hours sweeping, washing and wiping, along with cleaning all the pots and pans she used to prepare lunch and dinner.

One of her biggest challenges was keeping the gas cooker clean which was in almost daily use to cook a wide variety of meals, including the boiling of a bacon joint purchased each week from the local butcher.

This simmered away on the stove for a large part of every Friday evening and always brought an audience of cats and dogs who parked themselves in front of the cooker, each salivating wildly as they anticipated being given a morsel when, after several hours, the joint was transferred from the saucepan to a carving plate.

Alice though, had recently received some alarming news from the local gas company informing her that, as the gas supply was being changed from coal gas to natural gas pumped out of the North Sea, her cooker would now have to be changed for a model that could cope with this new type of gas.

'Does this mean I shall have to have a new cooker?' she asked, passing Harry the letter.

Harry picked it up and read it through, while Alice poured out the tea. 'I think so,' he said. 'But there doesn't seem to be any offer to pay for another one.'

'Oh well, it's about time we had a new cooker. This one's been around for about twenty years, if it's been a day,' Alice said.

'Well, it doesn't have to do much, does it? Nothing that a shovelful of coal or a few lumps of wood couldn't do,' Harry said.

Alice tutted and turned to me. 'More tea, John?' She lifted the tea pot off its mat and held out her hand for my cup and saucer. 'If you want to set up a campfire on the lawn everyday just get on and do it. And while you're doing it, I'll order a new gas cooker.'

Harry looked around the room for support, but there was none. 'More expense,' he muttered and buried his head back in the newspaper.

Over the next couple of weeks, Alice spent a great deal of time on her knees scrubbing and scouring the inside of the oven until, like the hob and grill above, glowed with spotless cleanliness. No one but no one was ever going to accuse Alice of having a dirty cooker in her kitchen.

And it was one Tuesday morning, when we were having breakfast, I heard the rumbling of a sack barrow making its way up from the street and, when it eventually reached the level paving slabs that led to the backdoor, Alice looked out of the window.

'They're here,' she cried. 'And look, they've brought my new cooker.'

She turned and headed for the door. 'Mrs Wilcox?' said one of the men who was breathing heavily and, like his colleague, was clearly not used to having to push new ovens up such steep paths.

'That's right,' replied Alice. 'You must be from the gas company.'

The man nodded and gulped down another deep breath. 'Yes,' he said, looking up at the vehicles parked in the yard. 'We are and if I'd known there was another way into here it would have saved us having to drag this up that slope. It's a killer.'

But Alice wasn't listening. 'I should think you need to take the old one out first,' she said, leading the two men into the kitchen. 'And you'll find the stop tap in the cupboard under the telephone in the hall.'

While they turned the gas off, Alice gave her cooker, a New World Seventy Five, a last wipe with a cloth and checked to see the grill pan was still in the oven along with the instruction book she had spent a large part of yesterday looking for.

'I think you'll find everything is alright,' she said, when the men returned. 'It's not been a bad cooker; in fact, I'd say it's been a very good one.'

'You've cooked some prize-winning cakes with it, haven't you Alice?' contributed Harry. 'And let's not forget a thousand or more joints of boiled bacon.'

If only it was possible, I thought.

'Absolutely,' Alice said, placing a hand on the side of the hob. 'I think I'm really going to miss her; you will be sure to take good care of her, won't you?'

'Oh, we'll do that alright,' said one of the men. 'I'll fetch the sack barrow and we'll take her out now.'

And once it was outside they set about taking care of it with a sledge hammer and, as Alice looked on in horror, smashed it to smithereens. They then brought in the new one, connected it and left, leaving a pile of broken pieces which had once been a spotless New World Seventy Five gas stove.

'So, what do you know about farming now?' Harry asked, when Alice's breathing had slowed and some colour had returned to her face. 'And where do you think we're going wrong? Did they teach you how to plough?'

My year at college had made me aware of so many things but I felt this wasn't the time or place to try and tell Harry what I thought he should be doing with his farm.

'I'm not sure you're doing anything wrong,' I said.

27

'And you'll be relieved to know I did have some instruction on using a plough.'

'Oh, that *is* encouraging.' Harry's eyes were on the ceiling. 'Mind you, it'll probably take a few more years yet before we manage to remove the closing furrow you left in Forty Acres, and only then if the stream can be persuaded to take its original course. But I thought you would be telling me to sell the pigs, sheep and hens, triple the size of the dairy herd, install a thirty-point herringbone milking parlour and invest in a cheese factory.' He picked up the carving knife and started to sharpen it against the steel.

'Well, you can sell the pigs,' I said, helpfully. 'And a few more cows to milk wouldn't be amiss.'

Harry finished carving the boiled bacon and slid my plate, complete with the mandatory two slices on board, along to me.

'We'll see, boy. We've a bit of catching up to do before then, like the pigs need a good clean out and there's about fifty acres of hay to make.'

'And you haven't told us how Elizabeth is yet,' Alice said. 'Is she alright?'

'Yes, she's fine but her term doesn't finish for another couple of weeks.'

CHAPTER THREE

Hay making

IT TOOK A FEW days but by the end of the week I was moving back into the routine of milking the cows each end of the day and, more importantly, they were gradually settling down and beginning to show signs of returning to become the sweet sociable girls I used to know, but there was still a long way to go. The volume of slurry they were depositing in the collecting yard was still on the deep side.

With a period of fine weather forecast, when the sun beamed down from a clear blue sky and temperatures crawled into the mid-80s, haymaking became the priority; the pigs would have to wait a little longer.

'If you take the David Brown with the mower down to Long Meadow and make a start, I'll sharpen a couple more blades and bring them down to you,' Harry said.

It looked as if it was going to be yet another hot day, so I filled up a couple of bottles with water and dropped them into the toolbox before making my way over to the diesel tank to fill up with fuel.

Then came the task of attaching the mower to the tractor. I've no doubt, in time, having had lots of practice, it would be possible to reverse up to an implement and be able to stop the tractor in precisely the right place and simply slip the linkage arms on to an implement's shafts and secure them with lynch pins. No pushing and pulling, no kicking, no second tries at lining the tractor up, no moving the tractor a few centimetres forwards or backwards, only to see it roll back to where it was, and no trying to lever big implements into position with long poles.

Compared to some heavier implements, such as the plough or a wide cultivator, I discovered the mower is a relatively easy piece of kit to shunt around but, as I also found out, with its cutter bar stored in the vertical transport position with a heavy wooden swathboard on the end of it. The whole machine was liable to fall over backwards when it was manhandled. Which is what happened.

Lying prone, like some slayed porcupine with its feet in the air, try as I might, I couldn't lift it back up again – and it was all the more annoying because I had been so close to attaching it to the tractor before it fell over.

'Thought you would have been down in the field by now, boy,' Harry said when he walked into the shed where the mower was kept. 'I think you'll find the cutter bar needs to be vertical when it's connected to the tractor.'

'Well, it was but then something slipped and it fell over backwards.'

Harry sighed. 'I know the top link extends but I don't think it has much chance of reaching that far,' he said. 'Come on. Let's lift it back up to how it should be.'

I went around to the end of the cutter bar and

grabbed it with both hands.

'Keep your fingers away from the blade because if it drops down you'll be counting them to see how many you still have,' Harry warned. 'There's more than a few farm workers missing a full set of fingers, I can tell you.'

'What, from being cut off by a mower blade?' It sounded a bit of an exaggeration to me.

'The most frequent finger removing accidents happened when cutter bar mowers were pulled by horses and the drive came from a wheel running on the ground," he explained. 'When the cutter bar was blocked up or maybe a section had broken off, they'd bring the horse to a halt, jump off the seat and then go and start poking about with their fingers to see what the problem was. And then, for something to do, the horse would take a step forward and that was it.' He made a chopping movement with his hand. 'You can't wonder they never learned to count properly after that.'

I moved my hands further away from the blades and waited for Harry to find something safe to hang on to. And then we lifted together and as the cutter bar reached its vertical position again, it settled onto it stand.

'You're miles away with the tractor,' Harry said, when he tried to connect one of the linkage arms to the mower. 'Not even in the same field.'

I looked over his shoulder and, while the linkage arm was still a few inches away from where it needed to be, it wasn't as bad as Harry was making out.

'I'll give it a push and see if I can get one of the arms on,' he said.

And I heard him grunt as he heaved the mower

forwards until the linkage arm could be attached. 'Where's the bloody lynch pin?' he shouted. 'I can't hold this for ever.'

The pins were in the tool box and should have been in my hand ready to clip on to prevent the linkage arm slipping off.

'Hurry up, boy. It's starting to slip off.'

I ran around the tractor to the toolbox, grabbed three lynch pins and headed back to Harry but as I arrived there was a long groan and the mower slipped rearwards, pausing only briefly before it toppled backwards on to the ground again.

'I've got two lynch pins,' I told Harry.

'Oh good,' he said. 'I'm sure they will come in very useful at some time today. Did they teach you anything about using a scythe while you were at college?'

'How would it be if we lifted it up again and put the top link on first,' I suggested. 'That would prevent it falling backwards while we attach the lower linkage arms.'

Harry thought about it and while he did, a shadow moved across us, accompanied by a smell of stale tobacco. It was, and could only be Ronny.

'Here's the man of the moment,' he said. 'Ronny Adcock, rides to our rescue.'

'Hello, Harry. You having trouble?' Ronny drew hard on a needle-thin, self-rolled cigarette and then let the smoke trickle out of his left nostril. Dressed in a collarless shirt, which revealed the remains of some form of undergarment, along with jeans and wellingtons, it could never be said Ronny wasn't prepared for sudden climatic changes.

'Hello Ron,' Harry said. 'Is it right what I hear?

You've decided to float the company on the stock exchange and go public; I thought you were all set to accept ICI's offer?'

'Cut the crap,' Harry.

'Only if you help us get this mower sorted out.'

'What's the problem? Doesn't usually take three people to hook a mower on a tractor.'

'Yes, well John's been having a few problems putting the tractor in the right position, so if the calf will not come to the teat, the teat on this occasion must go to the calf,' Harry said. 'We'll all get together and lift the mower over to the tractor. And if we could do it now, we might just manage to get some grass cut before lunch time.'

With the added help of Ronny, the mower was finally hitched to the David Brown tractor and, with the two extra knives on board, wrapped in sacking to keep them safe, I set off for Long Meadow.

I had almost forgotten how good it felt to be driving down the track once more, passing through the green fields I knew so well. There was also the tractor's long red bonnet and bright yellow exhaust pipe to enjoy along with a clear blue sky and a light warming breeze. If I could have been sitting on anything but a wet sponge seat, my happiness would have been complete.

A couple of fields further down the track, at the top of Piggy Hill, I looked out across the meadows spreading for miles before me until, on the horizon, they merged into an impenetrable haze as the heat rising from the ground did strange things with the light. A gentle drive down the hill to Forty Acres and it was not long before I arrived in Long Meadow.

Being July, most of the grass had gone to seed

33

which, while making the grass easier to make into hay, did not have the feed value of grass cut a few weeks earlier in June. Good though to see it was all standing – probably due to the low levels of fertiliser that had been applied.

I removed the spare knives and lent them up by the gate, and then released the cutter bar and lowered it to its horizontal working position. I would need to change knives after about three or four hours, or sooner if a knife section tried to cut a rock and sheared the rivets holding it on.

As its name suggests, Long Meadow is a long, narrow field which is reasonably flat and easy to work in that there are good long runs to be made without having to lift the mower and waste time making hundreds of headland turns.

The first-time round is always something of an exploration of how the grass is going to cut and also a good time to find any unexpected fencing posts or boulders that have appeared since the field was shut up earlier in the year to allow the grass to grow and bulk up.

And having survived the first time round, there is always the back cut to look forward to; when the mower is used to cut the outside edge of the field the tractor ran on while making the first cut. This can be a real pig because the mower is having to cut grass flattened by the tractor's wheels and, to make matters even more testing, it is also the longest way around the field.

After about an hour, though, I was going well. As I moved through the crop, the cut grass was falling back over the cutter bar and the wooden swathboard at the end of the cutter bar was deflecting about twelve inches of it from the end of the blade to leave a clear path for the tractor wheels to run on when I came round again.

Harry always warned me never to become too complacent when mowing. There was always something waiting to go wrong; the connecting rod sliding the blade from side to side may come loose or bent, the fingers it slides through to create the scissor action can twist or their points become bent, a knife section can lose a rivet and start flopping about, and the whole cutter bar can suddenly swing back should it hit an obstacle rather more solid than standing grass.

Well, about halfway round on what was perhaps the twelfth circuit, when I was thinking what I would be writing to Elizabeth about this week, there was a loud crash and all Harry's can-happens suddenly happened.

When I stopped, a trail of unidentifiable metal bits came to a halt behind me and when I say came to a halt, I didn't include the drive shaft which continued to rotate and flop wildly about, not doing a lot. Looking from the tractor seat, it looked to be an expensive sort of mess and I was forced to concede this mower may have just cut its last stem of grass.

To make matters worse, I spotted Harry heading down the hill in his Land Rover and I could see from the direct and determined way he was driving, he wasn't that pleased with what he was looking at.

'Never reckon to drive into a field and find anyone working,' he said, as he stepped out of the Land Rover and walked passed me. 'They're always stopped for some excuse or another and, if I may say so, it looks as if you've discovered a totally new reason. If I'd thought, I would have brought the yard broom and a shovel with me.'

He stepped forward and took a closer look at the debris which lay before him and started poking at bits of it with the toe of his boot.

'Didn't any of your college teachers say anything about making sure you put the lynch pin in when you attach a top link? You know, those little spring-loaded things you use to stop the pins dropping out while you're mowing and prevent the whole machine from becoming detached and disintegrating into a thousand little pieces?'

'But I took some out of the toolbox,' I said. 'Three of them – two for the linkage arms and one for the top link.'

And then I felt in my pocket and found a lynch pin.

'Well, there you go,' Harry said. 'Never liked this mower anyway. Hook off what's left of it and take the tractor up to the farm and bring a trailer back down to pick everything up. I'll go and see if I can get us another mower from somewhere.'

As I watched the Land Rover drive away there was no avoiding a low feeling. Back from college, all fresh-faced and raring to go, and I was making a complete mess of everything; the cows, the trouble I created putting the mower on the tractor this morning and now, due to my stupidity, we didn't even have a mower. All it wanted now was for the weather to crack.

Steeped in thought as I mulled things over, I drove the tractor up to the top of the hill and hardly noticed someone holding the gate open for me. In fact, if I hadn't had to turn my head to avoid an overhanging branch I would have driven straight on regardless. Instead I looked to my right and saw Elizabeth.

The brakes on the David Brown were not one of its

better features but to be fair, they were probably as good or as bad as most other tractors. Even so, despite my best efforts, it was several yards before I managed to stop, apply the handbrake and knock it out of gear.

'Elizabeth,' I shouted, as I swung my leg over the steering wheel and jumped down. 'What are you doing here? I thought you still had another week to go before the term ended.' I made to give her an embrace, but she held her arms out, pushing me away.

'No, John. Don't even think about coming near me with those clothes,' she cried. 'I've enough washing to do already.' But then she laughed. 'I suppose I could risk just one small kiss, though.'

I ignored her and put my arms around her and pulled her close. 'How did you get back? I was planning on driving north to pick you up.'

'Yes, I know you were but with not a lot happening in the last week of term, I thought I would head home. I caught a train down to Birmingham and then took another to Northampton. I then caught the bus and here I am.' She shrugged her shoulders and gave me that smile again.

'Aren't you the little globe trotter,' I said. 'Anyway, it sounds as if you've been having a better time of it than I am.'

Elizabeth's face darkened. 'You haven't told Alice you've developed an allergy to boiled bacon, have you? She'll be devastated and I shouldn't think the butcher will be best pleased either. But then, there may be a few pigs feeling happier...'

'No, it's nothing like that.'

'Well tell me, then,' she said. 'Or is it one of those 'boy' things you find difficult to talk about?'

'Elizabeth! I thought the people I've been mixing

with for the last year were bad enough, but your lot seem worse.'

She laughed again and put her arms around me. 'I'm sorry. I'm being unfair. If there's something you want to tell me, of course I'll listen.'

'No, it's nothing. Just me being silly.' I took her hand and pulled her towards the tractor. 'Come on, let's get back to the farm. We've the whole summer in front of us and I'm looking forward to it.'

CHAPTER FOUR

Shearing the ewes

AT BREAKFAST THE next morning, Harry seemed very pleased with himself; which was strange. On the few occasions when he had shelled out a packet for a new machine he made a big point of telling me there probably wasn't anything wrong with the old one, the new one wouldn't be half as good and the chances of it lasting anywhere near as long, were remote.

And then he would say he didn't know what had possessed him to even think about buying it and let me know that when the old one was new it cost less than half as much, before picking up the invoice, holding it up to the light and making a big thing about counting the number of zeros he could see.

But this time it was different. He seemed almost happy, unnaturally so.

'We won't be long knocking down a few acres with this little beauty,' he said, rubbing his hands together. 'There're only a handful of these in the country and we're talking seriously about ten acres an hour, not your piddling ten acres a day, if you're lucky. No more wasting hours sharpening blades, this one has only four reversible blades and they cut everything – and no more struggling to cut the outside swath.'

'Four? How can that work?'

'It's a drum mower – the blades are fixed to the edge

of two drums which rotate at some incredible speed. It's like I've always said, the cutter bar mower is so out of date. With today's powerful tractors there's no need for such an antiquated system.'

'Sounds good. When are they delivering it?' I asked.

'They said it will be with us this afternoon and I was rather hoping you might be able to use it to finish Long Meadow, that's assuming you can hook it on to the tractor without wrecking it.'

Alice came to my assistance. 'Harry, are you having a top up?'

'Just half a cup, please.' He pushed his cup down the table. 'Probably best if you take the tedder and give what you've already cut a shake-up and when you've finished that, leave the tedder down there and get back here and we'll see where we are then.'

'Are you having another cup before you go, John? Alice asked.

'No, I'd better get on, thanks, but I'll take a bottle of tea with me.'

I did as Harry suggested and spent about an hour fluffing up the grass I cut yesterday; it was a good drying day and the hay was making well. Such a pity I didn't manage to cut all of it before the mower fell to pieces, but I decided not to dwell on it.

Even so, as the tines of the tedder clattered round and lifted the grass, it was good to see the water vapour rising up from where it had been lying and there was also a sweet scent in the air of grass in the making.

Less than two hours later I was back at the farm and I rather hoped the dealer had delivered the new mower but I was to be disappointed. Instead, I noticed Harry had brought about a hundred ewes into the orchard.

'I think you'd better give me a hand with the shearing for a few hours until the mower arrives,' he said, after he'd inquired what I thought the state of the cut grass was in Long Meadow. I told him I thought it was making well but wouldn't be ready to bale until tomorrow afternoon at the earliest.

Harry had set up a holding pen for the ewes having a small hand gate which exited onto a small area of ground he'd spread a tarpaulin sheet on. Tied to the hurdle on one side of the gate was a tall post from which an electric motor was suspended, and this powered the shearing head, the drive conveyed to it in a flexible tube. It was switched on and off by pulling on a cord.

'You catch and roll, and I'll shear,' Harry said.

'You want me to do what?'

'Catch and roll,' he repeated. And then more emphatically: 'Catch a sheep and bring it out here so I can shear it and then roll the fleece up when I've finished shearing it. Got it?'

'I think so,' I said.

'Alright then, let's make a start.'

There was a small hand gate in one corner of the pen containing the ewes and it was through here I assumed Harry wanted me to deliver a sheep to him. So I went into the pen and grabbed the nearest ewe and did my best to guide it to the gate. But the sheep was having none of it and try as I might I couldn't get her to move in the right direction.

'That's right, boy. Push her along. Don't take any trouble from her. Assert yourself so she knows who's boss. Whatever you do, don't be intimidated.'

It was not a good start. After several minutes I was sweating and exhausted but the sheep I was hanging

41

on to still refused to move towards the gate.

'Perhaps if you opened the gate so she can see where to go,' I suggested to Harry.

'If that's what you want me to do,' he replied, reaching for the latch and pulling the gate wide open.

No stranger to gates and hurdles, this sheep did not need any second bidding; spotting the open gate, she suddenly took a lunge towards it. But Harry was too quick for her and managed to close the gate just as she arrived.

All was not well though. When she crashed into the gate she managed to drag the hurdles along the ground for a few feet with some of them becoming unhooked from each other so that the once captive ewes were soon spread out all over the orchard.

'Bugger that,' Harry said as I felt another black mark creep onto my gross-incompetence record sheet. 'I take it you didn't do sheep handling at college, then?'

'We did but they had smaller sheep and bigger hurdles,' I said.

We rebuilt the holding pen, rounded up the sheep and started again. This time things went slightly better and I managed to pass a ewe out to Harry who took it and, in one deft movement, pitched her onto her rear end, reached for the shearing head and pulled down on the cord to start the motor.

I watched as he started at the throat and took a single cut from her belly up to her chin and then worked on one side until he had cleared the wool off her head and down to her shoulder. The wool fell away from him as he worked the shearing head from right to left in an almost casual manner, revealing some remarkably clean looking wool as he did so.

'This is the point where you can either carry on

taking the blows from the stomach to the back bone or choose the modern way, called the Bowen method, which, after you've trimmed off the flank, allows you to take longer blows along her body from back to neck,' Harry explained. 'There are those who say the Bowen method is quicker in that the shearing head spends more time cutting with longer blows, but I find it creases up your back on these big ewes so I use the English method.'

With the sheep half shorn, Harry kicked the cut fleece to one side and pulled the ewe upright so he could cut the wool away from her other side, gradually working down towards her rump where, with one final blow the last of the wool was off, and the ewe walked away leaving the fleece lying on the tarpaulin.

'Now this is where you have your moment,' Harry said. 'He picked up the fleece and threw it so it opened out on to the ground with the outside upside. 'You bring the sides in to the middle and then roll it as tight as you can from the tail up to the head and then, just before you get to the end, you kneel on it, grab a good handful of wool and twist it to form a thick rope which you use to wind around the wool and tuck the end in to hold it all firm. And then you place the roll in the big sack I've fastened between the hurdle and the tree. Got it?'

Harry made it look easy but I had a suspicion, it wasn't going to be when I tried to do it. 'I hope so,' I said.

'Good, and while you think about it, get me another sheep to shear.'

And so it started. As soon as Harry had nearly finished shearing a sheep, I would dive into the holding pen and drag another one out through the narrow gate and hold it until Harry had kicked the fleece from the sheep he had been shearing to one side and then pass my sheep over to him. I would then set about folding and rolling the fleece and, having placed it in the big bag, prepare myself to catch the next one.

It was draining work and, in the heat, I found the sweat running off me. Harry said the oil was running well; the lanolin in the wool was helping the shearing head, with its reciprocating head and comb, to cut freely through the fleece and it also made my hands soft and my trousers oily.

'Hang them up tonight and you'll be able to step straight into them tomorrow morning,' said Harry, while pausing to take a mouthful of water. 'The lanolin solidifies when it cools down, but it makes your skin as soft as a baby's bum.'

It was very nearly lunch time before Harry suggested I had a go at shearing and, to help me get started, he had placed a sheep on the tarpaulin and then told me where to stand to make the first blow. The shears, when I held them, felt heavy and cumbersome and when I pulled the string to start the motor, they tried to twist in my hand.

I made a tentative start by making the opening cut from her belly up to her chin, as Harry directed. And I was awaiting further instructions when Harry announced he had just remembered there was a telephone call he needed to make.

'Just finish that one and come on in for some lunch,' he said, as he headed for the orchard gate. 'And whatever you do don't drop the shearing head, you'll damage the comb and cause all sorts of expensive problems.'

I wish he hadn't said that because I thought I had enough problems without adding to them by pointing out things like that. Already the sheep was restless and I was struggling to restrain her from twisting herself round and escaping. If I was to have any lunch today, there was nothing for it but to carry on.

After I had trimmed around her head, it was a matter of working from that point around her body, cutting the wool from her stomach to her back bone until I reached her tail.

While this phase seemed to have proceeded reasonably well, I realised I had allowed the sheep to slip so she was now lying down with my boot over her neck, To have any chance of shearing the side she was lying on, I would have to somehow pull her back up to a sitting position and to do that I would need both hands which meant putting the shearing head down and I couldn't do that without pulling a cord I couldn't now reach.

I scrabbled to my feet and used my left arm to try and lever the sheep's torso back into a sitting position, but it was a hopeless task, particularly as she had had enough of being mauled about and was now kicking out wildly.

Reaching for the cord I managed to stop the motor and place the head on the floor, but I was now too late to hold her still. Her feet had found the floor and she now had some traction and she used it to scamper off in to the orchard, the cut half of her fleece trailing behind her, pieces catching on the ground and being torn free so that it looked like some sort of manic paper trail.

What to do? In desperation, I reached into my pocket and found a few feed nuts I normally reserved for the

45

cows and placed them on the ground to distract her while I reached out and grabbed her.

The only thing now was that I had grabbed a handful of fleece I had already cut so as she made to move away, the fleece shredded, and if I hadn't been able to react and take hold of some wool still attached to her, there would have been a half shorn ewe running around the orchard for evermore.

I knew I had her when I heard her groan; that 'Oh if you must' type groan. And having wrestled her back to the shearing area and into a sitting position, I reached for the shearing head and pulled the start cord.

Harry was just finishing his apple crumble when I made it into the kitchen.

'Didn't break any world records with that one, boy,' he said. 'That's assuming you didn't carry on and shear the rest of them.'

I washed my hands and splashed some cooling water onto my face and arms. 'No, I think I need a little more practice before I could claim to be any good at that job,' I said. 'And it's pretty back aching work.'

'Before we had the machines we used to cut the fleece by hand with shears,' Harry said. 'Spring loaded shears that had blades about ten inches long. If you think your back aches, just think what your wrist felt like after hours of working those shears. But we still got through them, not that we could cut as close to the skin as we do now.'

I sat down and Alice passed me a plate loaded with pie, potatoes and cabbage which I wolfed down before setting about a healthy portion of apple crumble, followed by two cups of tea.

'Any news on the mower?' I asked, as Alice passed

me my second cup.

'Not yet but if they leave it too late it won't be worth taking it down there today, what with the milking and everything else. We'll carry on with the shearing and see what happens.'

CHAPTER FIVE

The new mower

'WELL, I CAN SEE the one you sheared from here,' Harry said as we approached the orchard gate. 'The way you've left the wool on the legs and the top of its head you could mistake it for a poodle. And what happened to its tail?'

'Not a lot. It got up before I could do that bit,' I said.

'It's a good job I spent a few days dagging them all then. This time of the year they're likely to get maggots and all sorts of horrors around the backend if you don't trim them out in that department.'

I released the latch on the pen gate and waited while Harry sorted himself out with the shearing head, giving it a good brushing to clean it, turning a spring-loaded adjusting screw to change the pressure the blade placed on the comb, and then giving everything a generous squib of oil.

'Right then, boy. Let's be having our first customer.'

I don't know whether the sheep had resigned themselves to being sheared, but they all seemed to be in a calmer mood than they had been this morning and certainly more compliant when I invited them to leave the pen and handed them over to Harry.

Most of these girls had been sheared before in previous years and, while sheep are not renowned for their long-term memories, it seemed reasonable to assume they had some inkling about what it was all about. Perhaps it was the warmth of the day and the relief they would have when their thick winter coat was removed.

It remained a mystery but, during the afternoon we managed to work our way through about forty of them, a number which Harry seemed to be quite pleased with.

'Are you going to have another go?' he asked me as we were thinking about calling it a day.

'Well, if you think it would be a good idea,' I replied, instantly reliving the nightmare I'd endured at lunch time and not particularly wishing to repeat it.

'I think it would be a good idea. Get you into the swing of it so when we set about doing the other two hundred, I'll be able to leave you to it.'

'Not a good idea,' I said.

'Well may be not this year, eh?'

I smiled, not knowing what to say.

'Right then, I'll get you a sheep and we'll see if you can finish it before we need to fetch a torch.'

I took my stance by the electric motor as Harry dived into the pen and brought out a sheep.

'The first thing is to sit it down on its arse with its back leaning to you,' he said. 'And as a general rule, you want to make the sheep work for you in the way it moves so you don't need to struggle all the time. That just upsets the sheep and wears you out.'

I held the sheep and thought about the best way of getting her sitting down, as Harry had described. Although I had seen it done countless times this afternoon, I couldn't for the life of me recall just how he had managed it. I decided to go for one of the front legs and pull her over but that resulted in her scrabbling up onto her hind legs and very nearly falling backwards on top of me. Which would not have been a very good start.

'Grab her flank with your right hand and have the other around her neck,' said Harry. 'Then lift with your right hand and push across with your knees.'

It was like preparing to play the accordion, not that I ever had, but the result was probably very similar in that, as Harry had predicted, the sheep slipped over onto her bottom and, as I pushed across with my left hand, took a more upright posture.

I was now ready to start shearing and, with the motor running and the cutting head buzzing and vibrating I took the first cut from her belly up to her jaw.

'You really should just trim round her teats before you start shearing the main chunk,' Harry said. 'But make sure you keep the skin tight so you don't risk cutting off anything important.'

Bending well over the head of the sheep I delved as instructed down to the ewe's nether regions and by pulling the soft skin with my left hand set about removing wool from where wool shouldn't be – well not on all breeds of sheep. But I soon returned to the neck and began my trawl down one side, making successive blows from her belly across to her backbone.

'Don't let her sag against you or you'll be cutting through slack skin,' Harry warned.

I stuck my knees into her side to straighten her up and continued until I had her hind leg and tail completed.

And then came the big moment when I needed to work on the other side and while Harry seemed to make the change over in a relatively seamless fashion, I had yet to discover how to perform such a move.

'Just push her up so you end up with her looking to your left and then the wool will fall away from you as you work down to her tail again cutting from her backbone to her belly and, with the job completed, you stand up and let her walk out from between your legs.'

I tried pushing her up but for some reason I was wrong-footed and Harry had to step in to help me until I had her in the required position.

'That's right, boy, you're on the home straight now. Try and keep the blows at or just above skin level so you don't have to double cut the wool – which reduces its value.'

With some final tidying up around the tail the job was done and, as instructed, I stood up to allow the sheep to walk away between my legs, which would have been a good way of ending the day if she had just walked. But no, clearly angry at the way she had been treated she took off at a pace and took my left leg with her.

Harry sucked in air through clenched teeth. 'Oooh, nasty; you alright, boy? I hope she didn't catch the old wedding tackle, did she?'

I shook my head and rolled over onto my front, so I could get to my feet. 'No, but it was close. I think I might just dispense with the walk-through finish next time.'

It was time to fetch the cows in for their evening milking, so I left Harry clearing up and set off, albeit at a gentle pace, to Farm Close where the girls were still grazing a new grass ley that had been under sown into a crop of barley last year. But before I could make it to the top of the yard I met the dealer's lorry with our brand-new mower on board.

'Where do you want it?' the driver asked, leaning out of his window.

'Does it need to be undercover?'

The driver shrugged. 'Dunno, mate. It's up to you. As long as it gets off my lorry you can have it just where you want, but that doesn't include up in a loft or somewhere like that.'

Useful. I looked for a suitable spot for him to drop it off. 'I think there's an empty bay up under the Dutch barn you could put it in. Follow me and I'll show you where it is.'

The lorry had a crane on board which was good because there was no way we could have lifted the mower off without it. I should have left him to get on with unloading it but I was keen to see what our new mower looked like.

'So this is the latest thing in mowers?' I said when he had lowered it to the ground.

'Not just the latest. This is the *very* latest,' replied the driver. 'The very first one we've sold in the county. I reckon your boss must be something of a trend setter?'

I declined to answer and took a closer look. The cutting department comprised two round drums each about a yard in diameter and each had a pair of small blades attached to their rims, they couldn't have been more than three inches long. The base of the drums rotated at some wild speed using power from the tractor and the gearing was such that the blades when

52

they were rotating did not make contact with each other.

It all appeared to be so simple and obvious which made me wonder why the reciprocating blade mower had been used for so long. It must have been the lack of available power, I surmised but then, with no hydraulic lift arms to raise it off the ground at the end of the row, there may have been other difficulties.

Either way, it looked as if tomorrow could be an interesting day but first I had to finish this one.

I was pleased to see at least some of the cows had made their way up to the gate when I arrived in Farm Close. Thrifty was there standing next to Matty and I gave each of them an ear tickle as I walked passed them. Horns was doing her best to be a good girl, and Lucy was sort of standing by the gate, but she was still too shy to mix with elder members of the herd.

I asked her why the rest of the girls weren't waiting for me, but she went all bashful and put her head down to grab a mouthful of grass for something to do.

As I walked down to the end of the field I found myself agreeing with Harry: having cows which needed rounding up every time they had to be milked put hours on a day, hours which could have been spent doing more important things. I could have started bringing some ground barley to bribe them to be by the gate, but it was a negative move which, once started would be hard to stop.

No, I thought. They would have to make their own minds up about this and hopefully they would come round to my way of thinking once more: like, I don't want to have to walk all the way across a field to fetch them when they are quite capable of walking up to the gate to meet me.

And then I recalled the phrase I had come across when I had been with them before: 'For cows to love you, you have to love them first'. And it was so true and I was aware that, at this moment in time not all of them came anywhere near to loving me. Perhaps they had felt jilted when I disappeared out of their lives the last time I was here. It was something I was going to have to work on.

With them all gathered up by the gate, I opened it and waited for them to saunter through. 'Come on girls,' I said. 'It's been a beautiful day; let's see if we can all keep it that way.'

When Pauline, one of the Red Polls strolled passed and stopped she turned her head to look at me and I thought I had found a new friend but then she lifted her tail and dropped a bucketful of poo at my feet.

'Nice one,' I said. 'I thought I had taught you better manners than that.'

She turned and looked at me again, and then coughed, which fired a plume of slurry towards me. It was close, too close, but it missed.

Oh well, give it time, I thought, as I pulled the gate closed. Time changes everything.

With the cows in the collecting yard, I ran down to the house to get the bucket of warm water and the udder cloth.

'Are you going to have a cup of tea before you make a start, or are you in a hurry to be finished?' Alice asked when I had placed the bucket in the sink and turned the hot tap on.

I glanced up at the clock which was just coming up to five o'clock and considered I had just about enough time for a cup. All that effort with the sheep had made me thirsty.

'Sit yourself down then and I'll make a fresh pot.'

'Is Harry still clearing up?' I asked.

'Well, I think he's about finished but he did come in a few minutes ago looking for the trussing needle.'

'Not the dreaded trussing needle. What on earth did he want that for?'

'I don't think he wanted it for the reason you're thinking.'

'I should hope not.' Memories of being awoken by Harry pushing that long needle through the bed covers still lived with me and I hadn't overslept since.

Alice laughed. 'Well it seemed to have worked. But no, he wanted the needle to stitch the large sack up, the one the rolled up fleeces are placed in.'

'Oh right,' I said, recalling it had been just about full when we finished.

The tea was poured, Alice pausing after the first few drops had left the spout to tilt the pot backwards and ensure the water was evenly mixed with the tea leaves before continuing to fill the cup through the strainer.

'Have you seen Elizabeth lately,' she asked, adding a splash of milk and passing the cup over to me.

'I met her down the fields the other day but we've both been a bit busy. I was hoping to pop down and see her this evening, you know, just to see how she's getting on, that's assuming she's going to be there.' I took a sip of tea.

'Well, I haven't heard that she's not,' Alice said. 'Why don't you give her a call?'

'No, I won't, thanks; I'll just turn up and see. Give her a surprise visit.'

'If you're sure, but you know you can use the phone if you want to.'

'Yes, I know. Thank you.' I drained the last of my tea and stood up. 'Anyway, I'd better get these cows milked. That's the first job.'

I collected the bucket from the sink and made my way up to the collecting yard where the cows were beginning to get restless and I could hear the dull plopping of slurry landing on concrete as they registered their protest.

'Oh, come on, girls. Give me a break,' I said, as I walked through them. 'You've only been in here ten minutes.'

The Lister engine started on the third turn of the handle and then, when I was ready, I placed a scoop of ground barley into each of the four feeders and opened the gate to let the first four cows in.

CHAPTER SIX

Artificial insemination

AS USUAL, AT half-past six in the morning I met Harry padding around the kitchen making a pot of tea. We didn't speak much but I managed a 'Good-Morning' as I pulled out a chair and sat down at the table and waited for the tea to be poured. Harry slid my cup across and then disappeared down the hall with a cup of tea for Alice. I could hear him opening doors and climbing the stairs as he made his way through the house.

I took a sip and stared out of the window to see what the weather was doing. Already the sun was climbing high in the sky and it looked as if it was going to be yet another warm day.

Across in the orchard I could see Pedro taking his morning constitutional, pausing to lower his head to have a sniff at where the sheep had been penned as they waited their turn to be sheared. It wouldn't be long though, before he retreated to the shade provided by the large oak trees bordering the top end of the orchard, and where he would spend the day perusing the meaning of life while using his tail to keep flies on the move.

Harry returned to the kitchen and sat down to drink

his tea. 'I should keep an eye on the red and white Friesian; she's getting pretty close to calving and I saw one of the heifers bulling yesterday evening so if you keep her in the yard after you've milked her, I'll give the Artificial Insemination man a call.'

'Right,' I said. 'Are you fetching the cows in or are you off shepherding? I don't mind if you are.'

'No, I'll fetch them in and then pop down to check on the sheep. I'll also have a look in Long Meadow to see where we are with the hay.'

Harry set off up the yard, Ross and Bob he'd let out from their kennels jumping happily around him as he headed out towards the top gate. I wandered over to the dairy and retrieved the bucket for the hot water.

I don't know why, but there was a marked change in the cows this morning when they walked into the collecting yard. They were holding their heads up higher than they had been for the last couple of weeks and, if it's possible for cows to do it, there seemed to be almost a bounce in their stride.

Thrifty walked passed me and gave me an acknowledging glance, Lucy was mingling happily with the other girls and even Pauline was keeping her tail clamped over the rear-mounted canon she had used to try and cover me with slurry a few days before. All of which was very welcome but a little unexpected; perhaps, at long last, we had turned the corner.

And milking too was almost like old times. Thrifty took a handful of ground barley while she waited to come into be milked and then gave me a big rasping lick as I stroked her ears and the top of her head. Horns was back to her cheerful self and spent the time gazing dewy-eyed at me and making silly snorting

58

noises whenever I looked back at her, and the whole herd appeared to be in good spirits. Better still, no one crapped on the floor and no one started messing about and kicking milking machines off.

There was a surprise too when I noted how much more milk we had – an increase of nearly four gallons on yesterday. I felt great and so proud of them all. When I went in for breakfast, having endured the wrath of Miserable Old Sod on the churn lorry for having to wait a few precious minutes while I brought the last three churns down, I told Harry how different the cows were.

'Well, I told you they would be,' he said. 'You've a good way with them. Well done. Did you remember to keep the heifer in, the one which was bulling?'

'Yes, I did, as long as it's the right one,' I replied. 'Sometimes it's a job to see which one is bulling.'

'You can usually tell by the way she looks and her temperament and you should also have some idea which one it is from her records.'

I nodded. Harry was right and I made a note to see if I could introduce a better recording scheme than just scribbling notes down on a calendar. The only detail which I regularly recorded was the amount of milk sent to the dairy each day. Individual cow yields, calving dates and rations were virtually non-existent.

'Have you rung the AI man?' I asked.

'Yes, just before you came in. He said he would be with us by ten o'clock and probably earlier.'

'That's prompt service.'

'Well they have to be if they're going to achieve a good first-time pregnancy rate. If every cow needs a second service, weeks of production can be lost.'

'You've never thought of having a bull on the farm,

59

then?' I asked. 'One that could run with the cows and just get on with the job when required?'

'We used to have a bull, a big Hereford, but he was cantankerous old devil who you could never trust,' Harry said. 'We'd put him out in the field so he could enjoy some grazing and to stop him roaming too far, we hooked a long chain through his nose ring and attached it to a cast iron hub that had been used as the front wheel of a Fordson tractor. It weighed a ton but it didn't prevent him moving about because he used to hook his horns into it and lift it off the ground.

I met him coming down the yard one day with this load on his head, and he started to paw the ground before he chased me into the barn and it was only the loft steps which saved me. I was up there for hours before he decided to move on. The next day I loaded him into a lorry and sent him off to market; I thought it would be safer if he was in a pie with a piece of pastry on top of him.

'But it was when we changed over to artificial insemination the fun really started. You remember what happened, don't you Alice?'

Alice looked up from her tea and sighed. 'Harry I've heard this story so many times, do you really have to tell it again?'

'Well I think John should know.'

'I can't think why,' Alice said.

'What do you think I should know?' I asked.

Harry drew a breath and looked down the table at Alice, but if it was support he was after, there was none on offer from that direction. Alice was at the sink filling the kettle.

'It was the first time we were using AI,' he started. 'And I'd rung up the AI man and he couldn't say when he would be with us but as it was a market day, I had to tell him I wouldn't be about to help him. Instead, I said I'd arrange for someone else to be there. Well, the only person I could find who was available was a lady who kept her pony with us. Mildred was her name, wasn't it Alice?'

'Yes, and she was a perfectly respectable lady who was always keen to lend a helping hand,' she said.

'I met her walking up the field, so I explained we had this man coming to serve one of the cows and I asked her if she wouldn't mind helping him. I have to say she looked a bit put out but she agreed to do what she could,' he continued. 'Anyway, she clearly thought she was expected to help out somehow so when the AI man arrived she met him by his van and told him she'd managed to put the cow in the crush and screwed a hook into the wall for him to hang his trousers on, and there was a bucket of warm water for him to wash himself afterwards.'

Harry collapsed onto the table, his face awash with tears and his laughter rolled out in ever louder waves. 'Oh boy, I should think he dined out on that one for years,' he gasped.

I noticed Alice was smiling. 'You might spare a thought for Mildred who felt she had to move away from the village shortly afterwards,' she said.

'Yes, but how about Lord Shmuck,' Harry said, wiping his face. 'He was even worse.'

'Get on with it then, tell John all about it and then perhaps we can settle down to some boiled bacon,' Alice said, pouring the tea.

'Who was Lord Shmuck?' I asked.

'Well that wasn't his real name but that's what everyone called him due to him being so hoity-toity and speaking like he had a couple of plums in his mouth.'

'What happened to him then?'

'He bought some land with a few buildings just off the Stratton Road, you know, the one which goes down to the reservoir, and he had the idea of starting a pedigree herd of Charolais cattle. So he goes and buys a dozen heifers and then relies on AI to get them in calf, but it didn't go well and try as he might he couldn't seem to get the timing right and not one of his heifers actually managed to get in calf.

'Anyway, one day he happened to be in the field when he spotted a heifer bulling, so he rushes home and gets on the phone to the AI and they send out a man who arrives before Lordy can make it back to the farm. When he meets the man on his way out and he asks him how it all went and the man tried to speak like he was being spoken to so he told him it went: "Absolutely top hole, old boy," and Lordy looks at him aghast and replies: "So, that's where we've been going wrong".'

The sun was warm on my back when I walked up the yard and the day had all the signs of being another scorcher. I'd left Harry to make his peace with Alice although I suspect that while admonishing Harry for relating such tales, she was not above enjoying them herself just to see Harry looking so cheerful.

I was heading for the David Brown tractor and, once I had filled the fuel tank and checked the oil and water, I was to hook it up to the new mower. And I have to say, I was rather excited, yet relieved Harry would soon be on hand to help me.

The mower still had a layer of wrapping around it

which I needed to pull off before the machine was fully exposed and I could see the drums and the drive which led to them from the power take off. Rolled up and stuck to the side of the mower was the operating manual and I carefully prised it free. A few minutes reading through it could pay dividends in the future, I thought, but Harry turned up before I had time to open it.

'Well, this looks simple enough,' he said. 'The lower linkage arms slip onto these pins here and need lynch pins placed through these holes here to hold them on.' He gave me a stare. 'And the top link slips in here, again with a lynch pin to stop the retaining pin from dropping out.'

Another wide-eyed stare.

'The pto shaft looks alright but we'll have to check it's not too long or the frame could be bent when the mower's lowered. Right then, boy, reverse the tractor onto it and let's see if we can hook it all up.'

It was my cue to climb aboard the tractor and attempt to drive the tractor back so the lower linkage arms could be attached without any mega amounts of pulling pushing and swearing. And I have to say, on this occasion, it wasn't too bad.

'Not bad, boy. Not bad at all, for a change,' Harry said as he pushed the linkage arms on and then made a big thing about securing them with their lynch pins. 'See how those lynch pins just seem to clip in to place, boy? It's just so easy, almost unforgettable if you think about it.'

I grunted a reply.

'That just leaves the pto shaft,' he said. 'To allow it to lengthen and shorten, there's a tube sliding in a larger second tube but it's important there's sufficient room for the mower to be raised and lowered without the tubes running out of space.'

'We covered that at college,' I said.

'Oh, that's good.'

With everything attached I pulled the hydraulic lever on the tractor and slowly raised the mower into its transport position.

'Do you think we should try it before we take it down the field, boy?'

'It would be as well,' I replied. 'It's a long way to walk back again.'

Harry released the catch which swung the two drums into their offset working position and then, after a close look at everything, asked me to engage the pto, a task requiring me to press the clutch pedal down as far as it could go and then reach behind and move the lever by the pto shaft.

'Do you want the high or low ratio?' I asked.

Harry thought about it for a few minutes while I remained stretched out with a clutch pedal on the tip of my boot at one end of my body and the top of a lever between my fingertips stretched out at the other. 'Try it in high ratio, boy. It all depends on what engine speed we're going to run at.'

I pushed the lever away from me and selected 'high' and then slowly allowed the clutch pedal to rise. Then engine speed dipped as the drive engaged and the drums began to turn, rapidly gaining speed and starting to whine as the blades sped round at some phenomenal rate.

'Give her more throttle,' Harry shouted at me. 'Look on the dial and set the pto speed at 540 rpm.'

And the whining noise became louder and the dust and loose straw beneath the drums began to lift of the floor and swirl about us as we watched and listened to the mower's howl increase until it reached its full operating speed.

After a couple of minutes we could stand it no longer and Harry waved his arms about, gesturing to me to shut the tractor down. But even when the tractor engine crawled to a halt, the drums continued to turn for some time before they finally stopped rotating. And then, as the dust and strands of straw floated back down, everything was quiet again.

'Well, that sounds as if it's working alright,' Harry said. 'Is there anything in the instructions regarding lubrication we ought to know about?'

'I don't know. I haven't had a chance to find out yet,' I said. 'Probably best to have a look though, I would have thought there was something to grease up or an oil level in the gearbox to check.'

I opened the operator's manual and found the daily lubrication chart. 'It says here there's two grease nipples on each of the drums with the usual ones to grease on the universal joints, and to check the oil level in the gear box we need to remove the small screw as marked.'

'Anything else?' Harry asked.

I turned over the page to find an item on out of season care which was a bit premature.

'No, I think that's about it.'

'Right, if you grease up and check the oil, you can set off down to Long Meadow,' Harry said. 'I'll follow on behind with the Fordson and the baler along with the sledge.'

Oh no, not the man sledge, the one which nearly caused me to collapse with heat exhaustion and inflicted on me such deep blisters on my hands, I still have the scars?

'Which sledge are you bringing down?' I asked, fearing the worst.

'The new one, the one we just drop the bales in and pull a rope to release them,' he replied. 'Why, do you want to use the other one?'

'No, the new sledge will be fine.'

'Oh, right. I'll do that then.'

Harry headed off for the tractor shed while I found the grease gun and, after a few pumps with the handle, was relieved to discover it wasn't empty; I had discovered filling a grease gun from a twenty-five pound tub could be a messy job.

With every bearing lubricated and oil levels checked, I set off down the field and was surprised to see how much weight the rear mounted mower took off the front tractor wheels; they bounced a few inches off the ground every time the rear wheels dropped into a dip in the track and the steering was really light. I supposed it was because, for transport, the drums were carried in a position which put them in line with the tractor and were some distance away from the rear wheels.

The solution would have been to put some front weights on the tractor but apart from having to be careful not to open the throttle too quickly, it was not too difficult to navigate my way down to Long Meadow.

I couldn't deny a sense of excitement, mingled with a degree of trepidation as I drew to a halt in the field. Jumping off the tractor, I moved a few paces away and saw a brand-new and as yet unused machine.

Removing the pin which held the drums safe during transport, I swung them into their offset, working position and heard the over centre lock click into place. I had noted the drums needed to be level when in work, so I lowered the mower and adjusted the top link to tilt them back a little and then wound down the adjustable linkage arm a couple of turns.

All set, I clambered back onto the tractor and I raised the mower clear of the ground and headed off to the point where the old mower had disintegrated. Starting the drums rotating called for my usual stretching act between boot and fingertips, but soon they were spinning at full speed, the whining noise not quite so deafening in an open field.

So, this was it. I lowered the mower, engaged high-second gear, began to move forwards into the crop and then, to my joy and surprise, watched the grass disappear under the flexible skirt at the front and re-emerge at the rear of the mower as a nice, tidy swath. It was terrific.

With Long Meadow being a good flat field, I wound up the speed until we were travelling at an incredible rate, probably three times the speed the old mower could be used at. The mower just purred its way through everything it ran into.

At one point I was moved to stop and take a look to make sure it was cutting all the grass but there was no mistake; when I pulled the grass back across the swath there wasn't any uncut blade to be seen. And when I set about mowing the dreaded back swath – the one on the outside edge of the field that had been run on by the tractor when I first started the field, it just did it. No fuss, no blockages, no nothing.

An hour into it and the field was finished, and Harry had yet to make it down here, so I fastened the drums back in their transport position and headed back up

Piggy Hill towards the farm.

I met Harry just as he was opening the gate out of Hollow Close and he didn't look to happy.

'Go on, boy. Tell me the worst. The top link pin has snapped, the blades have bent, and you've hit a gate post. Go on, tell me, I can take it,' he said.

'No, nothing like that,' I said. 'It...'

'You mean it's worse?' Harry's eyes glanced back to the mower, almost daring himself to take a longer look.

'No, there's nothing wrong with it at all. Believe me.' I stopped the tractor. 'Go and see for yourself.'

'But why are you coming back then? You've only been down there an hour and Alice has made you some lunch.'

'Well, the job's finished.'

'What, all of it?'

'Yes, all of it.'

'Well, I'll be buggered.'

He seemed lost for words.

'Right then, let's have a think what's for the best. If you go and mow the bottom half of Farm Close, the piece the cows are shut off, and then move into Signet that will give us another twenty-five acres to play with and leaves about another twenty acres which, if the weather holds, we can do later this week. How's that sound to you?'

'Yes, that would be good' I said. 'Might be an idea to see if we can pin down Ronny for a bit of bale cart.'

'Oh, he'll turn up soon enough. What was the hay like in Long Meadow? Do you think it will bale later today?'

'It's getting close, but I was thinking that if you ted the hay and then the grass I've just mowed, the hay could be ready to bale by the end of the afternoon,' I said.

I left Harry to it and headed for Farm Close and then remembered he said he had some lunch for me. Ah well, what's a sandwich of boiled bacon and a bottle of cold tea?

CHAPTER SEVEN

Sorting out the bully

IT HAD BEEN a good day and one I reflected on as I drove out of the rick yard with the girls' buffer feed on board. The new mower had worked faultlessly and had mowed more acres in a day than the old mower could have achieved in three or four days, and only then if it managed to stay in one piece. Better still, it had left the grass in a good fluffy swath which could only speed up the drying process.

Harry managed to have a good day too, working away in Long Meadow where, after tedding all the grass he had baled the half I had cut before D-Day, when the mower disintegrated. He had even stacked all the bales into groups of seven so they would get some air around them and be ready to load onto trailers.

I took the buffer feed across to the far side of the field where the cows had gathered. Just why they still enjoyed eating dry hay when there was so much grass about was beyond me, but it was probably a habit. And I was more than pleased for them.

With the bales cut and spread around so they could all have their share, I stood back and looked at them and noticed that little Lucy was still standing back and not joining in so I took a few wads of hay over to her.

And that was not a very clever thing to have done because before I knew it, Pauline, the big Red Poll strutted over and gave Lucy a head butt in her side and then pushed her away.

'What the hell do you think you are doing?' I shouted at her. 'You just get yourself back over there or you'll be looking over the edge of a pie dish.'

I shoved her in the direction of the other cows. 'And don't you ever do that again you great bully.'

After a few steps she stopped and I knew what she was planning. She lifted her tail and drew breath before giving a big cough and firing a jet of slurry. But I was ready for it and stepped out of the way before she could change direction.

I moved round and stood in front of her. 'You are one horrible cow,' I told her. 'Carry on like this and you won't be here.'

Back in the Land Rover, I drove over to the side of the field and parked up under the low branches of a weeping willow tree, turned off the engine and waited to see what Pauline was planning next.

And I didn't have to wait many minutes before she was heading off towards Lucy again. Bullying can be a big problem in dairy herds; the herdsman at college spent a lot of time splitting up groups of cows that couldn't get on with each other.

'They're just like people,' he had said. 'Groups form a social order and in the run of things, they can get on with each other, but occasionally you get a misfit who wants to disrupt things by picking on the most timid members of the group. If it gets really bad the only solution is to get rid of the offender.'

Although there was still plenty of hay where Pauline was, she strode over to Lucy and did her head butting thing again. And it made me so angry.

I started the Land Rover and drove as fast as I dared across the field and skidded to a halt a few yards away from her. Not pausing, I opened the door and stepped out and started shouting at Pauline like I've never spoken to a cow before. I told her exactly what I thought of her, how she needed to change her ways and warned her that if she was even considering using her rear end again to express an opinion, I would make sure she doesn't get any fuel to put through it for the next ten weeks; possibly longer.

Up to that moment, Pauline was intent on getting her mouth around the hay I had carried over for Lucy and, with Lucy now standing some distance away, all she had to do was take a step forward and start eating. But she didn't. Instead, she snorted her disgust and turned away, strolling slowly back to the main herd.

I think I could mark that one up as a victory to me, but I doubted the battle was over. What I needed to do was encourage Lucy to become more confident and assert herself more, because I had a feeling that if it wasn't Pauline doing the bullying, it would soon be one of the others.

I drove back to the farm and, as I turned onto the top road, I saw Elizabeth walking towards me. I pulled alongside, opened the window and stupidly, I couldn't think of a word to say.

'Hello, John,' she said. 'What was all that shouting about?'

'Oh, that was just me telling a bullying cow what I thought of her. I don't suppose she'll be any different for it though. Anyway, good to see you and what brings you up here?'

Elizabeth hesitated. 'Well, I just thought I wanted to see you, that's all.' She looked down at the ground and scuffed her shoe against a non-existent weed. 'It seems almost as if you don't want to see me anymore.'

I stopped the engine and climbed out. 'What! I been thinking you didn't want to see me, especially when I drove down the other evening and you weren't there.'

'I know. That was the one evening I had to go and visit Auntie Joan, you know the one who lives by herself in Brampton. If only you had phoned, I could have told you.'

'How about all the other times when we'd arranged to meet up after college and you didn't turn up,' I said.

'John, I told you how much work I have to do just to keep up with the course. Biomedicine isn't an easy subject, you know.'

'And I suppose farming is, then?'

'No, but...' She stopped and I saw the tears welling in her eyes. I had said too much and I moved closer and put my arm around her. But she shook me away.

'Go away,' she sobbed. 'I don't want you anymore.'

There seemed nothing I could say but I tried my best. 'We could go and have another look at the cows, if you want. The red and white Friesian's about to calve so...'

'Sod your bloody cows. Don't you ever think of anything else?' Elizabeth turned and headed for the cattle grid.

'Elizabeth,' I shouted. 'No, please don't go. Not that way.'

I ran after her but she was already making her way across the metal poles that formed the cattle grid and I was going to be too late.

Her scream was loud and penetrating and as I ran to help her I was thinking broken legs and worse. 'Are you alright?' I asked.

After years' of use, the poles had come loose in their sockets and could turn, making them next to impossible to walk across; as soon as they were stepped on they would twist and feet, and anything attached to them, would slip between the gap. And that is what Elizabeth had done.

'I think so. Just a bit bruised.'

I stood on the edge where there was a secure footing and leaned over to help Elizabeth climb out. Fortunately, the space below the poles wasn't very far down but the bottom had about a foot of foul-smelling slurry in it.

'Oh, bloody hell. Look at the state of my jeans,' she cried when we had arrived on firm ground again.

'I'll get some straw and give them a wipe,' I offered.

'No, don't go anywhere,' she said. 'Not now. Wait a minute.'

Her voice had softened and she was looking at me. And as I nodded, I held out my arms and she came to me. 'It sounds as if we've both been pretty stupid,' she said, as we met for a long kiss. 'We can go and look at the cows if you really want to.'

'No, it's alright. I'll go down and see them later.' I pulled her closer to me. 'Love you Elizabeth.'

'Love you too but I think I'm making your jeans dirty with all that crap in the cattle grid.'

'And worse than that,' I said, 'I think I'm now covering your jumper with pieces of hay,'

She laughed and took my hand and pulled me towards the rick yard. 'Come on, let's go and have a real roll in the hay together and then we can both think of an excuse to tell Alice.'

Awakening to a clear blue sky was becoming the norm and it was so easy to forget those dark, winter mornings when outside, an icy wind howled and moaned around the head stones as I sat on the edge of the bed and braced myself for the moment I would have to lower my bare feet onto a cold, lino floor.

Those days would return; of that I was certain, but in the meantime, with temperatures barely falling below the high seventies, staying cool and avoiding dehydration were the key objectives.

Not that such extremes ever appeared to trouble Harry, who always wore a cap and along with a shirt, vest and heavy calico work trousers, and only rarely was seen swigging water. Perhaps it was the extra half cup of tea he always had that made the difference.

'Going to be another warm one today, boy,' he said, as he removed the teapot lid and poured in the boiling water.

'It certainly looks like it. I heard it was the warmest day of the year yesterday.'

'Well I think today could be even warmer,' he said as he prepared to disappear out of the kitchen holding Alice's cup of tea. 'Oh, by the way, the red and white Friesian calved, a good-looking bull calf.'

'Yes, I went and had a look at her last thing and saw she had. Good strong calf and she looked well too.'

'That must have been late?'

'Well, it was a bit. I think you'd gone to bed when I came in.'

I sipped my tea while I waited for him to return and my memories went back to last night with Elizabeth.

'Ronny appeared from somewhere yesterday while you were milking and he tells me he's checked his diary and consulted with his secretary and can be with us today,' Harry said. 'So just on the off chance he actually does make it I'll run some trailers down to Long Meadow so we're all set to get the bales off the field, and if he doesn't turn up, we'll just have to press on without him.'

I made my walk out to the dairy to retrieve the bucket and fill it with hot water while Harry fetched the cows in. Surprised to see, when he came over to shut the collecting yard gate, he was covered fairly liberally from the chest down to his boots with slurry, fresh warm slurry.

'That frigging Red Poll,' he said. 'She lined me up and then gave a big cough so this happened.' He spread his arms out to show me the full extent of his covering which apart from a small area by his pocket, was just about complete.

'That will be Pauline,' I said. 'She's getting a bit bolshie at the moment and I think it's to do with the young heifer she's taken a dislike to.'

'Well, if Pauline, whatever her name is, carries on like that, she'll be toast big time,' he said, heading off to the house for a change of clothes.

I turned to face Pauline and stared at her. 'I hope you heard that. That was the boss and he can have you out of here just like that.' I clicked my fingers to show her just how quick.

With milking underway, I was pleased to see how the girls were continuing to be more relaxed and happier than they had been, and this was reflected in their milk yield although, with milking directly into the churn it was impossible to see how much each cow was producing.

For a few obviously low yielders this was their saving because I felt sure that in a larger and better equipped herd these under-performers would have been culled out and it was very likely dear old Thrifty would have been one of them – and that would not have been good.

Anyway, Harry was still convinced there was a place for dual-breeds and seven hundred gallons/year cows was acceptable, providing the calf she produced turned into a profitable beef animal.

For some reason, I thought the boiled bacon sliced off this morning's joint was particularly flavoursome, not that I was moved to ask for more. That would set a precedent which may have been hard to change and anyway, two slices with a round of bread and butter was normally more than enough.

'More tea, John? Asked Alice, holding out her hand for my cup. 'And how was Elizabeth when you saw her?'

'Oh, just fine, thanks. We got a few things sorted out, and well, it's all good.'

'Well her mother will be pleased. She's been telling me Elizabeth has done nothing but mope around the house ever since she came home from college.'

'That's a shame,' I said, not really wanting to take this conversation any further.

'Anyway, everything's alright now?'

'Yes, I think so.'

'Good. I have to say though, there was a lot of hay, straw and mud on the sofa when I came down this morning. I thought one of the dogs had been left in.'

'Yes, I'm sorry about that. I had a bale burst open on me when I was feeding the cows. I should have taken more care to have brushed it off.'

Alice gave me her, "I wasn't born yesterday look", and passed my tea over.

'Will you have another cup, Harry?'

'Just half a cup, please Alice,' he replied, sliding his cup down the table. 'Did you know you can now get overalls which hay and straw doesn't stick to?' he said. 'They call them Big Porky's.

'Right,' I said, draining the last of my tea. 'I'll go and see if Ronny's turned up.'

There was a smell of cigarette smoke in the air as I walked up the yard and I knew Ronny was about before he strolled out from the tractor shed, his folded down wellingtons scuffling across the yard's gravelly surface.

'Morning John,' he said, raising a hand which held the last vestiges of a self-rolled cigarette between the tips of his finger and thumb. 'How's you?'

'I'm very well, thank you Ronny,' I replied.

He took a final drag and then, as he exhaled smoke out of his right nostril, produced a tin from one of his pockets, flipped the lid open and dropped the remains of the cigarette in it. 'Can't waste them,' he said, waving the tin in the air. 'They're nearly five shillings a packet now and it won't be long before they're a quid; just you see if I'm not right.'

I thought at that moment I'd rather not see anything of Ronny's and even less smoke it, but I smiled sympathetically. 'That's life Ronny. It's getting to be an expensive world for all of us.'

'What's the plan today then?'

'Well, there're bales in Long Meadow to load up, there will be hay to bale, hay to ted and hay to row up. And then there will be some more to mow and more bales to load.'

'Sounds like a busy day,' he said.

A sudden squeal of excited dogs announced Harry's departure from the house.

'Morning Ronny,' he said when he had made it into the workshop. 'Haven't found any real boots to wear yet then, or are there enough holes in them to keep the air circulating?'

Harry didn't wait for an answer but turned to me. 'I've taken two trailers down to Long Meadow. What I was thinking is that if you and Ronny each take another trailer down we'll have enough to clear the field when we've mopped up the rest of the hay. You can get on with some tedding while Ronny and I load the trailers and then I can bale while you move on to mow the rest of the grass.'

It all seemed clear enough, I thought. 'But what does Ronny do while you're baling?'

'He can be rowing up in front of me and then go and row up in Farm Close. If he has any spare time he can come and throw a few bales onto the trailers we've brought down.'

'But aren't we a tractor short if he's going to do that? I asked.

Harry thought about it. 'I'll give Sam a call and see if he can let us have a tractor – he owes me a few favours. You go and sort the trailers out with Ronny and I'll see what I can do.'

I nodded. 'Right then Ronny, if you take the Fordson and hook on the big two-wheeler, I'll hook up the David Brown to the four-wheeler, but make sure you fill the diesel tank up first,' I said.

CHAPTER EIGHT

Beating the weather

THERE WAS SWEAT, there was dust and there were bales. It was one of those magical days when tractors mowed, tedded, rowed up and baled. Trailers were loaded and brought into the rick yard to await unloading and the air was full with the scent of freshly mowed grass, freshly baled hay and, thanks to Harry borrowing a TVO-powered Massey Ferguson tractor from Sam Jones, the never to be forgotten sweet aroma of the exhaust these tractors produced.

'It's the tractor they use for yard scraping,' Harry said when he arrived in Long Meadow driving a tractor which was just about covered in dried-on slurry. 'But it will be alright for a bit of rowing up.'

For my part, the mower worked amazingly well, the speed at which this machine could cut was just so impressive – and all with just four blades, each about the size of a couple of fingers. By lunchtime I had finished so, having dropped the mower off at the farm, I headed down the field to see how Harry and Ronny were getting on.

I know we were busy but I couldn't help pausing for a second or two at the top of Piggy Hill and look down to Long Meadow and see the borrowed tractor rowing up the swaths, Ronny driving it and the exhaust pot belching out a puff of dark smoke every time the governor opened and pumped more fuel into the engine. Meanwhile, Harry looked as if he was about to hook the Fordson up to the baler.

And that is something I didn't want him to do. Finding top gear, I tore down Piggy Hill, bumped across Forty Acres and then turned right into Long Meadow. Harry was just about to slip the power take off onto the tractor's shaft when I skidded to a stop beside him.

'Where's the fire?' he asked when I jumped of the tractor.

'I just wanted to see if you'd rather use the David Brown now I've finished mowing.'

'What all of it?'

'Yes, every last blade of it.'

'That's amazing,' he said. 'I would never have believed it possible.'

'I thought you might be better off with this tractor with its dual clutch – you know, when the clutch is pressed to stop the tractor, the pto keeps turning, unless you press the pedal right down. Pretty useful if you're baling.'

'You're right, boy. We'll do that. Let me get the Fordson unhitched and we'll hook the David Brown on. And while we're at it, you can stay down here with Ronny and do the baling and I'll take the tedder up to Farm Close and knock some life into that and then move into what you've mowed today.'

'Don't know whether Farm Close will bale today but I'll bring the baler round when I've mopped up this piece and we'll see.'

And that is how I filled the next two and half hours

81

of the afternoon. Not long after I'd started, Alice drove down and dropped off some boiled beef sandwiches and a bottle of tea which I shared with Ronny. I let him have the sandwiches while I drank the tea, which was still reasonably warm.

When Ronny had finished rowing up – putting two swaths into one for the baler - I asked him to hook his tractor onto a trailer and start loading as many bales as he could on to it and then put the rest of the bales in stacks of sevens.

'If we had a tractor loader we could lift all these bales onto the trailer without having to pitch them by hand,' he said.

I smiled at him and, while I knew he was right, convincing Harry was the biggest hurdle to overcome. I also noticed while he was speaking to me, the myriad of black spots of oil which now almost covered his face, arms and presumably his clothes.

When it came to changing fields I folded up the baler so the pick-up was in line with the tractor and chose to leave the sledge attached and tow it behind the baler. Ronny followed me with the borrowed tractor towing the rower up with its big offset spider wheels which, in transport position had a penchant for veering to the middle of the road making tight right hand turns impossible. I pointed this out to Ronny who said he would be careful.

The trouble was that, to get to Farm Close, involved some tight right hand turns, not least at the end of the village where the route required a turn off the High Street into Harbury Lane, a narrow road between two walls which, at best, was only wide enough for a single vehicle.

There was nothing I could do though, I had the baler

and sledge to squeeze through what seemed to be an ever-decreasing gap. But it eventually it widened out and it was only a few minutes before I arrived in Farm Close. Ronny arrived a little later and I couldn't help noticing the brick dust on the end of the tines and hated to think what the wall must look like.

As we set the baler up, Harry drove into the field with the Fordson.

'I think you'll be alright to bale this lot,' he said. 'But the other field still needs some making and will have to wait until tomorrow.'

We walked out into the hay and picked up a few handfuls. It was crisp and smelt sweet as good hay always does.

Three days later, the New Holland Super Hayliner 68 was parked under the barn and all that remained of haymaking was to load up the bales from the last field and stack them in the rick yard.

'I think two trailers should do it,' Harry said. 'There can't be more than a couple of hundred bales can there? I assume you looked at the counter on the baler?'

Counter? That was the first time I had heard about one of those. 'Where's the counter then?'

'It's by the knotters and it gets tripped every time a knot is tied. Haven't you seen it?'

I shook my head. 'No, I'll have to check on that. But if we take the two largest trailers and there's some left we'll have to go back again.'

'Did you cover that subject at college?' he asked.

'What, bale counters?'

'No. Stating the bleeding obvious.'

'Not really, not in any depth. I guess I'm just sort of

a natural at it.'

'Oh, be away with you boy. Just hook up the trailers and let's be out of here,' Harry said.

And we did just that. Harry took the Fordson while I climbed aboard the David Brown and, with the ropes and pitch forks stashed on the front of my trailer, the dogs running and barking beside us, we drove down to the field.

It wasn't quite so warm this morning and the air felt fresher. If the weather was to change now no one could accuse us of not having made the best of a solid period of good dry weather. We'd mowed and baled over fifty acres of hay and all of it had been beautifully made without a drop of rain falling on it.

There was just one caveat. When we were discussing haymaking Harry had told me that there was more bad hay made in a good time than in a bad time. And that he said was because, when the sun is beating down, hay can feel dry but it still hasn't finished being 'made'.

'It may look right but if it's baled too soon, it will heat up in the barn to incredible temperatures and cause a fire and all the horrors that go with a farm fire,' he said.

I wondered if we would see any barn fires this year.

Harry brought his tractor to a halt in the middle of the field and I waited for him to climb onto the back of my tractor. 'Reckon we've some rain on the way,' he said. 'That's how all these long dry spells end. A good clap of thunder and a good soaking. And we've still two hundred sheep to shear and the pigs to clean out.'

I stopped by the heap of bales furthest from the gate and Harry gave me the choice of stacking or loading.

'I'll stack this one,' I said. 'And I can tell you these headland bales weigh a ton.'

'Don't worry boy. The headland goes right round the field and there will be others.'

I had tried to drop the bales out of the sledge in something approaching a row which we could drive along but there was invariably the odd stack which required a diversion. But bit by bit, the bales came on board and I did my best to make a tidy stack I hoped would stay on the trailer until we arrived back at the farm.

Meanwhile, the sky had continued to darken and it seemed Harry was going to be right about the impending deluge.

'How many more bales can you count,' he asked when I had just about completed the fifth course of bales.

I stood up and looked out across the field and counted the stacks. 'Near as I can tell there's about twenty-five and if each of those has seven bales, that makes one hundred and seventy five.'

'More than I thought then,' Harry said as he plunged his pitchfork into the next bale. 'Better try and get seven courses on this one with a few on top and we'll see if the rest will fit on the other trailer.'

To make it easier for him, I left a gap on level five for the bales to be forked up to. I then grabbed them and started making two courses above, plus a few more. 'The birds are going to have to fly a bit higher to get over this one,' I said, as I grabbed another bale Harry hoisted up to me. 'Just finish that stack and that will about do it.'

With the last bale on board, I stood up and took stock of the weather. Already on the horizon I could see flashes of lightening and there was a distant rumble of thunder.

'You'd better come down,' Harry said. 'And we'll see about loading the next one.'

I watched Harry, pitchfork in hand, set off towards the Fordson.

'There's just one thing, Harry,' I shouted. 'Just how do I get down?'

'Lower yourself down to the back rave and then use it as a ladder for the rest of the way,' he said, without stopping.

The view to the ground looked intimidating and I couldn't even see the top of the rave from where I was standing. But there was nothing for it but to try and make it down. I lay on my stomach and slowly lowered myself over the rear of the load, my feet trying to make contact with the top rail of the rave, three courses below me.

I reached the point of no return and I still couldn't locate it and I was now in a spot of bother. Another inch and I felt I would be in free-fall, and the ground after all the sunshine was rock solid which wouldn't make for a soft landing. And just as I had resigned myself to dropping, one of my boots latched onto the rail and, as I stood on it, I gingerly reached down and grasped it with my hands.

'You managed it then?' Harry said, as he lifted another bale onto the flat bed of the next trailer.'

'Yes, no problem at all,' I said. 'I'll pass the bales up to you for this one, if you like?'

'No, it's alright, boy. I think I'm getting the hang of it now.'

'Well, if you're sure,' I said, using one of the bales still on the ground as a step to help me climb onto the trailer. As I straitened up I felt the first spot of rain and it seemed to send a message of urgency, instilling in me the need to stack the bales Harry had already placed on the trailer as quickly as I could.

There was a pause as Harry climbed on the tractor to move the trailer on to the next group of bales and I noticed he left the engine running as he returned to pitch the bales up to me at a rate which gave me little time to place them. Soon, I was having to stack them as he moved the tractor, making it even more difficult to build the load.

'It's starting to look a bit wobbly,' Harry said.

'I know. I think it's a case of more haste less speed.'

'That may be true but I don't know what it's doing up there with you but it's starting to get wet down here.'

In my attempt to keep up with Harry I hadn't noticed how much the rain had increased. It was now pouring down and the thunder and lightning was occurring more regularly and closer to us, to the extent I was beginning to feel nervous about being on the trailer. I looked across the field and couldn't see much further than the hedge, the rest veiled in a grey wall of water.

When I mentioned my concern about the lightning to Harry he assured me I would be alright because the trailer was on rubber tyres, which sounded as if it could be a convincing reason, but I wasn't entirely sold on it.

'Just try not to touch the end of the pitch fork or we'll both get it,' Harry said.

I was now up to the fourth course and a quick scan of the number of bales left to pick up made me think we would need another trailer, but Harry kept pitching them up until, once again, I had to leave a gap for him on the fifth layer so he could get them up to me.

I was now soaked through but like, Harry, I was determined to get these bales off the field. We hadn't worked our butts off mowing, tedding and baling all this grass just to see it get ruined in the rain.

'Just a two more stacks, boy,' Harry said, as he headed for the tractor to move us along the field. 'Have you room for them?'

'The sky's the limit,' I shouted after him.

And eventually, when we had eight courses on and a few more bales down the middle on top of that, we had them all on the wheels.

'That's it, you've got them all,' Harry said. 'You'd better stay up there while we rope it on.'

Which seemed a good idea because without a rope to slide down I was marooned on the top of the load and there was no way I wanted to stop up here for the ride home to the farm. I just hoped Harry could manage to lob the rope up to me; I guess I would be the best part of twenty feet off the ground.

I watched from above as Harry uncoiled the rope and found an end and after gathering a length up in his hand, he stepped back and threw it up towards me; and then I watched it drop back down to the ground again.

'It's the blasted rain,' he said. 'It makes everything twice as heavy and so you can't grip it. I'll tie a stone onto the end of it.'

Now, wait a minute. It's wet, I'm getting cold and now Harry wants to throw a stone at me. I looked over the edge of the load and saw Harry digging around for a suitably sized stone.

'Could I suggest something else?' I asked.

'What's that, boy?'

'If you tie the end of the rope to the pitch fork, I may just be able to grab it without you having to start throwing stones in my direction.'

'We can give it a go, but I don't think you'll be able to reach it.'

Harry pulled the pitch fork out of the ground where he had plunged it in after heaving the last bale up and looped the end of the rope between the tines. He then held it up towards me and I lay on my front and tried to reach down for it, but I was a good foot short.

'What you need is something to stand on,' I said.

'And dare I ask what you suggest?'

'A bale?' I replied and heard him groan as I said it.

'Go on then, choose a light bale, not a sodding heavy one from off the headland, and drop it down here. And I'll not be best pleased if you don't grab the rope after all this messing about.'

With the bale to stand on, albeit, its edge, Harry manged to poke the end of the rope up to me and, resisting a cheer, I set about laying it out so the load could be secured.

'If you could just tie off the end I can use the rope to get down off the load on the other side,' I said.' I was increasingly getting the feeling Harry had just about had enough. Like me, he was soaked though but he'd just pitched what must have been the thick end of three hundred hay bales in a short time. He must have been feeling shattered; I know I would have been.

'It's tied on,' he shouted, and I gave the rope a trial tug, just to make sure. I then hung onto it while I lowered myself over the side and began to slide down at an alarming rate. There was no way I could slow my descent; the rope was too wet and greasy so my arrival on the ground was harder than I expected.

'You alright?' Harry asked, looking down at me, flat out on the ground.

'I think so, a tad bruised but nothing broken.'

I picked myself up and headed over to the tractor and half an hour later we arrived back at the farm. Short of unloading the trailers, which could wait, haymaking was over for another year.

CHAPTER NINE

Harry and the ferret

'WE'LL GET THE pigs cleaned out today, boy,' Harry said. 'I know it's not your favourite job but it still needs doing. We've all got our worst chores and we all have our best chores and they all need doing to the best of our ability.'

It was breakfast time and Harry was in one of his philosophical moods which, I had noted on other similar occasions, usually coincided with him receiving the farm's monthly milk cheque. Not that it took a lot of working out because when it arrived, the calendar I used to note down the number of gallons I had sent away each day disappeared from the dairy and then, when I needed it, I had to retrieve it from his desk in the front room office.

'Life is full of ups and downs,' he continued, his tone now lower and one which portrayed a heavy degree of profound intellectuality. 'And who was it that said: "Love conquers all things"? Chaucer wasn't it, because I reckon he got it about right.'

'I think that was Virgil, and I don't think cleaning pigs out was what he had in mind,' I said.

'Virgil? Who the hell was he?'

'A Roman poet.'

'A Roman poet? What did he know about farming?'

I sighed and drank my tea 'I thought we were going to finish shearing the sheep?'

'No, I finished them last week,' Harry replied. 'Do you know, boy, I think you're wrong. I reckon it *was* Chaucer. Wasn't he the one who did Banbury Tales?'

'Close,' I said. 'It was Canterbury Tales, and I didn't see you shearing any sheep last week. We were up to our eyes in hay making.'

'I pushed them in with Smith's sheep and had them done by some contractors they had hired. Any chance of half a cup, Alice?' He slid his tea cup down the table. 'So, I was right all along then. And, if I'm not mistaken, Chaucer also did, "Love me not for my being, but for myself".'

As Harry spoke he nodded knowingly, a smile playing on his lips, magnanimous to the end. 'You see, boy, like I said, we've all got our worst chores and our best chores and they all need doing to the best of our ability.'

'Wasn't that Shakespeare?' said Alice.

'No,' Harry scoffed. 'That was me who just said that.'

'No, not that bit. When you said; "Love me not for my being, but for myself". That was Shakespeare, wasn't it?' Alice said. 'John, you having another cup, I think there's one left in the pot if you want it?'

'What do you reckon, boy?' Harry asked.

'I think I'll go and make a start on the pigs,' I said.

I hooked the David Brown onto the two-wheel flat trailer and brought it round to the old cow shed which now housed various groups of pigs in pens running the length of the building. The tops of the pens had boards on which straw bales had been stacked.

These served two roles; one was a convenient supply of straw to bed the pigs on and the other was a way of providing some insulation against the cold during the winter.

Convenient as the bales might have been, the down side was the difficulty in carrying several hundred bales into the building through a narrow doorway and stacking them while the pigs were running around, and having to work in the back-wrenching low space below them when cleaning the pens out. The more muck there was to clean out the smaller the space it became.

And today, with the added tasks of hay making delaying routine clean outs, the muck level was particularly high, probably a couple of feet thick in places which left only about three feet of head height to work in. But there was nothing for it other than to climb over into the pens and start loading up the barrow I used to wheel the muck outside, tip it on the floor and then fork it onto the trailer.

By lunch time I had managed to clean out three of the pens which left another eight to do and this meant I would still be cleaning pigs out tomorrow and possibly the best part of the next day too. What joy. If only it was possible to strike up a rapport with the pigs as you can with cows and the chore of cleaning them out would have been so much better and more interesting.

Cows you can talk to and have a positive conversation with on so many subjects; you can understand their moods and their expressions, their likes and dislikes, their happiness and their sadness.

93

But for pigs it's food in one end and shit out the other and that's all there is to them.

I was just about to put the fork down and make my way down to the house for lunch when Harry walked in on my grousing holding what looked to me like a ferret.

'How's it going, boy?' he asked.

'Not too bad, thanks. Three finished and eight to do.'

'Just been down to the bottom meadows and the barley's well on the turn, Give it another week and we'll be harvesting.' He turned to go.

'Harry?'

'Yes, boy?'

'Is that a ferret you're carrying?'

Harry looked down at the red eyed, slim-line, sandy coloured creature he had tucked firmly under his arm. 'What this?' he asked, pointing a finger at it.

'Yes, that,' I replied.

'Well, you're right, it's a ferret. Nothing to get excited about, just a ferret, that's all.' And with that he continued on his way down to the house.

I smiled and wondered what Harry was up to now. Whatever it was, the odds on him receiving the blessing from Alice for any plans he may have for keeping a ferret anywhere near the house were, I thought, absolutely zilch. I'd heard these animals were quite capable of squeezing through holes not much bigger than your wrist, could turn in their own length and kill a rabbit with a single bite to its neck.

Harry was settled down at the table in the kitchen when I walked in, having left my wellingtons outside the back door. A few minutes scrubbing up with blue soap and a bowl of water and I joined him.

'And how was your morning?' Alice asked me, as I

sat down and drew my chair up to the table.

'Well, nothing to report really, but overall, it's been alright, thanks,' I said.

'And you, Harry?'

'Not too bad. Like I said to John, the barley is well turned and another week should see us harvesting.'

Alice stooped down and opened the Rayburn's oven. With her hands clad in thick padded gloves, she reached in and pulled out a large pot which continued to sizzle as she placed it on a wooden board in the middle of the table. It smelt terrific.

The lid of the pot was removed and Alice lowered her ladle in its depths and carefully pulled out a large joint of mutton, cooked flesh already falling off as she lowered it onto a plate.

'There you go, Harry, carve some of that up and I'll fish round for the vegetables,' she said, clearly pleased with the way her creation had turned out.

Harry looked pleased too as he stood up and reached for the large knife he used to carve meat with. But as his hand landed on the handle, he gave a sudden gasp and clutched his leg.

'Are you alright?' Alice cried, clearly concerned.

Harry sat down and rubbed his thigh. 'Just a twinge,' he said. 'But I'm alright. I think I might have strained something somewhere.'

'Well you be careful. You should get John to give you a hand.'

'Yes,' I chirped in. 'You can always ask me; you know that.'

Harry stood up again and reached for the carving knife but before he could pick it up he gave another gasp of pain and sat back down, before starting to furiously rub his leg again.

And it was at this moment I could see something moving in his trousers which I soon realised was definitely not a leg or any other part of his anatomy.

'Oh gawd, Harry. Tell me you haven't put that ferret down your trousers, have you?' I asked.'

Harry started to speak but he was distracted when the ferret took another nip at his leg, this time higher than the previous two.

'The little bugger's getting hungry,' he cried. 'I think you'd better give me a hand to get him out.'

Alice, who had been concentrating on ladling out vegetables from the pot into a serving dish, looked up from her work. 'You still having problems, Harry?'

'You could say that,' he said, his voice now rather constricted. 'But don't concern yourself. John says he'll give me a hand to sort it out.'

'No, I didn't,' I retorted. 'And there's no way I'm putting my hand anywhere near your trousers, not with *that* in them.'

'Why's he being like that, Harry?' Alice asked, beginning to realise that Harry's problem could be rather more than a strained muscle. 'What are you hiding in your trousers?'

At this point Harry yelled out and started to pull his trousers off like a man possessed. 'It's going berserk in there,' he stammered while hopping about on one foot, pulling at his belt. 'It must have been the mutton.'

Harry dropped on to the floor and peeled off the last of his trousers before giving a large sigh of relief. 'I'm a bit sore, boy, but I think I just about got away with it.'

It was then that Alice let go a loud ear-splitting shriek. The ferret, freed from its confines, had run across the floor towards the window and was now climbing up the curtains.

Harry sat up and peeped over the edge of the table in my direction. 'I think we could have a problem here, boy.'

After all the fuss at lunch time, a few gentle hours cleaning out the pigs was almost therapeutic. I know it must appear trite, but I suddenly acquired an interest in loading a barrow with pig muck so it could hold its maximum load.

There was no point, I discovered, just dropping forkfuls in the middle of the barrow; the first few forkfuls needed to be placed around the outside because in that way the sides became more vertical and the potential volume of the barrow increased. And if I patted it down, to apply some compression, I discovered this too allowed more to be loaded and fewer trips needed to be made to the trailer.

I applied the same loading system to the trailer – working on building the sides up, rather than the middle - and reduced the number of times I had to drive off down the field to the muck heap.

As for Harry, I saw nothing of him. When I say nothing, that isn't quite correct because on the odd occasions I glanced down to the house, I could see him moving about. Sometimes he would be in an upstairs room, sometimes in one of the front rooms or the connecting corridor, but always, it seemed, on the move. Alice, I noticed, had taken the Land Rover out.

When the church clock struck five, I called it a day with the pigs and after dropping a few bales of fresh straw into the ones I had cleaned out and tidying up so they could be fed without anyone tripping over forks, shovels or barrows, I headed off down to Farm Close to fetch the cows in.

And after a day cramped up in the pig pens, it was good to be out and taking in the fresh air. The chestnut trees in the graveyard were now in full leaf and provided some welcome shade for a few sheep which spent their days grazing between the headstones. As I walked passed them they just stayed where they were, gently chewing the cud and perusing life as they always do.

When I arrived in Farm Close, I discovered the cows had also taken to the shade, which was a nuisance because their trees were at the other end of the field. I gave them a call as I walked across to them, but it had little effect; and while one or two put their heads in my direction, the rest of them remained where they were and ignored me.

'Oh, come on girls,' I said when I got to where they were sheltering. 'You know what time it is.'

I walked round them and patted a few rumps to get them moving but it was like pushing a piece of string; they would take a few strides and then stop and look at me. Thrifty, thought this was hugely funny and would move only a few inches every time I gave her a tap on her flank. Horns looked at me and I could see the laughter in her eyes too and it wasn't long before the whole herd was at an immovable standstill.

'Right then,' I announced. 'If that is how you're going to be, you can all bloody well stay here. See if I care.'

I turned away and walked off towards the gate, not looking back. I guess I had made it to about halfway across the field when I felt a push in my back, not a big push but just an "I'm here push". I ignored it and carried on walking but the push was repeated so I stopped and turned round. It was Thrifty and not far behind her were the rest of the girls.

'What are you doing?' I asked her. 'Have you finished having your fun then?' I tickled her ears and looked into her big brown eyes.

'You're one beautiful lady,' I said.

CHAPTER TEN

Pigs, ferrets and rats

'So what were you planning to do with the ferret?' I asked Harry, the next morning, when he was closing the gate leading into the collecting yard.

'Well, I had a bit of a job catching the little sod,' he said. 'I went round the house so many times I was beginning to worry for the carpets, but I eventually cornered him under the sink in the bathroom and only then because he slipped trying to climb out of the bath. But can't the little bugger bite?' He rubbed his leg as he spoke.

'Yes, but what were you doing with him in your trousers in the first place? Was it a bet?' I asked, vaguely remembering reading something about a person who had entered a competition for such a feat.

'No,' laughed Harry. 'It was just that I couldn't find anything secure enough to put him in, what with lunch almost on the table. I've put him in a tea-chest for now, but I wouldn't be surprised if he manages to gnaw his way out of that. Just hope he doesn't head in doors now he knows where the remains of the mutton are.'

I needed to be getting on with the milking so my

question regarding what Harry was planning to do with the ferret would have to wait. Instead, I turned my attention to the cows and, having let the first four in to the bale, I set about washing udders and putting the milking units on two of them.

When I was at college there was a big thing about stripping the fore milk – a sample of milk drawn by hand from each of the teats before the units are attached - to see if there was mastitis present. If there was, it showed as small clots in what could be some rather watery milk.

Some of the more conscientious dairies used a special fore-milk cup having a black rubber liner in it and this helped reveal the white clots in the milk. I used the concrete floor and it seemed to do the same job.

Anyway, mastitis was bad news all round – for the cow it was a painful problem which, understandably, made her bad tempered and very shy of anyone touching her udder, and for the dairy farmer it meant a loss of milk yield and a lot of hassle.

Infected cows had to be treated with tubes of antibiotics squeezed into their teats and this meant the resulting milk was not fit for use by the dairies and had to be discarded, although it was always rumoured that such milk commonly found its way into churns.

Fair to say, there wasn't a total understanding just what caused mastitis but most realised it was a problem which could be conveyed from cow to cow when the milking machine used on an infected cow was placed on another one.

Thankfully, I had yet to be troubled with a case of mastitis although it was always something to keep an eye out for.

What was concerning me this morning though, was that Thrifty was hobbling badly and she was clearly not happy about putting any weight on her right front foot. There was nothing I could do until I'd finished milking and although she had been through the milking bail I didn't expect her to move away very far.

When I'd shut down the engine, I pushed open the gate and walked round to the back of the bail and there was Thrifty. She hadn't moved above a couple of steps and that was where she had decided to stay.

'Come on old lady, let's have a look at that foot of yours,' I said sliding my hand down her leg until I reached the offending foot and then encouraged her to lift it clear of the ground.

It took a couple of attempts before she understood what I was asking her to do but eventually, with her leaning on me rather more than I really wanted, she lifted her foot clear of the ground.

As I expected, between her cloves was a generous amount of mud and muck and I did my best to dig in and clean it out so I could start to see what was troubling her. I ran my fingers down each side of the cloves and pressed around between them, working as quickly as I could; her weight was beginning to tell on me.

Just as I begin to think it might have been a muscular or even an infection, my fingers caught on something sharp - a slither of glass she had trodden on. Pointed like an arrow it had penetrated into her flesh by over an inch, I discovered when I managed to pull it clear. It must have been very painful.

'Well, I think I've just about seen it all now, boy,' Harry said.

'What's that?' I said, gently lowering Thrifty's foot to the ground.

'Normally when we're dealing with foot problems we have them in a crush and start using ropes and pulleys to lift legs; it's a hell of a game and doesn't usually achieve much at all apart from a mass of bruises,' he said. 'But it looks as if you've sorted this one out.'

'I hope so. I don't think the glass caused too much damage, but we'll have to hope she doesn't have any infection.'

We looked at Thrifty, now half a ton of happier bovine making her way across the paddock and joining the other girls by the gate into Church Close.

'She's walking a lot better than when I fetched them in,' Harry said. 'Good to see you getting back on side with them all again.'

After breakfast, I was in with the pigs again, forking out endless amounts of muck, working doubled up beneath boards which supported bales of straw while trying to avoid half a dozen young pigs wanting to get involved in the action.

About mid-morning, Harry walked in and he was carrying the ferret again.

'What *are* you planning to do with the ferret?' I asked him. 'You have to admit, it's a bit of a liability.'

Harry gave the beady-eyed weasel a stroke but had to remove his hand quickly when 'Blossom', as he had started to call it, took a lunge for one of his fingers.

'A liability? No, not at all, boy,' he said. 'These are amazing animals that can be used to catch rabbits and control all manner of vermin and this is why I've

103

brought him in here.'

'I'd have thought pigs were a bit out of its league,' I said.

Harry scoffed. 'Not pigs, it's rats we're after.'

I had often seen the odd rat scurrying around the farm buildings and while I always thought them to be pretty hideous creatures, I had accepted they came hand in hand with the farming scene.

'And how are you going to do that?'

'Well it's quite easy. I just put Blossom into a small gap between the bales and we stand back and wait until all the rats come running out. And in the meantime, we equip ourselves with a couple of shovels and prepare to clobber them as they come running past us.'

It sounded horrific. Being in a confined space with a hoard of terrified rats intent on escaping from a psychopathic ferret had no appeal at all. I watched as Harry released Blossom into the bales and I reached for a shovel, not for any rat clobbering but to provide me with some protection.

We didn't have to wait long before the first rat appeared. Clearly having a bad experience, it jumped down from the bales and scurried across the pen, through the bars at the front and into the passageway I was standing in. Harry, shovel in hand, stood at one end and I at the other and the rat turned towards me but thankfully it found a drain hole to disappear down before coming too close.

'Block that hole up with some muck,' Harry shouted.

And then, seconds later, bedlam broke out as a dozen or more large rats streamed out of the bales and threw themselves down into the pens before running blindly towards the passage way, their only escape route. Startled by this sudden invasion and all the other activity, the pigs started to kick up a deafening row but not quite loud enough to drown out Harry who I could hear shouting and banging around with his shovel.

At one point a couple of rats came running in my direction and I clamped my shovel directly in front of me but these rats were past caring and, in their panic, they both climbed over the shovel and would no doubt have continued climbing up my trousers if I hadn't dropped the shovel and found refuge in a feed trough.

'Did you get any?' shouted Harry, when the noise had subsided and he had joined me outside.

'No, they were too quick for me.'

'Same here but Blossom certainly did the job though, didn't he?'

I couldn't argue with that and I wondered what it must be like to crawl about in the dark waiting to come face to face with an adult rat.

'Where's Blossom now?' I asked, not that I was over concerned for its welfare. I just wanted to avoid the sudden appearance of any more swarms of rats while I was forking muck out from under the straw bales.

Harry stood in the passageway and looked along the stack of bales. 'He must be here somewhere,' he said. 'He's probably just having a snooze after all the excitement. He'll come out when he's ready. Just keep an eye out for him.'

I wanted to ask Harry what I should do if I spotted Blossom but I suspected the answer may have been beyond what was going to be possible. Harry strolled off towards the house and I wondered if Blossom, when he woke up, would be heading that way too.

CHAPTER ELEVEN

Harvest

SOMEWHERE ALONG the way, the year had shifted into August and the spring barley was just about ready for harvesting. Which was just as well, because the amount of barley left in the lofts was down to a few barrow loads; about a week's supply.

'Do you think she will start, boy?' Harry asked as we strolled up to the barn where the combine harvester had been stored for the last ten months.

'I shouldn't think so for a minute,' I replied, recalling the saga we had endured when we set about starting it last year. 'I think I might as well take the battery off the tractor now and save ourselves a lot of time.'

'Don't you be so sure. Sometimes these things can surprise you. It's all about if she wants to start, that's what makes the difference.'

I stood back and waited to be surprised as Harry climbed up onto the operator's platform and sat down on a wet foam-rubber seat before turning the ignition key and turning to look at my upturned face.

'This is it, boy,' he said as he opened the throttle and reached down to pull the handle which would engage the starter gear with the engine's flywheel and activate the solenoid to power the starter motor. 'I'm pulling it right now; come on girl, give us that roar, let's hear that beautiful music…'

Well, there was no denying I heard a click, but sadly, not a lot more that could have been described as beautiful music or anything else which came even close to sounding like enthusiastic engine noises. Harry gave the handle a few more tugs and then conceded defeat.

'Bugger it,' he said. 'I think we may need the battery off the Fordson tractor after all. I'll have a check round her while you sort that out.'

I was already on my way to the tractor shed and I could almost see the Fordson sigh as I grabbed a handful of spanners, prised open her hood and started to loosen her battery terminals. Then, standing on the front wheel, I lifted the battery out and carefully lowered it to the axle before jumping down to the ground and grabbing it with both hands; the last thing I wanted was to spill any of the acid.

By the time I arrived back at the combine, Harry had removed the drained battery so I hoisted the one I was carrying onto the operator platform and left him to it while I had a look around this enormous machine.

Behind the guards which shrouded the sides there was such a tangle of belts, pulleys and cables I couldn't begin to think how it was all put together. It looked like an awful number of sleepless nights for someone.

Thinking about it though, it was more likely the assembly of such a complicated drive system probably evolved with changes being included as harvesting technology improved.

With the engine running, Harry raised the cutting table and the sails which helped to feed the crop onto the bed, so he could squirt oil on the reciprocating knife. And then, after another all-round inspection and generous use of the grease gun, came the time to engage the main threshing drive at which point last year, we discovered a failed bearing on the sieves.

It was a big moment and I could see Harry was nervous. If I believed everything he says, this combine, despite about to start its sixth harvest, had yet to clock up a twelve months of work; the rest of the time it had stood idle under the barn.

But now was not the time to be reflecting on such matters. Harry gave me the thumbs up and pressed down on the large lever which would tension up the main drive belt and hopefully start every component of this mobile threshing machine working.

I watched and waited. At first there was a dull scraping noise and the engine speed dropped as the load increased. And then I could hear the threshing drum starting to run up to speed and there was the rhythmic churning of the straw walkers, the shaking of the sieves and the empty rattle of the augers and elevators.

Harry climbed down and set off on a tour to check on everything, glancing up at the pulleys and their belts and chains, ducking under the rear hood where the walkers released the threshed straw onto the ground and pondering over the amount of dirt which was now being delivered from the elevator into the grain tank.

'Sounds great,' he said to me as he pulled himself back up onto the platform. Once seated, he reached for the throttle and slowly pushed it until it was wide open, and then the noise and vibration really set in.

I looked up at Harry, happiness all over his face, or was it relief? Eventually he disconnected the threshing drive and shut the throttle, and slowly everything came to halt; a little moan here, a scraping noise there but all was well.

'We'll just try the unloading auger,' he said, opening up the throttle a little and pressing another lever. The auger began to rotate and delivered a mountain of dirt and goodness knows what else onto the ground beside me.

'She's a goer,' proclaimed Harry, standing at the top of the steps, when he had shut the engine down. 'But I'll tell you something, boy,' he added, as he slipped a hand round to the back of his trousers. 'I'm not going to sit on that wet sponge of a seat ever again.'

'How much have we to cut this year?' I asked.

'About the same as last year which was about ninety acres, give or take the odd acre, but we might get asked to help out at Smiths if they get behind. I think they've already made a start on the winter barley, which as you'll have learned at college, comes in a week or two earlier than spring sown barleys.'

I nodded. 'Would it be a good idea to go and have a look at the crops and see where we're going to start?'

'Just what I was going to suggest,' he said. 'But let's go and have a cup of tea first.'

An hour later and we were standing in the middle of the barley that had been planted in Forty Acres. As we walked though it there was a dry, arid smell about it and the straw was crisp and rustled. Most importantly, the ears of grain were now knuckled over and it was these Harry had given his bite test to ascertain its moisture content.

109

'It all depends on how much you want to go harvesting,' he said, as he selected another ear of barley and put it between his hands to rub the grains free. 'If you don't really feel like it you can always find an unripe ear to test, as you can a hard, ripe one if you're keen to get started.'

'What do you reckon about this field then?' I asked. 'Is it fit to cut?'

'Well, I think it's worth a try. It's when the grain is in the tank and all the dry grains are mixed up with the not-so-ripe ones you get the full picture; if the grain heaps up like a church steeple it's too wet.'

'So, we'll make a start?'

'Well, we've got to start sometime so it might as well be now,' he said. 'Come on, let's get back to the farm. We'll have a spot of lunch and then I'll fuel up the combine and set off down here and you'd better sort some sacks and string out and bring them down on a trailer. We'll sort the auger out tomorrow, unless you want to have another go at carrying the sacks up the loft steps.'

I smiled at him. If I hadn't untangled him from the broken loft steps and the hundredweight sack of barley he was trying to carry up them last year, I think he would have probably still been there.

'We should put the props under the floor joists as well,' I said, recalling how near we came to having the floors collapse as the auger had heaped the grain into the lofts.

'Put it on the list,' Harry said.

I watched the combine trundle out of the yard while sorting sacks out in the loft. I was looking through one of the long narrow vertical gaps in the stone wall which, like the others in this stone barn, had been placed to allow ventilation. Not that they were doing much in this afternoon's weather, which was both hot and without a hint of a breeze.

So, this is the start of harvest, I thought, as I through bundles of sacks down the loft steps. The end of the farming year when all the effort put into growing crops, the ploughing, cultivation, sowing, fertilising and weed control, come to fruition.

I hooked the David Brown onto a flat trailer and loaded the sacks and a handful of bale string to tie them up with once they had been filled with grain. As an afterthought, I decided to take down a couple of cans of diesel for the combine at the same time and, it was while I was filling the five-gallon cans from the large tank in the yard, I spotted Elizabeth walking up the path to the farm.

'I'll just pop in and say hello to Auntie Alice and I'll be there,' she shouted across to me.

I hoped she wouldn't be too long. I'd heard it said when I was at college that there is nothing designed to irritate more than to have a combine harvester standing still with a full grain tank with nowhere to empty it. And I imagined Harry could be more irritated than most.

With the trailer ready to go, there was nothing else to do other than to walk down to the orchard gate and have a few words with Pedro. He looked well as he trotted over to see me, pushing his muzzle into my chest and slobbering down my shirt as only he could.

'Hey, Pedro,' I said, reaching up to give his ears a rub. 'Who's a happy boy, then?' I'd discovered a long time ago, his favourite spot was just at the base of his ears when he would look at you with his big dewy

111

brown eyes and wait for me to tell him he was the best donkey in the world.

'I thought you would have been harvesting,' Elizabeth said, as she joined me by the gate.

'We've just started and I'm off down the field with the sacks. Harry's already on his way down there.' I put my arm around her shoulder. 'You could come with me if you don't have anything else to do.'

She turned and looked at me. 'Would you like me to?'

'You know I would.'

'Well, let's go then,' she said, giving me a short peck of a kiss. 'But only if you let me drive.' And with that she headed off up the yard and climbed onto the tractor. 'You'd better stand beside me in case I go wrong.'

As we came down Piggy Hill, I could see the combine harvester working its way slowly around the perimeter of the field, the header taking an eight and a half foot cut. I wondered how full the grain tank was and which way round we should go with the trailer.

But then I saw Harry stop and step onto the tool box and lean over into the grain tank and start pushing the harvested grain about, so he must be just about full.

'He looks as if he's about ready to unload,' I shouted in Elizabeth's ear. 'We'd better turn left in the field and go round to catch him up.'

The journey around the headland wasn't quite so smooth going as the grass fields we had driven across, so Elizabeth selected a lower gear and slowed down.

'Do you still love me?' she asked, as she tried to steer the tractor around the worse of the bumps.

It was a question I wasn't prepared for but I answered it. 'Yes, I do, very much.'

112

'That's good,' she said. 'Because I love you too.'

Harry had stopped the combine and then reversed a few yards to allow the straw working its way through the combine to be spread along the row rather than building up in one big heap. He'd also moved over a little to give us extra room to bring the trailer alongside.

'How's it going?' I shouted up to him.

'Not so bad. A bit damp on the headlands but that's to be expected. I see you've brought Elizabeth with you.'

'Hi Uncle Harry, I promise not to get in the way,' she said.

Harry smiled. 'You'll be alright. John will look after you.'

I'd been unrolling the bundle of sacks and was now ready to receive the first of the barley.

'Are you ready, boy?'

'I think so,' I replied, bracing myself for the wall of grain that was about to poor down the chute towards me.

'Here she comes then.'

Harry pressed down on the unloading lever and a few seconds later the barley gushed out onto the chute and headed for the sack I was holding open.

'That'll do,' I shouted as the grain reached about halfway up the inside of the sack. I knew from last year, the amount remaining in the chute would be more than enough to complete the fill.

Elizabeth passed me a length of string and I tied off the top of the sack and dragged it over to the rear of the trailer so I could have one to lean the next sack on without wasting time tying it up. Meanwhile Elizabeth had the next sack open and was waiting for the Harry

113

to start the unloading auger.

'You going to be alright?' I asked her.

'I hope so,' she said. 'It can't be that difficult, can it?'

Sad to report, as it turned out, it was that difficult because as the grain hurtled down the chute its force knocked her and the sack backwards with the result that most of the grain poured over the trailer floor. And I loved her for it.

'I'll clear that up when you're combining,' I shouted to Harry, who nodded and waited for me to get ready with the next sack.

'I wasn't planning on going bulk just yet,' he said.

We worked our way through the afternoon but by about six o'clock I could feel the damp starting to descend and it was not long before Harry called it a day. If we'd been at the top of the hill we could have carried on for longer but we'd at least made a start and everything appeared to be working alright.

With Elizabeth standing beside me, and Harry sitting on the sacks of barley, I hauled the loaded trailer back up to the farm and parked it under the barn. There was still the milking to do but Elizabeth said she would keep me company providing I give her a lift down to her home afterwards.

CHAPTER TWELVE

Learning to drive the combine

WITH THE COWS in the collecting yard and ready for their morning milking, Harry told me he would set off shepherding and while he was down there he'd grease the combine up and get her ready to start work.

I reminded him the combine still had the Fordson battery and suggested he take the now charged combine battery with him and swap them over.

'Will do, boy,' he said. 'And you'd better drop off the trailer load you brought up last night under the barn where we can off load it, and hook onto the baler. Look out some packs of twine and don't forget the sledge and we can hook the Fordson on to a trailer. Oh, and there's just one more thing, if Ronny appears from anywhere, grab him and don't let him go.'

And so ended the morning's briefing for machinery maintenance, implement usage, site location and staff allocation.

I started the Lister engine and listened out for the two pulsator units to start their rhythmic hiss and stop routine which caused the pressure on the two sides of the rubber liner in each teat cup to equalise and stop squeezing, and then, with unequal pressure, start

115

squeezing the teat again.

A cycle which took two or three seconds to complete, its action was to mimic, as far as is possible, the action of a suckling calf. Clever stuff when you consider there used to be horrific mechanical systems, some of which used rollers to flatten the teat and draw the milk out.

With the first four cows in the cubicles each munching away on a scoopful of ground barley while two of them were being milked, I wandered over to Thrifty and wished her good morning and asked her how her foot was. Not that I expected any reply but I was pleased to note she was now walking normally and didn't appear to have any infection problems.

Horns never seemed to take her eyes off me and whenever I looked over to her she seemed to adopt an 'all-knowing' expression which she coupled with a snort and a slight shake of her head. I just wish I knew what she was trying to tell me.

But, much as I really valued these moments, today there wasn't time to dally. The sun was beating down and two cows needed their udders washing, the clusters needed removing from the two cows which had just about finished being milked – apart from a bit of working down of the udder to make sure – and placed on the two cows I had just washed.

The two milked cows were now released through the rear doors and, after placing a scoopful of ground barley in the feed hoppers, I let another two cows in and put the chain across the rear of them to prevent them wandering off. It was then their turn for their udders to be washed.

And so it went on until all the cows had been milked, which took about an hour and a half – longer if there were any problems.

The cows were then free to wander across the paddock and begin munching on the grass in Church Close and start making some more milk but, as I expected on a day like today, most of them headed for the large water trough and drank their fill before settling down in the shade provided by the trees lining the side of the track. So much for ration assessment.

Cooling the milk seemed to take for ever this morning and as I lifted the cooler unit with its rotating pipes and water running everywhere from one churn to the last one, I could already hear Miserable Old Sod drawing up with his lorry.

He only had the evening churns down there so I hope he didn't think he had it all and drive off. I slammed three full churns onto the trolley, slipped the retaining chain on and pushed off down the slope. If I could just get through the hand gate before he set off and he could see me, I would be alright.

I was moving down a one-in four slope faster than I ever had with a trolley laden with well over three hundred pounds of milk on board and no brakes. And coming towards me up the slope concentrating on sorting the mail and blissfully unaware of the danger he was in, was the postman.

Lifting my feet off the ground and applying all my weight on the skid achieved little but I was shouting at the same time and it was this that probably prevented a more severe accident occurring. But even though in the last few remaining seconds available to him he managed to flatten himself against the fence, one of the trolley wheels caught him on his knee and brought him down.

For the briefest of moments I was relieved to see that

117

the lorry driver had seen me and had stopped but now he was parked right across the bottom of the slope, preventing any runoff across the road.

I don't know how fast I was going when I piled into one of his side panels which he had lowered in order to load the churns in off the ramp, but there was a fair dent and I doubted he would be able to clip it shut again when the panel was raised.

'That's it, you've buggered my lorry again,' said Miserable Old Sod. 'I'm only still here because I could see you coming. I was quite within my rights to have driven off and left you to it. And then you wouldn't have bent my lorry.'

'It's cruel, thankless world, isn't it?' I said as I heaved the churns onto the ramp.

'Too bloody right it is, and I don't think the postman's too happy about it either.'

I looked back up the slope and saw the postman, who seemed to have finished gathering up all the letters I'd knocked out of his hand, and was now hobbling as best he could up the slope towards the farm. When he reached the hand gate, he paused to take a good long look to check on what else might be heading his way before stepping through and carrying on up to the house.

'You're a bloody liability with that trolley,' he said. 'That's the second time you've hit me.'

'Three strikes and you're out,' I said. 'Anyway, if you'd parked the lorry so I could get on the road I wouldn't need to have hit you would I?'

'Are you saying it's my fault?'

'Yes, but I don't want you to worry about it. Our solicitor is a pretty decent chap really, and I don't think for a minute he would take you to court. After all, the trolley still looks usable and there was no milk lost. So you might just be alright. I really hope so for your sake but mum's the word and I'd just keep my fingers crossed that no one takes this any further, if I were you.'

'But…'

I held up my hand. 'No, I'm sorry, I don't want your money; it won't make any difference, not now. Let's just leave it there and see what happens. You should find out by the end of the year.'

'But…'

I placed three empty churns on the trolley and started pulling them up the slope leaving the driver to sort out his own problems. And then, as luck would have it, I met the postman coming back down and in answer to my 'Good morning,' he limped by and replied, 'Bloody idiot,' which I didn't think was very sociable.

When I made it to the house for breakfast, Harry was carving the boiled bacon and by the time I had washed my hands and sat down, there was a plate waiting for me with two slices and a round of bread and butter lying alongside it.

'I hope you haven't been upsetting the churn man,' Harry said, as he sat down to start consuming his own plate of boiled bacon.

'No, I don't think so. He just wants to cheer up a bit, that's all and the same goes for the postman who was a bit offish with me, I thought.'

'Well you had just nearly killed the bloke with the churn trolley,' Alice said. 'What did you expect?'

I thought it might be a good time to change the subject and asked Harry how the combine was looking.

'She's already to go; I found Ronny mooching about as I was about to leave so I had him do the diesel and the stone trap,' he said.

'So he's had the prickly awn and smelly diesel treatment then?'

'Not so you would notice,' Harry said. 'I had him swilling down the collecting yard while we're here, so he probably has other aromas about him as well now.'

'Along with a swarm of home-reared flies,' I added.

'He'll need dagging soon,' Harry threw in for good measure.

'You lot are awful,' Alice said. 'More tea, Harry?'

'Just half a cup please.'

'And you John?'

'No, I'm fine, thanks. I'll grab some water out of the dairy.'

I pushed my chair back and stood up. 'Is the battery back on the Fordson because we'll need it to take a trailer down with us?'

'Yes, boy. It's already to go.'

'Right then I'll go and sort it all out.'

As luck would have it, we all arrived down in the field at about the same time; Ronny with the Fordson and a flat trailer for the grain, Harry in the Land Rover and me with the baler.

For starters, Harry and I walked out into the crop and almost automatically started pulling the odd head of barley, grinding it between our hands and then blowing on it to separate the grain from the chaff.

And then, like Harry, I picked a grain and placed it in my mouth, crunched down on it with my teeth, grunted knowingly and then spat it out.

'About sixteen percent, boy,' Harry said. 'That's the

best I've found. How about you?'

'About the same,' I said, reaching for another. 'I'll just confirm it with this one.'

But this one went horribly wrong. The grain I picked up so casually and placed in my mouth still had its awn attached and awns have barbs which allow it to move smoothly in one direction and adamantly refuse to move in the other. And with the awn moving smoothly ever further into my mouth, I was in a bit of trouble.

Every time I tried to halt its progress, it just moved on, using my gum, tongue and anything else it could grip on, to ensure it moved relentlessly towards my throat.

'Problems?' Harry asked as saliva started to run down my wrist in my effort to extract the awn.

'Yes,' I said. 'I've an awn going the wrong way.' I opened my mouth and pointed.

Harry bent down and made a cursory look. 'Bloody hell, boy. That one looks nasty, sort of terminal, if you ask me. Good job it's not pay day'

'Do you think a mouthful of water would help?'

Harry grimaced and shook his head. 'Shouldn't think so. I should leave it for an hour or two and then it might be easier to try reaching for it from the other end,' he said. 'Anyway, what do you reckon to the grain moisture? Shall we make a start or not?'

I tried to swallow and when I spoke, my voice came out as a sort of husky croak. 'I think we should make a start.'

'I think you're right, boy. The way you sound you'll struggle to make it to lunch so we'll do as much as we can in the time that's left. 'Course, if it manages to turn round...'

121

With the straw still too damp to bale, Harry beckoned me to climb up onto the operator platform after he had started the engine and engaged the threshing system. 'We'll do a lap and see how the grain looks in the tank,' he said. 'If it's standing up like a church steeple, we'll have to stop.'

He opened the throttle to full and pushed forward on the lever which provided the variable forward speed. When we reached the edge of the crop, he lowered the header and the sails and then, as the crop was cut it fell on the table and was swept from either end of the bed to the central elevator by an auger. From there, it was pushed by tines into the combine's innards.

Watching the crop as it moved into the combine was bordering on the hypnotic and it was only when Harry lifted the header as we reached the first corner, I looked up as he brought the machine to a halt.

'Come on then, boy. You have to learn some time so sit yourself down here and we'll see how you cope.'

'You mean you want me to drive the combine?' I asked, incredulously.

'More than that, I want you to *operate* the combine.'

We swapped places and I settled down on the seat.

'Right then, engage the threshing system,' Harry said, pointing to the large lever that was low down on my right. 'As you pull it up and you'll feel the main drive belt tensioning and everything will start to move. Give her a bit more throttle before you do it or you risk stalling.'

I did as he asked and very soon the sails began to rotate along with the bed auger, while the knife slid from side to side and the drum wound itself up to speed. I wasn't too sure what was happening within the combine itself but Harry seemed to be untroubled.

'Now open the throttle to full and we're set to go,' he said. 'She's still in gear so push the drive lever forward and we'll start to move.'

Which we did and I performed a pirouette which brought me in line with the next cut.

'Slow down and lower the header so it's about six inches off the ground,' Harry instructed.

'How do I know when it's the right height if the crop's covering the knife so I can't see the ground?' I asked.

'That's the tricky bit, but you can get some clues by looking down behind the bed. It's almost instinctive when you've been going for a while. You'll find out as you go.'

I lowered the header and judged that if the barley and a length of straw was landing on the bed, the cutting height should be about right. But I was wrong.

'I'd like for us to be able to bale at least some of the straw,' Harry said. 'And I was kind of hoping to get more than one bale. You need to cut it lower.'

So I did and watched a barrowful of soil and stones suddenly build up on the header.

'No, we usually cultivate after harvest, not during,' he said. 'We had better stop and clean the soil off the knife or a few knife sections will be snapping off – not to mention bunging up the drum and the sieves.

Harry insisted I climbed down off the operating platform while he went round to the front to clean the field off the header. 'It's not that I don't trust you not to touch anything while I'm digging around at the front but I just feel safer if you're nowhere near the combine,' he said.

So while I waited for him to remove the soil, I looked back at the couple of hundred yards I had managed to cut and harvest and it was not a pretty sight. The length of stubble went from knee high to ground level in a series of waves; if it had been purple, it would have made a terrific Mohican hair style.

And as I was looking, Harry joined me. 'Don't worry, boy. It will get better.'

'Why don't they put the header on wheels or skids to allow it to follow the contours and keep the right height?' I asked.

'Well if the field was perfectly level and all the barley and wheat was standing and at a constant height, I dare say you could. But when some of it is has gone down and the ground levels are all over the place, you need to be able to adjust the height as you go along. This machine uses hydraulic rams to lift and lower the header but earlier versions had a winch and an electric motor to power it but after days of lifting and lowering all the time, the solenoid used to burn itself out.'

With everything cleared, we clambered up onto the operator platform once more and set the combine rolling. This time I felt more confident and by the time we had arrived back at the trailer with a full tank, I thought I had just about cracked it, which, with hind sight, was a pretty rash assumption. I had yet to fully understand how the innards of the combine really worked and to experience the dreaded drum blockage, the horrors of which Harry insisted on telling me about as we worked our way around the field.

I drew up alongside the trailer and Ronny stood there, sack spread wide waiting for the grain to cascade down the chute into it.

'Don't unload too much in one go,' warned Harry.

'There's a delay in it leaving the tank and arriving at the bottom of the chute so you have to be ahead of it.'

Even this task proved to be tricky to accomplish without over or under filling the sacks; a short squirt more and the result was grain all over the trailer while a short squirt less meant a half filled sack.

'Right then,' Harry said when the last of the grain found its way into a sack. 'I'll leave you here with Ronnie and start off baling. Ronnie, when you've tied up the sacks, you can stack the bales while you're waiting for the combine to unload.'

'Can do, Harry,' Ronnie replied, brushing away a swarm of flies which, having breakfasted well on the slurry caked to his trousers, immediately returned to the same feeding ground for an early lunch and a spot of breeding.

'Oh, and there's one thing to remember, boy,' he continued, looking at me. 'The combine has its steering wheels at the rear which means when you turn the back end of the combine swings out. Don't forget.'

I soon learned there were a lot of things not to forget when driving a combine and how it turns corners was not particularly high on the list when I moved off from the trailer. As I turned the steering wheel to the right, there was big shout from Harry which was followed by a dull scraping noise and, at that point, I realised what I had done: despite Harry's warning, I had driven the rear end of the combine in to the side of the trailer.

I instantly thought of the fuel tank and the guards which hadn't a hope of providing any protection from the powered side swipe I'd just given them. The pulleys and probably the shafts would all be bent, bearings destroyed, belts and chains running out of line, straw walkers would be seized, tyres ripped off their hubs, flattened unloading auger. I couldn't bring myself to take a look at the wreckage and I considered walking slowly away and finding a ditch to lie down in.

'Don't do that again,' Harry said, as I joined him, having taken the long way around the combine. 'I've only a small tin of red paint with not a lot left in it.'

I looked at the scratch and breathed a sigh of relief; the straw-walker hood was slightly higher than the trailer floor and, as I had turned it had slid over it until it had contacted the front board where it received a small scratch.

'You won't be that lucky twice,' Harry said, and then he walked over to the baler.

CHAPTER THIRTEEN

Pedro at the fete

'IT'S RAINING', Harry announced, as I made my way into the kitchen the next morning.

I looked out of the window and saw and heard the rain, driven by a strong wind, hitting the window; the glass panes rattling in their lead surrounds. 'That's a pity. I wasn't expecting that.'

Harry poured the hot water into the teapot and then splashed a drop of milk into each of the cups. 'I hope it's not going to be one of those stop-go harvests like we had to put up with last year when we were still harvesting at the end of September and the combine was stuck and we had to spend a morning pulling her out with the Marshall tractor.'

I thought back to that morning when the combine harvester buried itself up to the top of the tyres and instead of climbing down off the combine, Harry had to step up on to dry land.

Worse, in my efforts to get near her with the tractor and trailer to offload a full tank of grain and make her less heavy, I also became bogged down and it was down to the Marshall tractor and its winch to extract both of us from our watery graves.

'The holes we created are still there and they're always full of water,' Harry said as he poured the tea. 'Put a fountain in them and I reckon they would make a good feature.'

'Or even a swimming pool if we built some changing rooms alongside,' I suggested.

'I think they would make a better lake, but you'd have to watch the tides.'

Harry disappeared down the corridor with Alice's cup of tea and I started thinking about unloading the trailers of barley, emptying the sacks into a hopper so the auger could to take it up to the lofts, because one thing for sure, we wouldn't be harvesting today.

'Come on girls, let's be having you,' I said to them as I opened the gate to let the first four cows into the bail. 'If you're still tired you've the rest of the day to catch up. I know it's wet and the wind is blowing but look at it like this: the grass will grow much better, taste sweeter and you'll get more ground barley because you will be making more milk. How does that sound?'

I looked around for some response but apart from a few blank stares from one or two of them, the consensus was that no one could give a jot about the rain, the grass or the ground barley.

'Alright, have it your way,' I said. 'See if I care.'

'But you do care, I know you do,' said a voice behind me. Before I could turn a pair of hands slid across my eyes and I felt a big wet kiss land on the side of my cheek.

'How long have you been there,' I asked Elizabeth.

'Oh, not long, just long enough to hear most of your

latest bovine lecture,' she said, giving me that wonderful smile. 'You should come and give a talk to Dad's cows some time because a more belligerent, bad tempered herd would be difficult to find.'

'Sorry, I don't think that would be possible,' I said.

'I don't blame you,' she said. 'But don't you think we should make a start on milking?'

'Yes, of course, but what are you doing here so early?'

'Don't you know what day it is?'

'Saturday?'

'That's right and today's the day we're all going to the village fete, and if we don't get a move on with milking, we'll be late. And before you say anything, I know it rhymes.'

So, with the first cows' teats washed, together, we set about milking and I was surprised just how well the cows behaved, Normally, when they encounter someone new in the bail, they let their concerns be known by emptying their bowels all over the yard – twice if they can - but on this occasion, they didn't seem to fret at all; which was so different from when Harry was about.

And while we worked, I was trying hard to think of some suitable class to enter at the fete. I really didn't fancy a repeat of the Donkey Derby, which I had been talked into at last year's event and I didn't think Pedro would enjoy the outing anyway.

'Are you doing anything at the show?' I asked Elizabeth, during a quiet moment.

'Yes, I'm entered in the gymkhana.'

'What, throwing yourself over jumps and all that?'

'Well, the idea is you have a horse beneath you to do all that for you.'

'Yes, well I suppose you'd have to,' I said. 'I was just thinking what I might have a go at. I'm definitely not doing the Donkey Derby. Not again. Once was more than enough'

'That's not what I heard,' she said.

Any hopes that Elizabeth had been joking were dashed when I brought the churns of milk down to the dairy. Outside, Harry had put a halter on Pedro and tied him to the orchard gate so he could give him a brush down.

'Want him to look his best at the fete,' he said, pushing Pedro around so he could make a start on the other side. 'Are you all set?'

'What for?'

'The fete, boy.'

'I'm not doing the Donkey Derby, if that's what you mean.'

'Not that, boy; we did that last time. This year we're entering the 'Best Donkey in Show' competition, you know, when you lead him round the ring and the judges look at him and all that stuff.'

'Oh right,' I said, as waves of relief swept over me. 'We had better make sure he looks his best then.'

'That's what I'm doing now. Can't do much about his stomach but we'll do our best with his coat and oiled shoes. Oh, and I've looked out a proper bridle and saddle this time which should look better than the length of bale string we had last time.'

I found Elizabeth in the dairy, cooling the morning's milk, and I told her the good news.

She responded with a big hug and a kiss. 'I love you John and I'm really pleased for you. But listen, I have to go now. I'll see you there.'

She gave me a hug and set off to the house to say

130

good-bye to Alice. I hadn't a clue how she was going to get back to her parent's farm but I felt good and I was looking forward to the day ahead.

I have to say, Pedro looked really smart. Harry had worked his magic with the brushes, hair dryer and combs so that he positively gleamed from the top of his ears down to his mane and on down to shiny, oiled hooves. And he knew it too. He had adopted a sort of swaggering, look-at-me walk which demanded everyone made nice comments about him.

'Pity about his stomach, you can't change that in an hour's brushing,' Harry said. 'But I reckon he looks alright. All we've got do now is get him in the horse box without him stepping in anything nasty but just to be sure, we'll take all his grooming gear with us for a final touch up.'

It had stopped raining when we arrived at the entrance to the fete and I was relieved when we had. The rear pick-up section of the Land Rover, along with the piles of bale string, fencing posts, staples and a host of other assorted bits which seemed to accumulate in such places, was not considered to be a suitable area for the cakes Alice had worked so hard to bake.

But I was suitable cargo and, although it had been a relatively short distance to travel, try as I might, I could not find a comfortable place to sit that was not either too wet or had some lump of misshaped metal in it.

'Good morning, Harry,' said the man taking the entrance. 'I dare say it's been what, the best part of a year since we last met.'

'Well, it would have been, wouldn't it,' replied

Harry. 'How much are you looking for this time?'

'That depends how many there are of you?'

'Three and the donkey.'

'Oh, you haven't, have you?'

'What?'

'Brought Redrow; you know, the donkey. I'd have thought after all that to-do at the church the other year you'd have tucked him up in a large field with big hedges so no one could see over.'

'Well I haven't and, just so you know, it's Pedro. And here's three quid.'

Harry dropped three notes into the man's hand, slid his window shut and drove on into the field.

'Irritating little nerd,' he muttered.

'You say that about him every year,' Alice said. 'Are you going to drop me off at the cake tent?'

'That's where we're heading. The rain's made the ground a bit soft; should be interesting when the cars need to drive out. Hope you've brought your wellingtons, boy,' he said. And with that, the rain started to fall again and this time, with the grey clouds hanging low over the hills, it looked to have set in for the day.

Having helped Alice unload her cakes into the tent and left her there to set up her display, we continued down to the trees at the bottom of the field where we planned to park and tether Pedro to a tree while we waited for his class to start.

That was, if it had been dry, but with the rain falling, Harry suggested letting the rear ramp down and leaving him inside to munch on some hay we'd brought with us.

'He won't mind,' Harry said. 'I don't think he likes the rain any more than we do.'

I thought back to last time when the fete was held on one of the warmest days of the year and we had used the trees to provide some much-needed shade for Pedro. But with water and feed provided, he was happy enough and let everyone know he was by presenting a series of asthmatic, high-volume brays that after half an hour, made my ears ring.

As last year, we were not the only ones choosing to bring their donkeys down under the trees and while I didn't remember any of them, Pedro clearly did because once again he let fly a barrage of brays that shook the horsebox he was in and probably also those parked near-by.

Harry looked at his watch. 'Your event starts at two o'clock but before that there's the grand parade and before that you need to register for the event. So I reckon you want to be heading up to the main ring by about one o'clock or before. There's bound to be a long queue.'

'How about his bridle?' I asked.

'It's hanging in the front of the box and I've brought some cleaning stuff so you can smarten it up while you're waiting. I'm off now, I've some people to meet, but I'll see you later.'

With the rain now drumming on the top of the horsebox I moved in alongside Pedro and set about seeing what I could do with the leather bridle Harry had found in the garage. It was filthy and most of it looked as if a good tug would break the straps.

'Move over, Pedro. It looks as if we have a serious cleaning job to do,' I told him.

And then I made a big mistake; I took the bridle to pieces which would only have been a good idea if I had some idea of how it should be put together again.

Even so, I washed and burnished each of the components and by the time I had finished, it was starting to look reasonably clean.

I looked at Pedro's head for some inspiration and even held up lengths of strap against parts of it to discover if their length had any bearing on where they went. For the record, I discovered the distance around Pedro's nose is almost exactly the same as the distance from the base of his ears to his lower neck, and I wondered if this was the same for all donkeys.

After half an hour of trying to work out what went where, I conceded I was in a mess, a big mess. According to Harry's time table, I now had less than an hour to be in the main ring so Pedro could be registered in his class and I was beginning to think I would have to revert to the use of bale string again.

But then Elizabeth arrived. 'Hello John,' she said. 'Nearly ready to register?'

I walked past Pedro to the rear of the box where she was standing and gave her a big hug. 'Nowhere near ready,' I said. 'I took his bridle to bits so I could clean it and do you think I can put it together again? 'Don't suppose you know anything about them, do you?'

Together we made our way to the front of the box and Elizabeth started to look at the pieces I'd left hanging over a rail.

'Yes, I see what you mean,' she said. 'Are you sure this isn't a dog's collar or one of those harnesses they use on guide dogs in the Alps?'

'I really don't know. Harry gave it to me and said to use it, so here we are. If it's any help, one of the straps is the same distance around Pedro's nose as it is from the base of his ears to under his neck.'

Elizabeth started to laugh and then Pedro drew

breath and began another deafening braying session. 'I'm not sure this would fit him even if you managed to put it together,' she said. 'The distance from his ears to his nose is far too long; the nose band would be over his eyes. And as for the chin strap, well, you'd have to extend it with some bale twine for it to meet on the other side.'

'How about if we just left the rope around his neck and lead him from there?' I suggested.

'You wouldn't be able to hold him if he took off,' Elizabeth said. 'I think the only way round this is if I rode and neck-reined him, just like the American riders do.'

'Is that allowed?'

'I'm pretty sure it is. That's how some people choose to show their donkeys.'

'Well, let's do that then; neck-reining it is. You can explain what it is later when we have the time.'

Elizabeth grabbed the straps and it wasn't long before she had a nose band sorted out and a couple of smaller straps which led from the nose band to Pedro's ears to hold it in place.

'Are there any reins anywhere?' she asked.

'No. I don't think there are. If there were, I think you've just used them.'

'Then you'd better start platting up some bale twine.'

Time was getting short and I worked furiously with the twine I found in the back of the Land Rover until I had platted a length which I thought would be about long enough.

'Quickly, John. I can hear the tannoy calling for entrants to register for the Best Donkey in Show class. Everyone else has already gone.'

135

I cut the end of the twine and tied them on to each side of the nose band as Elizabeth instructed and then led Pedro out into the rain which, at this moment, was probably at its heaviest, but this did not deter Elizabeth who now stood at Pedro's side waiting for me to give her a leg up onto his back. I then stood back and looked at them; Elizabeth in her best riding clothes and Pedro groomed to perfection. What a team.

'How's everything look?' she asked.

'Wonderful,' I replied.

'What? Even his stomach?'

'Yes, even his stomach,' I said, 'Come on, we'd better be making our way up to the ring.'

I must confess, as the rain sheeted down and I hung onto Pedro's nose band I was having some qualms about Elizabeth's ability to steer him with just the reins, and even more concern regarding the absence of anything to do with stopping him, but she seemed confident and who was I to question things at this stage? After all, we were both getting thoroughly soaked.

'How did you get on in the gymkhana?' I asked her, as we splashed our way across the field.

'A third place but I should have done better. It wasn't his fault it's just that I made some silly mistakes in the final round.'

'Oh right, but you still have a rosette.'

'Yeah, but it's the wrong colour.'

By the time we arrived at the registration office, we were walking through puddles, and where there weren't any to walk through, the ground was soft and squelched with every step. Where people were queuing, the ground had been churned up in to a muddy mess and I gave up hoping Pedro's hooves would stay clean.

Indeed, his once carefully groomed appearance seemed to have taken something of a dive and far from looking immaculate he now looked more like an old nag that had been wintering on a Fenland marsh. His mood had also changed and instead of holding his head up for all to see, his nose was now only inches off the ground, water running off his muzzle. Elizabeth tried to pull his head up but he was having nothing of it.

'Name?' asked the bowler hatted man sitting in the shed.

'John Johnson with Pedro,' I replied.

'Class?'

'Best Donkey in Show.'

The man looked up and ran his eyes over Pedro and stifled a laugh. 'What, with that?'

'That's right. Is there a problem?'

'Well, look at him. He's…'

'He's what?' I asked.

'Oh, never mind. Here's your number and judging starts at two o'clock in the main ring, just after the Grand Parade. Nice bridle, shame about the stomach though.'

'What a horrible little man,' Elizabeth said as we headed for the centre of the ring where everyone else was gathering.

'All set?' Harry asked when we met up with him. 'I see you've teamed up with Elizabeth; good idea.'

'Don't think this weather is helping,' I said. 'Pedro knows he looks a mess and he's depressed.'

'Not to worry, it's the same for everyone. Just do your best.'

For about twenty minutes we mingled with the rest of the fete's competitors in what had been scheduled as the Grand Parade but what with the rain and the muddy conditions it was something which soon deteriorated into chaos as the organisers tried and failed to sort horses and donkeys from dogs, lamas and the occasional rabbit.

And all this was happening while the tannoy system pumped out loud crackly music, interspersed with frequent incoherent announcements which attempted to tell interested spectators, should there still be any, what might be going on.

Eventually, though, the ring emptied as competitors and their charges dispersed to other parts of the field. That is, other than the Best Donkey in Show entrants who would have the ring to themselves for the duration of their event.

'Are you ready for this?' I asked Elizabeth.

'We're here now so we might as well get on with it.'

I looked her and smiled. She looked as bedraggled as Pedro did, yet she smiled back at me and I loved her for it.

'We should have entered the wet T-shirt competition instead,' she said.

'We can do that afterwards. Come on, there's a bloke over there who wants us to move closer to him.'

As we gathered I had a look at the other entrants, all five of them, and it was a sorry looking bunch which looked more like beach donkeys on a wet Sunday afternoon. One of them, a small-scale donkey with black and white markings, had its owner holding an umbrella over it but the rest of them had water running down their once carefully groomed flanks, puddling where hooves met the soggy ground.

'Now, I want you to form a line spaced out by a couple of yards,' said the man with the bowler hat, white coat and umbrella. 'And then I'll spend a few minutes with each of you.'

There was some jostling for position, it seemed some favoured the end of the line, not that I was particularly bothered about it until Elizabeth leaned down and pointed out to me that the end positions were the ones judges always remembered best.

'Really?' I said. 'Come on Pedro, let's go down to the end.'

'If you're all settled, I will now start the judging,' said the man. 'And I'll start at this end and move along the row.'

'He's coming to us first,' Elizabeth gasped. 'Why did you move us here?'

'You said the end positions were the best.'

The judge arrived and went straight to Pedro's head, which was a mistake. Pedro, startled by such a direct approach lunged at him, his mouth open, his teeth bared.

'Whoa, fellow,' said the judge as he stepped backwards. 'I only wanted to have a look at you.'

If that was his intention, he'd blown it. From that point on, for Pedro, the judge was enemy number one. Every time he attempted to get near him Pedro would lash out. But I gave the judge his due; he didn't give up and kept trying to get close enough to run his hands over Pedro to check his conformation.

Which was another mistake because the final attempt at closing in towards the rump area, resulted in him receiving a double footed kick to the chest that dropped him on the ground.

Out of courtesy, I helped him to his feet and even

139

thought about trying to wipe some of the mud off the back of his white coat but, what with the two hoof marks on the front and numerous other muddy smears, I realised it would be a waste of time.

'Right then,' he said when he had recovered his breath and I had handed him his clip board and bowler hat. 'I shall need to make some notes. Perhaps you wouldn't mind holding my umbrella?'

'Of course, no problem,' I said, looking over his shoulder as he wrote.

'Conformation average; attitude wanting, coat could be better, hooves somewhere, tail unkempt, mane wild, bridle clean but shame about the stomach.'

'That doesn't sound too promising,' I said, but he ignored me and turned his attention to Elizabeth who had sat astride Pedro while he was being judged and had struggled to keep him under some control.

'Now, young lady, I want you to walk him away from me for a distance of about twenty yards and then turn left and canter for the next twenty yards, and then turn left again and walk briskly back towards me. Is that all clear?'

'I think so,' replied Elizabeth. 'Walk twenty yards away from you, turn left and canter for twenty yards, turn left and walk towards you.'

'That's right. Off you go then.'

Pedro was clearly pleased to be walking away from the judge; there was no love in that department, but when it came to the turn, the neck-reigning system was causing him some confusion. I could see Elizabeth trying to cajole him into a left turn but he wasn't having any of it; any direction which brought him closer to a bowler-hatted man with a clip board was to be avoided.

With only a slight deviation from the walk away direction, Pedro took off at a gallop and just kept going; twenty yards, thirty yards, forty and more, slowing only slightly when he spotted the rope which marked the end of the main ring to veer to the left and head down to the trees where the Land Rover, horsebox and some unfinished hay awaited.

'Well, that's a pity,' said the judge. 'I thought he was going to be a possible winner, but it was a shame about his stomach. I'll let you know if I need you to bring him back should I need to make a second assessment.'

Pedro didn't win the Best Donkey in Show award and from the bottom of the hill under the trees, we couldn't see who did win, but I wasn't worried. When I caught up with Elizabeth, she was laughing, and put her arms around me.

'What a farce that was,' she said. 'Poor Pedro wasn't enjoying one minute of it and I don't care what the judge thought of him. For me he'll always be the Best Donkey in Show.'

I had to agree with her. 'Of course he is, but where is he now?'

'I found him in the box with his head in the hay, slipped his bridle and saddle off and I left him there.'

'If he's all settled then, it could be a good to time to climb in the Land Rover and take the worst of these wet clothes off,' I said.

'Yes,' she agreed, taking my hand in hers. 'But only down to my T-shirt.'

CHAPTER FOURTEEN

Harvesting issues

IT WAS A GOOD two days before we were able to continue with the harvest, and only then because Harry decided to move operations to one of the top fields where the ground was drier and would carry the combine.

Retrieving the combine from Forty Acres needed a helping pull from a tractor and a chain and we both agreed the bales would have to stay where they were until we could take a trailer in without it getting stuck.

'It'll come right in the end, boy,' Harry said after I had moaned about the conditions. 'It always has done and always will.'

I wished I could share his optimism as I tried to hitch the baler onto the tractor from where we had left it before the rain arrived. The drawbar had sunk in to the ground and there was no more thread on the jack to raise it to the height I needed to connect it to the tractor. All I could do was lower the linkage arms and secure some rope to them after I had run it under the baler's drawbar. Lifting the linkage arms raised the drawbar and I found some large stones to place beneath the jack to provide it with some support.

It was then I noticed no one had reduced the pressure

in the bale chamber by unwinding the clamps that gave the straw the resistance to create a firm bale when the ram pushed another wad of straw into it. I unwound the clamps and then, as if by magic, the bale began to expand lengthways to the point I could reach in and pull it out of the chamber.

I had rather hoped, Harry would let me drive the combine but it was not to be. Clearly, I hadn't impressed him sufficiently to be let loose starting a new field. Instead, with the sun glaring down, I stood beside him as he cut around the barley that had been sown in Calvert Close, a ten-acre field near the allotments.

'It looks good, boy,' he shouted to me. 'A good even crop which I reckon will do twenty-five hundredweight to the acre – more if we're lucky.'

And then he asked me to have a look under the straw the combine was leaving in a swath and check on the number of grains of barley there were on the ground beneath it. I stepped down on to the ground and stood back as the machine rolled slowly past me, waiting until it was several yards in front to avoid being covered in chaff being blown off the sieves and the straw spilling off the end of the straw walkers.

I used my hands to brush the straw to one side while inspecting it to make sure all the ears of barley had been properly threshed, and then knelt down to discover how many grains I could find lying on the ground. I didn't know what to expect and while it seemed likely there would be some, I was at a loss to know how many represented an unacceptable loss and called for the combine's threshing system to be adjusted.

I looked carefully and found about six grains in

143

about a yard of swath which, bearing in mind the combine was cutting a width of eight and half feet, didn't seem to be excessive. I walked on a few yards and counted the grains I could find at a different location and the number was about the same.

Meanwhile, Harry had moved on and was now the best part of a hundred yards in front of me, so I set off at a jog to catch him up, the sharp stubble catching at my ankles and the occasional awn digging into my jeans.

He had just reached a corner of the field as I caught up with him and sprinted the last few yards to avoid being mowed down by the rear wheels which started to move out as I drew level with them. The rear of a moving combine was not a place to be when turns were being made. Back up on the platform alongside Harry again, I gave him the news.

'So, it's about a half a dozen grains in a yard of swath,' he said. 'That's just about acceptable. It doesn't want to be any more or we can start talking about hundredweights an acre, being lost, and an embarrassingly big green stripe appearing in the stubble when the grains begin to germinate and grow.'

'How can you reduce the number of grains being lost?' I asked him.

'Well the first thing you can do is drive a bit slower so the threshing system doesn't have as much crop to work on and makes a better job of it, but changing the sieve settings can also help. If they are opened up a small amount, less grain will fall over the back but the grain sample in the tank will suffer with more chaff in it. Similarly, I could increase or reduce the amount of wind being blown up through the sieves. It's all a balancing act between what is an acceptable grain loss and the quality of the grain sample in the tank.'

'And knowing what to do if one of them becomes unacceptable,' I added.

'That would help,' Harry said, lowering the header and starting a cut along the back side of the field.

I looked in the grain tank and noticed it was well over half full and we still had the best part of three sides of the field to cut before we could be back at the trailer for unloading.

'I think I'd better run back and bring the trailer round,' I said.

Harry stood up and peered over the edge of the tank and nodded. 'It's a better crop than I thought, boy. We're not going to make it all the way round. You go and fetch the trailer and I'll go as far as I can and then cut some room out so you can bring the trailer alongside.'

I climbed down and made my way back to the trailer, noticing a few rabbits making their way out of the crop and into the hedgerow as I walked. These, I considered, were the clever ones which, recognising their world was changing, made an early exit but there were always a few which chose to move into the middle of the field as it was cut until eventually, with only a small area of uncut crop left, they had no choice other than to make a dash for it.

Harry had told me about people lining up with shot guns to shoot the rabbits as they fled but it struck me as being a rather dangerous time for both the combine driver and the rabbits, even if it did put some food on the table.

By the time I had reached the trailer and started towing it around the headland back towards the combine, Harry had brought the combine to a halt and

I could see him using his arms to level out the grain in the tank and provide room for the grain still pouring into it as the threshing system separated out the last of the crop passing through it.

I also noticed the deep ruts the combine wheels were making, which was a bit worrying and I hoped there would not be any problems with getting stuck.

'All set?' shouted Harry, as I held open the first of the sacks and braced myself for the rush of barley as it left the emptying auger and cascaded down the chute towards me.

'Right, let her go,' I shouted back.

Harry pressed the lever and there was a short delay before the grain reached the top of the auger and began its slide, a wall of grain heading my way which threatened to knock me backwards when it arrived. But I stood firm and the sack filled at its usual alarming rate, as did the twenty or so other sacks that were needed to empty the tank.

'You don't think we should be looking to do away with sacks and start using trailers we can empty straight into?' I said after the last sack had been filled. 'We waste so much harvesting time filling sacks and even more when we have to empty them.'

Harry cleared his throat. 'It's something we could perhaps consider for next year, but it means purchasing hydraulic tipping trailers and all that sort of stuff. We'll have to think about it.'

'The trailers could be used for carting muck and so many other things too.' I said, 'It wouldn't be just for grain.'

I could see Harry becoming agitated. The day was getting hotter, the combine was ready to go, and this was not the time to be discussing future farm plans.

'We'll see, boy,' he said, preparing to move off to carry on harvesting. 'I think you'll find that's Ronny coming across to us. Get him to give you a hand sorting the baler out and then he can stack bales and tie sacks while you bale. You'd better send him back to the farm for the Fordson, we don't want a trailer loaded with grain sacks without a tractor to take it home should it start raining.'

And with that he engaged the combine's threshing system, sending its usual cloud of dust heading my way and continued cutting around the field. I tied off the sacks, stacked them so they would stay on the trailer and then did a U-turn in the space that had been cut, being careful not to catch the trailer's drawbar on one of the tractor's rear wheels.

As I drove, I thought about our conversation regarding the investment in grain trailers. If, I reasoned, it took fifteen minutes to empty a tonne of grain and the combine could, on a good day, harvest ten tonnes, that was two and a half hours it was spending unloading or, put another way, about a quarter of a day of lost harvesting time and taking the labour of two people to do it.

Ronny was waiting for me by the field entrance and, when I had stopped a little further along the hedge, he came over to me, his usual swaggering gate causing his rolled down wellingtons to scrape their way noisily through the stubble.

'Morning, John,' he said.

'And good morning to you, Ronny. How's the day with you?'

'Fine thanks,' he replied. 'But it will be different this time next week,'

He looked at me and I noticed some of his spots

were erupting. 'Why's that Ron?'

'Because I'll be twenty-one and I'll be a man.'

'You'll be a what?'

'A man,' he said again only with more emphasis. 'You know, a man.'

'Sorry, Ronny, you've sort of lost me there but never mind, Harry wants you to go back to the farm and bring the Fordson down and put it on the grain trailer. Make sure there's enough fuel in it. I'll put the David Brown on the baler and you can stack the bales when you're not helping Harry unload the combine. Got it?'

'Right then, John. I'll do that,' Ronny said, his eyes lighting up as they always seemed to when there was an opportunity to drive a tractor. 'You don't want me to bring a trailer so we can take some bales back with us?'

'Good thinking Ronny, we'll do that but don't be long about it; Harry will need unloading soon.'

Ronny set off at a jog while I set about unhooking the grain trailer and, to do this, I needed to find some large stones to spread the weight under the jack. The trailer wasn't full, but I had started stacking the sacks at the front, which placed all the weight on the screw jack.

I don't know whether it was the heat affecting me, but everything seemed to be taking longer than it should today. Before I'd hooked up to the baler, Ronny was back in the field with a four wheeled trailer and by the time he had dropped that one off and attached the grain trailer, Harry was stopped and waving his arms about.

'Looks like Harry wants emptying,' I said to Ronny.

'I'm on my way,' he said.

And he would have been, if he had remembered to

148

put the drawbar pin in the clevis, the key part of ensuring a tractor and trailer are connected to one another. The result was all the more dramatic because as Ronnie started off, the trailer came with him for a few yards and build up some speed before slipping off the drawbar and piling into the ground, followed by at least half a dozen sacks which split open as they hit the stubble.

'Oh shit,' he said.

'I don't suppose you brought a shovel with you?' I asked.

'Ronny shook his head.

'Probably just as well because if you had I think Harry would have knocked your head off with it.' I could hear the combine getting closer. 'Even so, I think it might be a good idea if you pop back to the farm and find one.'

Ronny could also see Harry heading his way. 'I'll go and get one right away,' he said, jumping on the Fordson and high-tailing it out of the field.

'Where's he buggered off to?' Harry asked when he'd climbed off the combine to have a look at the mess.

'To get a shovel,' I said.

'Bloody idiot,' he fumed.

'I'll carry some sacks over to the four-wheel trailer and you can unload there,' I said.

Harry turned back towards the combine. 'The sooner we have some proper bulk trailers we can empty into the better,' he mumbled.

It all took a bit of clearing up but by lunchtime things were back to normal and everything was going well. Harry was making good progress with the combine

149

and I was baling the straw behind him, stopping occasionally to give Ronny a hand with stacking the sacks. And, as it turned out, it was just as well we had the four-wheel trailer with us because it gave Ronny a chance to haul the trailer up to the farm when it was fully loaded without Harry having to stop combining.

Shortly after one o'clock Alice drove into the field and parked in the shade provided by one of the trees on the headland and I was pleased to see Elizabeth with her.

'If you can let the back of the Land Rover down, I'll spread it all out on that,' said Alice as I walked over towards her. 'And it would be good if you could drag a few bales over in to the shade for us to sit on.'

'You're too dirty to kiss,' Elizabeth said, as I grabbed a couple of bales.

'How did you know what I was thinking?' I replied.

Harry parked the combine a few yards away and came across to us, brushing dust off his shirt and trousers.

'Hello Elizabeth, how's my favourite niece?' he asked.

'I'm very well, thanks Uncle Harry.'

'That's good to hear,' he said. 'John needs someone to keep him on track.'

'How's the combining going?' asked Alice, as she reached into a bag and brought out a sandwich tin.

'Not so bad. It's dry enough but hellish dusty.' He looked around. 'Where's Ronny?'

'I think he's just popped behind the hedge,' I said.

'Oh right. Go and tell him lunch is served, will you?'

'I think he knows that.'

Alice offered the sandwiches around and the tin came to me, I hesitated, recalling the last time we had an in-field lunch there had been some strawberry jam sandwiches on offer.

'Come on John, help yourself,' said Alice and I dutifully obeyed and bit into a boiled bacon sandwich.

'Harry, are you ready for a sandwich?' she asked. 'Or would you prefer a piece of fruit cake, the cake I won the competition with at the fete.'

'Yes, a good-sized slice of prize winning fruit cake would be nice,' Harry said, slipping off the bale on to the ground so he could lean against it.

I felt Elizabeth's knuckle poke me in the side as I watched a plate loaded with wonderfully moist fruit cake being passed over to Harry.

'You know boy, there's few greater pleasures in life than a generous slice of fruit cake and a mug of tea to wash it down.'

'There may just be another slice, if you want it,' Alice said, revelling in Harry's adulation. 'But how about you other boys, there's another couple of sandwiches in the tin when you're ready for them.'

I took another bite out of my boiled bacon sandwich and nodded my thanks, and Ronny grunted.

It wasn't long before Harry was getting restless and I couldn't blame him. The weather was perfect; hot with just a hint of a breeze which caused the barley to gently sway with an audible rustle. Every so often there would be a stronger wind, a whirl-wind that drifted across the field picking up strands of straw and wafting them high in the sky before they ghosted back down to the ground.

'Come on, boy. We'll have a swap round this afternoon, you can combine and I'll bale; we might get some heavier bales that way and use less string.'

I needed no second bidding and was on my feet

151

before he had finished telling me.

'What are your plans for the rest of the day?' I asked Elizabeth.

'If it's alright with Uncle Harry, I'll have a ride around the field on the combine with you,' she said.

I looked at Harry and he smiled. 'Go on then,' he said. 'But don't let a bit of dust come between you two.'

'And if you think you're going to do Harry's trick of starting the combine while I'm still here you are mistaken,' Alice said. 'I've been covered in dust too many times for that. So, you just wait while I get cleared up.'

'It'll be alright, Alice. I'll drive it over to the standing crop before I start everything up,' I said. 'You should be safe from there.'

Well, she wasn't. When the combine's threshing system stops, all the dust and chaff settles down on anything it can find to settle down on and, in a dusty crop like this one it all adds up to a heavy load of dust waiting for a chance to escape. So when I engaged the drive and opened the throttle a dust cloud of monstrous proportions swarmed out of it and, as luck would have it, drifted as an impenetrable mass directly towards the Land Rover and Alice.

'Oh, that's such bad luck,' said Elizabeth.

'Oh shit,' I said.

'I can't see too well, but I think Alice is waving at us.'

'I bet she is.'

I lowered the header and watched as the crop began to fall on the bed and be swept along to the central intake where it would be taken up to the threshing drum. Half a minute later I heard the first grains landing in the tank and all seemed to be as it should be with the world.

'You alright?' I asked Elizabeth.

'Yes, fine thanks.'

She had one hand on the front railing and the other she had around my shoulder, and it felt good.

By the end of the afternoon, Elizabeth was long gone, the field was all but finished and there was a distinct dampness in the air which was affecting the way the crop entered the combine. It seemed reluctant to be cut and flow as easily as it had a couple of hours before.

If I hadn't nearly finished, I would probably have stopped and called it a day and, although I hadn't given the grain the bite test, I was pretty sure its moisture level must have increased.

Disaster struck when I had only a couple more runs to make to finish the field. There was a sudden screeching noise and the engine started to labour before everything came to a sudden halt. I disengaged the threshing system and let the engine tick over while I wondered what had happened.

Was this the dreaded blocked drum, Harry had been going on about? Instead of passing the threshed straw onto the straw walkers, the incoming crop had begun to wrap around the rotating drum and it only took a matter of seconds for it to have gathered enough straw for it to become blocked. I rather fancied this was the problem. And so, it seemed, did Harry who stopped baling and walked over to me.

'Oh dear, oh dear. You know what you've done?'

I nodded. 'Blocked the drum up.'

'Right on, boy. It could be a late night for you and

the cows.'

'What's for the best, then?'

'Well, the first thing to do is open the concave gap as wide as it will go, which should relieve some of the pressure. Then we have to undo the cover which will expose about six inches of the drum – a single rasp bar if you're lucky. And then you start cutting straw and pulling it out – one piece at a time.

'After about an hour, again if you're lucky, you might just be able pull the drum round a small amount to give you more straw to start cutting out. So, about midnight, there's a chance the drum will be free enough for you to have a go at engaging the threshing system, but more likely you'll have to keep cutting little bits of straw out one by one, by which time your hands will be sore and your knuckles horribly grazed and bruised.

'And when you do get it all clear and the drum is rotating properly, don't forget to close up the concave gap to where it was set because, if you leave it open there will be an awful amount of half threshed heads coming out the back.

'All set? I'll go and finish baling as much as I can and I'll be back to see how you're getting on. Oh, and here's my knife; lose it and you're dead.'

Having opened the concave and undone the clips holding the inspection cover, I looked to see a mass of straw so tightly compressed it was almost impossible to push the point of Harry's knife into it. And when I cut across it a few strands were released but there was no pulling them out, their ends were too tightly packed.

So, as Harry had said, I set about cutting straw strand by strand and it was slow progress, painfully so. Where I wrapped my fingers around them soon became raw and while the pile of straw I had managed to release grew larger, there appeared to be very little difference to the mass still in the drum.

Eventually, I uncovered one of the rasp bars and, with an edge to cut against, it all became a little easier but when Harry clambered up the steps and peered in, there was still a long way to go.

'I think it might be best if you go and milk the cows,' he said. 'I'll carry on down here for a bit and when it gets too dark, what's left will have to wait. When you're at the farm, just check to make sure Ronny's put the trailers of grain under the barn.'

I said I would and gave him back his penknife. Feeling less than happy, I stepped down off the combine and began to walk back, I'd bring the cows in from their field on the way. I hadn't gone many yards when Harry shouted after me.

'Hey, boy. If it's any help to you, there's not been a combine operator yet who hasn't bunged up a threshing drum, so don't feel bad about it. Just be careful and try not to do it again, and I might treat you to a penknife sometime. Right?'

'Thanks Harry. I'll try not to.'

CHAPTER FIFTEEN

Calving troubles

LOOKING AT THE calendar on the dairy wall, just above the desk I leaned on to fill out the churn labels every morning, there was a note that Matty was due to calve. Not that it was written in stone. A cow's gestation period can vary as much as for any other animal and I wasn't particularly concerned.

Even so, I made a mental note to have a look at her when I took the herd's buffer feed out to them later that evening after I had finished milking and cleaned up. Matty had been dry now for about ten weeks and while she chose to wander into the milking bail with the rest of the girls, she only stopped for a mouthful of ground barley and, I like to think, to have a few words with me.

And this evening things were no different, Matty came in and wolfed down her scoop of feed and then, when she had finished, I opened the door and let her out but not before I had noticed the pin bones near her tail had widened – an indication she was close to calving. But I hadn't realised just how close.

When I took their bales of hay out and spread them around so everyone could have their share, Matty wasn't with them, which I thought was strange and a little worrying, bearing in mind she seemed perfectly alright not an hour before.

It was getting dark and with Matty being an Angus cross, her black coat didn't help when it came to trying to find her in a fifteen acre field. But I drove the Land Rover around the headland with the headlights on and found her standing beneath one of the chestnut trees and looking totally out of sorts with herself.

I stopped and walked over to her. 'What's the matter old girl?' I asked, as I stroked her ears to see if she was running a temperature. Her eyes looked a little glazed over and she was far from happy. I wondered if I should try and bring her in for the night but thought she was probably better being left out here, at least for now.

And then she started straining and staggering about, clearly in some discomfort and I knew there was something wrong, seriously wrong.

'Don't you worry Matty, I'll go and get you some help. I won't be long,' I told her.

I drove down the yard to the house and ran into the kitchen. 'Harry,' I shouted. The door at the other end of the corridor opened and Alice came towards me.

'You alright John? Something the matter?'

'Yes, it's Matty, I think she's in trouble with the calf she's due to have. Is Harry about?'

'He isn't, I'm afraid. He's gone up the village to meet up with Sam Jones, Smith's manager, so I don't expect him back for a while.'

'Well I think we should call the vet,' I said.

'If that's what you think John, let's do it.' Alice said. 'I'll call them now and ask if someone can come out straight away.'

'That would be great if you could. Tell them I'm in Church Close, they'll see the Land Rover's lights.'

And with that, I set off back across to Matty who had now gone down and was lying on her side, taking short, painful breaths.

'Steady old girl, there's help on the way and we'll soon have you sorted out. Just you see.' I stroked her ears, I could feel her pain, and I wanted it so much to go away.

I'd left the Land Rover with its lights pointing back to the farm so the vet could see where to head for, but as I waited and no vehicle arrived I wondered if it would be too late. Matty was becoming weaker, her breathing was becoming more laboured and try as she might, I knew she was struggling to stay with me.

I began to think of the times we'd had together, our Sunday afternoons when I would go down to the field early so I had time to sit and talk to her, the big rasping lick of her tongue as she responded. She was so loving and so kind and she was Matty.

The lights when they arrived caught me unawares but when they turned into the paddock and headed for the gate into Church Close, my spirits rose.

'Their coming Matty,' I told her. 'They're going to make you better.'

The vet parked his vehicle so its lights shone directly on to us and came across to meet me.

'It's John, isn't it? I'm Roy McAllister, one of the vets at the practice. What's the problem?'

This is Matty, a Friesian who, according to our records, is about to calf. She was alright earlier on and, although her pin bones had moved, she wasn't showing any other signs of calving immediately but when I brought their buffer feed out she was away by

158

herself and, as you can see, not very well.

'Right then, let's have a look at her. It would perhaps help if you could turn the Land Rover round and shine its lights over here along with mine.

'Yes, of course. I'll do it now.'

I left them to it and went to the Land Rover and turned it round so it could provide the light Roy had asked for, and left the engine running to keep the battery charged.

'What do you reckon,' I asked when I made it back. 'Is she going to be alright?'

'We'll she's not very good. Her unborn calf is clearly presenting problems and that could be seriously bad news for both of them. What breed is she in calf to?'

'A Hereford,' I replied.

'Well that's one thing in her favour. It's not one of those big continental breeds we get so many calving problems with. I think the only thing we can do at this point is to have a feel about inside her and see how the calf is lying. If, as it looks, the calf is being presented incorrectly we'll see if we can sort it out.'

'Can you do it here?'

'Is there a choice? She's not going to make it back to the farm, is she? But anyway, let's not pre-empt things; let me see how things are.'

Roy went back to his wagon to get the equipment he needed while I stopped with Matty. 'This is it, old lady,' I told her. 'Just be brave and everything is going to be fine, just you see if it's not.'

'Right then. Let's make a start,' said Roy, who had donned some rubber overalls and was now washing his right arm in a bucket of soapy water he had brought over.

159

'Just hold her tail out for me and I'll slip my arm in and see what's what. I have to say, this job's a lot easier when the cow's on her feet, but we'll manage.'

Roy moved his arm about. 'I have a leg,' he said, at last. 'I'm pretty sure it's a rear leg which means the calf will be coming backwards. What I need now is to find the other rear leg and because it is being so difficult to locate makes me think it could be the reason why the cow is having trouble.'

He took his arm out and paused for a moment. 'I think what we'll do is slip a rope on to the leg I've found so we don't lose that one and then hopefully it will give me some clue where and how the other one is lying. The plan then would be to pull the calf out and take it from there.'

He reached into a bag and removed some calving ropes, soft ropes about a couple of yards long with loops on their ends. Having soaped up again, he pushed his arm in and after some more explorations, relocated the rear leg.

'Right, I've looped round one of the rear legs and that's now pointing in the right direction. Now all we need to do is find the other one which I think is probably tucked under the body of the calf and I need to push the leg I already have away from me so I can pull them both back towards me, if I can get hold of it.'

Roy squirmed and pushed his way in as far as he could. 'This is where you wished you'd been born with longer arms,' he said, struggling for several minutes before announcing he'd found it.

'That's it. I have my hand round it and I'm just making sure it is a back leg and not one of the front ones.' He paused for few seconds. 'Yes, I'm sure it's

160

the one we want so I'm pulling both back legs towards me and now, having them in the right place, I'm looping the second rope round it.'

He slid his arm out and took a breather. 'This job keeps you fit even if you don't have any friends afterwards,' he joked. 'But hopefully we're all set to pull the calf out and it might even be the cow will give us some help now we've straightened everything out. Just go and have a look at the front end to check she's still alright, please John.'

I moved round to her head and while it was clear she was not too happy about things, she was still with us. 'Not long now Matty. You can start thinking of names if you want to.' I gave her ears a gentle stroke and returned to where Roy was.

'Is she still alright?' he asked.

'I think so. She's not responding to anything much.'

'Right, let's see if can get this calf out of her. The point to remember with a breech birth is, unlike a normal birth, the calf's tail needs to be located and pulled out otherwise it will act as a hook and restrict the passageway. And the other detail is that we don't want to be hanging about with it halfway out, because at that point the umbilical cord is likely to be trapped and the calf is on its own.'

Roy pulled on the ropes and the hooves appeared before he paused briefly to find the tail and position it so it wasn't lagging behind. More pulling and the calf's mid-drift appeared.

'Right then John, give me a hand now and pull one of these ropes with me and try and pull slightly down towards the ground as if she was standing up.'

I did as I was asked and tried to grip the rope as best I could.

161

'Wrap it around your hand,' Roy said.

Together we pulled and then all at once, the calf slid out and Roy immediately went to its head to start clearing out the mucus that had accumulated in the calf's mouth and lungs.

'Try and hold it up by the back legs,' he asked.

I did my best to hold it while Roy stuck his fingers into the calf's mouth and throat until he got a reaction and the calf coughed and spluttered into life.

'That's it, she's breathing. You stay here and keep giving her a rub around her chest to keep moving that mucus. In a breech birth it doesn't get a chance to clear as in a normal birth when they come out head first.'

Roy moved over to the cow's head and encouraged her to get to her feet. 'Come on old girl, it's all over now and it's time to go and say hello to your new baby.'

Matty tried but got no further than lifting her head off the ground.

'Bring the calf round here so she can smell it,' he said.

I dragged the calf round and placed it inches away from Matty's nose and it was like turning on a switch. Her eyes opened wide and her nose moved over the calf and very soon she was licking her. And even the calf was responding as Matty's tongue moved over her.

'You'll notice I've left the placenta in there for her to expel, rather than taking it out which can be tricky to make a thorough job of and often leads to infection – not to say there isn't a risk leaving it in but I think it's a reduced one.'

Both Matty and her calf had yet to get to their feet

and Roy suggested moving the calf a few feet away from her to encourage her to stand up and, after a few false starts, Matty was vertical again, albeit a little unsteady.

'I've given her a jab containing some antibiotics and I think she should be alright and it looks as if the calf's about to try out its legs as well.'

It was trying hard but still had to make it onto four of them at the same time. Every time she managed to raise herself onto her front legs, her back legs seemed to collapse beneath her. But she was getting stronger and with a drink of Matty's colostrum, or "beestings" as Harry called it, inside her she would soon be running around.

'Well, that's us about finished.' Roy said as he washed himself down and watched Matty continue her licking. 'Ah, the magic of the tongue; it's a life saver for so many different animals.'

We stayed with them for a little longer until the calf had tottered round to her udder and begun to suckle.

'That's what she needed,' Roy said, pulling off his overalls and rolling them up. 'Does mum have plenty of milk about her?'

'She was springing up well, so I'd expect she will have,' I said.

'That's good. Well, if you don't mind I'll be on my way. If I'm quick I can just get a pint in at the George before last orders are called. Everything should be alright tonight but I'll call round tomorrow morning to give her a check over in daylight but if you have any problems before then, give me a call.'

'Thanks Roy.'

'No worries and thanks for your help.' And with that he climbed into his wagon and drove off across the field to the gate into the paddock.

I went back to Matty and her new calf. She looked a lot better than she did a couple of hours ago and I told her as much. I wondered if I should fetch her a wad of hay to chew on but thought she probably had other things to do.

Back in the Land Rover, I had one last look at her standing there in the lights, her calf had settled down and she stood over it, her tongue still moving gently over her new pride and joy.

How did you get on with the Friesian calving?' Harry asked as I walked into the kitchen the next morning. 'I gather you had Roy McAllister out.'

'That's right. Matty had got herself into a bit of a tangle with her calf, like it was backwards, and had gone down in what looked like a lot of pain, so Roy had to sort the calf's legs out before we could begin to pull her out.'

'What, in the dark?'

'Well, we had the lights from the Land Rover and his wagon and he also had some pretty powerful torches.'

'Sounds as if he did a good job for us. And the cow and calf are alright?'

'I had a look at her about midnight and everything looks to be as it should. The calf, a heifer, suckled and while moving a bit gently Matty seems to be alright. Roy said he would call in this morning and give her a check over, now he can see all of her.'

'That's good,' Harry said as he left the kitchen to take a cup of tea up to Alice. 'Been even better if it had been a bull calf.'

Harvest was drawing to a close and I had the privilege of driving the combine when the last straw was cut and disappeared up the elevator into the threshing system. Having had a fine spell of weather, which saw us harvesting almost every day, the finishing date was getting on for a fortnight earlier than last year.

'That's a good job out of the way,' Harry said as he clambered up the ladder and stepped onto the platform. 'Well done.'

'A bit better than last year,' I said.

'Well we haven't had to get the pop-pop fired up to pull the combine out of a wet hole, if that's what you mean.'

I smiled. 'It was almost worth it just to see the old tractor working.'

'There will be other times, you mark my words, boy.'

I didn't doubt him. Some of Harry's land lay wet even in a dry time, particularly the fields which ran alongside the old railway line where any drainage systems had been damaged when the railway was built.

'Perhaps we should be looking at having some of it drained,' I said, as I drove the combine over to the trailer for its final unloading.

'Oh, I don't know about that, boy. Putting pipes into the ground does not come cheap.'

'They told us at college there were some generous grants available from the ministry. We could have a look at what's on offer.'

'We need to have a look at it, but for now, let's get the combine unloaded and then you can set off back to the farm with the trailer while I try to get some more straw baled.'

165

Any thoughts that we had finished with the combine and the baler for this year proved to be hopelessly wide of the mark because as Harry opened a bottle of Davenports' light ale, one of a dozen Alice had delivered about twice a year, the telephone in the hall started ringing.

'That was Sam Jones, Smith's manager,' Harry said. 'He says one of his combines has fallen to pieces, the baler's eaten itself and how are we fixed to give them a hand for a few days?'

'And what did you say?' I asked.

'I told him we'd be there in the morning.'

'Oh right. That will be different.' Truth was, I didn't know what to think. On one hand I was excited at the thought of working in some different fields, in different crops, but on the other, I was almost disappointed that for us, harvest had not finished after all.

'It'll give the combine a chance to earn us a bit more money,' Harry said. 'More than it will generate sitting under the barn for the next ten months.'

'Providing it behaves itself and doesn't break down,' I said.

'Well, if it does, it's only doing to Sam Jones what it was preparing to do to us at the start of next harvest.'

Which I thought was a profound statement for Harry and one which really warranted a reply of equal tenor, but the moment failed me. Instead I asked him who pays for the fuel.

'They do,' he replied. 'The way it works is that we go there with full fuel tanks and when the work is finished, we leave with full tanks. Which is a fine and fair way of doing it until you start working for some small-scale farm who only has his diesel tank filled

166

once a decade by which time it's some pretty awful stuff you could hardly light a bonfire with.'

'So, the idea is we just roll up there with the combine and the baler and he tells us what to do and where to go to do it.'

'That's about it, boy. Should be good. Might even get a load or two of straw out of it.'

Later that evening I drove down to Rose Hill Farm to see Elizabeth and as I slowed to take the turning into the drive I wondered if anyone had spent the few minutes it would have taken to put a proper latch on the gate; one which worked effortlessly and allowed the gate to swing open and stay open.

But no, it was the usual tangle of bale twine, knotted in about a dozen places and wrapped around an oak tree which had been used as the clap-post ever since the gateway had first been created. Looking at the twine and the tangle which held it all together, I was tempted to save time and effort and just lift the gate off its hinges and run over it.

But I refrained and cut the string and took the weight of the gate as I pulled it open and returned to my pick-up and began the half-mile drive up to the house along a pot-holed track that weaved its way between hedges and the occasional out-building. The day was drawing to a close and I could feel the heat of the day being replaced with damper, cooler air as the light began to fade and night time beckoned.

Drawing up at the house, I noticed the cows were in the collecting yard and waiting to be milked. I wondered, albeit briefly, whether the cows were now being milked three times a day, something I had read about recently and a system which claimed to increase milk yield significantly.

As I stepped out of the pick-up I was met by William junior who told me he was just about to make a start milking the cows.

'You're late, aren't you?'

'Well not really. I was just watching the end of a film.'

Whatever, I thought, and wished him well as I made my way to the kitchen door which was open and I could see Elizabeth's mother working at the sink.

'Hello Kate,' I said, trying my hardest not to surprise her with my sudden appearance.

She turned to face me, her hands dripping soap suds onto the stone floor. 'John,' she gasped. 'Where did you come from?'

'Well I thought it was about time I dropped in to see you. How's everything going?'

'Fine, thanks. Just fine. Sit yourself down and I'll make a cup of tea.' Kate pointed to one of the chairs which surrounded the large table. 'But then, I suppose you'd rather have me seeing if I can find Elizabeth?'

I smiled. 'Well, if she's about.'

She finished drying her hands on her apron and headed for the door. 'You watch the kettle and I'll go and see where she is.'

Kate left me in the kitchen and set off down the long corridor leading to the other half of the house, a house which was home for three generations, of "Williams", the eldest of which, William senior, was snoozing gently in a large chair beside the wood-fired stove.

Having already seen William junior, I wondered idly, where dour William was and I wasn't long finding out when he strode in through the open kitchen door and headed straight for the sink to scrub his hands.

'What brings you down here?' he asked, as he dried his hands. 'Come to see our Elizabeth, I don't doubt.'

I looked at him and noticed not for the first time his thin, gaunt features which smacked of a lifetime of physical work. But while the high cheek bones, receding hairline and large ears were interesting, the main inescapable attraction was the ten-gallon dewdrop hanging from the end of his nose. Even as I stared, it seemed to increase in size.

'Well, that would be right,' I replied. 'But as I mentioned to Kate, it's been a long time since I saw you all.'

Dour William grunted, dropped the towel he was using on the draining board, pointed to the kettle which was now boiling and then set off down the corridor, leaving a trail of straw as it fell of his socks.

Kate was not long returning. 'Elizabeth said she would be down in a few minutes,' she said as she set about making a pot of tea. 'So, we probably have a good half hour for you to tell me all your news.'

I laughed and wondered, not for the first time, just how such a pleasant, fun-loving lady could have ended up married to someone as miserable as dour William. So, over several cups of tea, Kate and I talked away and while I didn't notice it at first, I became aware she was using the time to find out all about me; which with hindsight, was only fair and proper she should know who had fallen in love with her daughter.

'John!' cried Elizabeth as she crashed into the kitchen and flung her arms around my neck. 'I'm sorry but you should have let me know you were coming.'

Long golden-brown hair, white t-shirt, blue jeans

169

and trainers, she looked wonderful and I told her so.

'One of those impulsive visits,' I said, as she sat down beside me. 'I thought we might go out for a drive, or something, providing I can undo the string on the gate at the end of the track.'

And that is what we did.

CHAPTER SIXTEEN

Contract combining

'WHICH ONE DO you want to take up to Smiths?' Harry asked as we walked up the yard after breakfast. 'The combine or the baler?'

'I'll take the combine,' I said, and instantly felt apprehensive at the prospect of taking such a large machine on the public highway through the village.

'Right,' Harry said, not giving me a chance to have any second thoughts. 'It's the baler for me. Be sure to fill it up with fuel and don't forget to take some spare knife sections and rivets.'

It had only been less than twenty-four hours since I sat on the combine, but it could have been a life time. For the last three days I had been counting off the acres, willing everything to keep working as the end of harvest came ever closer. And when the last straw disappeared there was an enormous feeling of relief of a job completed.

And now, as I sat on a cold lumpy seat, holding a cold damp steering wheel and preparing to fire up the engine, it was like starting all over again, rewriting a contract with a machine after I had reneged on the first one.

171

'Come on, old girl,' I muttered. 'Let's go and do some more harvesting.'

I turned on the ignition and pulled the starter rod and the engine turned over a couple of times before it roared into life, a cloud of black, sooty exhaust smoke rising high in the barn before it descended and covered me in its shroud.

'Alright, you've made your point,' I said, when I could see and breathe again. 'Now let's see if you're up for a bit of serious work.'

I squeezed the bulk of the machine through the gateway at the top of the yard and steered for the cattle grid which marked the start of the top road. Having safely rumbled over the metal bars, I opened the throttle, risking a slightly faster pace and watched as the outer edges of the header grazed the grass embankment on either side.

Standing up and peering over the top of the grain tank, I could see Harry driving the tractor he'd hitched to the baler not far behind. Couldn't see the sledge so I don't know what his plans were for that.

Out onto the main road I drove the combine towards the centre of the village and hoped there wouldn't be too much traffic parked outside the newsagent which, as it turned out, was a forlorn hope. Not only were there cars on both sides but today, of all days, there was a large delivery lorry taking up more than half the road. There was nothing for it other than to stop and wait; while the lorry remained where it was, there was no route though the village in either direction and the traffic began to build up.

After about five minutes, I risked a peep over the tank and spotted a queue of traffic as far as I could see behind me and then, to my horror, I heard a siren and

172

very soon, trying to emerge from a road on my left and turn in my direction, was the fire engine with flashing lights and everything else blaring away.

People were starting to get annoyed. I could feel it and it wasn't long before someone was clambering up the ladder towards me.

'Where do you think you are?' he asked. 'In the middle of a field?'

I turned and looked at him and saw a well filled pinstripe suit. 'Have you ever driven a combine harvester that's over ten feet wide through a gap measuring less than three feet?' I asked him. 'Because here's your big chance to show me how to do it.' I stood up and waved for him to take my seat and then pushed past him and climbed down onto the road before walking away to see what Harry had to say about it.

'Don't worry, boy,' he said. 'It will all sort itself out when it's ready to. But while we're waiting just nip in the shop and grab me a newspaper, could you? And when you've done that ask the firemen to turn off that siren. Oh look, the police have arrived.'

I wandered off to the shop and bought Harry a newspaper and then, because the lorry looked like it had just about completed its delivery, I made my way back to the combine and climbed aboard and settled back down on my seat. This was definitely not a good start to the day.

But, as Harry had predicted, it all sorted itself out and the traffic started to move again. It took a bit of time but when the lorry had managed to wheedle its way back off the curb I found I had enough room to continue on through the village. As I did, I found myself directly alongside the silver Cortina driven by the fat man wearing the pinstripe suit.

Being a warm day, he had opened the sun roof and now, from where I sat I could see his big bald head, a pair of sun glasses and the car's immaculate white leather trim. This was just too good an opportunity to miss so I didn't think twice about it before pressing the lever that emptied the grain from the tank. There wasn't a lot, but what there was had become damp and stared to smell a little and there were also a few rat droppings mixed in with it; all in all, I'd say there was about a half a shovelful.

And it was all just so perfect; the positioning, the timing, everything you could have asked for and more. The grain arrived on the chute just as we started to move and, being damp and mixed with extraneous material, needed the movement to encourage it to start flowing. But down it flowed and at just the right time, emptied off the chute and into the car.

Sam Jones was waiting for us when we finally arrived at Smith's farm and he was clearly in no mood to hang about.

'There's no need to get off the combine,' he shouted up to me. 'Just follow me.'

And then he ran over to his pick-up and set off along tracks and through fields I had never seen before but soon we arrived at field of wheat which must have been over sixty acres, so big, it was a job to see the hedge over on the far side.

'Now then,' began Sam. 'This is where it all happens today. I've two other combines coming in to help us out and with a bit of luck there should be another one coming out from the dealer we can use on a sort of trial basis. But anyway, make a start on the headland and I'll get one of my chaps to follow you round with a trailer, so you can empty when you're full. Alright?'

I nodded. This was farming on a scale I had never experienced before, and I had been told there was over three thousand acres of it and over twenty-five men were employed. When it came to Friday pay day, Sam had them forming a queue outside his office and he'd call them in one by one, cap in hand, to give each of them their wages.

I was also told that Sam carried the employees' national insurance cards about with him in his top pocket so if he wanted to dismiss anyone he could give him his cards and tell him to get off the farm and that would be the end of it.

Harvesting wheat was a totally new experience for me and I hadn't a clue how the combine should be set up with concave gaps, drum speed, sieve settings and goodness knows what else. To my mind though, wheat didn't look that different to barley so, for a start, I thought the safest route was to leave everything as it was and see what happened. If it was a clean sample going into the tank and there wasn't much grain being thrown out the back of the combine, all must be well.

I tentatively pushed down on the big lever to engage the threshing system and listened as things started to move and speed up, the sound it all made was impossible to describe but somehow, I had discovered, it was still possible to detect when something was not quite right.

With the throttle set to its full, open position I lowered the header and nudged the variable speed lever forward and as we began to move the wheat started to fall onto the bed as it was cut before disappearing into the elevator and up to the threshing drum.

The big moment is when the grain starts to arrive in the tank and it seemed to me to be taking a long time to appear, to the point I was on verge of stopping to see where it was all going. I was having visions of it all pouring out on the ground, but then it finally arrived, flowing out of the clean grain elevator and cascading down into the base of the tank.

Not halfway round and I had to stop to unload and it was my first experience of unloading into a trailer rather into sacks and it was just so much quicker. The only problem was that the end of the chute wasn't high enough to clear the side of the trailer, so it had to be swivelled upwards to allow the trailer to drive under it and then released. I wasn't too sure how this would work if anyone wanted to unload on the move.

Eventually, I made it round to the start of the field again, having unloaded twice and with probably half a tank on board. And then I noticed for the first time, there were two swaths of straw which meant there must be another combine in the field.

I stood up and looked around and there, in the far corner of the field, was a dusty cloud beneath which I could just about make out a blue combine harvester and not far behind it was another tractor and trailer.

This was exciting stuff and I suddenly had thoughts of being part of a large team of combines working across the American prairies, each machine stepped out across the field, operating a few yards behind the one in front and taking vast swathes of crop with every pass.

Always wondered how so many combines managed

to turn when it came to the headland; it must have been an awful traffic jam until they were all sorted out and if the crop was dusty, working so close to other combines must have been a terrible place to be. It also occurred to me that, if one combine had to stop for one reason or another, all the others behind would have to as well, unless they managed to steer around it.

And on the subject of dust, I had discovered long ago that a wind blowing directly towards the combine as it moved across a field was a far better situation than a wind which simply followed the combine. When this happened, the dust would travel with you and it could become so thick, it was almost impossible to see what was happening on the header below.

By mid-morning there were no less than four combines working in my field and there were tractors and trailers running about all over the place as they raced around to ensure each combine's grain tank was emptied.

There was no order in where each combine was working, which was a shame and on a couple of occasions two machines would set off from opposing ends of the field and have to cross over when they met in the middle. But by and large, it was all working well and what was once an imposing sixty-acre field of wheat was swiftly becoming a field of straw swaths.

I wondered how Harry was getting on with the baler; I had caught a glimpse of him working a few fields away earlier on, but I was at a loss to know where he was now.

Just before one o'clock, Sam drove into the centre of the field in his pick-up and once he had climbed out he stood to one side and waved his arms about. I was unloading at the time and wondered what it was he wanted but then I noticed the other combines and tractor drivers had stopped work and were now driving their machines towards him.

As soon as I had unloaded, I did the same and by the time I arrived, everyone else was standing around munching through large sandwiches and drinking mugs of tea.

'Come on, boy,' Sam said. 'You'll be missing out if you don't get a move on.'

I needed no second bidding; I was both hungry and thirsty but also slightly intimidated to be in the presence of such experienced workers who had spent a life time working with farm machinery.

He passed me a sandwich, a great big door-stopper of a sandwich I could hardly get my jaws around and, as I chewed away, I couldn't help wondering what it was about boiled bacon that made it so popular in these parts.

'There you go, boy. Get on the outside of that and wash it down with a mug of tea and you'll be good to go for the rest of the day. Oh, and Harry asked me to tell you he'd be milking the cows this afternoon so not to worry about them.'

Not ten minutes after we had stopped we were on our way again, each of the combines creating a large cloud of dust as their threshing systems were wound up to speed once more.

The afternoon was hot, as hot as I could remember, and the sun glared down with an intensity which scorched the back of my neck and I should have been grateful for the protection a layer of dust afforded. I began to think how remiss it was of manufacturers of machines designed to be operated in the heat of summer, not to provide some element of shading.

I was still mulling this one over when a brand-new combine rolled into the field and it was colossal. I had never seen such a machine and nor, it seemed, had the crowd of people gathered around it. As I drove up the field towards it, the closer I came, the larger it appeared to be.

I turned on the headland very slowly and had a good look. The header was at least twice the width of mine, the grain tank looked big enough to hold several tonnes and the width of the rear hood suggested there were at least five straw walkers, possibly six. What a machine, and when I caught sight of it, the name on the side said it all: Giant Matador.

By the time I had made a return to the top of the field, the new combine had started cutting and it was soon obvious that its output far exceeded that of the three combines already working in the field.

It was not long before the field was finished and it was time to move onto the next one and by evening, we had managed to harvest over one hundred acres, Harry's acreage and a bit more in just one day.

'That was quite a combine harvester,' Harry said, when I met up with him as he prepared to take the buffer feed out to the cows.

'You're telling me it was,' I said. 'Its output was just something else.'

'You want to try baling behind it. There was so much straw in the swath, the baler was dropping a bale out every two or three yards and where it had stopped, I had to manually fork the mountain of straw it had created into the baler. Anyway, Sam says thank you for your help but he won't need us now he has the

179

new combine; they can hardly keep up with the amount of grain going into the barn as it is without us adding to his problems. I don't know how they would cope if some of it needs drying.'

'So that's us finished, again?' I asked.

'That's it boy. Harvest home for us - again. Take the feed out and we'll crack open another beer to celebrate.'

CHAPTER SEVENTEEN

Laying the hedges

WITH HARVEST COMPLETED, the grain heaped up in the lofts and the straw bales stacked high under the open-sided Dutch-barns, life suddenly took on a gentler, quieter pace with lunches taking a little longer and a chance to have a chat about things that didn't concern combines, balers or trailers.

As it happened, the end of harvest also coincided with a change in the weather which turned noticeably colder and more showery. Days were also becoming shorter and although it still wasn't dark at six o'clock in the morning, an overcast sky could result in a murky start to the day, one when it was good to have a coat within easy reach and wellingtons became increasingly the required footwear.

Out in the fields, the hedges were now covered with berries; hips, haws, slows, elderberries and even crab apples, although most of these were lying on the ground. They spread an amazing mass of colour throughout the countryside, a sign which Harry insisted indicated we were in for a hard winter.

'When bird feed is plentiful at this time of the year it's nature's way of saying it's going to be a long, cold winter with plenty of snow and ice,' he said.

'And what indicates a mild winter with plenty of frost free days and the occasional rain shower?' I asked.

Harry thought about it. 'Not so many berries,' he said.

'Oh, right.'

'Would anyone like another cup of tea,' Alice asked, lifting the tea pot and rocking it to gauge its contents. 'There's just about enough but I can top it up if you want more.'

'I'll just have half a cup,' Harry said.

'And you, John?'

'Yes, another cup would be good, thanks,' I answered, handing my cup over.

'How do you feel about a spot of hedge laying,' Harry asked, when Alice had refilled my cup and passed it over. 'I don't suppose they taught you how to do that at college, did they?'

'Well, not really. We had about half a morning trimming the principal's garden hedge, but I don't think that would really count. For the field hedges they used a mechanical trimmer attached to a tractor and we had the job of forking the cut stuff off the top of the hedges and then making a bonfire with it. It was pretty labour intensive.'

Harry scoffed. 'If you keep taking the top growth out of hedges, you end up with a load of stalks which cattle and sheep can walk through,' he said. 'For a hedge to be stock-proof, it has to be laid to get some heart into it. Otherwise you have to spend a fortune on back fencing.'

'Hedgelaying's a pretty long job though,' I said.

'We always reckoned on laying a hedge every twenty years, so the idea was to lay a length each year to ensure everything was laid within that time span. And it was good winter's job once you had the fire lit and started cutting.'

'How much could you lay in a day?'

'A good man could lay, stake and bind a chain,' he said. 'But it all depends on the hedge and how thick it was.'

'A chain? How long is that?'

'Didn't they teach you anything? A chain is twenty-two yards or four rods. It has one hundred links and ten chains is a furlong and eighty chains is a mile. An acre is ten square chains or, put another way, a chain wide by a furlong.'

'But who first decided a chain was to be twenty-two yards? Seems to me like an odd number. Was he a cricketer?'

'Don't know boy but I had a contractor once who was using a chain which, when I put it against my chain, was about a yard shorter so I was paying him for a yard a day he wasn't laying.'

'But really, who made the first chain?' I persisted.

'I don't know,' Harry repeated. 'It could all do with the size of an acre which I've always been told to believe, is the area of ground one man and an ox can plough in a day.'

'Well, that doesn't make any sense at all, either,' I said. 'Is it heavy or light ground and is the ox big or small? Too many variables and, another thing, how long was the day. That doesn't add up.'

'Now you mention it, I don't suppose it does,' Harry conceded. 'But it's in all the books as the definition of an acre and I have to say, the picture of the ox I have in my book is pretty impressive.'

I could sense Alice's interest waning and I was tempted to ask her what she thought about it but decided against it.

'I'm off up the village this morning to see the butcher,' she said. 'So, I'll be near to the other shops if anyone wants me to get anything.'

Alice looked around the table. 'No? Right, but that's where I'll be if you change your mind.' She started to gather the plates and cups up and I took the hint and prepared to leave.

'I've just the yard to give a swill down and I need to check on one of the Red Polls to see if she's calved. I'll be with you after that, if that's alright?' I said.

'Alright, boy. I'll be in the workshop.'

Duties completed I wandered back down the yard to see what Harry was up to in the workshop.

'How's the Red Poll?' he asked, when I had stepped through the doorway

'Oh, she's fine. A good strong bull calf up and suckling like a good one.'

Harry had not been idle. He had found all the hedge laying kit including billhooks, axes, slashers, sharpening stones, strong leather gauntlets and even a pair of goggles which, in my ignorance, I thought was a tad superfluous.

'The key to good hedge laying is to ensure everything used for cutting is razor sharp,' he said. 'I've known people take their billhook home with them and sit in the front room all night sharpening the blade with a wet stone.'

'Bit annoying if you're trying to watch television, I'd have thought.'

Harry ignored me. 'And these same people have been known to bugger off home in a huff if their axe of billhook happened to strike a stone or come across a nail someone had hammered into a tree.'

'It's that important to them,' I said.

Harry nodded. 'It may be a bit extreme, but it just shows how much people care about having a sharp blade to work with.'

We loaded all the kit into the back of the Land Rover and set off down the fields but not before we placed a can of diesel and a bale of straw in the back to help light the fire. Harry had decided to make a start on the hedge between Long Meadow and Forty Acre.

'I remember helping my father lay this one when I was about your age,' he said.

'So it's longer than twenty years ago?'

'Well yes, but most of it is pretty slow growing blackthorn and we'll be cutting all the elder out.'

We parked by the gateway and the first thing I asked Harry was which way we were going to lay the hedge? To my mind, there was a ditch on the side we were which, if we laid it to the left, would mean us standing in the ditch while we worked.

'On a level field like this one, the direction doesn't really matter,' he said. 'But when there's a slope, it's best to lay it so the branches point up the hill and not down it. Looking at this one we need to go to the other end and start there.'

'Doesn't that mean we will be standing in the ditch?'

'Yes, but if we work on the other side we have a barb wire fence to struggle with and we'll be working cack-handed.'

Harry set off with the long handled slasher with its

185

twelve-inch blade and began to take the side growth out and, reduce the bulk of the hedge, as he described it. There would also be wood available from which we could cut stakes that needed to be inserted every yard or so to hold the binders.

The part I was wary of arrived rather more quickly than I expected when Harry handed me a pair of leather gloves, a billhook and asked me to lay the first branch.

'You don't want to cut it off because it needs to keep growing, but just make a cut near the base of it and gently pull it over with your left hand. If you get it right, there will be a short spur near the split which you will need to cut off when you have it in position.'

Harry stood back and watched while I made a tentative chop with the billhook and just managed to nock a slither of bark off.

'It'll need a bit more than that,' he said. 'Go for about the middle of it and see how it bends.'

So, I went for the middle and it refused to be pulled over. So I gave it another incision, a deeper one which couldn't have left more than half an inch of wood to hold the two parts together.

'That's it,' Harry said. 'Pull it over nice and gently and lay it down where you want it to be and make sure you don't twist it, or you'll break it off.'

But something went wrong and it twisted, and it broke off.

'Never mind, boy. There're a few more branches we can use,'

By lunch time, we had about five yards of hedge laid and Harry had started knocking in the stakes he had cut out.

'This is where some people use bale string rather

186

than binders to keep the branches in place,' he said. 'But it's a terrible thing to do to a hedge and it looks dreadful. Don't you ever be tempted to use string boy.'

Lengths of thin branches that could be twisted between the stakes and keep the laid branches tight and firm were not that easy to find though, but Harry was convinced we would find enough for our needs, hacking them out of the tall bushy material he was removing from the sides of the hedge.

We went back to the farm for lunch and as I joined Harry in the Land Rover I tried hard not to recall how ineffectual I had been on my first attempt at laying a hedge. I think I must have chopped out at least half a dozen pieces which I had been trying to retain with just a gentle cut so they could be pulled over. At this rate, there was no question about having to leave the barbwire fence in place; without it the cattle and sheep could walk on straight through it and not know they had changed fields.

'You know you've got the dealer representative coming this afternoon to talk to you about tractors, don't you?' Alice asked, as Harry washed his hands.

'You're right, he is, and I'd forgotten all about it. Better not spoil his day by not being here.'

'Well I could talk to him if you're busy,' Alice said. 'I don't know what about, but I could make him a cup of tea.'

'There's no need for that. We're just making a start on laying the hedge between Long Meadow and Forty Acre, you know, the one I helped father lay all those years ago.'

'Yes, I do remember, only too well. That was the

afternoon you nearly killed yourself when the axe head flew off.'

'Well it won't happen again,' Harry said. 'They make them better these days.'

'I hope they do. Come on John; sit yourself down.'

I dried my hands and sat down as Alice opened the oven door and, after donning a thick pair of oven gloves, lifted out a large pie.

'If that pie tastes as good as it looks, we're in for a treat,' said Harry.

Alice smiled appreciatively and used a knife to make the first incision into the golden pastry crust. 'Hold your plate up Harry, and I'll ladle it on board. And John, you get ready for yours.'

A generous portion of beef pie followed by a steamed treacle sponge with custard was enough to set any man up for the day and most other things too, although swinging a billhook while doubled up under a prickly black thorn branch probably wasn't one of them.

'I take it you're not coming back down to the hedge this afternoon, then?' I asked.

'No, I've promised I would see this representative chap so you will be on your own, if you think you can do it. Just take your time and try and pull the branches down so they are angled slightly away from you. That gives the hedge a clean side which looks good and a bushier side where all the foliage is poking out.'

'I'll do my best.'

'And be careful with the axe,' Alice said.

As I drove the Land Rover down to the bottom of Piggy Hill I could see the hedge we had started laying and even though there had only been a few yards of work, it was quite dramatic how different it already looked.

And then it occurred to me that here was an opportunity to break with tradition and create a hedge with different shapes – well, at least with one different shape. Perhaps a bird or a cow, or even a donkey, an immortalised version of Pedro. The idea grew with me as I drove across Forty Acre and by the time I arrived, I was totally sold on the idea of a donkey.

Rather than stopping, I drove slowly back along the hedge looking for a likely spot, a place where the branches would lend themselves to be moulded into the shape of a donkey.

About two thirds of the way along there was a young ash tree which looked as if it could be persuaded to create the frame work and there was plenty of blackthorn available to trim and shape accordingly.

Grabbing the long handled slasher from the back of the Land Rover, I made a start. My donkey would be about twelve feet long and eight feet high at the shoulder and, I have to say, after a couple of hours when I stood back to have a look, it was definitely taking shape.

The location of a convenient clump of young cedar had made me change my mind which way the donkey was facing and I needed to lower the back end by about a foot as a result. Clearing out the space under it to create the belly was more than a little taxing and I ended up with deep scratches all over my arms.

But it was worth it. When it was time to leave, my 'hedge-donkey' was just about finished, although it was one of those projects where there is always just a little more that could be done.

Halfway up Piggy Hill I stopped the Land Rover and

stepped out to see what it looked like from a distance and I was impressed. I just hoped Harry would be equally pleased with it, but I had a gnawing doubt my creation would be met with any enthusiasm.

'How did you get on with the hedge laying,' Harry asked me, when I went into the kitchen to fill the bucket with warm water.

'Oh, not too bad. It's slow work but as you say, there's no rush,' I replied.

'I was planning on coming down to see how you were getting on, but I only made it to the top of Piggy Hill.'

'Really?'

'Yes. But then, as I looked in your direction, you won't believe this, but I swear I could see a donkey in the hedge – about two thirds along from where we started.'

'That's strange,' I said. 'It must have been some trick of the light, or something.'

'I don't know, boy. I think it could be time to have a trip to the opticians.'

'Yeah, well it comes to us all at some time,' I said, lifting the bucket out of the sink. 'I'll get on and with the milking.'

CHAPTER EIGHTEEN

Grey Fergie plus a cab

I DON'T KNOW HOW I missed seeing the Grey Fergie tractor although, to be fair, it was parked under the barn in the shadow of the combine harvester. Even so, I must have walked passed it a dozen times as I carried sack loads of ground barley from the stone barn to the cows' feed bins in the bail.

But there it was now. Not exactly gleaming but by all accounts, clean and spotless down to the last rivet in its cab.

And it was the cab which really caught my eye. This was the first tractor cab I had encountered at close range and I felt a desperate urge to climb aboard and discover what it was like to sit in one.

The only problem was the absence of a door, which was a tad disappointing and, for that matter, mystifying. After making a couple of turns around the tractor to be absolutely sure there were no hidden entrances, I was forced to assume the route into the cab was through the back of it which, rather than having the grey metal sheeting used by the rest of the cab, had a simple green-canvass cover suspended from the edge of the roof.

Before I could climb in though, Harry appeared.

'What do you reckon to her?' he asked.

'Well, she's pretty small as tractors go,' I said. 'What's the engine rated at?'

'About twenty something horsepower, I think, and it's a four-cylinder diesel.'

'That's about half the power of the David Brown.'

'Yes, but she's probably half the weight and she has some really advanced hydraulics on her. And before you say anything else, I've also arranged for her to be fitted with a front loader; you know, one which can be fitted with a large bucket or a wide tined fork.'

'That's terrific,' I said, as thoughts of loading muck onto trailers, loading bales, loading sacks, loading *anything* I wanted onto trailers flashed through my mind. 'And it has a cab too. That's just *so* good.'

'Well, I shouldn't get too excited about the cab. To my mind, it's a waste of money and I only said we'd have it to see how we would get on with it,' Harry said.

'Yes, but…'

'I mean,' continued Harry, 'how are we going to get under low roof beams with that cab sticking up so high? And, in the summer, you'll be sweltering.'

'Let's not rush into this,' I said. 'There's been hundreds of times when it's been raining, snowing or blowing a gale when sitting on a tractor has been an ordeal. You know yourself. And how about when the seat gets wet and water runs out of your arse from the sponge padding every time you sit on it?'

'Steady boy. All I'm saying is we'll see how we get on. Now why don't you go and get the cows milked and then you can give the tractor a drive, or whatever you want to do with it?'

I turned and headed off across the paddock to let the cows out of Church Close and when I reached the gate, I looked over and saw my girls waiting patiently for me, their tales swishing idly and their heads turning to make the occasional swipe at an irritating fly.

All of a sudden, I felt their love and respect and I was humbled. So what was having a cab all about anyway? Was it important, was it going to change anything? Probably not. These were the girls that mattered, not some warship-grey metal cab bolted onto a ten-year-old tractor.

'Come on girls, let's go and end the day on a really happy note, shall we? I walked on ahead of them and I knew Horns would only be a pace or two behind. But I teased her and pretended I hadn't seen her until she could stand it no longer and pushed her nose into my back.

'Horns, what are you doing?' I asked as I turned to face her. And then she gave me that silly head twisting snort of a smile as only she could. I reached into my pocked for a handful of barley and she licked it clean with a single swipe of her tongue. And then we were both happy.

We reached the collecting yard and the girls trooped passed me as I held the gate open for them. Matty, who had endured a difficult calving, was now looking really well, and Lucy seemed to be happier and more confident and was at last finding her place in the herd. I asked Pauline whether she had been a good girl, and she was followed by Thrifty, Sophie, Christine, Carol – the list seemed endless and I loved them all dearly.

As soon as I'd finished milking and organised the

churns, made sure everything was prepared for the morning milking and taken out the evening's buffer feed, I was back with the Grey Fergie.

Harry had left the owner's manual on the seat so, after I had climbed in from the back, I settled down to have a read through it and became engrossed with the tractor's weight transfer system.

This used a sensor on the top link which when, for example, a plough was attached to the tractor it could maintain a constant working depth by detecting the force being used to pull it.

If the force increased, the plough would be lifted slightly, adding more weight onto the tractor's wheels for extra grip and if it reduced, the plough was lowered by a small amount.

I was just on the control page when I heard a noise behind me. It was Elizabeth.

'Harry said this is where I'd find you,' she said. 'He told me to ask you whether or not you had managed to start the engine.'

'Hi Elizabeth, just looking at our new toy. And no, I haven't started the engine yet; is that a problem?'

'I don't know but by the way Harry was talking, it seemed he hadn't managed to find out how to do it.'

'Yes, now you mention it, when we were looking at the tractor earlier he looked as if he was having problems in that department, but I think I've discovered how it should be done. Do you want to go for a ride in it?'

'Well, only a short one. I have to be back in about half an hour to give you time to get ready.'

'Get ready for what?'

'Taking me out. I start back at university tomorrow, if you hadn't forgotten.'

I had forgotten. 'Oh right. I think I'd better leave the tractor alone then,' I said.

'No, you don't have to do that.' She slid further forward into the cab and somehow, found a place to stand. 'Come on, start it up and show me what it will do,'

I worked the magic with the heel of my boot, pushed the gear stick over to the start position and heard the engine turn over and fire up.

'Where do you want to go?' I asked.

'I don't mind. Preferably somewhere I don't have to get out and open gates.'

'I'll take it round to Farm Close then. Hold on.'

From then on, conversation was impossible as the sound of the engine echoed around the cab accompanied by a generous volume of rattles and vibration. Already I was thinking that a day or two working in these conditions would have my ears ringing.

We arrived at the top of Samuels Lane, the bridle path that went down the side of the fields, parked up and stopped the engine. The silence was just so welcome.

'I think we can walk from here,' I said.

Elizabeth nodded. 'I think that might be for the best.'

She bent over me and gave me a kiss before squeezing past and climbing out of the rear of the cab.

'Well, that was a memorable experience,' I said, when I too had extracted myself from the cab and made friends with my ears again. 'Let me know if you think I'm shouting.'

'Oh, it wasn't that bad,' she said.

'You weren't sitting where I was.'

'Pretty close though.'

I found her hand and we strolled off down the leafy pathway, brushing through the long grass, pushing aside the bushes, while a golden glow from the setting sun filtered through the branches above us. And every so often a cooling breeze stole its way through the trees, taking the heat of the day away.

'So, you're off back to York,' I said after we had travelled nearly to the end of the pathway.

'That's right. This will be the start of my second year and, sadly, this time you won't be there to keep me company.'

'I don't think they do repeat years at Askham Bryon.'

'Oh well, you'll just have to come and see me then.'

I stopped and pulled her close.

'Elizabeth, do you think there will ever be a time when we can be together?'

'But I thought we were together.'

'I mean properly together.'

'Yes, but I have my university course to complete…'

'I know and there's no way I want you to give up on that. I was just thinking ahead – you know – to when you've finished.'

'That's another two years away and who's to say what will happen in that time.'

'Exactly, that's what's worrying me,' I said.

'Then let me tell you, you have no need to worry about me and I hope I have no need to be concerned about you.' She sounded cross.

'That's all I wanted to know,' I said. 'I just love you so much.'

'And I you, John Johnson. Now, are you going to

take me out tonight or are we going to walk over to that broken bale and lie down and look at the setting sun?'

'If there's a choice, I think I'll opt for the broken bale.'

'They tell me Elizabeth is back at York today,' Alice said as she placed the bowls and plates out for breakfast.

'That's right,' I said, drying my hands. 'It doesn't seem as if she's been back home above five minutes and now she's going again.'

'Oh, you've seen a fair bit of each other, during the summer, haven't you?'

'Only when it rained, but you're right, we managed to be together whenever we could.'

'Who's taking her up to York?'

'I did offer but I think Kate shouted first, so they're making it into a family outing with her sisters, which should be fun,' I explained.

'Don't worry, Elizabeth will be back before you know it and she always writes to you.'

I smiled. 'Thanks Alice. I know she will.'

Harry barged into the kitchen and headed for the sink. 'Those bloody pigs,' he said, as he grabbed the tap and turned it on. Do you know, that Large White boar just tried to have me, came at me waving his tusks about like he meant it and it was only because I was carrying a bucket I managed to steer him away. He'll be finding out what a bacon rail is if he tries that again.'

'You should be more careful,' Alice said. 'You know how they can be.'

'Well that big sod will soon be learning how I can be

too.' Harry dried his hands and went and sat down at the table. 'How did you get on with the tractor, boy? Do you like it?'

'Well, it's a bit noisy, what with the all the metal sheeting in the cab. And I wouldn't want to be in it all day,' I said. 'But as a tractor, yes, it's fine.'

'They're delivering the front loader today so we'll find out what it can do pushing up the branches and brush we're taking off that hedge we're laying. We'll see, but if you take the Land Rover down and carry on with the hedge, resisting the urge to make donkey shapes, I'll bring the tractor down when they've fitted the loader.'

Harry reached for the carving knife and started to cut slices off the week's boiled bacon joint. He placed two slices on a plate and passed it over to me. Alice buttered the open side of a loaf of bread and then cut it off and dropped the resulting slice on to the side of the plate.

'I see in the book, they recommend having a weight on the back when using the loader,' I said, as I worked my way through the two slices wondering, not for the first time, why I don't just place the slices on the bread and make a sandwich of it. I might just have been able to secrete some brown sauce onto it too.

'Yes, I saw that. It makes sense because if the loader is lifting, it takes the weight off the rear wheels. I think there's a big block of concrete that comes with the loader and hooks on to a bar which fits on to the lower linkage arms, or something like that.' Harry said. 'Probably be quicker to use a hand fork anyway rather than wasting time fitting loaders and weights and then having to drive it down there and back again.'

198

'Don't forget to mention the cab,' I said, swallowing the last of my boiled bacon.

'Why should I do that?'

'Oh, it doesn't matter. I'll get on down there and see what happens when you turn up.'

'Aren't you going to have another cup of tea before you go?' Alice asked.

'No, I'm alright thanks. I'll go and make a start.'

'Just check on the cows when you go through Hollow Close. I think I saw that Red Poll laying into Lucy when I came up from shepherding the other day. She can be a right so-and-so.'

I walked up the yard to where the Land Rover was parked and made sure all the hedge cutting gear was still on board before I climbed into the cab. Driving up the yard, I suddenly heard my name being called. It was Elizabeth, her two sisters and Kate who had walked up from the street and were now standing just outside the house, waving their arms and shouting.

I left the Land Rover where it was and walked down to meet them.

'We've just popped in for Elizabeth to say good-bye to you,' Kate explained. 'So the rest of us will go and cadge a cup of tea off Alice and Harry and leave you to it for a few minutes. Come on girls.'

'Sorry about this,' Elizabeth said, when the noise had moved into the kitchen.

'That's alright. It was very thoughtful of you to drop in and see me.'

'Let's walk up the yard,' she said.

'Of course.' I held out my hand and she clasped it.

'I was thinking about what you said yesterday,' she started. 'And I think it would be a wonderful idea if we were to be together, properly.'

'So what are you suggesting?'

'Well,' she started. 'I don't have to go to university, do I?'

'But you must,' I said. 'You can't just give up like that. Look, I love you more than anything and I want us to be together for so many reasons but we can wait. It's only a couple of years and if you gave up university now, you would regret it for the rest of your days.'

I looked at Elizabeth and I noticed she was crying before she buried her head in my arms. 'I hoped you would say that, but I was just so worried you wouldn't wait for me and go off and…'

'Hey,' I said, pulling her closer to me. 'Don't cry, you'll make me cry too and then Harry would have a ball.'

Elizabeth laughed through her tears. 'Oh John,' she cried. 'I'm so sorry for being so stupid. Tell me you love me again.'

'I love you so much but how about this for a plan? When you come home for the summer we'll announce our engagement and then we can spend the next year planning weddings and all that go with them. But we must keep it a secret until then.'

'I will John, I will, I will, I promise.'

'Come on then. Dry those tears and kiss me good bye before the rest of them pile out of the house. And if you want to write me a letter when you get a minute that would be good. At least, it will keep Alice guessing about what's going on.'

We turned and began walking back down to the house and, as we were spotted, the noise reached yet another crescendo and it was hard to believe there were only three of them.

'You ready to go, Elizabeth?' Kate asked. 'Don't worry, you'll be seeing John at Christmas if not before.'

And I watched Elizabeth nod her head, take hold of her mother's arm and start to walk down to the street. Harry and Alice stood in the doorway and waved their good-byes and I stood at the top of the slope so I could see them climb into the car and drive away.

'Have you ever heard people make so much noise?' Harry asked me when they had finally departed. 'And there were only three of them; can you believe that?'

But I wasn't listening.

As Harry had requested, I stopped in Hollow Close to see how Pauline was behaving. She was easy to spot because she was the only cow who seemed to be continually on the move and it was quite noticeable how the other cows kept out of her way.

There was little doubt in my mind that she was a bully, not just to little Lucy, whose life she was making a misery but to all and sundry. I drove over to her and let her know I was watching, not that is seemed to make any difference; she just carried on moving through the herd.

But this wasn't just a random stroll. I could see she was gradually working her way closer to Lucy and Lucy was now aware of it. I was incensed with the devious way she was operating. I took the Land Rover across to be nearer to them, climbed out and reached into the back to see if I could find a stick or something, Short of using the long-handled hedge slasher, there was nothing suitable I could find.

It was as if I wasn't there. Pauline moved around totally ignoring me and when she had arrived at her quarry she gave me a look which suggested she was going to be unstoppable.

I stepped out of the Land Rover and discovered I was now between her and Lucy which was not a very sensible place to be. She snorted and stamped her feet and then began moving towards me as I shouted at her and waved my arms. But there was no stopping her.

Five yards away she broke into a canter and put her head down and came straight for me, half a tonne of twisted bovine on a mission to rid the world of an adversary who had blighted her life. As the gap closed I prepared myself to dive to one side and when she was within a whisker of me I did just that but I was a second too slow, a second when her head made contact with my shoulder and spun me round, the pain already arriving before I hit the ground.

I lay there and tried to regain my breath before taking stock of the situation. I'd never seen a cow so aggressive and when I put my head up I could see I was about to see a lot more.

Pauline had stopped and turned to face me, her face full of hate and anger. She was going to charge again and this time she was going to trample and really do some damage. And the way I was feeling, there wasn't a lot I could do about it.

She was now pawing the ground, savouring the moment before she unleashed what she clearly planned to be a decisive charge.

But then, just as I was beginning to feel the end was about to happen I saw a group of cows coming across from the main group. There must have been a dozen of them and their numbers were increasing as more and more cows joined the pack, all it seemed heading for Pauline.

And Pauline had also seen them, and they provided just enough distraction to allow me time to struggle to my feet and make it over to the Land Rover, climb in and slam the door shut before there was a fearful bang as her head piled into the door.

My shoulder was giving me some major pain and I had to use my left arm to start the engine and after that, I wasn't hanging about; I headed for the farm and just hoped Harry would still be there.

It was Alice who saw me first. I just managed to slip out of the Land Rover and hobbled round to other side when she came out of the house.

'John, what's the matter?' she cried, running over to me.

'It's that blasted cow, she had a go at me and managed to catch my shoulder.'

'You'd better come down to the house and let me have a look at it,' she said. 'Take my arm and we'll move as slowly as you want.'

And it was then Harry emerged from the workshop. 'Don't tell me, that old Red Poll has given you a shunt,' he said.

'That's right,' I said, wincing with the pain as I moved slowly towards the house. 'I got between her and the small heifer and she let fly at me.'

'What's the damage?'

'I don't know but it hurts.'

We made it into the kitchen and I lowered myself down into one of the chairs.

'You have a look at his shoulder Harry while I make a cup of tea,' Alice said.

Harry pulled down my shirt and had a look and a prod with his hand, which didn't help any with relieving the pain.

'Well, it looks alright from here,' he said, turning to Alice. 'Probably just bruised or something; might be a good idea to let the doctor have a look at it though, just to make sure. I'll make the tea while you give him a call.'

From that point on, my day took on a rather different format than I had planned. Alice's call to the doctor resulted in me being driven by Harry to the hospital to have my shoulder X-rayed but not before Alice had insisted on me changing my underpants and putting a clean vest and shirt on. Hospitals in her book were where people went to die and if I did, she wasn't going to be responsible for anyone discovering anything but clean, ironed underpants.

I suppose we were in the hospital for about five hours before a white coated doctor called me over and announced that while the x-ray had not revealed any breakages, there had clearly been some bruising and ligament strains which I would take a few days to recover from.

'The thing is, what are we going to do with the cow?' Harry said as we drove home.

'I don't think we've any choice,' I said. 'She'll have to go. I think we've tried to sort her out and there have been times when she seemed to be behaving herself, but I've always had my doubts she actually was.'

Harry thought about it. Losing a cow from some unavoidable medical condition was one thing but sending a cow to market because it had severe behavioural problems was different and one he hadn't experienced before, if you ignore his episode with the Hereford bull.

'I think you're right. We don't have a choice, Next time she could end up really injuring someone. We'll keep her in tonight and I'll get Petersons to pick her up in the morning.'

By evening milking time, the pain in my shoulder was starting to subside, helped no doubt by the aspirin tablets Alice had given me.

'You going to be alright to milk or do you want me to do it?' Harry asked.

'I think I'll be alright, but I think it might be a good idea if we both went and fetched the cows; just in case she's still being aggressive.'

We set off down the field and found the cows waiting for us by the gate leading out of Hollow Close. After a few welcoming strokes, Harry opened the gate and they started to wander through, but Pauline was not with them.

'She's not here,' I said as the last cow left the field.

'Not here?' Harry looked back into the field which, as far as I could see, was now empty of cows. 'Where's she disappeared to, then?'

'I don't know. She must have got through the hedge somewhere and goodness knows where she will have gone.'

'You take these up to the farm and I'll go and have a look round,' Harry said.

I set off after the cows while Harry pulled the gate shut behind him and went in the opposite direction. As I walked along the track it occurred to me that if it hadn't been for the cows distracting Pauline when she was about to charge at me for the second time, I might not now be here. Those cows had probably saved my life.

Milking with a badly bruised shoulder was not a very comfortable or pain-free thing to do. Squatting down and placing the teat cups was particularly difficult but slowly I worked my way through them and after about two hours, I lifted the door release rod and let the last one out.

Harry walked into the yard as I was shutting down the engine and I looked at him for any signs of success, but he shook his head.

'I found the place she pushed through the hedge and I tracked her across the next couple of fields down towards Forty Acre but after that she could have gone anywhere,' he said. 'We'll have another look tomorrow; there's a chance someone might see her and give us a call. But she might be miles away by now. There's no telling where she is.'

'Well at least she's not causing any more trouble here,' I said, rubbing my shoulder.

'That's true but after tomorrow she wouldn't have been causing trouble anywhere else either. Come on, I'll give you a hand with the churns and we'll see what tomorrow brings.'

CHAPTER NINETEEN

Pauline on trial

'HOW'S THE SHOULDER doing?' Harry asked when I arrived in the kitchen. 'Don't suppose you had a lot of sleep.'

'No not really. I couldn't find a way to lie down without it hurting but I kept taking the pills and they helped to soften the pain. Anyway, did you hear anything about our missing cow?'

Harry poured out the tea. 'Not a word,' he replied. 'She's probably found a nice piece of quiet woodland and settled down in there. Someone will see her but that doesn't guarantee we'll get to know about it.'

'Do you think you should let the police know she's missing? I mean, if she causes a traffic accident there could be some come back if we haven't been seen to have made some effort finding her.'

'Good point, boy. I'll let them know.'

Harry disappeared with Alice's cup of tea and I drank mine before slipping on my wellingtons and walking over to the dairy for the bucket.

'I'll give the police a call right now, so if you want to fetch them in…'

'Yes, I'll do that,' I said.

I carried the bucket of hot water up to the bail and pushed it under the gate before setting off across the paddock to where the cows had spent the night.

'Come on girls,' I shouted when I was halfway across. 'It's that time of the day again. Come on!'

I watched as a few of them lifted their heads and started walking towards the gate and then a few more joined them and gradually the whole herd was on the move, so by the time I opened the gate most of them were ready to go.

There was one big surprise though: Pauline was back with us. And I couldn't believe it. How on earth did she get back in with the other cows? I looked at her as she walked passed and she gave me half a stare but otherwise she was just another cow and gave all the appearance of a good natured, placid girl that would have walked around a butterfly.

I slid the bolt across to secure the collecting yard gate and walked through the cows to the hand gate at the other end where two steps down put me on the drive down to the yard, and the house beyond. Harry had just left and was walking up towards me.

'I've given them a call and all the details about how she looks and I also told them to be careful if they do find her,' he said.

'Well, have I got news for you,' I said.

'Oh no. Don't tell me she's turned up?'

'Correct,' I said. 'I don't know where she came from but she's walking about as if nothing has happened, looking as placid as the rest of them.'

Harry gave his cap a shuffle. 'So, what do we do now?'

'I don't know but I'd better make a start milking or

208

they'll all be going psycho.'

The shoulder was marginally better this morning and, while it still hurt, it had at least lost that throbbing pain which was there when I milked yesterday. Handling the full churns was a steady job though, and as for taking them down to the street on the trolley, I had to ask Harry to do it.

'You can cheer up Miserable Old Sod while you're down there,' I said to him as he set off down the slope with three full churns on board.

'I'll tell him he'll soon be out of a job and really make his day,' Harry shouted back to me.

With the milk all sorted we made it into the kitchen for breakfast.

'So, what have you done with the Red Poll?' asked Harry, when he had finished carving the boiled bacon.

'Pauline? I've let her out with the others. She came in to the bail to be milked and was no trouble at all, so there didn't seem to be any reason not to let her out.'

Harry rubbed his chin. 'It's a tricky one. We know what she's capable of and do we want to live with a cow that has a potential to cause serious injury? What do you reckon, Alice?'

'I honestly think she should go,' she said. 'Next time it could be someone walking in the field she attacks, and then there would be all sorts of problems seeing as you knew what she can do.'

'I think I have to agree with Alice,' I said. 'Pauline's a time bomb waiting to go off and it's not worth the risk of keeping her in the herd.'

'Right then, that's agreed,' Harry said. 'I'll give Petersons a call and see if they'll pick her up tomorrow.'

'Where will they take her?' I asked.

209

'To the abattoir.'

'I don't suppose you'd consider having her put down on the farm, would you?'

Harry looked at me. 'I know what you're thinking boy, but…' he faltered. 'If you think it would be for the best, then that is what we'll do. It will probably have to wait until tomorrow seeing as today's Sunday.'

I nodded my thanks and reached for my cup of tea.

For the rest of the day I couldn't get Pauline out of my mind and I asked myself just what had made her so aggressive yesterday and then, today, back to being a normal member of the herd. Was it, I wondered, something about Lucy that upset her so much? After all, until Lucy arrived, Pauline hadn't shown herself to be anything other than a pleasant and compliant young lady who was happy to be loved and cosseted along with the rest of them.

After lunch, I strolled down to their field and stood by the gate and watched them. Most, including Pauline, were lying down enjoying a siesta in the warm afternoon sun, taking the opportunity to take time out for some serious cudding.

Lucy, I noticed, was one of the few who remained standing and she was on the move, plodding nonchalantly around the field until she came close to Pauline and then, surprise, surprise, she lunged forwards, thumping her head into Paulin's flank.

This is madness, I thought. They're each as stupid as each other. I was tempted to go into the field and give both of them a talking to, but memories of yesterday's events held me back.

Instead, I walked back to the farm and found Harry in the workshop.

'It's not Pauline causing all the trouble, it's also the heifer you bought off Sam Jones,' I said. 'Can you remember why Sam wanted to sell the heifer, after all, they have their own dairy herd which needs replacements?'

Harry put down the hammer he was using to straighten out the Land Rover's door. 'Now I think about it, he did mention something about not wanting to risk having her in the herd if she turned out like her mother. But I'd never heard of such a thing and ignored him.'

'Well, that's it then,' I said. 'It really looks like Lucy is the problem. Before she arrived, Pauline was as good as gold and now she's having to put up with goodness knows what from some little upstart of a heifer whose mother has a bit missing in the head.'

'Are you're sure?' Harry asked.

'Well, that's the way it's seems to me. I just saw it happen; Pauline's lying down cudding away surrounded by her colleagues and Lucy walks over and rams her head into her flank for no reason. And bearing in mind Sam's reason for selling her... What more can you say?'

Harry thought about it for a little longer before he spoke again. 'I'll tell you what we're going to do boy, we'll go and see Don Tater.'

'Who is Don Tater?'

'He's a small holder who runs about thirty acres just off the Stratton Road, quite near Lord Shmuck's place. Been around for years and while he's a good stockman and knows his stuff he talks a load of bollocks on most other things.

'I don't know whether he still is, but he was a part time fireman for the village fire brigade and because he only had a push bike to speed his way to the fire station when the alarm sounded, by the time he arrived the fire engine had usually all crewed up and left.

'He then started lingering around the station on the off chance the alarm would go off and he would be close enough to be included in the crew but even then, the one time the alarm went off, Don had pedalled off down the shops for a sandwich and with only a couple of hundred yards to reach the station, he had a puncture and missed the call again.

'And on the few occasions he did manage to join the crew it was a disaster. At one farm fire, he jumped on a tractor with a loader with the idea of moving some burning bales away from a diesel tank. Anyway, he lifted the bale so high, it tumbled back down onto him, so it was a case of "Water on Tater" and even then the tractor was burnt out.

'But the worst moment was when he was part of a crew which attended a traffic accident when two cars, a top-of-the-range Mercedes had bumped into an old Ford Anglia. There was hardly a mark on either of them but Don, trained as he was to avoid fires, goes round the back of the Mercedes and puts his axe through its fuel tank.'

'He sounds as if he's not quite cut out for the fire service,' I said.

'Too right, he's not. But if you start speaking to him keep away from the subject of Russia; Don always maintains he's been an MI6 secret agent and has been trained to kill with his bare hands and to speak fluent Russian, Polish and Uzbekistan with an understanding of German, Dutch and Australian along with a smattering of Welsh.

'Anyway, he's always on the lookout for cows he can put calves onto suckle and usually buys the old cows which have run their course in commercial dairy herds, so he could be very pleased to get a nice young first-calver. Come on, we'll go and see if he's about.'

'Don't you think you should put the door back on the Land Rover before we go anywhere?' I asked.

'Yeah, perhaps you're right. I'll just finish knocking the impression of a cow's head out of it and we can drop it back on.'

Harry went back to his metal bashing while I headed for the barn where the Grey Fergie was parked now complete with its loader, which looked interesting, as did the large concrete block hanging from two hooks attached to a bar on the rear linkage.

It was too good a chance to ignore so I climbed into the cab, trying not to jar my shoulder too much and started the engine before using my bruised shoulder, arm to gently pull the hydraulic lever back. But nothing happened even when I tried it for the second and third time.

And then it dawned on me. I had my foot pressed down on the clutch pedal and that not only prevented the drive going to the rear wheels but also to the power take off and the drive to the hydraulic pump. When I released the clutch pedal and pulled the lever, two hydraulic rams began to extend and lift the loader arms and continued to push the loader higher until I moved the lever in the other direction for it to sink to the ground.

The loader was fitted with a tined fork attachment used to load muck and, to empty it, there was a rope that fed back into the cab which needed to be pulled to release the catch and allow the fork to swing

213

downwards. The muck, or what ever happened to be on the tines, then slid off into a trailer or a muck spreader.

This was going to be fun, I thought as I stopped the engine; a cab to keep the weather out and a loader to do all the heavy lifting. What could be better?

I could hear Harry shouting from the yard, so I struggled out of the cab and broke into a trot to see what he wanted.

'Just give me a hand to line up the hinges so I can get the door back on where it belongs,' he said. 'We can have a play with the loader another time.'

The drive to Don Tater's place was not far at all. In less than five minutes we were driving up a pot-holed track which terminated outside an ancient caravan which lounged in front of a set of wooden buildings that wouldn't have been amiss in some foreign shanty town.

'Is this it?' I asked.

'Yes, this is it but don't be misled by appearances. I know a lot of farmers who would give their eye teeth to be able to produce beef cattle as fine looking and as well finished as Don manages to do.'

'Oh right.'

'It's just a pity he's such a bull-shitter.'

Before Harry could say anything else, there was a rattling of a chain and from across the yard and from the side of the caravan a large German Shepherd dog emerged and hurled itself across the yard at full pelt, his jaws open wide, the chain dragging behind him.

'Stay where you are, boy. I think he runs out of chain before he gets as far as we are,' Harry said, stepping back a few paces. 'Well it did the last time I was here.'

Suddenly the chain went tight and the dog came to a violent halt a few feet in front of us and I wondered how he had avoided breaking his neck or at best crushing his throat, but he was still barking and growling and was clearly intent on tearing us to pieces.

'Where does something like that sleep?' I inquired.

'Anywhere it wants to, I should think,' Harry replied. 'Oh look, here's Don now.'

I peered across the yard through the dust kicked up by the dog and the chain, and saw a man stepping out of the caravan.

'Does he actually live in there?'

'I think so, unless the dog decides to.' Harry started waving. 'Don, we're over here at the end of the chain.'

Don looked across and started walking towards us, his boots shuffling through the gravel, kicking up small clouds of dust with every step. 'Who's that?' he shouted, his voice gruff and uncontrolled.

'Don, it's Harry Wilcox. If you could call your dog off, we could come over and speak to you.'

'Harry who?'

'Harry Wilcox.'

The dog's barking and lunging at the end of his chain suddenly stopped and the dog turned and walked back to his place by the side of the caravan. It looked as if he had some sacks to lie on and a large bowl of water beside them.

'Oh, Harry Wilcox,' Don said. 'Of course, you are. Couldn't see you for the dust and who's this with you?'

'This is John Johnson who has been working with me for what, about eighteen months now.'

215

'Oh really, I'd have thought we would have met before now.'

'No, I don't think so,' I said. 'I'm sure I would have remembered if we had,'

'Anyway, what do you want?'

I looked at Don and beneath the unshaven, gaunt appearance I could see a man who, in some strange way, cared about what he did. That he had an amazing shock of blonde hair, bale string around his trousers and a faded orange shirt which had lost all of its buttons several years before, couldn't change that, and I thought it was good.

Harry cleared his throat. 'Well Don, I was wondering if you would be interested in a freshly calved Friesian heifer we have.'

'How freshly calved?' he asked.

'Only about three months and she's probably already in calf again.'

'How much do you want for her?'

I looked at Harry and wondered where he would pitch the price. Start too low and he'd never get what he wanted, but too high and he would be shown the door.

'How does eighty sound?'

'Bleeding' awful,' Don replied, screwing his face up in disgust. 'If you're not going to be sensible, I've a lot of other things I can be doing.'

'Where do I need to be then?' Harry asked.

Don cleared his throat and spat on the ground. 'I think fifty would be generous.'

'Oh, come on Don. Get real. You know, and I know she has to be worth more than that.'

'Alright I'll go sixty but that's it.'

'I'll meet you half way and call it seventy.'

'Seventy and give me a couple for luck.'

Harry held out his hand. 'It's a deal. I'll bring her over tomorrow.'

'You'd better come and have a drink on it,' Don said, turning back towards his caravan.

'Alright but only half a cup.'

This morning's milking marked the end of Lucy's stay with us and I just hoped she would be alright with Don who I considered to be a kind man and would look after her well.

As a suckler cow, she could look forward to years of rearing her own calves and having a long, happy undemanding life grazing meadows, laying under trees in the shade, spending the winter in a deeply strawed yard and not being bothered twice a day for milking.

I told her all this as she waited to be milked for the last time and gave her a handful of ground barley to chew on while she thought it through. I made sure she was the last one to come in to be milked so when I let her out she could be kept in the collecting yard.

Meanwhile, Harry had backed the horsebox up to the bottom of the two steps and lowered the ramp for Lucy to walk up, which she did with no trouble at all.

'Bye Lucy,' I said to her as Harry lifted the ramp and put the pins in to lock it closed. 'Be good and be happy.'

'Right then, I'll take her round to Don's while you sort the milk out,' Harry said. 'You sure you're able to handle the churns?'

'Yeah, no worries,' I replied.

'I'll tell Don you'll be round to see her sometime.'

'That would be good.'

And then I watched Lucy leave the farm and head off to her new life. 'Be happy, little girl,' I whispered.

Moving the churns about was more painful than I thought it would be and when it came to taking them down the slope on the trolley, I elected to only take two full ones chained at the back of the trolley. Apart from having less, unstoppable weight hurtling down the slope, there was now more weight on the skid to help provide some braking.

Great theory, but one which did not work too well in practice. And if it hadn't been for the side of the churn lorry, there had been a good chance I would have ended up across the street in the stream.

'Oh no, not again,' said Miserable Old Sod. 'Not another flaming dent in my side panel.'

'Looks like it,' I said.

'Why?'

'I don't know.' My shoulder was really hurting and I could do without any hassle. 'I've another three churns for you so just stay where you are,' I said. 'But if you had any goodwill in you, you would be giving me a hand, rather than just standing there moaning all the time.'

And then something remarkable happened. Old Sod jumped down off the lorry and grabbed the trolley, loaded three empty ones on it and began hauling it up to the dairy. Once there he offloaded the empty ones and replaced them with the three full ones and set off down to the lorry.

I was impressed and was even more so when he crashed the trolley into the same side panel as I had.

'Never mind that, boy,' he said as he loaded the churns onto the lorry. 'Shit happens and we all need some help at times in our lives.'

218

With that he shut the lorry up and drove off up the street and I didn't get a chance to thank him.'

Harry arrived back in the yard as I walked up from the street and I asked him if everything went alright.

'Yes, no problems. Don was there to help me unload her and I think she will be fine and he said you can come along anytime you want to have a look at her.'

'That's good, thanks.'

When I walked in to the kitchen there was a letter for me on the table and I could see by the writing on the envelope, it was from Elizabeth. I washed and dried my hands, sat down and opened it and pulled out what must have been four pieces of paper.

'How is she?' Alice asked. 'Is she settling in to the new term?'

'Yes, she seems quite happy about things apart from when she heard about my run in with the cow the other day. I should think Kate must have spoken to her, or something.'

'Oh, that's good. You must make plans to drive up and see her for the day. I'm sure Harry wouldn't mind milking for you.'

'Harry wouldn't mind doing what?' Harry asked as he walked into the kitchen.

'Doing the milking for John if he drove up to York to meet Elizabeth for one day.'

'No, of course not. About time you had a break, anyway. When are you planning on going?'

'I'll have to let you know on that one. But thanks for the offer.'

CHAPTER TWENTY

Muck spreader revisited

I HAVE TO CONFESS, until Harry mentioned it, I hadn't realised the farm even had a muck spreader. And when Harry told me where it was, I wasn't totally surprised I hadn't seen it.

'It's at the back of the orchard, behind Pedro's stable,' he said. 'I thought we could get it out and have a go at spreading the muck heap we've been unloading trailers of muck onto for the last decade.'

I felt I should ask him why it was at the back of the orchard behind Pedro's stable, but changed my mind. For whatever reason it was there and why it was there really didn't matter. Instead I asked him, when it was last used?

'It's been a few years,' he said. 'But I'll tell you when it was; it was when Prince Andrew was born and that was when, Alice?'

'I think it was in 1960 wasn't it? That was the same year Princess Margaret married that photographer fellow.'

'Antony Armstrong-Jones,' I said.

'That's right, 1960. It was on the television,' Alice said. 'But what does this have to do with a muck spreader?'

'That was the last time we used it,' Harry said.

'Well that's not a very nice way of remembering something like that. How would you like our wedding year to be linked to the last time you used a muck spreader?'

'Well, there was no need to after we were married.'

'No need to what?'

'Remember when I used the muck spreader. Actually, the year we were married was the year I purchased my first pig, the one with the floppy ears. Do you remember that?'

Alice sighed. 'I think we'll stop this conversation if all you can talk about is muck spreaders and pigs,' she said. 'Now, does anyone want more tea?'

'I think we also bought that teapot in the same year,' Harry added.

It was time to make a move. 'So it's in the orchard behind Pedro's stable?'

'That's right, boy. It might need a good grease up and a bit of attention but it was working when it was parked there. I remember it was because…'

I didn't linger to hear anymore and pulled on my boots and set off for the orchard. As I left the house I was met by a blast of wind which had increased quite noticeably since I went in for breakfast.

Pedro was up and about when I lifted the latch on the gate and pushed it open to let myself in. He strolled up to me and placed his wonderful velvety muzzle on my arm and stared into my face with big brown dewy eyes.

'What's the matter, old fellow,' I said, reaching up and stroking his ears. 'I guess you must be feeling a bit lonely now the cade lambs have all left you.' I left him to it but not before I had dug out a handful of barley meal for him to scoff.

The muck spreader, when I found it, was enmeshed in an impenetrable tangle of nettles, thistles and briars and it took some wild thrashing about with the long-handled hedge slasher to uncover it sufficiently for it to be seen.

And I was surprised how small it was. The hopper in which the muck was loaded was only about ten feet long, four feet wide and no more than two feet deep. At the back of it were two horizontal beaters which spun the muck out, and were fed by a chain and slat system that moved the muck held in the body of the spreader towards them.

The whole system was driven by the wheels it ran on and of the two levers at the front one was responsible for engaging the drive to the beaters and the other to the chain and slats. On this particular lever, there were a number of positions which could be used to change the speed of the slats using a ratchet – the further the lever was lowered, the further the slats were moved with every move of the ratchet.

Although I had cleared most of the restraining briars and all the other nasties, there was no way the spreader was going anywhere unless its tyres were inflated. I decided to bring a tractor round and use the pto powered air compressor to inflate them, assuming they hadn't any punctures, and I was just perusing what size of pin I needed for the drawbar when I heard some rustling behind me.

I turned expecting to see Pedro but it wasn't him, it was Ronny. 'Well, the wanderer returns, long time no see,' I said. How's it all going?'

'Not so bad, thanks,' he replied. 'And yourself?'

'Yes, fine thanks. I'm just working out how to get this spreader working again, Any suggestions?'

'Well you could light a bonfire under it,' Ronny said.

'I don't think that's quite what the plan is. Have you seen Harry?'

Ronny reached into his pocket for his tobacco tin and then sat down on the edge of the spreader to roll himself a cigarette. And when it was completed, he raised the creation to his lips, lit it and took a long, lung-filling drag before expelling it in a cloud which flowed out of his mouth and nostrils at some alarming rate.

'He told me where you were and to give you a hand,' he said, at last.

'Oh right, well if you're available we need to get a tractor round here with the compressor to inflate the tyres,' I explained. 'So if you bring the Fordson round from the rick yard, I'll fetch the compressor.'

'Will do, John,' Ronny said, taking another drag from his cigarette.

'And put that cigarette out before you even think of going near the rick yard,' I added. 'With this wind blowing it could go anywhere.'

We walked round to the workshop and while Ronny carried on up to the rick yard I rummaged about for the compressor and found it under a pile of old plough shares which I then had to move somewhere else. One day I'll sort this mess out, I thought.

The tyres were so flat they seemed to take an eternity to even start filling. I wondered at one point if there was even an inner tube in them but eventually they started to fill and the muck spreader slowly began to lift.

'Always amazes me that most tractors these days can pump out forty horsepower or more and they choose to put a pathetically small compressor on the power take off which would take an hour to inflate a balloon. With that sort of available power there should be much higher capacity pumps about. What do you reckon Ronny?'

'I reckon you must be right, after all, you've just finished college,' he replied.

'Well that wasn't the only subject they taught,' I said, unsure whether Ronny was trying to be funny.

At last, the wheels looked to be reasonably well inflated, not that I had a clue how much pressure they should have in them.

'Give them a kick and see what you think,' I said.

'I rather not, these are my best wellingtons.'

Fair enough.

The next task was to hitch the tractor on to the drawbar and that had been on the ground for so long it had sunk below surface level and even getting anywhere near it without being stung by nettles, lacerated by prickly thistles, or ripped apart by briars was a challenge.

Only by a lot of stamping and tramping did we manage to locate the end of it – a ring that would fit in the clevis of the tractor's drawbar, providing we could raise it high enough.

'See if you can find a chain or something we can loop under it and attach to the linkage arms,' I said. 'And while you're doing that I'll try to dig down under it to make room for the chain.'

Ronny set off for the workshop, taking the compressor with him and returned five minutes later with some chain he'd removed from an old pulley.

'Just the job. Lower the tractor's linkage arms and we're in business.'

Ronny raised the spreaders drawbar until it lined up with tractor's clevis, and then I dropped the pin in and the job was done.

'Brilliant,' I said. 'Now we can see if it moves. Just edge her forward a few feet and I'll have a look to see what's turning.'

One of the wheels skidded for a short distance before it began to rotate and for first time in about seven years, the muck spreader was on the move. 'Take her round to the workshop and we'll give her a onceover there,' I shouted up to Ronny.

'Well, that's given us a bit more space in the orchard,' Harry said when he walked across the orchard to meet me. 'But where did this wind come from?' He pulled his jacket round him and reached into his pocket and drew out a length of baler twine. 'Didn't think I'd need to do this,' he said, putting the string around his waist and tying a knot. 'Still can't think why we parked it here, though.'

'It seems a strange place to leave it,' I said. 'But then, where else could you grow such magnificent briars, thistles and nettles?'

'That's true, boy. Conservation has always been a priority with me.'

We walked back and ran into Pedro who appeared to be enjoying the morning's activity in his orchard.

'It's about this time we get a visit from the vicar,' Harry said. 'Seeing Pedro has just reminded me.'

'Not the harvest festival; surely not after the last time?'

'The vicar has either a short memory or he can only retain the good bits,' he said. 'But then, when you're in his business I should think you have to be an optimist as well as a believer.'

'I didn't think there were any good bits to retain.'

'That's why he wants to do it again.'

Dragged out into the yard, the muck spreader was beginning to look as if it might actually be made to work so, ever hopeful, we set to freeing up everything that was meant to move and applying generous volumes of grease and oil to bearings and chains.

'The biggest problem we had when it was working, Harry said, 'was with the slats which are connected to two bed chains and pull the muck into the beaters. If one chain jumped a cog, the slats started to move at an angle and then the chain broke and the whole system collapsed into a tangle of bent slats and twisted chains. And then you had to fork out whatever was left in the spreader before you could begin to sort it all out.'

After about an hour it was time to give the spreader a run, which meant towing it up the yard and putting the drives in to gear. We started with the beaters, which seemed to be spinning as they should and then engaged the floor slats and, lo and behold, they began to move as the ratchet drive propelled them rearwards along the floor a few inches at a time.

'Sounds good,' Harry said. 'Brings back memories. All we need to do now is take the spreader and the loader down to the heap and give it a real go. Ronny can take the spreader and you take the loader. I'll meet you down there.'

These were exciting times. The first outing with a tractor plus hydraulic loader, plus cab, plus muck spreader; it will be really interesting to see how it all works.

The muck heap, which was in the corner of the field that led into Piggy Hill, wasn't so much a heap as a low-level store. At its deepest it was no more than three or four feet and as a result it covered far more land than it should have.

Perhaps now we had a loader it would be possible to push the heap together and if we ever have trailers that can tip their loads off, this too will help to contain the muck in a smaller, tighter area and reduce valuable plant nutritional losses which just leach away every time it rained.

'Where shall we start?' Harry asked. 'I should get Ronny to park the spreader at an angle so you don't have to keep driving around him to fill it.'

I waved at Ronny and directed him to the position we thought he should be and looked at Harry for confirmation.

'Give it a try, you can always tell him to move. And by the way, have you put a clip in the bottom of the drawbar pin? When the muck is moved to the rear of the spreader, there's a point when it's heavier at the back than the front so the spreader lifts on the drawbar. Without a clip, you'll lose the pin and very soon after that, the spreader as well.'

I checked all was well with the drawbar pin and then climbed aboard the Grey Fergie and instantly thought how much better it was to be in here out of the wind although, to be fair, with no floor panels and an open back, there were still more than a few drafts blowing about.

'This is it my little grey friend,' I said. 'Your time has come to show us what you can do.'

I pushed the hydraulic lever to bring the fork down to ground level and drove forwards into the muck and when I considered I had a full a load as was possible, I pulled the lever and then remembered I needed to be in neutral with the clutch pedal raised. The loader arms began to lift and, when it was clear of the ground, I engaged reverse gear and carried on lifting as I reversed out of the heap. When I was clear, I turned and headed for the spreader and with the fork tines directly above it, I reached out and pulled the rope to drop the muck into the spreader.

It was as I was reversing away and preparing to change into second gear and drive back into the heap for another forkful it occurred to me I had already depressed the clutch pedal five times and if, as I suspected, the spreader needed about ten forkfuls and we managed ten loads before lunchtime, that would require me to press the pedal a minimum of five hundred times or about a thousand times in a day.

For the next two or three forkfuls everything continued to work well and the loader operation was becoming almost a routine series of actions. But increasingly, I was running on land that had been covered in muck, and grip was more difficult as a result, despite the weight provided by the large block of concrete hooked on to the linkage arms. Everywhere I drove I was now leaving quite deep ruts and it wasn't long before the ground was so chewed up, it was becoming difficult to tell where muck ended and soil began.

Difficult, but while I soldiered on, there were worse times ahead. There was always a temptation to drive in the ruts created when I reversed out simply because they exposed relatively dry soil, and they ran in the direction I wanted to go.

There was a limit though and when I looked round

228

and saw the big concrete block lying in the mud several yards behind me, I knew I had reached it. The ruts had become so deep, the block had made contact with the ground which then as the tractor sank even deeper raised the hooks off the linkage arms and parked the block on the ground.

The tractor, now with no extra weight on the drive wheels, quickly became marooned and, try as I might, it was going nowhere.

'I thought you were just about getting the hang of it, before that happened,' Harry said. He picked his way through the mud and stepped up onto the concrete block. 'Not enough ground clearance, that's the problem.'

'Have you a chain or a rope in the back of the Land Rover?'

'No, but we can soon get one. Let's see how Ronny gets on spreading what you've loaded first; just in case we need to bring anything else down here – like a two-thousand ton walking drag line with a thirty ton bucket on it.'

'Yes,' I said. 'Sounds good to me.'

'Alright Ronny, take this load to the top of the field and we'll start spreading it from there.' Harry and I climbed into the Land Rover and followed him.

'This wind cuts into you,' I said, pulling my coat around me.

'Well, you've a cab to keep you warm. You should be alright,' Harry said.

We watched as Ronny turned to drive across the field and we walked over to him.

'Pull this lever first and then drive on to get the beaters rotating and then, while you are still moving, put this other lever down a couple of notches and that

229

will start the bed chains and the slats moving,' explained Harry. 'You alright with that?'

'I think so, Harry,' Ronny replied.

'So, it's this lever first for the beaters, start driving forwards and then it's this lever down a couple of notches,' Harry repeated. 'Right then, off you go.'

We walked away and watched as Ronny leant backwards and pulled the first lever and started to drive forwards, the beaters turning as they were designed to do.

'Have you noticed which way the wind is blowing?' Harry asked.

I hadn't really thought about it but now he'd asked the question, I realised it was blowing away from us, towards Ronny. 'It's blowing in the direction he's travelling,' I said.

'Exactly,' Harry confirmed. 'At least it won't land on us.'

It was then Ronny managed to engage the bed chains and slat drive and for a short while nothing seemed to happen, but then the first of the well matured muck arrived at the beaters and as they took hold of it, the muck was shredded and thrown up into the air in what I thought was a pretty impressive spread pattern which must surely provide an even covering when it lands on the ground.

But alas no. The wind took nearly every particle and thrust it forwards for it to land on Ronny, so before a dozen yards had past, he was having to wipe his eyes to see where he was going, and his hair, coat and trousers were covered as thoroughly as if he had rolled in it.

'Oh dear,' I said. 'That's unfortunate.'

'It's only shit landing on shit,' Harry said, turning

away. 'I think it might be a good time to fetch a rope to pull you out with.'

CHAPTER TWENTY-ONE

Dagging and tupping

WE DECIDED TO leave the muck spreading for a couple of days to see if the ground dried out and allowed the Fergie to work without getting stuck and the concrete block dropping off. Instead, Harry decided it was getting close to the time for the tups to be in with the ewes and brought all two hundred and fifty ewes up to the orchard, so we could tidy up their rear ends by removing any mess that had accumulated in that area.

In preparation for the ewes' arrival we had placed some gates across the yard to guide them into the orchard and I had shut Pedro in his stable while we fetched them up from the bottom fields.

'Are we all set?' Harry asked as he walked out with his two sheep dogs bouncing around him.

'Who are you taking?' I asked.

'Ross and Bob. They could do with a good run.'

I gave Ross a pat and he jumped up and, as usual, splashed his great long tongue across my face and while I wiped the saliva off I inquired whether we were walking or taking the Land Rover.

'Alice is taking us down there,' he replied. 'So, if

you're set to go, I'll go and see if she's ready.'

I climbed in the Land Rover and shunted myself across to the middle seat, never knowing whether to straddle the gear box with my legs or to stay squeezed up on one side of it. There wasn't time to peruse the question because both doors opened simultaneously and Harry piled in from one side and Alice from the other, albeit more sedately.

'Where did you say we're going?' Alice asked.

'Just drop us off in Abbots, the large grass field on the other side of the brook and we'll take it from there,' Harry said. 'And if you can leave the gates open on the way back to the farm, that would be good.'

'Won't the cows start to roam if I do that?'

'They shouldn't do, but you're right. Leave the two at either end of Hollow Close closed and then we'll be sure.'

We drew to a halt by the bridge where we'd had so much trouble the last time I was involved in moving sheep and, as we climbed out, I was tempted to ask Harry if he had brought a change of clothes this time.

'I'll see you back at the farm then,' Alice said. 'And I hope you're feeling fit, John.'

I smiled and watched her drive away up Piggy Hill.

'Are they all in this field,' I asked.

'They are now. I've been trying to save some fresh pasture for them when we bring them back and split them into groups for the tups,' he explained.

'Oh right. So it's just a matter of rounding these up and taking them back with us.'

'That's about it, boy. Before I send the dogs round them, I'll stand here and rattle this bucket and with a bit of luck they should all come charging towards us

233

after that.'

Harry strode about thirty yards into the field and started to rattle the bucket and I have to say, with the possible exception of one or two wagging ears, its effect on the sheep was less than encouraging.

'Oh well, we'll do it the hard way then,' he said, giving me the bucket.

With a couple of sharp whistles, Ross and Bob set out to gather the sheep and with a field which was quite half a mile long, they were soon little more than dark patches racing across the grass in the far distance.

But they were doing their job and the sheep were now coming towards us with Harry giving commands for Ross and Bob to lie down when they were pushing the sheep too hard.

'That's the trouble with some dogs,' he said. 'They push sheep too hard and the sheep can't handle it. You just want to bring them on at a steady, controlled trot.'

Gradually, the ewes came towards us and Harry walked back to open the gate.

'You go across the other side and rattle the bucket out in the field where they can see you,' Harry said. 'We want them to cross the bridge nice and steady; and I don't want them to push me into the brook, like they did last time.'

Under Harry's control, the ewes flowed across the bridge and before I knew it, he was shutting the gate behind them. I also noticed Ross and Bob dropping into the brook for a drink and a cool off.

'That's the first bit completed. All we need to do now is walk them up to the farm. Most of them will know the way, but you just walk ahead of them with the bucket and we'll be fine.'

If I had learned anything when working with sheep is that nothing but nothing is predictable or 'fine' as Harry put it. And, just to prove the point, it seemed, a low flying Chinook helicopter chose the moment to fly over us at about a hundred feet and scattered the sheep everywhere.

But the dogs did their work and it was not long before everyone was making their way back up Piggy Hill in an ordered file.

'Bloody army,' Harry shouted. 'Bugger off and spend my tax money somewhere else.'

There were a couple of hold ups when we had to take the sheep through Hollow close where the cows were grazing, but it was not long before they were across the paddock, down the yard and, with just a few wrong turns which the dogs corrected, into the orchard where Alice was waiting to close the gate.

'Just like that,' she said, as she stood back. 'It doesn't get much better than that. Does it?'

'It could if the army would stop flying their damned helicopters over us,' Harry said. 'But you're right; they came up very well.'

Harry then turned to me. 'A quick cup of tea and we'll get the hurdles in and make a holding pen and then we can get started. That alright with you?'

'Sounds good,' I said, following him towards the house.

'Have you ever used dagging shears before?' Harry asked me when we had run about a dozen ewes into the race. He was holding some rather cumbersome scissor like cutters made from a single piece of metal which doubled round on itself so that when the blades were overlapped and squeezed, it caused them to slide

235

against each other and cut wool or anything else that was in the way.

'They've been around for years, if not centuries, and before motorised clippers were available they were used to shear sheep; and a steady old job it must have been,' he said. 'These days though, we just use them for trimming or shaping coats or, as we are, cleaning up rear ends to remove the daglocks.'

Harry handed me a set of shears and I gave it a squeeze and heard the two blades slide against each other.

'I suppose there's an element of self-sharpening when they're used,' I said. 'And you must work up some tremendous wrist muscles if you use them all day.'

'You'll find out, boy,'

Harry had moved into the race and was holding a ewe between his legs, facing its rear end. Bending down he set about using the shears to trim all the soiled wool away from under and around the ewe's tail.

'It not only cleans them up but also helps to prevent blowfly laying eggs and forming maggots which can eat into the flesh and cause all sorts of problems, not least a lot of pain for the sheep,' Harry said,

'Sounds awful,' I said.

'Regular dagging is all part of shepherding. Come on, it's time you had a go. Get yourself in a comfortable position and be prepared to get your hands filthy – and be careful where you put the points of the blades.'

I have to say it really was a mucky task but I could see the purpose of it and how important it was to do. Some sheep were a lot worse than others and took

236

time to trim properly but gradually, I fell into the swing of it and while Harry always seemed to be quicker, I reckon I was not too far behind.

'What happens to all the trimmings?' I asked Harry when we had a moment to fill the race with another dozen sheep.

'Not a lot these days. There was a market for it when people came and collected it to make a liquid fertiliser for plants – they'd wash all the muck out of it and put it in bottle and sell it. They used to say it was good for tomatoes, but no one has been round for years now, so it all ends up on the muck heap.'

By the time we stopped for lunch I think we had done about a third of them and my wrist was starting to feel the strain, and I was also beginning to discover muscles in my legs and other parts of my lower half which were starting to complain about what was happening to them.

Harry looked at the sheep we had left to do. 'I don't think we're going to finish them all today,' he said. 'But what we'll do after lunch is take the eighty or so we've finished and put them in Long Meadow. And then we'll do the same with the next eighty and put them in Abbots and that should leave us about the same number for the third group to run in Piggy Hill. We'll sort out the tups after that. Do you agree?'

'Yes, that would work well and give us a break too. I'll just make sure Pedro has enough water before I go in.'

Scrubbing my hands clean was a good challenge and, however hard I tried to use the nail brush, it still looked as if I had just finished sweeping a chimney. I think my nails were stained. And when I held my hands up to my face I could still smell sheep muck.

237

'How's it all going,' Alice asked.

'I think it's all going very well,' Harry said. 'What do you reckon boy?'

'Yeah, I think you're right. It will be a good job to finish though.'

Harry laughed. 'I can remember when we'd be dagging for weeks at a time. Father used to rent us out to do it for other flocks in the county – a sort of contracting – and I think he did very well out of it. Not that he ever got his hands dirty.'

'It must have been a joy,' I said.

'Well you didn't have to queue at the bar much when you stopped off for a beer on the way home,' he said.

Alice had made a roast and for one moment I thought it was a bacon joint, but it turned out to be beef and, with cabbage, carrots and potatoes, it was just so good. Too good to be dagging sheep on.

With that inside me, a generous slice of apple pie and several cups of tea, the thought of bending down staring at a sheep's back end wasn't high on my wish list, but there would be an opportunity to walk it off when we took the first batch of eighty ewes down to Long Meadow.

'Right then boy, you ready?'

I stretched. 'Yes, let's go and do it.'

'Will you be able to pick us up, Alice? We'll be coming back from Long Meadow.'

'Yes, I'll just do the washing up and I'll be down there.'

Ross and Bob were with us again not perhaps with the same level of enthusiasm but still pretty keen, and we set off down the track, the sheep behaving themselves.

'I think they look a lot better now,' Harry said. 'Dagging is one of those jobs which it's so easy to forget or delay doing but it really is important.'

And I have to say, they did look cleaner and I also noticed the rattling sounds I had heard when we brought them up had disappeared.

'Will they be having any supplement feed now?'

'Yes, they need to keep their condition so I'll be giving them some ground barley each morning along with a few minerals from now on. It's also a good time to check on how the tups are working.'

And then the Chinook helicopter went over us again, possibly lower than before and with very much the same effect on the sheep which scattered all over the place. Harry waved his fist at them and I think I saw someone sitting at the open door, waving back.

'Get his number,' Harry shouted.

'You can't see it from here,' I said.

'Not the bloke sitting down, the blasted helicopter. I think they must be doing it on purpose.'

'It's a bit of a coincidence,' I said. 'Perhaps it's Don Tater off on a secret mission for MI6.'

Ross and Bob had the sheep back on track within minutes but Harry was still seething.

'Isn't the country big enough, or the sky high enough for them?'

We reached Long Meadow without any further problems and I was relieved to see Alice heading our way in the Land Rover. When she arrived, we clambered in and headed off back to the farm.

'Did you see that helicopter,' Alice asked.

'See it? We were nearly in it,' Harry replied, 'And the sheep were everywhere again.'

'Oh well, everything's alright.'

Everything apart from Harry, I thought.

It was back to the dagging again and we managed to get another eighty finished before I had to stop to fetch the cows in.

The final group of ewes vacated the orchard just after lunch on the next day and Pedro, who had been confined in his stable for a day and a half, was as pleased as I was dagging had been completed.

When I opened his door, he marched out and immediately headed for the oak trees and settled himself down in the shade, but not before swiping an apple off a low branch of one of the few eating apple varieties the orchard held, and then giving his, "What are you going to do about it," look.

'Nice one, Pedro,' I said. 'Enjoy the day.'

'We'll take these down to Piggy Hill and then set about putting the tups in,' Harry said.

'Where are they at the moment?'

'The boys? Our fine-looking Suffolk tups with their big black Roman noses? Haven't you seen them? You've been sleeping next to them for the last couple of weeks.'

'You mean they're in the graveyard? I guess I haven't been that way lately.'

'I've been giving them some extra feed to fuel them up for the weeks ahead and I reckon they look pretty fit,' Harry said. 'They needed to be close to home and it's useful to train them so they'll come to the bucket. Anyway, first things first. Let's get these ewes down where they should be and then we'll sort the boys out.'

It had become almost a routine to be taking ewes down the track both not only for Harry and me, but also Ross and Bob who trotted alongside them, only occasionally bringing the odd wayward wanderer back into line.

'Can you hear what I can?' Harry said.

I stopped and listened. There was no mistaking it: a Chinook helicopter.

'They must have been waiting for us.'

'It would seem so.'

This time there was not one but two of them and together they roared over the top of us at a ridiculously low height which made me almost want to duck down. But the strange thing was the sheep hardly moved.

Not that the same could be said for Harry, who was waving his arms about, shouting and making rude signs just in case the helicopter crews were in any doubt what he thought of them.

'Bastards,' he roared. 'What the hell do they think they're doing?'

'I think the sheep must be getting used to them, though,' I said.

'God knows why.'

As I slipped the catch shut on the gate at the top of Piggy Hill, I felt as if we had done a good job which had, apart from helicopter intrusions, gone smoothly. Men and dogs working in harmony, I thought.

Harry looked over the gate at the sheep which were now spreading out across the field and I could see the pride in his eyes.

'They have fresh grass to go at and a good water supply. It's time to bring in the boys,' he said.

Back at the farm, we hooked the Land Rover onto the horsebox and took it up to the top of the yard and reversed it towards the gate which opened into the graveyard. With the ramp down and the gate tied to the guide on one side and a hurdle to the other, we were ready to load.

But then Harry queried whether we should take them down three at a time to avoid any mishaps occurring when we unloaded them.

'We could take six down and try and drop three off in to two groups,' I suggested. 'But it could all end in tears if we can't prevent all six charging out in one field and we have to spend the rest of the day trying to sort them out.'

'Might be better to take three down at a time,' he said. 'It's only one extra trip.'

And then I remembered the marker paint for their chests and asked Harry when he was planning to do that.

'After the difficulties we had the last time we tried paint, the fact there are still smears of it all round the inside of the horsebox and that I had to buy a completely new set of overalls, I think we'll try a different system this year,' he said.

'And what's that?'

'Come with me, boy and I'll show you.'

I followed Harry around to the back of the Land Rover and watched him reach in and pull something out that looked vaguely like a horse harness

'This is the latest thing,' he said. 'It's a raddle harness which you strap around the tup's chest and it has this coloured crayon which marks the ewe when he's doing it. And you can change colours every two or three weeks to keep a check on which ewes are not taking or if one of the tups isn't working.'

'Sounds to be a good idea. Have you tried putting

one on yet?'

'No, I think they could be too big for me and I'm not very keen on the colours. I only picked them up the other day, but I have the instructions.'

All of a sudden, I was hit by a sense of concern. Harnesses of any description can be a difficult puzzle to work out even when you have a calm, placid Pedro prepared to be messed about, but trying to fit one to a ram whose mind is rapidly filling with lustful thoughts, could be a greater challenge.

'Do you not think it would be better to fit them on here, before they catch sight and scent of some freshly dagged sheep?' I inquired. 'Or whatever it is that takes their interest?'

Harry thought about. 'You could be right, boy. I'll bring three of them and we'll use the yellow crayon. See if you can get them penned in the horse box and we'll give it a go.'

I actually managed to pen one of them in the back of the horsebox but I wasn't concerned; I thought we would need all the space available to sort out the harness for the first time.

'Right then,' Harry said, when we had climbed in and shut the small door at the front. 'This is the harness and these are the instructions. Do you want to read them out while I put the harness on the ram, or would you have me read them out and you slip the harness on him?'

'It might be better if we both learned how to do it,' I said. 'So, if you read the instructions I'll have first go.'

Harry passed the harness to me and then opened the instruction booklet. 'Here we go then. Step one: Locate the front and rear of the harness. From the diagram it looks as if the crayon piece runs lengthways and there are two straps coming off from one end of it and two off the other end.'

'But which are the front straps?'

'It looks as if the front ones could be marginally longer than the rear ones.'

I gave the straps a quick measure and discovered which were the long ones and as such, were presumably positioned at the front of the harness. So far, so good.

'Step two: Place the crayon on the chest of the ram and secure the rear straps around the body taking care not to twist the straps which may cause sores to occur,' continued Harry.

'How can I hold the crayon on the centre of his chest between the front legs and do the straps up?'

'Don't worry boy. Keep calm. I'll hold the crayon while you do the straps. Alright?'

Harry bent down and held his hand out to hold the crayon in place and it was about at this time the patience of the ram expired. It was either that or he could now see Harry's stomach as an unmissable target right before his eyes, but either way, the result was Harry receiving a pronounced head butting to his solar plexus.

'Bloody hell, boy, what happened then?' he groaned.

'Probably best not to stand in front of him,' I said. 'But if you could just hold the crayon steady, I'll carry on doing these straps up.'

Harry tried again and came at the crayon from a reverse direction and I managed to clip the two ends of the strap together.

'Right, that's those straps secured. What's next on the list?'

'Step three: Avoid standing directly in front of the ram.'

'Doesn't it mention anything about the other two straps?'

'Patience, boy. Bring up the remaining two straps between the front legs and, crossing them over, attach them to the clips on the rear strap.'

I took hold of the straps and asked Harry to read out the instruction again.

'Step four: Bring up the remaining two straps between the front legs and, crossing them over, attach them to the clips on the rear strap.'

'But the straps don't reach that far,' I said, pulling them hard. 'They're about four inches too short.'

'Have we put it on back to front?' Harry asked. 'There seems to be plenty of extra strap left over on the rear one – the first straps you clipped together.'

'But we checked we had the shorter straps at the rear,' I said

'Well something's not right. Let's take it off and try it the other way round.'

So we did that and this time the front straps were about eight inches short.

'How about putting the crayon further forward so there's more strap available at the front,' Harry suggested.

'But that would place it somewhere under his neck and I'm not sure these fellows are into that type of relationship.'

Harry thought about it. 'No, you could be right. Look, take it off again and I'll go and get another one from the Land Rover and we'll see if it's a bigger version. Could be I've picked up the wrong size, or something.

While he was gone, I unclipped the straps and took a long look at the harness and it was then I realised the straps lengths could be adjusted by repositioning the clips which locked onto them.

So I started again and with a ram that seemed to have passed the point of caring what I did to him, placed the crayon on his chest and connected the two rear straps around his middle and then, having moved the clips to allow more length of strap, brought them up between his front legs, crossed them over and attached them to the clips on the rear strap; easy.'

Harry returned and told me he'd had a look and they were all the same size, but he too had discovered the straps could be extended by moving the clips

'Oh, you've done it, boy,' he said, running his hands around the straps. 'Do you think it will stay put?'

'I don't know. Time will tell. It's something that will have to be checked on when you give them their rations.'

Harry gave the straps a final inspection. 'I know paint was messy, but at least you knew it was there,' he said. 'Like you say, we'll have to keep an eye on these and if there's any doubt or hassle, we'll get the paint out.'

With three tups having had their harnesses fitted we drove down to Long Meadow and delivered them to the girls and then we had to make two more trips before the job was finished.

As we stood looking at the tups we had released into Piggy Hill, one of them mounted a ewe and, when he'd finished, there was big streak of yellow on the ewe's rump.

'Well, they work,' Harry said. 'Let's hope they keep working.'

246

CHAPTER TWENTY-TWO

The lost hour

LATE OCTOBER, AND with the clocks going back an hour there was an opportunity for an extra hour in bed which I had been looking forward to, deliberately going to bed an hour later to gain the full benefit. But Harry was having none of it.

'The cows don't have wrist watches so all they will think is you're late starting, and we can't have that, can we?' he said.

'Oh, I don't know,' I yawned. 'When I'm milking them an hour later this evening they won't be too upset about it and they have to get used to it sometime and anyway, you don't make a fuss about it when we lose an hour's sleep in the spring.'

'That's different. Anyway, you're up now so you might as well milk the cows and you have an extra hour to give the yard a good swilling down.' And with that, he exited the kitchen with Alice's tea.

When I came in with the bucket for the hot water, Harry was still in the kitchen. 'Don't make too much noise getting the water,' he whispered. 'Alice is still fast asleep.'

'I can fetch the cows in if you want me to?' I offered. 'That's if you have something else to do.'

'No, there's no need for that. I'll catch you up in a minute.'

I walked up the yard with the bucket of water and, having checked through the milking machines, went round to the engine department and cranked up the Lister, being careful as ever not to hold the starting handle with my thump wrapped round it. Every so often, the engine would give a vicious kick back when I was trying to start it and such a grip could dislocate the thumb and not know anything about it.

Eventually the cows began to wander into the yard and they didn't look to happy.

'Good morning, girls,' I greeted them as cheerfully as I could muster. 'This is your *very* early morning call and the start of a wonderful new day for you.'

I looked at the dull, eye-sagging expressions on their faces today as they mooched by me and you could be forgiven for assuming they had been out on the town all night.

'Oh, come on. What are you all looking so glum about?' I gave Horns a stroke on her neck as she sauntered passed, but there was next to no response, and even Thrifty seemed happier to be left alone.

'What's the matter with them all?' I asked Harry when he brought the last of the cows into the yard. 'They don't seem to have a lot of go about them this morning.'

'I was just thinking the same, boy. Have you checked their mineral licks lately?'

The salt licks, which also contained a multitude of other minerals, came in large blocks weighing the best part of twenty-five pounds. A hole through the middle

248

of them allowed them to be secured to a post or, if it was strong enough, a rail where the cows could spend time licking it.

'I think they've just about finished the two we had out in the paddock and there used to be one in the collecting yard by the crush,' I said. 'But I think that's all but disappeared.'

'Well, I should make sure they have one and I'll see about getting some minerals we can mix in with the ground barley. Failing that, I'm not sure what the problem could be, unless there's going to be a change in the weather.'

Harry walked off down the yard to take the Land Rover, complete with a few bales of hay and a couple of bags of ground barley, down to the sheep and I walked round to the front of the bail, listening out for the pulsators as they began their rhythmic "hiss-and-stop" routine.

A scoop of barley in each of the feeders, and I went to the gate to let the first four cows in, so the morning's milking could begin.

Breakfast time seemed a long time coming and, although it was good not to have to worry about getting the churns down to the street on time, it was as if my whole day had been seriously disrupted.

I had finished the yard cleaning by half past eight and then I remembered I needed to put some fresh mineral blocks out for the cows. About five years ago, or even longer, Harry had ordered several tons of salt blocks and they had all been stored on the floor at the back of the stone barn, and anything that takes up residence in such a place invariably becomes covered first with a heavy layer of dust and then sacks containing goodness knows what along with bags of linseed cake, grass seed, mineral supplements and all manner of other commodities which needed to be stored for one reason or another.

As a result, digging out the salt licks was a dusty, time consuming task which saw me becoming plastered with the white floury dust that leaked from the hammer mill when it was used to produce the barley meal. Eventually though, I found them and they were not in the best condition,

Salt attracts moisture and being wrapped in cardboard might have seen them being delivered in good condition but a year or two down the line and they had become sodden and filthy, the packaging surrounding them now rotting away.

Putting my hands around one of them to lift it out was not a pleasant experience and as soon as I had heaved it out onto the open floor, I was looking for some sacking to wipe my hands on. I pulled a couple more out and stood back to inspect them.

Strangely, once the wrapping had been disposed of and the salt lick had been exposed, they were not in too bad condition. So I grabbed a wheel barrow and loaded three of them into it and headed off to deliver one to the collecting yard, one to the paddock, which I placed next to the large water trough, and the third I placed beside the track in a circular feed trough.

When I made it back to the farm, I looked back and was interested to see that several of the cows had already found one of the licks and were standing around it, their heads swaying about as they used their tongues to rasp across its surface.

Harry always said cows, like many other animals, know instinctively what they need to eat to stay healthy and by the way they were setting about the block I had just put out, it would appear there had been a deficit of some much-needed minerals in their diet. According to the packaging these salt licks also contained a raft of minerals including the essential calcium and magnesium. I made a note to ensure they always had a lick available to them in the future.

'Goodness, what have you been up to?' Alice asked when I walked into the kitchen. 'Look at you, you're covered in dust and something else pretty horrible. If you want to change into something clean, I'll put them in a bucket to soak.'

'I think that's a good idea,' I said. 'I've been rummaging about in the barn for the salt licks.'

'Looks like they were well buried.'

I went to my room to find something clean to wear, but not before I had pulled off my outer clothing. I didn't think Alice would have appreciated a trail of dust and slime through the house.

'If you want a quick bath, the water's warm,' Alice shouted up the stairs.

'Thank you.'

'Good to see you getting to grips with the job,' Harry said when I returned, having bathed and changed into some clean clothes. 'Those blocks are pretty yucky. If we ever get through them all, I'll order a smaller number next time.'

I grabbed a magazine to read and tucked into my cereals.

The Fordson tractor, hooked up to the muck spreader was where I left it, when I arrived with the Grey Fergie. Harry had given me the choice of hedge laying or muck spreading and having considered that we'd had a couple of days when the weather had been dry, I said I'd have another go at finishing the spreading.

'If you could get it finished it would be a good job out of the way,' he said. 'We can keep going down to the hedge laying as and when we can, but that muck spreading is starting to hang on a bit too long,'

'Well, I'll give it my best and just hope I can keep moving this time.'

I reversed the spreader into a good filling position and began loading it. As usual, the first few loads when the ground was at its driest were the easiest to do but, I don't know whether it was because I had now moved onto firmer ground, the tractor now seemed to be staying more on top rather than sinking and creating deep ruts everywhere. Which was good news and I just hoped it would last.

I hadn't noticed the arrival of Ronny and the first time I saw him was when I was preparing to climb out of the Fergie to spread a load.

'I'll spread this one,' he said, clambering up into the driver's seat of the Fordson, not even looking to see if the seat was dry, which it probably wasn't.

'Go for it,' I shouted at him.

After his experience with the spreader which had seen him covered in black well-rotted muck when the wind had blown it onto him, I was surprised to see him come anywhere near the muck heap, let alone the spreader. I wondered how he had managed to clean himself up but then, when the muck had dried he'd probably just brushed it off.

It took just about ten minutes for him to make it back to the heap and by then I had a forkful of muck waiting for him to drive under and release into the spreader.

From then on, with the better traction we were managing a load every seven minutes for a total turn round time of about fifteen minutes and felt we were, at last, making some serious progress. If we could carry on at this rate, there wouldn't be much left at the end of the day.

Mid-morning and Harry stopped by on his way down to the sheep, to see how we were doing.

'What's the grip like?' he asked

'Not too bad at all,' I told him. 'We now seem to be on firmer ground.'

Harry looked where we were and nodded. 'That's where the old track used to go when they were carting the iron ore down to the railway,' he said. 'And that's where the muck heap was meant to be, but it seems to have spilled over into a larger area. How much longer do you think it will take?'

'If we carry on like we are, we could just finish it today, if you felt like milking or driving the loader.'

'That's not for me, boy. I'll milk for you if it means we can finish it. They talk of rain tonight, so you know what that will mean. Are you alright for diesel?'

'I think so but it might be worth bringing a can down when you pass next time.'

'Will do, boy.'

Harry slipped the Land Rover into gear and drove on down to Piggy Hill to his sheep.

The day went well and, with the change to the clocks, it was just starting to get dark as I scraped up the last of the muck and loaded it into the spreader. I felt we had made a good job of it and, apart from a brief refuelling stop for the two tractors and a short break for a boiled bacon sandwich and a bottle of tea Alice had made for each of us, we had worked virtually non-stop.

The only casualty was my left knee which was now feeling the pain after pressing the clutch pedal on the Fergie over a thousand times. When I climbed out of the cab to wait while Ronny spread the last load, I found I could hardly walk without it threatening to give way.

At that point, I convinced myself it must have been a loader driver who invented the 'live-clutch' which provided a constant drive to the hydraulic pump and power take off without affecting the drive to the rear wheels.

'Well done, Ronny,' I said, when he arrived back to the heap. 'That's a good job done and you're still almost clean.'

Ronny reached into his jacket, pulled out his tobacco tin and began to roll a cigarette, not speaking until he had lit it and smoke began to pour out of his mouth and left nostril. 'It's like this, John: muck waits for no man, and it's never finished until it's spread.'

'You mean like Marmite,' I said, helpfully.

'Sort of.'

'Good, well that's all sorted then. I think we should make our way back to the farm while we can still see the way.'

The cows were already in Church Close when I drove through the field but I couldn't see any hay that had been put out, so I assumed Harry was still dealing with the churns in the dairy.

We parked up under the barn by the combine harvester and then, in the darkness, walked down the yard and met Harry topping up the jug for the house milk.

'Here're the workers,' he said, as we stood by the

254

door, the light shining out into the yard. 'How did it go? All finished?'

'It's all done and dusted,' I said. 'But it will take a bit of working down when we come to cultivate it.'

'That's to be expected but you've done well and it's a good job to get out of the way. Well done, Ronny,' he shouted out the door into the darkness.

'Thanks, Harry,' came the reply.

'Right then. If you take the feed out to the cows, I'll take this milk to the house and we'll call it a day. Oh, and you'll be pleased to know the cows seemed to be a lot better this evening, so I think the salt licks must be doing their job.'

CHAPTER TWENTY-THREE

Quality rubbish

WHEN I CAME into the kitchen the next morning the sun was already climbing into the sky and I had made my mind up to point it out to Harry after yesterday's debacle when rather than gaining an hour's extra sleep, I had actually lost an hour.

'Morning,' I said. 'Nice and bright this morning and it's still only just six o'clock. It's a bit different to yesterday.'

'You wouldn't think you could get two days as different, would you boy?'

I knew there was an answer in there somewhere but it was too early. Instead, I picked up yesterday's newspaper and started reading it.

Meanwhile, Harry set out the cups, lifted the teapot and the strainer and started pouring. And then, after placing it back on the tray, lifted the jug and added a splash of milk into each cup. He pushed one over to me and then scooped another up and headed off down the corridor.

'Before I forget,' he said as he came back into the kitchen. 'We've had a request.'

'What's that; not the vicar again.'

'Not that, at least, not yet. No this is from Rose Hill, Alice's place. They're planning to put on a bit of a do for bonfire night and they want us to bring them a load of rubbish to put on the bonfire. Don't ask me why because they probably have more rubbish than they know what to do with, without us bringing them more of it. Still, if that's what they want I dare say we could contribute a trailer load for them.'

'There's not that much. I had a good clear out when you were having that do with the fire extinguisher man.'

Harry smiled. 'Yes, that was good fun, wasn't it? The old boy was good sport and did his best but we had him beaten from the start.'

'He didn't have a chance, that fire burned for the best part of a week and you could feel the heat from it for days after that,' I said. 'But I suppose I could give the yard another search through and there's probably something in the orchard we could use.'

'Go steady in the orchard, boy. I know it seems everything ends up in there but there's some valuable stuff which is best left where it is.'

I felt the urge to ask him what sort of valuable stuff he was talking about, but something held me back. It was safer to stay out of the orchard, I thought.

'Anyway, if you can put what you can on a trailer and take it down there this morning, I think they would appreciate it,' Harry said.

'Right then, I'll go and make a start on the milking.'

'Oh, that's the other thing we need to sort out. It's time we started the cows on the kale, now the grass has all but stopped growing.'

My spirits dropped. Memories of cutting kale

returned to haunt me – the Marrow Stem kale which grew quite six feet tall and had stems nearly as thick as your wrist, the cold shower of icy water I received when I cut the stem, and the loading of a trailer which seemed to take for ever.

'You look worried, boy.'

'I was just thinking back to how we had to cut and cart it the other year, that's all.'

'Well we don't have to do it that way this time,' he said. 'I've grown about ten acres of it just below the old allotment field, so we can strip graze it.'

I felt better. 'When were you thinking about starting that?'

'If you take down stuff for the bonfire this morning we can sort out the fencing this afternoon,' he said. 'Alice and I are out this morning but we'll be back for lunch.'

'Somewhere nice?'

'I doubt it,' Harry replied as he disappeared through the door.

After breakfast I went and hooked the David Brown onto one of the two-wheel trailers on the basis that this tractor's brakes, while being far from efficient, were still better than the Fordson and, for that matter the Grey Fergie.

For the Fordson, road travel was a matter of slowing down and hoping nothing would require any violent stops to take place. It was all in the planning and being prepared, but even then there were times when it was necessary to steer into the kerb to try and increase the braking.

The Grey Fergie's brakes were even worse, but this was countered to some small extent by the fact that

258

the Fergie was much lighter and this combined with less power, resulted in most road work taking place in one of the lower gears.

Driving up steep hills needed a low gear because the tractor hadn't the power to get up them in a higher gear and, to descend steep hills, it needed to be in a low gear because you couldn't stop it.

Harry tells the tale of the time he was washing out the Fordson's air filter with diesel and when it was replaced in the canister, the diesel drained down into the oil bath which is designed to catch the dust and muck to stop it entering the engine.

'When I started the engine it sucked this diesel in and the engine began to rev faster and faster and there wasn't a thing I could do to stop it,' he said. 'It was totally out of control, roaring away like there was no tomorrow and if I'd been driving it, I don't know what would have happened.

'In the end, I went and hid in the workshop, convinced it was going to blow itself to pieces but all of a sudden, it started to shut itself down and came to a halt.'

'Had it damaged the engine?' I asked.

'That was the strange thing. It must have been revving at ten thousand rpm and more, which is something you only do with a diesel engine when it's in a hire car, but no, it wasn't damaged at all and, as you can see, it's still running today.'

With the trailer attached I worked my way around the yard stopping and picking up anything which looked remotely combustible. There were plenty of paper bags and handfuls of string but I had yet to find anything with any bulk in it which would help fill the trailer.

I had just about completed a circuit of the main yard and was heading for the rick yard, where I knew there were some rotten railway sleepers that didn't look as if they were of any further use, when my eyes alighted on a pile of old tyres which had to be a must for a bonfire, if not for the barbeque.

They were wet and there was water in their wells which slopped about and managed to drench a good part of me before I had the first one on board. And then I asked myself why I was struggling to lift these stubborn rounds of decaying rubber when there was a tractor and loader not a dozen yards away.

And did it make light work? I could have taken all morning to get those tyres aboard, yet the loader lifted them effortlessly and placed them just where I wanted them to be on the trailer in less than ten minutes.

With those on board I was getting pretty close to a full load but I couldn't resist using the loader to pile the rotten railway sleepers on top before I used a rope to help ensure everything stayed where it was.

I drove out of the yard and headed for Rose Hill farm, a route that took me up to the top of the hill where the entrance to Smith's farm was. For the descent down the fearsome Copse Hill, I was prudent and engaged a low gear but even then, the weight of the trailer started to push me and I needed to use the brakes to slow down to what I considered to be a safe speed.

My slow progress down the hill caused a number of cars and vans to form a queue behind and when the road levelled and became wider they overtook, one of them slowing down when he drew level to ask me when I was going to get back in the field.

I drove up to the farm and was met by William

junior who looked as if he had just about finished milking and I wondered what time their churn lorry arrived. Whenever it was, it must be a good couple of hours later than ours.

'Good morning, William,' I said as I stopped the tractor, swung a leg over the bonnet and jumped down.

William grinned. 'What brings you down here?'

Clearly, communication wasn't high on the priority list. 'Harry asked me to bring down some stuff you can use on your bonfire,' I replied.

William's eyes shifted to the trailer and its contents. 'Bonfire? Don't know anything about that,' he said.

'Well is your father about anywhere?'

'He's up the field.'

'And Kate?'

'She's in the kitchen.'

'Right. I'll go and speak to her then.'

William shrugged his shoulders and wandered off, his wellingtons splashing through ankle-deep slurry.

I walked round to the front of the house and, as I did, there was a wonderful smell of frying bacon which had my mouth watering before I even reached the kitchen door.

I gave it a knock and pushed it open. 'Kate,' I called, not wanting to just walk in. There was no reply so I stepped inside and tried calling again but not before I spotted the frying pan on the stove in which there must have been a dozen rashers of bacon sizzling away. This time I heard some doors being opened and in walked Kate.

'Hello, John. Everything alright?' She went across to the stove and picked up a slice and began to turn the bacon over. 'What brings you down here and how's

261

your shoulder mending?'

'Harry asked me to bring down a load of stuff you can use on the bonfire,' I said. 'And the shoulder's now a lot better, thanks.'

'Bonfire? I'd thought we had enough rubbish already down here for a dozen bonfires without bringing anymore.' She gave the bacon a final turn and then lifted the rashers out onto a plate before popping them into the oven to keep them warm.

'I don't know anything about that but sit yourself down and I'll pour you a cup of tea; they'll be in for breakfast in a minute or two and you can find out then.'

As I sat down, the kitchen door was pushed open and dour William shuffled in and headed for the sink.

'Look who's here,' Kate said.

William, who was scrubbing his hands and arms with a brush I'd rather use to polish shoes with, looked round at me. 'What brings you down here?' he grunted.

'Harry said you had asked him to provide some suitable material for your bonfire, so that's what I've brought down,' I said, trying to match the abruptness of the man. 'But I can take it back if you don't want it.'

'Bonfire?' he grabbed for the towel and rubbed it vigorously over his hands and arms, which I thought now didn't look much cleaner despite all the rubbing and scarifying he had given them with the brush.

'Yes, bonfire,' I said. 'I gather you're having a bonfire do tonight. You know, it's November fifth, bonfire night.'

'Oh, that will be nice,' Kate said. 'I'll make some sandwiches and hotdogs.'

'What have you got, then?' William asked.

'Anything I could find. There are some old tyres and a few rotten railway sleepers along with bags and other bits and bobs.'

'So we've now got all Harry's rubbish?'

'Well, that's one way of looking at it,' I said. 'But you can pick it through if you think there may be anything of use.'

Kate was spreading slices of bread with melted butter and when she had completed about half a loaf she returned to the stove and removed the bacon from the oven. 'Are you going to have a bacon butty, John?'

'If you can spare one,' I said. 'That would be very welcome, thank you.'

Dour William sat down and put his hands around the cup of tea Kate had just poured him, took a sip, and then tipped some of it into the saucer and began to blow on it. 'You'd better unload it in the middle of the paddock,' he said, looking at me over the top of the saucer he was about to drink from, the perpetual dew drop now so close to joining it. 'It'll save us a job, I suppose.'

I munched into the bacon butty and it was just so good. It was an idle thought, but I wondered if Alice could be persuaded to change her breakfast routine and accommodate a similar feast.

Young William arrived and, like his father, set about scrubbing his hands for minutes on end before giving them further punishment with the towel.

'Give John a hand unloading his trailer in the paddock,' said his father. 'And don't put it too close to the hedge.'

'Have you heard from Liz, lately?' Kate asked.

'Yes, I had a letter from her only last week. She seems to be more settled this year, don't you think?'

Kate thought about it. 'Yes, I think you could be right. She's certainly happier than she was this time last year.'

'Does she call you much?'

'Usually on a Sunday evening; just for a chat really, you know how it is.'

'Oh, that's good.' I finished my tea and turned to dour William. 'Well, I'll get the trailer unloaded then. You say you want it in the middle of the paddock?'

'That's right. William will go with you.'

I looked across at young William who was working hard on his third bacon butty. 'There's no rush,' I said, helpfully. 'I'll be outside when you're ready. Thanks for the butty, Kate and I'll see you all later today.'

'Bye John,' she said.

I climbed on to the tractor, and as I waited for William to arrive, I thought about Elizabeth and tried to imagine what sort of childhood she must have had living in such isolation. In many ways it was idyllic and one I would have gladly swapped with my council estate upbringing, but while there was an abundance of open fields, animals and fresh air to enjoy, it was also restrictive and in some ways unreal.

'I'll open the gate into the paddock for you,' William said, breaking into my thoughts.

'Oh right. Thanks,' I muttered, starting the engine and driving on.

'Do you think this is about the middle?' William asked, when he finally stopped walking.

'Near as makes no difference,' I replied, looking around.

Together, we heaved off the sleepers and the tyres

264

trying to keep the pile tight and high, rather than loose and flat.

'Are you planning on adding some of your own rubbish?' I asked him.

'Might drop a few bags of string on top but we haven't got that much to go at,' he said.

'I suppose it depends on what you class as rubbish,' I said.

William grunted and kicked off the last of the bags before jumping off the trailer.

'That's it then. Thanks for your help; I'll just coil the rope up and I'll be on my way.'

All in all, I reflected as I motored along the open road, in top gear and the throttle wide open for a heady fourteen miles an hour, it had been quite an enjoyable visit, even if they did seem a bit introverted and reluctant to speak.

I just wondered how they would take the news when Elizabeth and I announced our plans to become engaged. I even tried to imagine dour William making his, "Welcome to the family", speech and failed.

CHAPTER TWENTY-FOUR

Electric shocks and exploding rockets

I TURNED ONTO the top road and made my way along to the farm, slowing first for the cattle grid and then again to avoid the usual gaggle of hens scratching around on the track, before I could drive into the yard.

The next task Harry had mentioned was to load the trailer with some electric fencing so the cows could start strip grazing the kale. With a bit more planning, I would have put the fencing battery on charge before I left this morning but I hadn't and there wasn't much I could do about it. Even so, I clipped the charger leads onto the battery as soon as I could and hoped it wasn't totally flat, but suspected it probably was.

The fencing stakes, with their twirls of insulated tops the wire passed through to keep it off the ground, and bottom plates you were meant to stand on to push them into the soil, were bundled up in tens, which was about as much as I wanted to carry. I hadn't a clue how long a fence we needed so I put four bundles in to the trailer.

These were followed by wire and the fencing unit itself which, when running, gave off an ominous ticking noise as it pulsed high voltage, low amperage current along the wire to provide a deterring yet hopefully memorable harmless shock to any cow who should come into contact with it.

Electric fencing units always seem to hold a fascination for Harry. And this manifested itself the other year in the machinery dealer's premises when he managed to wire up the brass measuring ruler running the length of the serving counter and gave an almost fatal electric shock to both the storeman and the customer he was serving.

There was also the time when he advised a local man suffering from an arthritic elbow to grab hold of the electrified wire for as long as he could, on the premise it would do him the world of good. But the occasion which caused him the greatest amusement and he recanted at the drop of a hat, was when a dog lifted his leg and started to urinate on the live wire.

Harry and Alice returned home just before lunch and Harry came up the yard to see how things were progressing.

'How did you get on delivering the bonfire?' he asked.

'Well I took it down there and the first thing Kate asked was why I was bringing stuff to burn when there was already more than enough around their own buildings for a dozen bonfires,'

'I could have told them that,' Harry said. 'But William insisted he didn't have enough to build a decent fire and needed us to help him; the thing is, they've lived with it for so long, they can't see it's there anymore.'

'Well they now have a heap in the middle of the paddock to not see,' I said.

'And how are we fixed with the electric fencing kit.

267

All set?'

'Pretty much. I'm not sure how long the fence needs to be but I've loaded as much as we have. But I was thinking, if the kale is as tall and as thick as it was last time, how are we going to put a fence up that doesn't short out on the crop?'

'And there lies the big question,' Harry replied. 'There're two ways we can handle it. One is to physically cut a couple of rows every ten yards or so, and the other is to try and run the tractor down a row so the wheels push down on the kale and create a gap for the fence that way.'

'Will the crop stay down if we run on it and will the cows still eat it?'

'Depends on the crop. We'll have to see when we get there but for now, we'll stop for a bit of lunch,' Harry said. 'That's assuming Alice has managed to put anything together.'

I had an inkling she had and I sort of knew what it was going to be, but I didn't want to spoil the moment.

'I put a few potatoes in the oven before we left this morning and I think they should be alright,' Alice said, 'And if I do a few peas and Harry carves us some boiled bacon that will have to do us.'

'Sounds fine,' I said.

'And how were they all down at Rose Hill?' Alice continued. 'Was Kate on form?'

'Oh yes, she was in charge with the teapot in one hand and a frying pan in the other and everyone seemed to be their normal selves. I don't know where the girls were, I assume they were at school?'

'That's right, the bus picks them up from the end of the track about quarter past eight and takes them into

Storeton Green and then drops them off at about five,' she explained.

'They have a long enough day then?'

'Yes, but Kate always takes them down and waits with them for the bus to come in the morning and she is there when they're dropped off, so it's not too bad.'

Harry who had been attending to his dogs came in to the kitchen and then, a few minutes later Ross and Bob trooped in after him and flopped down under the table.

'Harry,' Alice said. 'Get those dogs out of here.'

'They haven't seen me all day. They won't hurt.'

This was defiant talk from Harry and, for a few moments, I thought he was holding his ground well but then I caught the first whiff of a dog with flatulence problems and I immediately switched my allegiance to Alice.

'Good grief, Harry,' she cried, her hand over her nose, as the smell filled the kitchen. 'Get those dogs out of here. I can even taste it.'

'Just open the window a crack, boy. It'll soon clear,' Harry said.

It was a pious hope. If opening the window had any effect on the concentration of the smell, it was soon topped up by further deliveries.

'Perhaps you had better open the door, boy,' Harry eventually conceded.

'I think that may be for the best,' I said, 'But what's that noise?'

There was a dull rasping noise coming from beneath the table where the dogs were lying.

'Oh my God,' Alice cried. 'Is that snoring, or something else?'

'I don't know and I'm not going down there to find

269

out,' I said.

'It's probably just one of the cats,' Harry said.

With lunch over, I headed back up the yard and took the battery off the charger while I waited for Harry to put his dogs away.

'Are we all set?' he asked, running his eye over the kit I had put in the trailer. 'We might need some end posts or something if we can't find anything to secure the end of the wire to in the hedge or fence. If you drop the post knocker into the trailer, I'll fetch a couple of posts round from the rick yard.'

The post knocker was a fearful piece of equipment and comprised a wide metal tube which was about ten inches wide and three foot long. At one end there was a sizeable block of metal welded inside the tube, which gave it the weight and, on the outside, four long handles had been welded. The idea was to lower the open end of the tube onto the top of the post and then lift the tube up and power it back down onto the post to knock it into the ground.

It needed at least two people to operate and the general rule was to take it in turns to lift it off the post which had been knocked into the ground to a required depth and position it on to the of the next post. The muscle power required to keep going all day was totally exhausting top but I often thought a gymnasium looking for the perfect body building machine need look no further than a post knocker, if only because it made every muscle in the body ache.

The kale field was once part of the allotments used by people living in the village, but with a decline in interest for home grown food and an increasing interest in television, more and more plots had become neglected and overgrown. A couple of years ago, the society which ran the allotments made a decision to sell off what amounted to nearly ten acres of land and offer it to Harry, who took it on.

'It was a pity you weren't here when we started clearing it,' he said, 'There were old sheds, broken forks, wire mesh, and goodness knows what. We had about a dozen trailer loads of rubbish off it before we could even begin to put a tractor and cultivator anywhere near it.'

'What's it like now?' I asked.

'Not bad. It's good easy working soil but getting rid of the rhubarb patches has been a bit of a challenge. I've ploughed it and sprayed it but they still keep coming up. It's amazingly resilient stuff, but it tastes awful.'

Harry climbed off the tractor and went and opened the gate into the kale field and I drove in just far enough for him to close the gate again.

'I don't think it's quite as tall as the other crops,' he said. 'This free draining land suffers from drought which can make it struggle if we don't get the rain, but it's not too bad. And the ground will hold the cows without them poaching it too badly.'

I walked into the kale and, not ten yards on, I turned around and saw nothing but kale stems. It was like being in a forest.

'Seems tall enough to me,' I said, brushing droplets of water off my jacket. 'And wet enough too.'

Harry thought about it. 'I don't think this is going to work,' he said. 'Even if we cut a couple of rows down there's going to be too much foliage for an electric fence, and every time we want to move it, which will be pretty frequently, we'll have to reel it all in and

271

pick up the stakes and start again.'

'So, we're going to have to cut it like last time,' I said.

'Looks like it, unless you can think of another way.'

'How about if we cut and cart a strip every ten yards or so and use that for the electric fence while they graze on the kale in front of it? That would save us having to cut, cart and feed so much.'

Harry nodded. 'It could work boy. But we would still have to take down the fence and put it back up again.

'If we have enough wire and stakes we could put up a second fence and just move the unit on it. We could always be one fence ahead.'

'Yes boy. We'll give that a try. So we need to cut and cart four rows every ten yards then?'

'If you think ten yards is enough?'

'It should be alright for a couple or three days and they will always be able to come back on to the grass field if they want to.'

We left the stakes and wire on the edge of the field and took the battery and unit back to the farm where I could finish charging the battery.

The drive down to Rose Hill in the Land Rover was a little cramped, despite Alice opting to sit in the middle passenger seat. I tried to give her as much space as I could, but with door handle sticking into me and wearing a big thick coat, there just wasn't the room.

But we endured it and it wasn't long before Harry drew up to the gate which marked the start of the track. It was the gate I had driven through this morning and I had deliberately made the effort to tie the gate up with a knot which could be easily loosened and untied. But no, there had been others coming this way who had managed to tie a real tangle of a knot.

'Cut the bugger open and use a fresh bit of string,' Harry shouted out of the window. I could hear him, but the headlights stopped me seeing him. 'And if you haven't enough string leave it open. That will teach them.'

'You can't do that,' Alice said.

'Then why can't someone find time to put a latch on a gate like every other farm has?'

I found a fresh length of string and, when Harry had driven through and I had closed the gate behind him, I wrapped the string around the post and tied it in a big bow.

'I'll give William a gate catch for Christmas,' Harry said. 'Either that or plans for a cattle grid.'

Alice said nothing and I thought she was probably right.

'Don't see you for months and then you come twice in one day,' Kate said as I walked through the door into the kitchen. 'And what have you done with Alice and Harry?'

'They were behind me but they've seemed to have disappeared somewhere,' I said.

'Never mind, you know where to go.'

I walked through the long corridor still with its low power lighting and knee-level dog stains on walls and turned left into the living room and suddenly my world exploded.

'Surprise!' everyone shouted. I looked around the room and there, sitting on the sofa was Elizabeth and her two sisters, Elsie and Emily.

'Elizabeth,' I cried making my way around the furniture. 'No one told me you would be here. That's wonderful. When did you get here?' I reached out and pulled her up off the sofa and into my arms.

And there we stayed completely oblivious to all the shouting and cheering which was going on around us.

'I only arrived back about an hour ago,' she said. 'And I couldn't call you to say I was coming because I didn't know if I was going to make it, what with exams and all that.'

'That's terrific,' I said. 'How long are you staying?'

'Until Monday, so we have the whole weekend.'

'It just gets better.'

'You've found each other then,' Alice said when she walked into the room with Harry.

'You mean, you knew Elizabeth was here?'

'Yes, they wanted it to be a surprise.'

'And I didn't know anything about it,' Harry said. 'Honest I didn't.'

Kate clapped her hands. 'Now listen everyone, they're lighting the bonfire now, so we'll give it a little while to get going and while we're waiting there's some hot dogs to get stuck into in the kitchen.'

The room emptied rapidly and very soon it was just Elizabeth and me.

'I've been bursting to tell mum our secret,' she said.

I smiled. 'If you really want to, then I wouldn't mind.'

'No, it's alright. I can wait. Come on let's grab a hot dog and if there's only one left we'll have to eat it from both ends, at the same time.'

'Sounds fun,' I said, following her out of the room.

With everyone in the kitchen it had become pretty cramped, and it didn't get any better when dour William and William junior joined us and demanded their sausage rolls.

'What's it like to have a bonfire made with quality rubbish for a change?' I heard Harry asking dour William.

'Quality? My arse. We've better quality rubbish than that anywhere you choose to look on this farm,' he replied.

'I need to try harder, then,' Harry said.

'Too right you do.'

At Kate's insistence, we trooped out and strolled over to the bonfire which, I have to say, looked impressive and I could feel the heat as soon as we made it through the gate.

'What have you put in there?' Elizabeth asked.

'I think it must be the old railway sleepers and the tyres,' I said.

Harry had brought a large box of fireworks with us and he set about letting them off as we stood around the bonfire soaking up the heat. And, as the rockets streamed into the air, the jumping jacks danced around our feet and the night air did battle with the Roman candles, I slipped my arm around Elizabeth and told her I loved her.

'I saw dad with a crate of beer if you fancy a bottle,' she said as yet another large rocket exploded overhead, showering everyone with bursts of golden sparks. 'Shall we go and see if we can find them?'

'What a great idea.'

CHAPTER TWENTY-FIVE

A sudden drop

By NEXT MORNING the weather had become much colder, to the point a layer of frost covered the ground and, as I walked up to the milking bail, bucket of hot water in hand, I looked up at an overcast sky.

'It looks as if winter's on its way,' I told the girls as they strolled into the collecting yard. Not that it seemed to trouble them. These girls were hardy and the weather would have to be really harsh for them to start to complain but should it be so, there was always a barn they could shelter in.

I only wished I could cope with such cold weather as well as they did. My feet became painfully cold and while I could warm my hands by pushing them up the side of a cow's udder, it wasn't a practical solution for my feet. And no matter how I stamped and ran on the spot, they just became colder and colder.

On this particular day I almost willed a cow to make a slurry deposit in the yard so I could go and stand in it and feel the heat seeping through my wellingtons, but not today. I've seen the yard covered inches thick in the stuff but today there wasn't a suggestion of any. Perhaps the cows were in a heat retaining mode too.

Having completed all my milking jobs, I was glad to

make it in to the kitchen where the Rayburn was pumping out mega loads of heat and I could sit down and stretch my feet out on to the front of it and leave them there until the socks began to steam; such exquisite ecstasy.

'Bit fresh today, boy,' Harry said. 'A coat and a bale string colder than yesterday and you may recall me pointing out the large number of berries there were this autumn and to be prepared for a cold winter as a result.'

'You certainly did say as much Harry and I didn't doubt you for a minute,' I said. 'If it stays like this, we'll be breaking the ice on the water troughs.'

'It's when the cows come in with frost on their whiskers, you know you're going to have do that. Never mind, you'll soon warm up when you start cutting a few rows through the kale.'

I shuddered. Hacking my way through head-high, leafy kale just waiting to deposit a pint of iced water down my neck, was definitely not something to look forward to.

'And make sure you take a waterproof coat with a hood,' Alice said. 'At least you'll stay dry then.'

'I've been thinking about this,' I said. 'If I cut two rows and lay them with their stalks facing away from where we're going to place the fence, the cows will still be able to eat them, the fence should be clear of any foliage and we won't have to cart any of it. What do you think?'

Harry thought about it. 'You'd have to make sure the cut stems are well away so it leaves a clear path for the fence,' he said. 'But give it a go and see how it looks.'

Buoyed with the thought there was now a chance I

might not have to spend the next month cutting and carting kale, I set off with the tractor and trailer, the freshly charged battery and the fencing unit on board the trailer along with a selection of cutting tools, most of which we had been using to lay the hedge.

My plan was to cut one row and place it to the right of where the fence was to run and then cut the other row and lay it to the left, which should leave a nice open pathway.

And that is about as far as I went because, as I drove into the field and turned to run along the headland, the ground suddenly opened up beneath the rear wheels and the tractor immediately dropped about three feet but left the front wheels on firm ground. The trailer, which was still also on firm ground was now at a steep angle, but its drawbar had at least prevented me slipping any further into the hole. I climbed off and looked at the tractor and noticed there was no soil whatsoever under the rear wheels. In fact, it was impossible to see just how deep the hole was.

'That's bloody allotments for you,' Harry said when I had made my way back to the farm and told him what happened. 'There's no saying what everyone got up to. I suppose this hole is an old pond or something.'

'It was a deep pond if it was,' I said. 'By the time I left, there was nothing under the rear wheels; just fresh air.'

'So what's it going to need to get it out?'

'About ten days and a miracle.'

'Sounds like a job for the Marshall, then.'

'I think it could be our only hope of seeing the David Brown again, unless you know anyone in Australia, that is.'

278

We headed down to the orchard and crossed over to the shed where the Marshall tractor spent its retirement years. Harry's father had bought it new in 1937 and when he took over the farm, he says it became the main workhorse, spending long hours either working in the fields or powering threshing drums from its belt drive.

'At really busy times of the year I would use the Marshall to power a threshing drum all day, and then take her cultivating for most of the night,' he said. 'She's had some long days, I can tell you.'

It had been sometime since I had looked in the shed and it was good to be reacquainted with her – her tall exhaust pot, the enormous, exposed flywheel, the large-bore, horizontal single cylinder engine and the cone clutch system. Its major asset though, and the one that guaranteed it an outing most years, was the winch with its steel cable, winding drum and generously sized anchor plates.

'She's still all there,' I said.

'She is that,' Harry concurred, rubbing his hand gently along the bonnet. 'There's a few years left in her yet. Right then, you get a couple of buckets of clean water for the radiator and I'll get the blotting paper. You'd better bring down half a can of diesel as well.'

I fetched the diesel first, seeing as the tank was further up the yard and it was there I ran in to Ronny.

'Morning John,' he said. 'Where is everybody?'

I put the nozzle into the top of the can and turned the tap on. 'We're in the orchard preparing to get the Marshall out,' I said.

'The pop-pop? What have you got stuck this time?'

I turned the tap off, removed the nozzle from the can

279

and straightened my back. 'The David Brown has found a big hole to drop into where the kale is,' I said. 'If you take this diesel down to the shed in the orchard, I'll fetch some water to fill the radiator.'

If there was anything you didn't need with the Marshall it was a funnel. The hole for the water was as wide as the bucket itself and there was also a sizable orifice for the fuel to be poured into, but even this did not prevent Ronny splashing diesel all over the place.

'Bloody hell, Ronny,' Harry said, as he stepped back to avoid the worst of it. 'You got the shakes or something?'

'Sorry Harry. It just came out a bit fast.'

Harry ignored him and set about rolling up a piece of blotting paper and inserting it in to a cap at the front of the tractor where it would smoulder away and warm the fuel before it entered the engine.

'Give me your lighter, Ron.' Harry held out his hand and Ronny dug into his pocket and produced his petrol fuelled cigarette lighter.

'Go steady with it, Harry. It's the only one I've got,' he said.

Harry looked at it. 'How does this work, then?'

Ronny took it back and flicked open the top, pushed his thumb sharply across the flint wheel and a flame appeared on the wick. He then held it out to Harry who held the blotting paper over it until it started to glow at the edges.

'That will do Ron,' he said and screwed the brass cap and its glowing blotting paper into its socket. He then reached for the starting handle and I'd forgotten just how large it was; at least, when it was compared to the one I used to start the milking bail's engine.

This was two-man giant of a handle which fitted into the centre of the fly wheel, but even with two people winding it, the engine needed to be decompressed to allow sufficient speed and momentum to be attained, and this used a threaded groove on the edge of the flywheel in which a small jockey wheel ran. When this wheel was on the flywheel a lever system opened a valve and decompressed the engine and when the grooves wound it off, the valve closed and the engine compression returned and hopefully fired it up.

'Shall we go for four turns or five before compression?' Harry asked as he slipped the handle into the fly wheel.

'I think four would be a good start,' I said. 'Ronny looks reasonably fit.'

'Four it is then, he said. And I watched him lift the jockey wheel and place it on the fourth groove.

'Alright, I've checked the oil, fuel, opened the throttle and you've filled the radiator,' Harry said. 'Who's having first go and don't forget to watch out if the starting handle sticks in the flywheel when it starts. If it does, run and hide somewhere.'

It was this warning which caused me some concern when we last started up the Marshall. The thought of a handle of that size flying through the air in some unpredictable direction was not one I particularly relished.

'I'll have a go with Ronny,' I said, making sure I was not the one standing closest to the flywheel.

'Alright?'

'Yes, let's do it, Harry,' Ronny said.

'Go!'

Pushing hard at the top, pulling hard at the bottom, the flywheel slowly picked up speed but I knew we weren't going anywhere near fast enough. When the fourth turn was completed and the compression came in, it was like hitting a brick wall; the flywheel came to an abrupt halt.

'That was poor,' Harry said. 'A really poor effort.'

'I think,' I gasped, 'you need to put the jockey wheel on at least six grooves.'

'Any more than that and you'll have peaked before it drops off the flywheel,' he said. 'I'll put it on five. Come on Ronny, your turn.'

'I've just had a turn,' he said, coughing up something green and spitting it out.

'Lucky you, two turns in a row,' Harry said.

Harry and Ronny took their places on the starting handle and, on Harry's shout began to wind up the flywheel. By the third turn, they were going well and when the jockey wheel dropped off on the fifth turn they managed to keep it turning despite the compression tripping in.

And then the engine fired, just the once and I was convinced it was going to stop.

'Come on Ronny,' screamed Harry. 'Keep turning.'

On every other stroke the engine fired which was just about enough to keep the flywheel turning and after about the fourth time, it fired consecutively for a few strokes and then, after that, as a great cloud of black smoke filled the shed and beyond, it started firing on every stroke.

'Close the throttle,' Harry shouted to me, and I slipped down the other side of the tractor, leaned over the mudguard and slid the quadrant into a notch or two above its closed position.

'Doesn't she sound wonderful?' Harry asked, his face beaming.

I listened to the steady, rhythmic pop-pop as the piston slipped back and forwards at a speed you could count to and nodded. I then looked around to see where Ronny had ended up and saw him sitting on the floor coughing and wheezing and, as the smoke cleared it was good to see he was also holding the starting handle.

Harry climbed onto the back, gripped the steering wheel in both hands and then pressed the clutch pedal down and pushed the gear stick in some direction to engage a gear. And then, as the clutch was released, the engine's governor opened the throttle and pushed yet another cloud of acrid black smoke belching out of the exhaust stack and the tractor began to roll out of the shed into the orchard.

'I think we will need some boards to have something for the tractor's wheels to move over when we pull it out,' I said, after we had driven the Marshall over to the workshop.

'Well you and Ronny put what you think we'll need in the Land Rover and I'll take the pop-pop down to the field and we'll meet up there.'

'I shouldn't go too close to the hole,' I warned. 'Fall in that and the chances are we'll probably never see you again.'

Ronny and I loaded the back of the Land Rover with everything we could think of that might help with the extraction of the tractor. Along with boards, we put in jacks, shovels, ropes and even a water pump before we left to meet up with Harry.

And when we turned into the field, Harry was standing looking down into the hole beneath the David Brown's wheels. In our absence I was worried the tractor might have carried on sinking but it had remained as I left it, with its rear wheels dangling over a bottomless hole, supported at the rear by the trailer drawbar and at the front by the base of the engine and the front wheels.

'Never seen anything like it before and I hope I never have to see anything like it again,' Harry said, when I joined him on the edge of the chasm. 'There must have been a fault or something when they put the top soil on after they had taken the iron ore out. It's a wonder no one's been killed. How on earth are we going to get it out?'

I detected a sense of despair in his voice and I was anxious to help with at least one idea. 'How about hooking onto the back of the trailer and see if the trailer will provide some lift for the rear of the tractor as we winch it back,' I said. 'Failing that, we need to get an excavator in here to build a ramp for the tractor.'

'You don't think the trailer chassis will bend if we just try tugging it out, do you?' Harry said. 'And won't the front wheels of the tractor just drop in the hole as it comes back?'

'Well it's a risk but I think it's worth a try before we start spending big money on excavator hire.'

'Perhaps if we shovel down a few feet off the edge it might just reduce the amount of strain,' Harry said.

So we took the shovels out of the Land Rover and started digging down in an attempt to turn what was a vertical drop into more of a slant.

'What do you reckon, Ronny?' Harry asked.

Ronny leaned back on his shovel. 'Don't know, never seen anything like this since our kid dropped his toy tractor down a drain.'

Useful information if it had been required but not perhaps entirely appropriate at this time. After half an hour's digging which seemed to have created a slope of sorts at the rear end of the hole we stopped and connected the chain and shackle around the axle of the trailer and then drove the tractor away from it to run the cable out. When it was as far as the length of cable allowed, a distance of about forty yards, Harry stopped and set about unhooking and lowering the anchor plates.

The anchor was designed to dig into the ground and prevent the tractor being dragged backwards by the winch, rather than the winch pulling along whatever was connected to the end of the cable. It was a sort of tug of war which the tractor usually won.

'What do you reckon, Ron? Do we give it a go and see what happens?'

'I don't think we have a choice, Harry,' he said. 'It has two chances – it will either come out or it won't come out and, if it doesn't we'll have to think of another way of doing it.'

Harry walked off towards the Marshall which had been gently ticking over while we talked and I was struck, not for the first time, by the way the tractor bounced on its tyres as the natural rhythm of the tractor coincided with that of the single cylinder sliding back and forwards.

'There have been times,' Harry said, 'when the bouncing had been sufficient to cause the catch holding the clutch pedal down to slip off and the pulley, which was part of the cone clutch assembly, to suddenly start rotating. Not much fun when a threshing machine starts up when you're not expecting it.'

I shouted to Ronny to stand back as the cable slowly tightened and then, when it had reached a critical force, started to pull the Marshall backwards, the anchors digging ever deeper into the ground. And when the anchors were almost fully buried and a wave of soil had been pushed up, the tractor stopped moving and the trailer started to move towards it. I ran round to the front to see if the David Brown was moving with it.

It was but it wasn't coming out; the tyres were just making dents and being flattened in the side of the hole. I waved my arms at Harry to stop pulling.

But I was too late: a second or two earlier and the trailer axle would have still been attached. Instead, there was a loud ripping noise and the sound of bolts breaking before the whole axle came off and headed rearwards in Harry's direction.

'Nice one,' Harry said, as the wheels veered to one side and careered on past him. 'I guess that didn't work, then.'

'The tractor was moving but it wasn't being raised. It was just being pulled into the side of the hole.' I explained. 'It might be better if we hooked the cable on to the front of the tractor and pulled in that direction.'

'What happens if we pull the front axle off the tractor?'

'Well, at least we'll have salvaged something.'

'Let's give it a go,' Harry said, resignedly.

So we did that and this time the tractor decided to rise up out of the hole, helped by the rear wheels dropping even further into the chasm before they were eventually heaved over the side on to firm ground. I looked into the hole and estimated it had to be a good thirty feet deep.

'Could have been a lot worse, boy,' Harry said when he joined me on the edge and looked in. 'And if it hadn't been for the Marshall and its winch, it probably would have been.'

I didn't want to spoil the moment by adding that, if it hadn't been for the Marshall and its winch, we would still have a trailer with an axle attached to it.

CHAPTER TWENTY-SIX

The vicar calls

BREAKFAST THE NEXT morning was a rather subdued, yet relaxing affair with Harry burying his head in the newspaper while I scanned through a copy of the Farmer and Stockbreeder magazine which had arrived some time during last week.

Yesterday, after all the hassle of extracting the David Brown tractor from its premature grave, Ronny and I set about cutting a couple of rows of kale to make space for the electric fencing wire.

And, to be fair, it didn't take that long although it was back aching work which was also cold and wet when the big kale leaves emptied icy water on top of us.

More importantly, I was pleased to see there was more than enough space for the wire to be positioned without it shorting out on any wayward foliage and the battery-powered fencing unit worked well as Ronny will vouch for.

All in all, then, it was a long day and by the time I had milked and taken the cows' feed out to them I had had enough and was ready for bed.

This morning, a chill wind had brought the dogs and two or three cats into the kitchen, much to Alice's annoyance, including the cat which spent most of its life curled up in a bowl on top of the washing machine and somehow managed to sleep through the vibrations when the spin cycle kicked in. As for the other cats though, as the dogs snoozed gently away soaking up the heat from the Rayburn, they dared themselves to snuggle into the warmth between them.

Apart from the hissing of the kettle simmering gently away on the hotplate, and the slow hypnotic ticking of the large wall clock, it was an unnaturally calm and peaceful start to the day, when even boiled bacon was bordering on being acceptable and, at a stretch, almost palatable.

When it came then, the loud, firm knock on the back door was not only a shock to the dogs, who struggled to untangle themselves and get to their feet while the cats fled in all directions, but also for those of us who were in a semi-comatose state of mind and were now being forced to pay more attention.

'If that's the vicar tell him to bugger off,' Harry drawled, not bothering to lift his eyes from the newspaper.

Alice went and answered the door. 'It's the vicar, Harry,' she said.

'Who?'

'Simon Fanshaw, the vicar,' Alice repeated. 'He's here to speak to you.'

'What, now?'

'Yes now, Harry.'

'Come on in, Simon and sit yourself down and I'll make a fresh pot of tea,' Alice said.

'Good morning vicar,' Harry said, looking up and folding the newspaper as he stifled a yawn. 'How good to see you again. Any news we should know about; any good juicy gossip you want to share or unburden yourself with?'

'I shouldn't think so for a minute,' he replied, settling down in his chair. 'But tell me, we had one of those parish ladies' afternoon tea do's the other day and one of the guests was wearing a coat she insisted was made of mole-skin, which I haven't seen in years, possibly since before the war.

'So, it seemed entirely appropriate for me to ask how an attractive young lady like her gets expensive mole-skin coats these days and she said the same way moles get moles and, for the life of me, I didn't understand what she was trying to say.

I heard Harry smirk and watched him wipe a hand across his mouth. 'No, vicar, that's a difficult one and I don't understand it either,' he said, reaching for his handkerchief. 'But I shouldn't worry about it as long as she paid for her tea.'

'And talking of tea,' Alice said. 'Here's a cup to keep you going.'

'Oh that's wonderful, Alice. Thank you so much.' And then he turned to me. 'John, isn't it?'

I nodded, smiled at him and tried not to think of moles getting moles.

'How are you doing? I gather you were away at college last year and now you're back to tell Harry how to do it all.'

'Not quite,' I replied. 'But we're all getting on just fine.'

'That's good. Now Harry, I think you know why I'm here and I hope you're feeling in an affable and generous mood; more so than is usual, perhaps.'

I could see Harry's face dropping. 'If it's about Pedro taking part in the nativity play, I'm not too sure

290

he really wants to go this year.'

'Why do you say that? In previous years he's done a wonderful job and everyone has loved having him. He epitomises the whole spirit of Christmas and the nativity play wouldn't be the same without him. As you know, he only has a small walk-on part and not a lot to do other than stand there for what amounts to a couple of hymns and half an hour at the most.'

Harry looked to Alice for support. 'What do you reckon Alice,' he asked her.

'If it's only half an hour I think it should be alright,' she said. 'And if everyone enjoys him being there, why not?'

Harry looked as if he was on his way to the gallows and I knew by the sideways glance he gave me what he was going to say next, it was his last lifeline.

'I think it's only fair if we ask John what he thinks, seeing as he is the one who would probably be in charge of him. How about it, boy?'

'I don't mind,' I said weakly. 'But only if Pedro's up for it.'

'That's all decided then,' said the vicar, getting to his feet. 'It's seven o'clock on the fourteenth of December and we'll see you there. Don't forget the shepherd costume; that really makes it, and thanks for the tea Alice. I can see myself out.'

There was a silence when the door closed which was only broken when Harry spoke. 'Thank you for your support everybody. I feel as if I've just been "moled".'

November eased its way into December almost unnoticed. Had it not been for the sudden influx of seasonal advertising and a shower of snow, which had everyone talking about a white Christmas, I don't think I would have been aware of what month it was.

But it *was* December, and as of this day, there were just three weeks until Christmas Day, which was a monstrous realisation. On the bright side, Elizabeth should be back home within a few days although, in her last letter she said she would be staying over with one of her friends when the term ended.

'I think we should make a start with the winter ploughing,' Harry announced as I was pulling my boots on after breakfast. 'We've a few more acres to turn over this time and we don't want to push ourselves into a corner with no time to make a job of it.'

So, the day had arrived when the plough comes out and I can look forward to weeks of sitting on a cold tractor, exposed to the elements, pulling a plough up and down fields sustained by endless lunches of boiled bacon sandwiches and cold bottled tea.

'Probably the best thing to do would be to hook on the plough and bring it into the workshop and slip some new shares on and give it a good check over,' he said. 'And while you have the tractor in the workshop, drop its engine oil out, change the filter and then refill it with fresh oil. But before you start all that, we'll drive down to see how the cows are getting on with the kale and then pop into town and pick up a few spares I think we'll need.'

And I thought I was going to have a relaxing day on the hedge laying; I'd already planned where to have the fire and was looking forward to some toasted boiled bacon sandwiches and explore the possibilities of being able to re-heat a bottle of cold tea.

When we arrived in the kale field the cows looked as if they were enjoying themselves and had spread out through the ten or so yard strip they had been allocated. Thrifty stood there with a stalk in her mouth munching into it and Horns was doing much the same, but she also had a large leaf to cope with and try as she might, she couldn't get it into her mouth.

'Have you tested the fence?' Harry asked, interrupting my observations.

'Not today but Ronny tried it last night and the way he yelled suggested all was well.'

'Come on, we'll test it now, just to be sure. I'd hate the cows to get through it and start roaming and trampling over all the rest of the kale.'

On his way over to the fence, Harry selected a long stalk and pulled off any remaining leaves so by the time we arrived he was holding just a long stalk about two feet long.

'What you do,' he explained, 'is to hold one end and then place the other on the wire. The resistance of the stalk means you only get a very small percentage of the full current. Look, I'll show you,'

And then he placed the end of the stalk on the wire as he held the other.

'I can just feel a tingle,' he said. 'If I push the stalk further on to the wire the current increases and I can feel more. You find a stalk and have a go.'

'Well, if you're sure,' I said. I looked around and found one which looked about right and, having stripped it of any leaves I placed it on the wire and received one of the biggest, arm jerking shocks imaginable.

I turned round and saw Harry laughing his head off. 'There's one thing I forgot to tell you,' he said. 'You always want to make sure the stalk isn't too wet or you'll get the full kick.'

'Nice one Harry. Is there anything else we need to check, like how deep is the hole we discovered yesterday?'

'No, but you did drag the axle-less trailer over the top of it, didn't you?'

'Yes, that should be safe enough.'

'Good, well everything looks to be alright down here. I should think they've enough to last them a few more days before we have to move the fence and give them some more, but always remember to leave the gate open so they can get back onto the grass when they want to; there's no water in here.'

'It'll be interesting to see how the kale affects the milk yield,' I said, as we drove back across the field and turned out onto the top road.

'The aim with winter rations is to at least maintain the milk yield but you have to bear in mind it's costing you more to feed them to achieve it,' Harry said.

'Doesn't the dairy pay more for milk in the winter?'

'Yes, but it's not that much and it certainly won't pay for all the extra feed costs.'

We arrived at the dealers and parked in the yard which adjoins the showroom where it is always worth a walk through to see the latest machinery developments and what we might see on Harry's farm in ten years' time.

Instead of walking into the show room though, Harry headed round the back where there was a yard full of older machines that I assumed had been traded in at some time for newer ones. I was beginning to wonder what Harry was planning when he stopped alongside a David Brown tractor fitted with a cab.

'What do you reckon to this one?' he asked.

I looked more closely. It was the same model we already had but, with the shiny unscratched red and yellow paintwork it was probably newer.

'Climb up and have a look inside,' Harry said. 'And you don't have to crawl in through the back, this one has a door at the front.'

I opened the door, reached up for the steering wheel and climbed in. Once seated, I looked around and noticed the canvas cover and cladding which must surely be less noisy than the metal sheeting in the Fergie cab. There were also the floor panels which would go some way towards stopping the draughts.

Harry opened the door. 'Pretty good eh?'

'Very good,' I said. 'Is it identical to the one we have at home?'

'Just about. It's done a lot less hours and there are one or two changes to the load sensing system, but not a lot.'

'Are you thinking of having it?'

'I thought I'd trade the Fordson in for it, if you agree.'

'But won't you won't miss the Fordson?'

'No, not really. She's been with me a long time but I think it's about time she moved on.'

'I think it would suit us very well having two tractors of a similar build, and don't forget the two-stage clutch for the power take off and the gearbox.'

'My thoughts too. Let's go and have a few words with the man, then.'

The new tractor was not due to arrive for five days to allow time for it to be checked over and serviced by the dealer, which meant I had a few days ploughing to look forward to in falling temperatures and in an icy north wind.

'Did they give you any tuition with the plough at college?' Harry asked.

'A little, mainly about plough adjustments and that sort of thing; not a lot on setting out and finishing though.'

Harry reached into his pocket and pulled out a book. 'Well, if that's all you did, you'll probably find this helpful,' he said.

'The beginners guide to ploughing – making it brown without tears,' I read off the front cover before opening it up and scanning through a few pages. 'This looks to be just what I need,' I said. 'Thanks Harry, that's very thoughtful.'

'I'm only thinking of the memorable finish you made in the Forty Acre which was more of a deep ditch and it still carries water down it you could float a barge in.'

'Yes, you've mentioned it before; several times. Well, I hope I can do better than that now.'

'You mean even deeper?'

I laughed. 'No, not if I can help it.'

It was after lunch before I could take the plough down to Forty Acres. By the time we had arrived back from the dealer there was only time to make the engine oil change Harry had asked me to do, and there were still the plough shares to change.

Even so, I was looking forward to setting out the first land with the two-furrow Ransome plough. I had the marking poles tied in a bundle and secured to the plough and I had the book which was going to tell me how I should do things properly.

CHAPTER TWENTY-SEVEN

Ploughing

I WAS NOT LONG DISCOVERING that words, diagrams and the occasional picture in a book about ploughing were not that easy to follow and, at one stage, I even began to wonder whether I was looking at one of Harry's jokes.

The first run I made, according to the instructions given, was meant to be shallow with just the rear mouldboard turning over a "suggestion" of a furrow. The return run was with the two mouldboards and would be deeper to turn over the ground beneath the small amount of soil turned over on the first run and then the third run would place a turned furrow on top of that.

The trouble was I couldn't seem to work out where the tractor should run to achieve all this. According to the picture of the completed opening, there should have been four furrows but I only had three, and I didn't know why or where I had lost one.

Not that such divergence from the correct way of ploughing seemed to bother the seagulls which had suddenly appeared from nowhere. An extra furrow here and there meant more worms to devour and they set about it with some gusto, flying as close as they could to the mouldboards as the soil was turned over to reveal the worms.

And while I was looking at these pearly white flying machines I remembered Harry telling me there was a world of difference between match ploughing and what he called commercial ploughing – like taking an hour longer on the opening – and I didn't feel quite so annoyed. I also realised that once ground had been ploughed, it couldn't be unploughed and remained there for all to see; you only have one chance to do it the right way.

Well, be that as it may, I ploughed on and by the end of the second day, like it or not, the time was approaching when two ploughed lands were coming together and the all-important 'finish' needed to be made. It was time to stop brooding about the opening and to concentrate on creating a good finish.

I parked up on the headland and reached for the book to search for advice. Page sixty-eight explained that, some time ago, I should have been measuring the distance between the ploughed lands to ensure that when they finally met, they would be parallel and of a distance that was a multiple of the ploughing width, plus one furrow, and straight.

Of the three, I think I was pretty close on being parallel, in that, while there was some convergence, both furrows where definitely heading for the same hedge and it wasn't wildly off the mark. But as for distance between lands, I had no idea and straightness was something that had deteriorated with the day, despite my efforts to prevent it happening.

For all this, I shut the book and chose what I thought to be the straighter furrow to work off and then shallowed the plough so it was only turning about four inches of soil to leave a shallow furrow. And then I kept on ploughing the other side, running along the headland to plough back on the other side of the land.

It was then I noticed Harry driving down Piggy Hill and I thought that if there was ever a time when I wanted to be alone, this was it and not to have Harry making comments on my work. But there was no preventing his arrival and it was not long before I saw him driving along the headland, looking out of the window at my work before turning around and drawing to a halt a few yards away from where I was ploughing.

'How's it going, boy?'

'Not so bad.' I stepped down from the tractor and walked over to the Land Rover. 'Just finishing off these two lands and then I'll be setting another one out,' I said.

Harry climbed out and started to walk along the headland until he came to the finish zone I was still working on.

'Not bad,' he said. 'Good to see you've shallowed this one up and you've avoided the temptation to make another ditch. What are you going to do now?'

'Plough down until my offside wheel drops into the shallow furrow and lift the plough up and lower it down again when the offside wheel isn't close enough to be in the furrow. And then, having ploughed back up the field on the other side of the land, I'll set the plough to run shallow and plough down with the off side wheel in the shallow furrow which should, according to page seventy three, I held the book up, leave me a single furrow width of unploughed land to plough out on the next run. And that will be the finish.'

Harry nodded and grunted his approval. 'Sounds as if it could work but keep it shallow,' he said. 'I'll just go and have a look at the sheep in Long Meadow and I'll be back to see how it finishes up.'

No pressure then, I thought as I set about doing what I had just explained. And at the end of it all, I have to say, it wasn't too bad. Not over straight and perhaps a little deep in places, but all the ground had been turned over which, at the end of the day, is the object of the exercise.

By the time Harry returned I was marking out the next land using the poles and trying to get them lined up so I could make an arrow straight mark with the plough; get this one wrong and you have bends which become gradually worse with every pass of the plough. It is the little tweaks, grabbing or losing the odd inch where it is required, that helps to keep a furrow straight, it says on page ninety-one.

'Not bad, boy. Not bad at all,' Harry said when we stopped and wandered over to take a look at my finish. 'Keep that up and you should be alright.'

And then he drove off leaving me to it: a two-furrow plough, forty acres and a thousand seagulls.

The new tractor arrived on the back of a lorry a few days later and, with the ramps lowered the tractor was rolled off to meet its new home.

'She looks very smart,' I said to Harry.

'Not for long I shouldn't wonder,' he replied. He turned to the delivery driver. 'Is it all serviced and ready to go?'

'As far as I know it is,' he replied. 'But if you really want to be sure you could always ring the yard and they'll tell you.'

Harry reached along the side of the tractor chassis and pulled out the dipstick. 'Oil looks clean, it's up to the right level and the filter looks new, so we'll assume it has been serviced,' he said.

The delivery driver held out his clip board for a signature: 'Just to say I dropped it off at the right farm,' he said, tearing off the top copy for Harry to keep. 'Now all I need is a Fordson tractor to take back with me.'

I gave the new arrival a once over while Harry set about driving his Fordson out of the shed and then up the ramps onto the lorry. He was driving it for the last time and I wondered if he was feeling cut up about it.

'All things have their day, whether it be cow, tractor or man,' he had told me; stalwart words they might have been, but I noted the sad look in his eye as he watched the driver raise the ramps and prepare to drive out of the yard.

'Well, there she is, boy,' he said when he strolled over to inspect the new tractor. 'After breakfast you can put the plough on her and give her a go.'

'Isn't there an owner's manual or something?' I asked.

Harry lifted the lid of the tool box and removed it, tapping the side of his nose in a knowing sort of way. 'Always in the tool box or under the seat,' he said. 'Never fails.'

I took it from him and wandered down to the house for a read while we had breakfast. Alice had the bowls of cereal on the table and the joint of boiled bacon was waiting to be carved.

'You're both a little late this morning,' she said. 'Is everything alright?'

'John's new tractor has just arrived,' Harry said.

'And I couldn't pull him away from it.'

'You boys and your toys,' scoffed Alice. 'If it's shiny, powerful and makes a lot of noise, you just have to be there.'

'That's about it,' Harry replied, tucking into his cereal. 'Have you discovered how the hydraulic sensing works, boy?'

'Well, I've found the page but, to be honest, I've yet to understand a word of it; something about the top link and a wire cable.'

'Well that all seems pretty straight forward,' he said. 'No bother there.'

I looked up at him and smiled. 'It will be interesting to see how it works.'

'A bit different from when we had horses to plough with. Those boxes up the side of the yard we now use for calves, used to be full of horses and most of them spent the winter and early spring with a plough behind them, working six days a week.'

'What happened on the seventh?'

'That was Sunday and my father wouldn't have any field work done on the Sabbath even if we were haymaking and it was the first dry day in weeks. The plough horses had the day off and come Monday, many of them were lame because they had stood about all day with no exercise after six days of hard ploughing. The vets called it the Monday morning disease.

'I was too young to actually plough but I used to go down to the fields with the men and they'd let me sit on the horses. When it was really cold, they put clay drain pipes on each of the plough handles when they went home to keep the snow off, but they were some tough men; walking all day behind a couple of horses

302

handling the plough wasn't that easy.'

'How many acres did they manage to do in a day?' I asked.

'If it was light land, like our top fields, a couple of horses could get over about an acre and a half but it would be down to one acre or even less on the heavier clay soils,' Harry explained. 'A lot depended on the horses and how they were and how they felt. They had good days and not so good days like the rest of us and if the mares were in season and horsing about, the only way to sort them out was to grab a handful of nettles and stick them under their tails.'

I winced at the thought. 'Yes, well, perhaps it's just as well we now have tractors,' I said.

'That's right, boy. Now we just sit on wet seats all the time.'

'Not any more, now we have a cab to keep the rain off.'

With the plough hitched up, the wire cable attached to the top link and the operator's manual in the tool box, I set off down to the field. Strangely, I had felt rather guilty, when I took the plough off the tractor I had spent so many hours on, and when I parked her under the barn, it seemed I was pensioning her off so she could make way for younger blood.

There was the usual frost lying on the ground and, as I drove along the headland, I rather hoped the wind would strengthen so I could, for the first time, watch it all happen while cocooned in a cab, rather than having to ward off an icy wind seeking out every gap between the buttons on my coat, numbing my fingers and deadening my toes.

When I hitched the plough on to the tractor, I had

altered the settings so, after a few yards, I had to stop and alter the length of the top link and adjust the heights of the linkage arms. It took a few stops and starts before I felt I had things about right, but as Harry had said, it was so easy to keep tweaking things and end up making them worse, rather than better.

But it wasn't just the plough I was trying to sort out. There were the hydraulics and, miraculously, after pulling and pushing a few levers, the traction improved noticeably and while I still didn't fully understand how it was doing it, we were travelling well. So I left well alone.

Lined up at the start of the furrow, I lowered the plough and the shares slid into the ground, lifting the soil on to the long sloping mouldboards which, with the aid of the skimmers, inverted it and buried all that remained of last year's crop.

I settled down in the cab and noticed that the seagulls had joined me and were, as usual, squabbling around the plough, fighting to be the first to get the worms as they arrived on the surface. And for the first time when I was ploughing, I wasn't dreading the moment when a gull would decide to empty its bowels on top of me.

'You can shit all you want,' I screamed at them.

Having said that, the back of the cab was wide open and it would only want a following wind and I could be in trouble again. Without stopping, I had a cursory look at how the rear canvass cover could be unrolled and secured.

Compared to the cab on the Grey Fergie, this cab was a mega improvement. There was more room, it had a door, it was quieter and it was less claustrophobic. All I longed for now was a force ten gale, sub-zero temperatures and a blizzard.

It took until lunchtime for my wish to come partially true and it certainly wasn't as extreme as I had hoped for. It was windy, yes, but my two remaining wants were sadly denied me. Instead, there was a heavy shower of rain which almost made up for it as I heard the rain peppering down on the outside of the cab.

And to think, that without the cab, I would have either been trying to find shelter under a tree or driving pell-mell back to the farm; either way I would have been drenched. All of which was very satisfying but I was rather disappointed to note that no one had thought to fit a windscreen wiper, perhaps that was only available for the deluxe version, should there be one.

I stopped on the headland and, as the rain hammered down and the gulls stopped flying, I set about devouring a boiled bacon sandwich and swigging cold tea from a bottle: some things change and some never do. I also took the time to continue reading through the operator's manual which had been joined in the tool box by Harry's 'How to Plough' booklet.

After about thirty minutes reading through both of them, and learning nothing I considered to be of any major interest, I put them under the seat cushion and restarted the engine.

I was amazed how conditions had changed since I stopped. The rain had made the field surface greasy and the only grip to be had was from the wheel running in the furrow, and even that was skiddy. I pressed the differential lock pedal to prevent the land wheel from spinning and clawed my way down the field.

It was just the same when I started back up on the

other side of the land, but when I returned to the top of the downside again, the furrow wheel was working in dryer soil and the grip improved. The lesson learned was that, when ploughing in rain, it was best to keep going and don't allow the open furrow time to get too wet.

Eventually though, as the rain continued to fall, conditions became too difficult and it was showing in the ploughing which was not turning over and burying as well as it should have, and the going was becoming impossible.

So, at about half past three, I picked up my marking poles and headed for the farm. There would be another day. The weather had been grim, but for once, I had stayed dry.

CHAPTER TWENTY-EIGHT

Strip grazing the kale

'YOU HAVEN''T forgotten this evening is when you take Pedro to the nativity play, have you?' Harry asked when he walked into the dairy as I was preparing to take the churns down to the street.

'No, I've had it marked on the calendar ever since the vicar called,' I said, while trying to gauge how many gallons there were in a churn I was looking down into. There were indentations on the outside of the churn which marked the number of gallons and, by looking into the churn at the milk it was possible to put a finger on the outside at the same level.

'Oh, that's good then. I think it starts at about seven, so you need to be there by about quarter to.'

'Could be milking a bit early then. I'll need to have a bath and all that, and I think Alice said she was looking out some shepherd's clothes for me.'

'That's the spirit, boy. You have to look the part.'

'If I must,' I said. I loaded the churns onto the trolley and set off down the slope. Miserable Old Sod was waiting for me and ever since the kindness he showed me when I had bruised my shoulder, I'd tried to have the churns down to him in good time.

'Slipping into bad ways again, I see,' he said.

'Yes, sorry about that. What did you say your name was?'

'I didn't but if you need to know, it's George.'

I loaded the empty churns onto the trolley and started off up the slope. 'See you tomorrow, George,' I said.

'How big a speaking part have they given you?' asked Harry, placing a second slice of boiled bacon onto my plate.

'I haven't any words to say at all,' I replied. 'All I have to do is hold Pedro and look like a shepherd.'

'That's no good. You want to build your part up a bit; you know, make it your own. Surely you can think of something to say - you don't know who might be watching.'

'And what do you suggest?'

'Well, how about: 'It's a clear night tonight. Good for a bit of star gazing,' or even, 'Pedro and I have walked miles today and we're just fair worn out.'

'Not really show stoppers are they?'

'No not yet but we need to work on it. Alice, help the boy out with some ideas.'

'I should think John will have more than enough to do just standing there holding Pedro without having to make a speech, or whatever,' she said.

'Oh, I don't know. It's a good opportunity and it would be a pity to miss it. How about a few, "Fear not for mighty dreads", or give them the "I had a dream" speech. That was by Churchill, so it's bound to go down well.

'I think you'll find it was by Martin Luther King

308

when he was campaigning for civil rights in America,' I said. 'Doesn't sound too Christmassy to me.'

'No, perhaps not, but there must be others that would fit the bill.'

'Such as?'

Harry paused and thought about it. 'How about, "We chose to go to the moon". That one would floor them. Old Lynden Johnson knew how to tell them.'

'I think that one may just be getting closer to Christmas, but you should know it was a speech made by John Kennedy before he was assassinated.' I said.

'Well, it would have been,' Alice said.

'Would have been what?' Harry asked.

'Made before he was assassinated.'

'I would have thought that would have gone without saying. Anyway, boy, you have a think about it. We'll try and be there to support you. How about, "This lady's not for turning?" or even "One small step for man…".'

After breakfast, I walked up the yard. It was time to move the electric fence in the kale field and, after the episode with the concealed hole, I was cautious about taking a tractor anywhere near the field, let alone, along the headland.

My plan was to put up the second fence before taking the first one down and it was a plan which would probably have succeeded better if I hadn't let the cows through to the kale. I had to say, they had made a good job of clearing most of it and there were only the short woody stalks and a few leaves remaining where they had been grazing.

Their eyes were now set on the beautiful lush, untouched crop that awaited them behind the single strand of electrified wire and I knew I needed to get the second fence up as quickly as I could. The thought of having to round up a herd of cows rampaging through a crop of kale did not appeal.

It was a good job we'd taken the time to cut down another two rows and leave a clear run for the wire and, after I fixed one end to a straining stake next to the hedge I set off with the wire, the winder spinning around so fast I had to keep my hand on it to brake it whenever I slowed down.

Two hundred yards later, I arrived at the far hedge and looked back expecting to see the cows. There weren't any but that was not to say they weren't on their way. I tensioned up the wire and secured the winder to the hedge before running back to the other side of the field to grab as many stakes as I could carry and push them into the ground at fifteen-stride intervals.

And then came the big moment; the removal of the fencing unit from the first fence along with its battery and then hooking it up to the fence I had just put up. I wondered if the cows would realise I had disconnected it and then start to push the wire down. Were they that astute? I would soon find out.

I paused for a few seconds to get my breath back and then lifted the lid of the unit and switched it off. The lead attached to the fencing wire was disconnected and I picked up the unit and the battery and headed through the kale to the new fence.

It was then I heard the crashing noise as forty-four hungry girls discovered they could lean over the wire and not receive an electric shock. And they didn't just lean, they pushed until the wire was down and they could step over it.

All of a sudden, ten yards seemed to be a long way

to go and I felt sure the cows would make it to the wire before I had a chance to connect the unit up. I clipped the lead onto the wire, pushed the fencer's stand into the ground and, having checked the battery connections, lifted the lid and switched it on.

Nothing.

It wasn't clicking and I dared myself to touch the wire and there was not a hint of anything. Check the battery terminals, check the lead, check the switch. Yes, the switch. It had felt a bit loose when I turned the unit off so I gave it a few toggles off and on and then I heard a click and the unit became live and working.

Grabbing a long stalk, the longest I could find, I pulled off the leaves and then held it at one end while I lowered the other onto the wire. And received a belter of a shock for my trouble, just like the last time. I was beginning to think Harry had brought down a stalk he had dried out somewhere. But hey, the fence was working and the cows were still the right side of it. All I needed to do now was collect the stakes and wind up the wire of the first fence.

'Do we have a spare battery?' I asked Harry when I made it back into the yard.

'How did it go, boy? You managed to sort them out?'

'Yes, but next time I'll close the gate to keep them out before I start to put up another fence and move the unit. They were within a yard of breaking through at one point and I swear they know when there's any electricity flowing through the wire because as soon as I disconnected it, they were pushing on it and treading it down.'

'They're some clever girls,' Harry said. 'But yes,

311

there is a spare battery but it probably needs charging and, if I remember right, it doesn't hold its charge too well.'

'Would it be better to get a new one?' I asked, thinking again how difficult it would be to remove cows from a field of Marrow Stem kale they were very keen to stay in.

'You can get one if you want. The dealer should have some in stock, and while you're there take a look at the trailers. It's about time we had a trailer we can empty by tipping rather than forking or shovelling everything off.'

I went into the dairy to give my boots a wash down with the hose and as I scraped, brushed and swilled them clean, Elizabeth walked in.

'Elizabeth! Where did you come from?' I dropped the hose I was holding and opened my arms.

'Hello, John,' she replied, as I wrapped my arms around her. 'Harry said you wouldn't be long.'

'Yes, but I thought you were back home on Tuesday,'

'Well take a guess at what day it is today.'

'Tuesday?' I offered.

She smiled and nodded her head. 'Right on. Now give me that kiss you always promise me in your letters.'

Elizabeth climbed into my pick-up and we drove into town to purchase the fencing battery and it felt so good to be together again.

'How was the stay with your friend?' I asked.

'It was very good. She lives near Kendal in the Lake District and it was the first time I had seen the mountains and the lakes, they were fantastic and I'd I think you would have been impressed with them too. Mind you, it's a bit bleak at this time of the year.'

'We'll have to see if we can make it there sometime,' I said. 'When's the best time of the year?'

'Christine, that's my friend, says spring time when everything is still fresh and perfect and there's thousands of daffodils everywhere, but it's a good place to be at any time of the year.'

'Oh right. Perhaps we should plan to go when you're back at Easter.'

'That would be terrific if we could. We may be able to stay at Christine's place.'

We made our way through the town's traffic and headed for the cattle market, Singleton Jones' yard, was just opposite and we parked in their yard.

'Have you been here before?' I asked her.

'Not for a few years. I think we used to come here with dad but I don't really remember much about it.'

We made our way into the show room and began to walk through the machinery display.

'They've some interesting pieces of machinery in here,' Elizabeth said, stopping by a large, red piece of kit with strange wheels. 'What's that one do?'

'That is a potato harvester,' I said.

'And how do you know that, clever clogs?'

'Because I just read what it says on the label.'

I weathered the dig into my ribs and we walked on until we arrived at the counter.

'You're not looking to test another electric fencer on my measure, are you?' asked Chris, pointing to the long brass rule that was fixed to the counter and ran from one end to the other.

'No, not this time,' I replied. 'I've just come for a battery we can run one off.'

313

'Well that's a relief,' he said. 'I'm still a bit wary of being anywhere near it, let alone touching it. I'll fetch you a fencing battery from the store. Won't be long.'

I turned to Elizabeth. 'Harry also wanted me to have a look at the trailers, those that can tip loads off using a hydraulic ram.'

'What's a hydraulic ram?' she asked. 'Is it something to do with sheep?'

I laughed. 'No, it's a cylinder into which oil is pumped and that forces out a piston to push the trailer body up,' I explained.

'Oh, right.'

'Do you do grain tanks for trailers?' I asked Chris when he returned to the counter.

'What, ones you can fix on the flat bed and can take off after harvest?'

'Yes, that sort of thing. A tank which could hold about three or four tonnes.'

Chris reached for one of his catalogues and thumbed through it. 'There's one here which looks as if it could be the sort of thing you're looking for,' he said, twisting the book round so I could see it.

'What's its capacity?'

He looked closer. 'It says it will hold four tonnes of wheat, so it's about what you want.'

'Well if you could give me a leaflet or whatever you have, we'll think about it,' I said.

I signed the receipt for the battery and tucked my copy into my top pocket as I lifted it up.

'What do you want to do now?' I asked Elizabeth when we had made it back to the pick-up.

'It would be nice if you took me out for lunch but I think we should be heading home. Harry tells me you have your nativity thing in the church with Pedro this

314

evening and I should think you'll have to spend some time cleaning and grooming him.'

I sighed. The nativity thing with Pedro was looming as large as ever and, after the disaster at the harvest festival service, it was not something I was looking forward to, but Elizabeth was right, of course.

'We'll head for home then,' I said. 'Lunch will have to wait for another day.'

'Well we don't have to rush home. They say the reservoir looks very good at this time of the year, yet no one bothers to go there.'

'We'd better go and have a look then. I'll treat you to some fish and chips and we'll take them there. No point everyone missing it.'

CHJAPTER TWENTY-NINE

Pedro's nativity disaster

ELIZABETH HAD TO leave shortly after we arrived back to be with her family and Kate called round on her way back from town to pick her up. Before leaving though, she told me she would see me later in the church because everyone had decided to be there to see Pedro.

'It would be just too good to miss,' she said, and that made me feel a lot better.

I then set about smartening Pedro, a task which started with a good wash he seemed to enjoy, followed by a long session with towels to dry him, which he sort of tolerated. What he didn't like though, was all the combing and brushing I had to do to untangle his mane and try and make some sense of how his tail should look.

At the end of it all, when I had managed to paint some hoof oil on to make his feet glisten, I stepped back and looked at him. And I thought he looked good.

'Is that Pedro?' Harry asked as he looked over the gate. 'You've made a good job of that, boy.'

'Yes, he looks to be a new donkey,' I said.

'What are you going to do with him now? If you let him loose the first thing he'll be doing is having a good roll in something horrible and you'll be back to where you started.'

Harry had a point. Pedro had never been averse to enjoying a good leg kicking roll and I could just see him doing it now and all my work would be ruined.

'Probably best I put him in his stable,' I said.

'Yes, but I'd give him a bale of clean straw. At least if he has a roll then all you have to do is brush him down.'

I walked round to the pigs and grabbed one of their bales and carried it round to Pedro's stable. 'Now you make sure you keep yourself clean,' I told him as I pulled off the strings and shook it out to make a good deep bed and hopefully keep him out of anything dirty.

It was as I was shutting and bolting the door I noticed the look he gave me and at that moment I realised he knew where he was going and what he was planning to do when he got there. Worrying.

Although I was an hour earlier than normal, I went and fetched the girls in for the evening milking and they also knew what time it was and could see no good reason why they should come in so early.

Instead of them walking towards me, as they normally did when they spotted me, I was ignored and I had to walk round each of them to start them moving, which they eventually did. And with half an hour already wasted and the nativity service starting at seven o'clock, I would have to get a move on.

Matty and Thrifty must have thought it was one of those Sunday afternoons when I came down to the field early and settled down beside them to have a few words about the world and share some secrets. They were some enchanting moments for all of us and when I made to stand up, one of them would turn her head and give me a big leisurely lick.

'Come on ladies, I need to be finished early tonight, so if you wouldn't mind getting to your feet…' They looked at me before beginning to raise themselves off the ground.

Pauline and Horns, who I noticed appeared to be getting on with each other, were waiting for me at the gate when I succeeded in gathering them all together. Try as I might I just couldn't instil in any of them any sense of urgency and they drifted casually across the paddock towards the collecting yard as slowly as I've seen them go. Once they were in I raced down to the house to fetch a bucket of warm water along with a clean udder cloth and while I was filling it I noticed some clothes Alice had looked out for me – the shepherd's uniform – were on the back of a chair.

Back at the milking bail, I pushed my way through the girls, slid the bucket under the gate and went round to start the engine. And, with that barking away, I returned to the front of the bail and dropped a scoop of barley meal into each of the four feeder boxes before opening the gate to let the first cows in.

At about half past six, when I still had a dozen cows to milk, Harry walked across the yard to me.

'You're pushing this a bit close, boy. You need to be there in less than fifteen minutes.' He looked round the yard at the remaining cows and shook his head. 'You'll never make it. You'd better go and get ready while I finish up here.'

Digging into my pockets I removed my watch and looked at it. Harry was right. At this rate I wasn't going to make it.

'Hell, is that the time?' I gasped.

'That's what I make it too, boy.'

I swore again and high-tailed it down to the orchard and was just about to open the gate when I saw Pedro tied up to the fence. At least that was one job out of the way.

'You've just about enough time to slip into these clothes and that's about all,' Alice said, pushing the shepherd's clothing into my arms.

'But I need a wash,' I said.

'Too late for that. You'll look like a shepherd and you'll smell like one. Just keep close the Pedro and no one will know.'

I tore off my jeans and pulled on the white floppy trousers which were several sizes too large for me around my waist but about six inches too short in the leg, and then I reached for the t-shirt with horizontal black and white stripes along with the red scarf.

'That looks good, just like a shepherd,' Alice said, passing me the hat, a round beret-like thing. 'Harry said you would.'

I was past caring and just pulled on a pair of trainers and ran out towards the orchard, untied Pedro and headed off down to the street.

'Good luck, John,' shouted Alice, from the kitchen.

I waved my reply and when we had made it down to the street we made a right turn and then after a hundred yards another right turn took us up to the church.

'Come on Pedro. Let's just get this over with and then we can forget all about it,' I told him. 'Just be yourself and relax and enjoy. We won't be in there for very long and everyone thinks you're wonderful, just like I do.'

The organ was playing softly when I walked in through the door at the back of the church; a hint of a Christmas carol perhaps, but not one I recognised. The pews were full though and there was a lot of talking as everyone waited for the nativity service to begin.

'You're late,' said a man sitting on the end of a pew nearest the door. 'But don't worry, we wouldn't have started without you, what with most of us having come just to see the donkey and see what he gets up to this time.'

I ignored him and looked a little further up the aisle and noticed people were now turning around to have a look at us. And among them I spotted Elizabeth, who made a little wave at me, as did Kate and her two younger daughters.

As we walked along the back of the church towards the central aisle, some of the congregation were pointing and making strange nasal sounds and then I realised for the first time that Harry had given me clothes which were closer to resembling a French onion seller than a biblical shepherd.

I could see the vicar beckoning me to make my way to the front and as we moved towards him, I kept a tight grip on Pedro. The last time we did this, he suddenly took off and grabbed a mouthful of carrots, scaring everyone witless with his gnashing teeth.

But there was no food on offer this time, if you discounted the holly decorations and the candles, and we made it up to the front of the church without any incident. What was strange though, was the laughter that seemed to follow us as we made our way towards the vicar. It started as a ripple and then gradually became louder until, when we had reached the front and stopped in front of the vicar, it had become almost hysterical. And we hadn't done anything.

I looked round to see people wiping tears from their eyes and others, who were in the outer pews, were now leaning over to catch a sight of us and then also bursting into laughter. I smiled politely back at them and hoped they would soon quieten down.

Rev Simon Fanshaw held up his hands for quiet and it gradually simmered down until somebody shouted out particularly loudly and the laughter started all over again.

'What did he say?' I asked the vicar.

'I'm not sure but everyone seemed to enjoy it. Which is good, it's Christmas.'

'Beats me,' I shrugged. 'You'd better show me where you want us to stand.'

He gestured over to his left where there was a small cradle containing the infant Jesus half surrounded by a boy and a girl who must have been Mary and Joseph. Behind them were some shepherds, the three wise men and a few animal-like structures which may have been goats. Standing a few feet above them all, stood the Angel Gabriel with a halo that seemed to bounce about above her each time she moved her head, which was frequently, due to her having to balance on a narrow stool hidden beneath her gown. It all looked very Christmassy.

'What I suggest John, is you stand to one side of Gabriel; you'll see we've left a space for you and Pedro.'

As I walked over towards the chosen spot I heard the vicar snort and stifle a laugh behind me, but I ignored him and concentrated on getting Pedro lined up and facing the right way round. And he did it beautifully.

'What do you reckon so far, Pedro?' I whispered in one of his ears and I stroked his nose.

The vicar turned to his congregation and smiled at them. 'Let me welcome you all to our annual nativity service,' he started, pausing for the words to land. 'And, as many of you will have noticed, this year we're joined once more by Pedro the donkey and John, his carer who has so kindly offered his time to look after him during the service and, may I say, appears to have made a big effort to dress so appropriately for the part.

At which point there was another wave of laughter from the congregation which the vicar tried to subdue.

'Please everyone, thank you,' he said, holding his hands in the air. 'Thank you everyone, quiet please.'

Gradually the church quietened down but there was still a rumbling of talk and laughter.

'So, let's start proceedings by turning to hymn number twenty-one and we'll all join in to sing that wonderful nativity carol, Away in a Manger,' he said.

I have to say, I took no notice of the hissing noise to start with but when I heard it for about the third time I looked round and discovered it was the Angel Gabriel, who was trying to catch my attention.

With the organ now playing the introduction, I turned to her and asked her if she was alright.

'I just wanted to ask you what, "Hung like a donkey," meant,' she asked. 'And why are there two of them?'

I smiled at her. She was such a sweet girl and had clearly been chosen for her key role in the nativity scene because of her innocent appeal. 'Why would you ask that?' I asked, totally confused.

'Because on your back you have: "We're both hung

like donkeys", written in big yellow letters.'

'I've what!?' I said, suddenly fearing the worst.

'We're both hung like donkeys,' she repeated in a voice that carried at least as far as the second row, even though the singing had started. 'It's written in big yellow letters on your back.'

Harry, I thought. I looked out at the congregation to see if he was here, but I couldn't see him.

'Oh right,' I said. 'Never mind that now.'

'Yes, but what does it mean,' she insisted, stamping her foot while her halo bobbed violently up and down.

'Be careful or you'll fall down,' I said, and three more stamps of her foot later and that is what happened. The stool toppled over towards me and she followed, the sudden movement startling Pedro.

And then, shortly after, I caught a whiff of something pungent and knew it was Pedro who had decided he wasn't having a good time of it any more, what with girls collapsing onto him and the church organ bellowing out unfamiliar noises.

It all had a familiar feel about it and I wasn't sure which we were going to suffer first, noise, gas, liquid or solids – Pedro had them all in his armoury – and I resigned myself to experiencing them all.

As it happened, he chose noise, and as the last verse of 'Away in a Manger' faded away he struck out with a series of brays giving them all the power of a fog horn. People closest to us covered their ears with their hands and worried parents pulled their children to them and held them tightly to try and provide some acoustic protection.

Having brought his braying to a halt, there was a gushing sound behind me as Pedro emptied himself on the tiled floor, the liquid flowing and being channelled

323

towards the crib, where it splashed briefly against its side before carrying it a few yards across the stone floor and becoming grounded on one of the central heating grills. Thankfully, Mary and Joseph had stood up and headed for higher ground.

Meanwhile, the vicar was trying to establish some order. 'Thank you everyone, thank you,' he said, clapping his hands. 'Please, everyone, just settle down and we can continue with our service.'

'How do you follow that?' someone shouted out, causing another surge of laughter.

'Alright, alright, that will do.' The vicar paused until everyone was silent, and then started to speak. 'Well that was fun, wasn't it? But we should perhaps use it as an example of the hardships Mary, heavy with child, and Joseph had to endure when seeking somewhere safe to give birth to baby Jesus and we should be proud and thankful that, Pedro has been able to provide us with that experience, an insight which brings us closer to how life must have been at that time. And for that we should feel grateful. And now, with that in mind, let's move onto the second carol for this evening which is 'We will rock you'.

As the organist began to play, I could tell Pedro was not happy; far from it. His flatulence, always an indication of how nervous he was feeling, had returned with a vengeance, and those seated in the front few rows were now holding handkerchiefs to their noses.

But that was not all. As I held firmly onto his halter I heard the dull splat as Pedro lost control of his bowels, a sound which was soon accompanied by loud gasps and no small amount of cheering.

He then lunged forwards, taking at least half a dozen

steps before I could even begin to restrain him. Without pausing, he dipped his head into the crib, and rummaged about in it clearly confusing it for a feed trough. He then raised his head and what he was now holding between his teeth and swinging about made my nightmare complete.

I led him down the aisle towards the door and weathered the comments from the congregation which flowed out from all directions as 'We will rock you' played on.

'The best one yet, boy,' someone shouted, and there was a cheer of agreement. 'Encore!' chanted another group, and before I knew it, the whole congregation was on its feet clapping, stamping and cheering.

Someone opened the door for us and we slipped out into the night, just as the congregation had united to chant 'Pedro, Pedro, Pedro...'

CHAPTER THIRTY

Cutting the Christmas tree

'I HEAR THE nativity play went well,' Harry said, as he poured the tea.

'Pedro was on form, if that's what you mean,' I said. 'How did you hear about it?'

'Elizabeth rang up and gave us the news. She asked to speak to you but you had already gone to bed. Anyway, that's all out of the way for another year.'

'I should think it's out of the way for the next century.'

'Could be right, boy, but we'll see.'

Harry pushed a cup of tea over to me and set off down the corridor to take a cup up to Alice. I looked out of the window and noticed there were flakes of snow starting to fall; the first snow of winter had arrived.

'Time we sorted out a Christmas tree,' Harry said, when he returned. 'We'll take the chainsaw up to Barns Cover and see what we can find.'

'Sounds good,' I said, getting to my feet. 'Better be getting on with the milking first, and while I think about it, Sofia, the Ayrshire cross, is not far off calving, and I've put her in a box and strawed her down. If you could keep an eye on her when you're going that way that would be useful.'

'Will do, boy.'

Barns Cover was a small woodland of about five acres at the farthest point away from the farm and was right in the middle of nowhere. Who actually owned it was something of a mystery and it was strongly rumoured to have been planted by iron ore workers in the late eighteen hundreds, perhaps with the aim of providing fuel to help ignite the coal used in the production of calcined iron ore which took place nearby.

Since then, with the decline in iron ore mining, the trees had matured, and Harry had over the years planted new ones to replace those that had been either felled or simply rotted away, and among these younger trees was a row or two of spruce.

The snow, which had been gradually increasing, was now clinging to the windscreen and when we finally arrived at the gate into Barns Cover, it was verging on being a blizzard.

'That was further than I thought it would be,' I said.

'It's a good walk,' Harry said, staring out of the window. 'And the men who used to work down here had to do it every day and then spend ten hours filling train carriages with iron ore rocks by hand. It made old men of them.'

'I'm not surprised. It must have been a tough life.'

'Right, then,' Harry said. 'We'll be snowed in if we don't get a move on. Let's go and have us a Christmas tree.'

I reached into the back of the Land Rover, lifted out the chainsaw and then followed Harry into the wood.

'The spruce trees are all over on the other side,' he said, marching on. 'It's only about a hundred yards.'

It may have been only a hundred yards, but it was a hard hundred yards. With no paths it was a case of finding ways around fallen trees and branches, some of which whipped back into my face as Harry pushed them clear and then let go of them.

'Here we are,' he announced at last. 'The shorter, bushier trees are on the outside edge because, unlike those within the wood, they receive sunlight all the way down and don't have to keep pushing their tops out to get a share of it.'

'What are we going for then, shorter bushier or taller skinnier?'

'I think after the issue we had with the kitchen window the other year, we might be better with a shorter bushier job.'

Sharing the kitchen with a Christmas tree that was several yards away on the lawn had not gone down too well with Alice's perception of seasonal décor, although I thought at the time the branch going across the ceiling was quite attractive, once it had been decorated. But I would have to agree with her that its overall appearance had been marred by the leaded window frames which had broken when the tree toppled over towards the house, several of which were still hanging on it.

I followed Harry as he walked up the row of spruce trees, inspecting each one until he stopped by a particularly bushy example which was about twelve feet tall.

'Now that is a beauty,' he said. 'Get that sunk into the ground and it will make about ten feet and that should be just about right. Fire up the chainsaw, boy.'

I turned on the fuel, set a bit of choke and gave the chord a pull and very much to my surprise, it started;

misfiring at first until I turned the choke off and gave it some throttle but from then on it roared away like a good one.

That is until I had crawled under the lower branches and took up a rather uncomfortable position so I could cut the tree off at its base, because that is when the chainsaw stopped.

'Pass it out here, boy,' Harry said. 'I'll have her re-started in no time at all, now she's already had a run.'

Well, he tried but after what must have been getting on for a hundred pulls of the starting cord, during which he had made various adjustments to the carburettor, he finally admitted defeat.

'It would be quicker if we used the bow saw,' he said. 'Stay there, I'll fetch it.'

'Might be an idea to bring the Land Rover round to this side as well,' I said.

I listened as Harry made his way back through the undergrowth and, for something to do, I picked up the chainsaw, flicked the 'on' switch and gave the rope a tug and away it went. This time I made sure I kept it running while I made my way back into a cutting position and, having taken out a small 'V' section to help it decide which way to fall, continued to cut until I felt it was set to topple and then scrambled out.

The tree thought about it for a moment and then slowly fell onto its side. It wasn't a giant Canadian Redwood but it was still a tree and I felt a sense of accomplishment.

'So you managed to get the chainsaw going, then,' Harry said when he drew up with the Land Rover. 'You'd better let me in on the secret.'

'Well it's all about having the right clothes, you know, a t-shirt with black and white horizontal stripes, baggy white trousers, red scarf and a black beret. Oh, and don't forget to have something memorable written on the back in big yellow letters like, let me see, 'We're both hung like donkeys'. How does that sound as suitable attire for a nativity church service?'

'Sounds as though Alice gave you the wrong clothes,' he said. 'Those are the ones Sam Jones and I wore when I was best man at his stag do. We went to Paris and had a mega session. I wonder how that happened?'

He started to laugh. 'Bet that went down well. I wish I'd been there now. What did the vicar say?'

'Nothing but I did hear him stifle a laugh at one point.'

'Anyway, enough of that, how did you start the chainsaw?'

'I switched it on,' I said.

'You mean it has a switch?'

I nodded. 'It's on the back, near the handle,'

Together, we dragged and rolled the spruce tree out towards the Land Rover and then, having stood it up, reversed under it and lowered it onto the roof so the branches pointed backwards.

'Good job we're not going on the road,' Harry said as we tied it on. 'As it is, you'll have to help me see where I'm going, what with the snow as well.'

The snow had now completely covered the tracks we had made coming down, and with visibility severely impaired by branches almost covering the windscreen, Harry drove alongside the fence which led to the bridge we needed to cross in the corner. Soon though, we were on our way up Piggy Hill and then on the track which would take us back to the farm buildings.

'Can't you just be normal, for once in your life,'

Alice said when she caught sight of the tree we had brought up. 'I mean, a little three-footer in a bucket in the corner of the front room would have been more than enough. Where are you going to put that?'

'We'll find a home for it. Anyway, you owe John an apology. You gave him the wrong clothes to wear last night; the ones I wore for Sam's stag do in Paris.'

'Not the ones that had the black and white stripes...' she held her hand up to her mouth and gasped. 'But they had something terrible written on the back. John, I'm so sorry. I found them in the cupboard when I was looking for something you could use as a shepherd and I brought them down to wash. And what with the rush you were in... I'm just so sorry. Look, I'll go and explain everything to the vicar.'

'Oh, there's no need for that,' I said. 'It gave everyone something to laugh about, not that they were short of things on that score with Pedro up to his usual tricks.'

Alice came over to me and gave me a hug. 'Only if you're sure, John.'

'I'm sure, 'I said. 'Don't worry about it.'

'Right then,' Harry said. 'If we all still love each other, we'll get this tree off and planted in the hole I dug for the big one last time, and it should be just about here.' He stamped his boot on a patch in the middle of the lawn and was met with a hollow sound. 'Told you so,' he said.

Christmas Eve, and Alice spent her day baking dozens of mince pies, sausage rolls and other assorted cakes and other delicious sweet things I really didn't recognise. The mistake she made was to leave them out on the table to let them cool and it became almost routine to sample some of the goodies whenever I came into the kitchen. We also had strict instructions to keep all cats and dogs out, so it was difficult to blame them for the missing items.

Harry had worked hard to set the tree up on the small piece of lawn outside the kitchen window, and then lather it with lights to the extent that when they were switched on, the television picture shrunk and the house lights dimmed. He had now taken himself off into the workshop to finish making Alice's Christmas present.

When a few days ago I had wandered in there to see what he was making he became very secretive but I could see it involved bicycle wheels and a lot of welding.

For my part, I had spent a couple of days placing feed around the farm so that, come the big day, there would only be the minimum amount of work to do. Sofia had calved a few days ago and now, looking at the calendar pinned to the dairy wall, I saw Thrifty was due to calve in the next day or two and, looking at the size of her, I felt sure it wouldn't be any later.

There were still a few days grazing left in the kale, but even so, I spent an hour or two cutting a gap in which to erect the second fence. Have to say, I was well pleased with the way the strip grazing had worked and apart from the first time I tried to move it with the cows in the field, it had all gone very well. Better still, the kale they were eating had helped to maintain milk yields and reduce their dependence on hay.

Harry reported the ewes were looking well and he was taking them down some ground barley to keep them in good condition. He also said he was pleased with the way the new raddle harnesses had worked and the ease with which he could change the crayon colour.

I went down to the bottom of Piggy Hill with Harry to see how he put out the barley for the sheep, just in case he was otherwise engaged at any time over the Christmas period. It was at this time I discovered that sheep aren't always the placid, timid animals most would believe them to be.

Before I had even lifted the bag out of the back of the Land Rover I was being jostled by the ewes and with their heads at groin height I proceeded with some care. I emptied the first bag in a line across the field and then it occurred to me it was possible to spell a name out in sheep depending on where the barley was placed.

So, with the second bag I moved quickly dropping a small pile of barley in a pattern I hoped was spelling out 'Elizabeth' but I ran out of feed before I could finish the 'b', which was a shame but when I looked back at them I thought it was a promising attempt.

'Something on your mind, boy?' Harry asked, when he returned from feeding the ewes in Long Meadow, and cast his eye over the ewes I had just fed.

'No, just thought the ewes might appreciate a bit of variety when they were fed.'

'Well, if you'll take my advice, you'll feed them in a straight line. That way you have a chance to count them and make sure they are all here and that they each still have four legs.'

It was a valid point but I thought it had been worth a try.

'Mind you,' he continued, 'Sam Jones had a bust up with one of his tractor drivers who then filled the sprayer with Gramoxone and used it to spray: "Sam sucks", right across the middle of a field of wheat.'

'That must have gone down well,' I said.

'Wouldn't have been so bad if the bloke could have used the correct spelling.'

Later that afternoon, Harry invited me into the workshop and unveiled Alice's Christmas present. Pulling a sheet off a strange looking shape which gave no clue as to what was beneath it, revealed a tandem bicycle.

'What do you reckon to that?' he asked.

I moved closer to it and told him I liked his use of scaffolding tubing for the main frame and that the inch-wide chain, something akin to the main drive on the combine harvester, would last for years. Complete with bicycle wheels, a couple of tractor seats with hay cushions and everything finished in Fordson blue, it looked interesting.

'Fancy a go?' he asked. 'We could take it along the top road for a short ride while Alice is still cooking in the kitchen.'

Not waiting for my reply he pushed his creation out of the workshop into the yard. 'See how well she moves?' he said. 'Hardly needs any effort at all to get her going.'

I refrained from pointing out that the tandem was on the slope out of the workshop and would probably have rolled out on its own anyway, and helped Harry push it to the top of the yard and onto the top road.

'All aboard,' he said when we had reached the other side of the cattle grid. Harry clambered into the front seat and I sat down on the rear one and instantly felt a sharp pain.

'Bloody hell, Harry. You could have found some

hay without thistles in it.' I turned the cushion over and tried again. 'Anyway, who has the brakes?'

'I've got them up here,' he said. 'Two on the handle bars as you would expect, and a third on the crossbar.' He pointed to a lever lying flat against the tubing between his legs. 'All set? Right let's go.'

I pressed down on one of the pedals and we began to move and before long, after a number of gear changes, we were tanking along towards the junction with the main road.

'Do you think you should try the brakes?' I shouted.

'I am trying them,' he replied.

I looked over his shoulder and saw him squeezing the brake levers to the point his knuckles had turned white.

'I don't think we're going to stop,' he cried.

'Try the third brake,' I shouted.

'That's only for emergencies.'

'And this isn't one?'

I saw Harry move his right arm and pull the lever attached to the crossbar.

'Brace yourself,' he shouted.

There was a rattling of chains and, out of the corner of my eye, I saw a wooden block fall in front of a rear wheel and I just knew this was going to be a violent stop and there was nothing for me to hold on to.

Sparks shot out from the wheels when they locked up and we veered off to the left, the front wheel impacting with the curb as we hurtled over the ditch and headed for the drystone wall.

As Harry pointed out later, when we were dragging the remains of his tandem back along the top road towards the farm: 'It could have been worse, boy.'

I couldn't disagree. That we were both still able to

walk and talk gave some weight to this sentiment but the same could not be said for the tandem. The rear wheel had suffered the most damage when it had hit the wooden block and chain braking system. Not only had it buckled but had taken on a sort of oval shape. The front forks must have been bent when the front wheel hit the curb but as for the rest of it, the scaffolding tubes looked totally unscathed.

'Good job we had the third brake or we could have ended up under a lorry,' Harry said.

'Pity we didn't have any other brakes that worked,' I said.

'I'll soon have them fixed. All we need is a couple of wheels and we'll be back in business.'

'Well you only have today if the present is going to be ready for Christmas Day,' I said. 'I think I'll go and make a start with the milking; it's the midnight carol service tonight.'

'How's the Angus cross doing?' Harry asked.

'Thrifty? Still no sign of a calf. I'll have a look at her when I fetch them in.'

I hadn't discussed it with Harry but I was becoming increasingly concerned about Thrifty. She didn't seem interested in anything anymore and while she tolerated those moments when I made a big fuss of her, I had the feeling she wasn't really enjoying them. And now, as she was close to calving, her whole attitude appeared to have changed to one of sadness and apathy on a major scale. I just hoped she would be back to how she was after she had calved.

CHAPTER THIRTY-ONE

Close call for Thrifty

THIS EVENING WHEN I brought the girls in for milking, Thrifty lagged behind and I was almost tempted to leave her where she was. There seemed little point in her walking all the way into the collecting yard just for a scoopful of barley meal, but I thought it might be for the best if I had a closer look at her.

'Come on special lady,' I encouraged her when she was halfway across the paddock. 'Just a little further.'

As I closed the gate behind her and I could see she was panting from her exertions and was far from happy, so before I started milking, I slipped down to the workshop to find Harry.

'I'm worried about Thrifty,' I said. 'She's made it into the collecting yard, but I really think she should be somewhere we can keep a better eye on her. I'd hate her to go down in the yard.'

Harry stopped what he was doing and found a bit of rag to wipe his hands on. 'Let's go and see what's for the best,' he said, and started off up the yard.

'Well, you're right, she's far from being herself,' Harry said, when we stood by Thrifty. He went round to the back of her and felt her bones. 'I'd say they've moved a bit, but not a lot.'

I looked at him seeking a solution. This was Thrifty, the girl who showed me so much love and made me so happy when I was with her. And now she was unwell and I was helpless to make her better.

'Probably the best thing to do would be to keep her in and I'll give the vet a call to see if they can offer any advice or even come over, if they think she needs it,' Harry said. 'You get on with the milking and I'll make the call and prepare a box for her with some fresh straw.'

We put Thrifty in one of the old stables and rigged up a couple of lights, running the wire from the workshop using the extension cable.

'The vet said he would try to get here as soon as he could,' Harry said as we looked over the door at her.

'Did he give any time?'

'No. I asked him but he couldn't give me one, he's tied up with another calving problem. Have you had any tea?'

'No, I haven't. I'll just keep her company for a bit and then I'll be down.'

Harry turned to go but only managed a couple of paces before he turned back. 'Looks like you have company,' he said.

'Elizabeth!' I put my arms out for here and she came to me and before I knew it the tears were pouring out of me. 'It's Thrifty.'

'Hey, it's alright,' she whispered. 'She'll be fine. Just you see.'

'But look at her, she's so unwell.'

'John, she's going to get better,' she said, firmly. 'Believe it, for her sake and listen; I can hear a car.'

And then a car drove into the yard and parked near where we were standing.

'Roy?' I said.

'Hi John. Sorry I took so long but I had a problem calving to sort out. And according to the message I received from Harry, there's another for me here. Let's have a look and see what we have. Oh, and who's this?' he asked looking at Elizabeth.

'Sorry Roy, I should have introduced you. This is Elizabeth, my fiancé.'

'Pleased to meet you, Elizabeth. Please stay if you want to; we might need some extra help.'

'I will,' replied Elizabeth, giving me a frown before leaning closer to me. 'You said you wouldn't say anything to anybody,' she whispered.

I unlatched the door to the stable and we walked in and Thrifty didn't even turn her head or twitch an ear while Roy examined her.

'We'll she's not very good. Her unborn calf is clearly presenting problems and that could be seriously bad news for both of them. I assume she's in calf to a Hereford?'

I nodded.

'What I'll do is have a root about inside her and see how the calf is lying. If, as I suspect, the calf is being presented incorrectly and I can't sort it out it might be better for her to have a caesarean.'

'Can you do one here?'

He had a look round. 'I should think so. A crush would have been better but I should think that's out of the question. But anyway, she seems very quiet so, let's not pre-empt things. Let me see what she has in there.'

He went back to his wagon to assemble the

equipment he needed while I stopped with Thrifty. 'This is it,' I told her. 'Just be brave and everything is going to be fine. And better still, there's a chance you'll have a big scar to show off to all the other girls.'

'Right then. Let's make a start,' Roy said, who had donned some rubber overalls and was now soaping his arm. 'Here we go then,' he said as he slipped his arm inside Thrifty and began to explore.

'Oh, that's interesting,' he said, eventually. 'Unless you have a calf with two heads, this young lady is carrying twins.'

'What?' I said. 'Twins? Are you sure?'

'As sure as I can be,' Roy said.

'Does that mean she'll need the caesarean?' Elizabeth asked.

'I think, bearing in mind the present health of the mother and the strain it would put on her to try and calve her, I think a caesarean is the route to take, both for the calves and their mother. So, shall we make a start?'

I stood back and waited to be told what to do.

'I need to give her a haircut where we're going to make the incision on her left side and for that, I've a small, battery powered trimmer. If you can just stay by her head and keep her company while I do it that would be good.'

'Can you see alright?' I asked, looking up at the two forty-watt bulbs Harry and I had fixed up.

'It's difficult to work in your own shadow, but I've a pretty powerful light which fits into a headband I can use when we get down to the cutting and pulling bit. There's also a torch I'll be asking you to hold for me.'

Roy completed his trimming, a long vertical shaved

340

area that must have been twenty inches long that
started about half way down from her hip bone, and
then set about scrubbing the area until it was
spotlessly clean. It's a good job I carry plenty of water
around with me,' he said. 'And we'll give the area a
final disinfecting with a strong alcohol solution when
we've finished with the scrubbing.'

He then produced a hypodermic syringe and fitted a
long needle to it. 'I'll inject some local anaesthetic
into her spine which will freeze the area we're going
to be working on and hopefully keep her more settled.
Can you just lower your light a little so I can see
where to place the needle?'

With that task completed Roy pulled on a pair of
surgical gloves and reached for the scalpel which he
broke out of its sterile wrapping. 'Right then, all set?'

I moved the light back to the working area as he
began to run the scalpel's blade down Thrifty's flank,
cutting through skin and the abdominal muscle; it was
an incision about sixteen inches long.

'And this is when we need the extra lights I was
telling you about,' he said.

'Are they here or do you want me to fetch them?'

'No, stay where you are. I think I've brought
everything in we need.'

He reached into his bag and pulled out the light with
the headband and slipped it on, adjusting it so the
beam fell where he wanted it to, and then gave me a
large torch which weighed a ton but produced a light
that could probably outshine a car's headlight.

'I always make sure I keep these charged because
some farmers expect you to work in the back of a barn
which has nothing more than a dusty old bulb hanging
from the ceiling,' he said. 'How's the girl doing at

341

your end, Elizabeth; is she breathing alright?'

'Yes, she's breathing but it's not easy breathing, if you know what I mean,' she said.

'I know. She just wants us to have her calves out and be done with it. We'll be as quick as we can.'

The cut had followed the centre line of the shaved and disinfected area and I was surprised how little bleeding there was.

'That's the first cut made. Now we need to locate and try and pull as much of her uterus out as is possible but not too heavily, just gently as far as it will comfortably go.'

He reached into the abdominal cavity and eased out the uterus which contained the calves. 'Now I need to locate one of the calf's rear legs, which I have, and now cut into the uterus and tie a calving rope to it so you can hold onto it while I find the other rear leg, hopefully on this occasion belonging to the same calf.

I moved closer and prepared to hold onto the rope.

'Move the light over here more,' Roy said. 'This is going to be the tricky bit and we don't have much time to do it in. We now have a calf's two rear legs attached to the ropes and I've cut the uterus open to make space for it to pass out. And when I say pass out that doesn't mean anyone fainting.'

I passed the torch over to Elizabeth and took the weight on my rope and waited as Roy prepared to make the lift.

'Are you ready?' he asked.

With all the mucus covering it, the rope was difficult to hold but I gripped it as tightly as I could. 'I'm ready,' I said.

'Right then, now lift but try and keep it vertical so the calf doesn't damage the incisions.'

We lifted and slowly but surely, the calf appeared, its head hanging down as it made its way out of a warm, safe cocoon into the evening air.

'That's good, lower it to the ground and we'll see about getting the other one out. Elizabeth, while we do that could you clean the mucus away from the calf's nose and make sure it's breathing alright, please?' Roy asked.

'We repeated the extraction process for the other calf but this one didn't look quite so healthy. As soon as we placed her on the straw, Roy was pulling the mucus off the calf's nose and rubbing her up and down.

'Another heifer and one which seems to be reluctant to take its first breath,' he said. 'Come on you stubborn so and so, start breathing, life smells good out here.'

Roy stopped rubbing her and reached for her back legs to pick her up and then he gently swung her and then lowered her quickly to the ground. And then it was back to the rubbing and nose wiping. At one point he stopped and blew up each of the calf's nostrils.

'Oh, do come on.'

I could sense there was an element of desperation creeping in. And then just as I thought he was on the verge of giving up, the calf gave a splutter and out poured a stream of mucus.

'That's better girly, have another good snot or two and clear your pipes; I'll let you use my shirt sleeve if it helps,' he said.

A few minutes later both calves were breathing and scrabbling to stand up. And I discovered I was breathing again too.

'That's very good,' he said. 'Come on John, this is

the last lap, I'll need another bucket of clean water, warm water if you have it, to give her abdominal cavity a good clear out and try and keep things as sterile as we can before we start stitching.'

As directed, I took the bucket down to the house and filled it with warm water. 'Do you want to put anything in it?' I asked him when I returned.

'I'll just put a drop or two of disinfectant to help kill any bugs, but I'll also be giving her an antibiotic jab when we're finished,' he replied. 'Now just hold that light steady while I wash out her abdominal cavity and you had better get ready to fetch me a second bucketful. You can't be too careful; infection setting in after a caesarean can be a serious problem.'

With the cleaning completed, Roy made a start stitching up the uterus. 'I've left the placenta in there for her to expel, rather than taking it out which can be tricky to make a thorough job of and often leads to infection.'

The uterus was then pushed back inside and a start was made putting stitches where the opening incision had been made. 'I'll need another bucket of water when I've finished so, if you wouldn't mind John…'

'Of course not,' I replied and turned to watch Elizabeth with the two calves. 'How are the twins?' I asked.

'Oh, just fine. I hope Thrifty knows what she's let herself in for.' I laughed and set off for the water.

'What do you want in it this time?' I asked Roy when I had returned.

'I've some iodine,' he said. 'We'll make up a solution and splash it over the incision.'

I winced as painful memories of having neat iodine applied to cuts surged through my mind. 'That will make her tingle,' I said.

'No, not really. The anaesthetic will be starting to wear off but she's a big girl and big girls don't cry.'

I watched as Roy placed the final stitch and then tipped the last of the iodine solution on to them, gently dabbing with a tissue to ensure they weren't weeping. 'I'll give her the antibiotic jab and then we can bring mum and twins together.'

Together we took the calves around to Thrifty's head end and instantly she became aware, smelling her calves and rubbing her nose over them and then, shortly after, she started licking, her big tongue working its magic across each of the calves' heads.

'Do you think, she will get up soon?'

'She'll not be long. Look, she's thinking about it already.

We stayed with them for a little longer until Thrifty had made it onto her feet and both of her babies had tottered round to her udder and begun to suckle.

'That's what they needed,' Roy said, pulling of his overalls and rolling them up. 'Does mum have plenty of milk about her? You'll know how important it is for the calves to receive that first milk from their mother.'

'Yes, we were told about the importance of colostrum at college but I think she was springing up well so I'd expect she will have,' I said.

'Well, that's us about finished here. If you don't mind I'll be on my way; Christmas Eve and all that. But twins eh? What a way of bringing in Christmas; couldn't be better and if you think about it, a stable and a birth; better keep an eye out for the three wise men. See you.'

'Thanks Roy and have a good Christmas; you've

certainly made ours,' I said.

And then he slid into his car and drove up the yard while I went back to Thrifty and her twin calves and, with my arm around Elizabeth's shoulder, I wondered if I had ever been happier.

'That worked out better than I thought it would,' I said.

'You worry too much,' Elizabeth said.

'Maybe, but do you know what the time is?'

'No, tell me.'

'It's five minutes to midnight.'

'So?'

'We've less than five minutes to get around to the church for midnight mass.'

She gave me one of her looks and suddenly took off down the yard. 'I'll race you.'

And as she sped away I couldn't resist it. At the top of my voice I yelled that word: 'Fiancé!'

CHAPTER THIRTY-TWO

Christmas Day

'HAPPY CHRISTMAS, boy,' Harry said when I walked into the kitchen, still a little bleary from the night before. 'Did you get Elizabeth back home alright?'

'Yes, we were a bit late and her father was waiting for us, which didn't go down too well but yes, she made it home alright.'

'What time was that?'

'I'm not sure but it was gone one o'clock, probably nearer two.'

Harry laughed. 'I wouldn't have wanted to meet William at two o'clock in the afternoon, let alone in the morning. He's a dour old sod.'

'Well he wasn't particularly welcoming and a bit short on any Christmas greeting, I have to say.'

'Never mind, boy. I gather we now have twin calves on the farm and that's good news.'

I brightened up. 'Yes, Thrifty came up with the goods albeit by caesarean but Roy did a mega job and it all went well. I had a quick look at them when I got back and they were fine.'

'He's a good vet is Roy McAllister,' Harry said, passing me my cup of tea. 'Knows his stuff and he's good with the animals.'

When Harry made his way down the corridor with Alice's tea I went across to the dairy for the bucket and returned to the house to fill it with warm water.

'Well, it's not a bad sort of day,' Harry said, as he pulled his boots on. 'Cold, dry and bright with a clear blue sky and they don't come much better than that at this time of the year. Come on, let's get the chores out of the way and then we can start Christmas.'

On the way up the yard, I looked in to check on Thrifty and she turned away from the hay she was eating to greet me.

'Hello, old girl,' I said, rubbing her ears. 'Happy Christmas. How are you today and how are your twins?' Her calves, which had been lying down together, now struggled to their feet and wandered round to Thrifty's udder for their first feed of the morning and it was so good to see.

The rest of the herd wandered into the collecting yard and I wished them all a Happy Christmas too, as they walked by me.

'It's Christmas Day girls, and you can all have the day off,' I told them but there wasn't a great response.

Halfway through milking Alice made her way across the collecting yard towards me holding a mug of tea and a sausage roll.

'Happy Christmas, John,' she said. 'Put these down somewhere and you can have a hug.'

I took the tea and sausage roll and she put her arms around me. 'Have a great day, John,' she said, giving me a kiss.

'Thanks Alice, I hope you do to.'

With milking over, I sorted out churns and labels in the dairy and headed off down to the street with three full ones in the trolley where I dropped them off on the ramp and then returned for the other three I had been cooling.

I had said to George I would try not to keep him waiting and it looked as if I was going to be alright. As I started off down the slope, I could hear him coming round the corner into High Street and, as I skidded to a halt, he drove alongside the ramp.

'Morning George, Happy Christmas,' I shouted to him.

'Good job you weren't late this morning, or I would have driven past you,' he said.

'That's not a very festive thing to say.'

'Bugger the festive. I'll be pleased when it's all over and then folks can stop pretending to be nice to me. No one really cares if I have a Merry Christmas, do they? Doesn't make any difference to them if I do or I don't.'

'Oh George, you really are a miserable old sod,' I said.

'There you go. Christmas Day, it's not even eight o'clock and you're back to calling me a miserable old sod, just like they all do.'

'You won't be wanting you're present then?' I said.

'Too right I won't, but you can put it in the cab if you must.'

I walked round to the cab door and opened it. The first thing I noticed was a pile of other small presents on the floor and I laughed as I placed mine alongside them. George, you old charlatan, I thought.

As I began to pull the trolley up the slope with its three empty churns on board, I turned and told George I'd see him tomorrow.

'Yeah, I suppose you will, boy. Have a good day.'
'And you.'

I don't know when or who did it but since leaving the kitchen first thing this morning, someone had been busy hanging a pile of decorations up; colourful paper chains which stretched across the ceiling and dangled down walls. And they looked really good.

The table too, had been given a festive look with table mats depicting Christmas scenes, a sprig or two of holly and a glass of hot mulled wine at each setting.

'It all looks and smells terrific,' I said to Alice. 'But how did you manage all this in that small amount of time?'

'I had a helper,' she said.

'Oh really?'

I felt that familiar dig in my ribs and knew it was Elizabeth. No one digs me in the ribs quite like her. 'Elizabeth,' I said without turning. 'How did you get here?'

'Uncle Harry picked me up this morning. He said you were looking like a wasted whale and were desperate for some help. Anyway, I need to have a quick word with you, if Alice will excuse us for a few minutes.'

'Of course you can,' Alice said. 'Go through to the front room. You won't be disturbed there.'

We went down the corridor and, as Alice suggested, turned into the front room and Elizabeth shut the door. And then she took my hands in hers.

'I don't think this plan of yours is going to work,' she said

'What plan is that?'

'Where we don't tell anyone until next summer we are planning to get married after I leave university.'

'What do you want to do then?' I asked.

'I think we should tell everyone now. When I'm

350

with my parents I feel as if I'm deceiving them all the time and it's too much to ask.'

'Alright then, let's tell everyone. We'll do it today when we're all together.'

'You do mean that, don't you John? You're not just saying that to please me or anything?'

'No, you're right. We should tell everyone. I think they're probably expecting it, anyway and there isn't going to be a better time to do it.'

Elizabeth tugged at my hand and I could see the tears welling in her eyes. 'And then the tears started to flow and we held each other for a long time, not wanting this moment, of all moments, to end.

'Please don't cry,' I said, softly.

'But I'm so happy and just so relieved.'

'That's good, really good and I'm so sorry I've upset you. That wasn't the plan, I promise you.'

Elizabeth smiled a smile I hadn't seen for months.

'Come on then,' she said, taking my hand. 'Alice will be wondering what we're doing in here.'

After all that, the day seemed to pass in a haze. Elizabeth and I fetched the milking equipment down from the bail and cleaned and sterilised them, a task usually performed by Alice but today she had enough to do preparing lunch.

We then let Thrifty out into the paddock for some fresh air and some gentle exercise, her two calves running along beside her. We gave her a good wad of hay to eat and it wasn't long before they all settled down together, enjoying the warmth of the wintery sun.

And then it was a brisk walk down the field to makes sure the cows were behaving themselves on the kale and the electric fence was working as it should.

'I'll take your word for that,' Elizabeth said, when I invited her to test it.

We had just made our way back to the top of the yard when the first car rolled in as Elizabeth's family arrived for their Christmas lunch.

'What are you going to say to them?' Elizabeth asked as we followed them into the yard. 'And when are you going to say it?'

'Oh, I'll pick a time,' I said. 'Don't worry.'

Elizabeth squeezed my hand and said she hoped so.

The first car had Kate, the two girls, William senior and his wife on board plus an enormous sack of presents which just about filled in the boot.

'Ah, John,' Harry said when he spotted me. 'Come and give grandad a hand getting out of the car and lead him down to the house without dropping him or at least, if you do, not where we would have to step over him.'

'I heard that, you miserable bastard,' said William senior, waving his stick about and pointing it at the Christmas tree. 'And you call that a Christmas tree, I've seen better in a knocking shop window.'

'A little too much information, I think,' Harry said.

'Too much information, my arse,' muttered William as I led him into the kitchen.

Then, when dour William and William junior had arrived in their pick-up, it was present time. On Elizabeth's insistence, I remained with them although I really wanted to leave them to it.

Soon the floor was a sea of wrapping paper as present after present was unwrapped accompanied by squeals of laughter. Then suddenly, out of the blue, Harry passed me a present. 'Here you are, boy, it's from Alice and me.'

I thanked them and began to open what was a reasonably small parcel and I couldn't begin to think what it was but two layers of paper down and it was revealed; a penknife. I held it up for everyone to see.

'And now you can stop borrowing mine,' Harry said, with a smile, and Alice can stop counting the knives in the kitchen draw every day.'

Alice, who was on her knees picking up discarded wrapping paper looked up at me. 'That's Harry telling porkies again, John,' she said. 'Don't listen to him because the truth is, I only count them once a week.'

I laughed as did everyone in the room and I looked round and saw Elizabeth. 'Now,' she mouthed to me and my stomach turned over. And if now was the time…

'Excuse me, everyone,' I started, as I rose to my feet and paused until the noise abated and I was surrounded by a lot of staring people. 'If I could have your attention for a few minutes, I have an announcement to make and I wanted to make it while we were all together so you could all hear it at the same time.'

I drew a breath and looked for support from Elizabeth who smiled and nodded encouragingly.

'The news is that I have asked Elizabeth to marry me and she has said yes.'

There was a gasp from Kate and, if I wasn't mistaken, a groan from dour William. But I continued.

'As you all know, Elizabeth is currently attending university in York and it is our intention she completes her course before we actually marry. This will mean a longer engagement than we had hoped for but it is a route we both agree is for the best.'

There was now a strange hush in the room and I held

353

out my hand for Elizabeth to join me.

'I wanted you all to know that for those who haven't yet realised it, John is a fine caring person who I love dearly and want to share my life with,' she said, reaching up to give me a kiss.

And then the room exploded. Harry was the first to congratulate us, shaking my hand and Alice was a close second with a firm embrace and a kiss for both of us. 'That is good news but I have to say, not entirely unexpected,' she said.

Kate pushed her way across the room and became very generous with her kisses and platitudes, while her younger daughters began a serious ear-splitting screaming session while jumping up and down on the sofa.

Dour William though, looked positively unmoved which was just as well because the perpetual nasal dew drop appeared to have just about reached maximum capacity and looked set for departure. I was beginning to wonder if I should have approached him on the subject before announcing our plans, but I doubted such impending news would have had made any difference.

Harry found a crate of brown ale from somewhere and proceeded to ruin Alice's crochet table cloth when he poured the beer too quickly and the froth bubbled over the top of the glass and what with everything else, it was not until nearly three o'clock before we sat down to devour the Christmas dinner Alice had prepared.

After a generous helping of turkey, vegetables and all the trimmings that make for that special meal, I collapsed onto a sofa with Elizabeth and dozed away the afternoon until milking time, trying not to think about having to do it all again when we drove down to Rose Hill Farm later this evening.

CHAPTER THIRTY-THREE

A busy spring

NEW YEAR AND the cold weather which had set in over the Christmas period continue and, if anything, it was now even colder with hard frosts which struggled to lift during the day.

It was though, a good time to get the plough moving and for most of January, I was taking the David Brown and the two-furrow plough out to turn over all the ground we planned to sow with spring barley.

These days had almost become a routine: after breakfast I filled the tractor with diesel, checked the engine oil level and greased up the plough, while Alice made me a boiled bacon sandwich and a bottle of tea. And then, having collected them from the house, I climbed into the cab and placed the bottle of tea on the gearbox in some futile attempt to keep it warm, and set off down to the field.

It felt really good to have finally finished ploughing the Forty Acres; I'd spent the last day and a half ploughing the headlands which seemed to take for ever.

Today, though, I was further up the hill on lighter land and it was an altogether different type of ploughing. For starters, I was in a higher gear and by opening the plough out I could increase the furrow widths by a couple of inches and it was surprising just how much that small amount contributed to an increase in output.

And I think the seagulls also enjoyed the higher speed because it produced a greater number of worms, but it didn't seem to stop the amount of squabbling as they fought for every one of them.

After my initial excitement of sitting in a cab and enjoying the protection it provided against the wind and the rain I began to think there was still a long way to go before it could be a working environment that was anywhere close to equalling that of say, a lorry or a car. It had also crossed my mind during one particularly steep manoeuvre that should the tractor roll over, the structure of the cab would not be strong enough to prevent it collapsing with the weight of the tractor on it and with no way of jumping off, it could all be very nasty.

But it was a welcome improvement and while it hadn't totally eliminated the need to stop and warm my hands and feet over the exhaust pipe, it could, with adequate clothing, keep me from suffering from the worst of the cold. More importantly, the cab meant I was able to keep ploughing longer and achieve a greater output.

By the start of February, I was able to move into the last of the fields, the one which we had used to grow the kale. As I drove into the field I became increasingly concerned about the ground opening up and dropping into a deep hole, as I had done when I had driven in with the fencing gear a couple of months before.

There was no way of telling where such holes might

appear, if indeed there were any more of them to fall into, so there was no alternative but to set out a land and keep ploughing and hope for the best.

But this was light land and, without encountering any deep-hole experiences, I managed to plough it in just over two days, and I have to say, it was the straightest and most even ploughing I had achieved, with almost perfect openers and half acceptable finishes.

'You're improving,' commented Harry, when he came down to see how it was going. 'There's just a chance we'll make a ploughman of you yet.'

And just in case I had any ideas that I had finally mastered the art of ploughing and to show me how far I still had to improve, Harry and I went to see the local ploughing championships where the county's finest set about competing for a place in the national championships.

Talk about skill; their ploughing techniques were just so good and the pains they took to ensure everything was right and perfect at every stage was pretty mind blowing, even if it did take half a day to plough an area which wasn't much larger than a tennis court.

Winter moved quickly in to spring and there were busy times ahead. The ewes were now only a couple of weeks away from lambing, the drilling of the spring barley could begin as soon as soil conditions allowed, and it wouldn't be long before the cows could be let into the first of their spring grazing, and the area where they had been wintered allowed to recover.

A spell of dry weather in March enabled the spring barley to be drilled into some good warm seedbeds.

'Soil that falls off the end of your boot, Harry said. And to help prevent moisture loss, all the fields were pressed using a set of Cambridge rolls, the slowest and dustiest job of the year.

One by one though, we worked our way through the spring jobs: chain harrowing the grass fields to pull out the matted grass, spread cow pats and level out the mole hills, top dressing the grassland with a sprinkle of artificial fertiliser, and applying weed killer to the barley crops.

A local farm sale enabled Harry to purchase our first hydraulic tipping trailer but he missed an opportunity to buy a second one at the same sale when he was seriously outbid by a neighbouring farmer. Harry was furious but only until he found out the price paid was greater than that of a new trailer.

I had a discussion with him today about re-seeding some of the grass fields which have been in permanent pasture since time began, but he didn't warm to the idea. 'I think they're best left as they are,' he said. 'They've done us alright for the last seventy years when they stopped digging iron ore out of it and they'll do us alright for a few more.'

I let the matter drop. That there were grass varieties now available which would be so much more productive, didn't seem to register with Harry. If the grass is green then all was well with him.

There were by now, about four hundred lambs running about the farm with their mothers trailing around behind them. Kind, clement weather had resulted in lambing being a fairly straight forward event although it wasn't without its upsets, not least being the loss of three ewes when a stray dog ran riot amongst them early one morning.

As ever though, lambing had called for some long hours and I tried to do my share of the night time inspection visits, always expecting Harry to be doing his ghost impression whenever I needed to climb over the style into the graveyard to look at ewes being kept in there. Memories of Harry and a white sheet at one o' clock in the morning still linger with me to this day.

But now, the days were becoming longer and summer was approaching, and Elizabeth was back home, having completed her second year at university.

'We should be celebrating our engagement,' she said as we walked hand in hand down the track one warm sunny evening. 'And while we're on the subject, are you planning on giving me an engagement ring any time soon?'

'What, like this one?' I said reaching into my pocket and producing a small presentation box.

'Oh, John, you haven't, have you?' she asked.

'Open it and see,' I said. 'I was going to give it to you later but…'

'John, it's wonderful,' gasped Elizabeth when she removed the ring from the box. 'And it fits perfectly too, look.'

She held up her hand for me to see and I had to agree it looked wonderful.

'Thank you, John,' she said as our lips met.

'Now, I just wondered if you'd like to come with me and see how the cows are? One of the Red Poll's is close to calving and…'

HARRY ME, AND BOTTLED TEA......

Harry, me and bottled tea is the second book to feature John Johnson as he tries his best to learn all he can about farming. It is, as most will know, the sequel to the incredibly popular *Harry, me and boiled bacon* and I really hope you have found them both to be good, fulfilling reads.

I would be very grateful if you could spare a few moments to provide a review for *Harry, me and bottled tea* – an opportunity to. register your thoughts on what you have read.

Thank you

ANDY COLLINGS

If you're looking forward to the next novel from Andy Collings, you can get the first chapter to read before anyone else by heading to:

andycollings2018@outlook.com

Printed in Great Britain
by Amazon